Listening In

Listening In

Kevin Chandler

Published by Accent Press Ltd – 2009

ISBN 9781906373658

Printed and bound in the UK

Cover Design by The Design House

This novel is dedicated to
the late great John Martyn,
and to Leonard Cohen;
for the songs, and the words.

Chapter One

December 23rd …

WHEN YOU EARN YOUR living by the hour providing an intimate service for total strangers, you develop a keen feel for the passage of time, and he sensed that hers was almost up. A deft glance at the clock confirmed as much and he smiled inwardly. He watched in silence as she filled out his cheque, savouring the elegant swirls of permanent black glimpsed beneath the blood red flashes of her nails. She had barely completed the signature when a raft of hail clattered the window, putting paid to his reverie and making her shudder to the core; such child-like reaction in so painstakingly beautiful a woman he found almost touching. Loosing the cheque, she wafted it back and forth, pursed her lips and blew long and seductively across the surface as if it were a hot tasty morsel she was preparing to pop into an infant's mouth. He found himself both engrossed and amused by this ritual, despite her eyes for once being trained, not on him, but on events outside.

"There," and satisfied the ink was dry she gave the cutest smile. "I must say I like your taste in paintings," Gina declared, gesturing to the two Degas prints upon the wall between their chairs, as she leaned forward to hand him the cheque, forcing him to avert his eyes from the first subtle hint of her cleavage. "Far more conducive than the weather."

Seeing no need to apologise for the weather, and resisting his desire to enquire what she saw in the Degas prints, he simply thanked her politely, stashed his fee inside his week-to-a-view diary, confirmed time and date of her next appointment and led her out into reception. Hearing her groan as another blast of hail scatter-gunned the pane, he turned to be confronted by her handbag, proffered as she made to don the black p.v.c. trench-coat draped across her arm. Ignoring the bag, he seized the coat and held it open invitingly. He noticed how her body acquiesced, the way her spine arched towards him allowing her shoulders to press against the heels of his palms much as a cat brushes the legs of its owner, and for one fleeting moment, he almost regretted not taking the handbag after all. Raising the collar about her neck she craned to look back at him.

"Mmm, the perfect gentlemen, thank you, Patrick," she purred, and her eyes cast him a kiss, "… and to think, one of my girlfriends told me to watch out; she said 'therapist' also spells 'the rapist'!"

Patrick's smile was tight-lipped.

Despite Gina's long coat depriving him of his customary glimpse of her fine legs, his eyes followed her along the landing until she disappeared from view down the stairs, at which point he quietly closed the office door and retreated to the safety of his desk. Removing her file, he opened its buff cover and shook his head. No sooner had he written the date than there was a loud knock on the outer door and he let out a sigh. 'What is it this time,' he thought, rising wearily from his chair, 'car keys, fountain pen, or the card for her next appointment? Any ploy to exact a little more than her due, and of course, it always works.'

"Neil!" Patrick's jaw dropped. "I thought you were …"

"Dead? We're all dead, Patrick, it's just that some of us don't know it yet. I imagine you still allow half an hour between clients? By the way … she's hot! How do you keep your eyes trained on her psyche when what you really want is to look up her skirt? Well, are you going to let me in or do we have to conduct our conversation on the doorstep?"

Patrick closed his mouth, swallowed hard and swung the door wide allowing his deceased ex-client to step across the threshold where they both loitered uncomfortably.

"Er, shall we, go through …?" Somehow Patrick stuttered out the words that seemed required by his role as host.

"To the therapy room? I know I haven't got an appointment, but I hoped I could rely on a good pro like you turning a trick for a sad old punter like me? It'll be just like old times, eh, Patrick?"

They settled in their accustomed positions and Patrick's hands fidgeted for something to grasp. Normally at the start of a session he would place his diary, symbolising both the promise, and limitations, of the therapeutic alliance, down upon the coffee table and commence proceedings with his customary word of introduction, 'Welcome'. But this was no scheduled appointment and his diary lay alongside Gina's notes out there on the desk. Instead, Patrick's elbows located the flat wooden arms of his therapy chair, allowing his hands to interlock and support his chin in a futile effort to establish a degree of comfort. Duly settled, he focused upon the young man whose own hands lay quiet and still in his lap, from which the long, black nozzle of a silencer lay trained in Patrick's direction.

"Neil, that's not funny."

"Quite right."

"Is that thing real?" Patrick enquired softly.

"Real as that hole in your wall," replied Neil, shifting his head a touch to the right. Patrick half-turned to follow Neil's line of sight and as he did so a muffled crack rang out and a neat hole appeared in the wall just behind his head surrounded by a ring of crazed plaster. In slow motion, Patrick's hands parted, lowered and gripped the arms of his chair as if they were handrails on a rope-bridge.

"Neil …" Patrick had no idea how the sentence would end, let alone this impromptu session with a dead client. Suddenly, Neil's words came back to him, 'We're all dead, Patrick, it's just that some of us don't know it yet.' And Patrick realised his own life was about to end in the very place where he had chosen to live the best of it, here in his therapy room, staring down a barrel of malaise.

Chapter Two

Two months earlier …

MOST WOMEN LEARN THAT there are two things to be wary of criticising in a man: his driving and the size of his penis; but then Patrick Chime was not your typical man. His Saab convertible had seen better days, and, should a boy racer cut him up, Patrick would simply emit a self-satisfied sigh at having no need of reckless point-scoring to shore up his maleness. As for his genitals, he knew there was nothing the matter with his cock even if Maggie no longer cherished its presence inside her. Besides, Patrick understood better than most men that female sexual desire and fulfilment owe less to the gauge of a man's penis than to the sensitivity of his tongue, whichever use he puts it to. No, as far as criticism was concerned, Patrick's Achilles heel was not to be found in his garage, or in his underpants, but in the fact that despite total strangers happily paying substantial sums of money to have him hear their woes, his own wife's abiding complaint was that he never really listened.

The spat with Maggie culminated in Patrick departing for work half an hour earlier than usual, un-availed of breakfast and leaving no goodbye in his wake. Along the three-mile route he sought comfort voicing every obscenity he could think of for the wife whose ace had already trumped the lot. The exercise at least served to let off steam and by the time he tired of repeating himself he had reached the roundabout a half-mile from his destination, the converted West Yorkshire woollen mill that was home to a wine merchant, reproduction furniture hall, fitness centre & café, craft shop, computer repairer, upholsterer, and nail salon-cum-tanning centre, as well as his own consulting rooms tucked away up on the second floor. Parking in his assigned place, nose-to-the-wall, rather than reversing in as was his custom in the days when he held more enthusiasm for the homeward journey, he snatched the keys from the ignition, climbed out and gave the door an unnecessarily harsh slam. Such was the closest Patrick ever dared veer towards domestic violence.

Examining the pile of post on the mat behind the mill's outer door, he removed the single item addressed to him and carried it up to his small suite of rooms. After inserting his key he gave the brass plate outside his office door its customary affectionate tap, *PATRICK CHIME, M.A., MBACP ~ Therapeutic Counselling and Supervision Services, Est. 1994,* and stepped into an intense ray of light as the low autumnal sun streamed through the IKEA wooden blinds. He adjusted the angle of the slats, set up the espresso machine and tore open the envelope to reveal, not as he'd hoped, a cheque from an ex-client who had reneged on their final appointment still owing him for two sessions, but circulars for two forthcoming training courses: *Transpersonal Agendas in the Therapeutic Alliance: An Experiential Workshop* and *Maximising Your Potential: How to Establish a Successful Private Practice.* The waste-bin was already full but the heel of Patrick's boot easily created the necessary space.

He poured his first coffee of the day, whose absence of *crema* caused him to swill it down the sink and set about grinding fresh beans. His second attempt proved satisfactory and he wandered through to the therapy room and settled by the window to overlook the still quiet car park. He preferred this time of day, before the other outlets opened and the stream of delivery vans, wine buffs, tan seekers and middle-aged wives bent on showing their reluctant husbands the reproduction table that would go a treat in their hallway, began to arrive. Even then, he was able to shut most of it out, his domain a calm, still point in the busy material whirl. He treasured the look of surprise whenever a new client crossed the threshold to be struck by the airy light, the soft hues, warm sofas, unassuming desk, and tidy kitchen corner of the reception area; and on into the inner sanctum of the therapy room, with its deep secure armchairs, the wall adorned by two carefully chosen prints: the agony of inter-personal estrangement portrayed by Edgar Degas' *L'Absinthe*, contrasting so well with the precious pearl of intimacy, captured in *Au Café,* by the same artist. Installed in place when he first opened his private practice, he felt they symbolised the essence of what his work is about, the struggle between intimacy and isolation, and he was always pleased when a client passed comment on them. Given the motley exterior of the rest of the mill, Patrick knew it was hard not to be impressed by the insulated little world he had created up here, conveying such promise of the peace and harmony lacking in his clients' lives. Of course, some arrived so wrapped in their own misery they failed to notice much at all on their first visit. But even for those with such little awareness of their surroundings, Patrick held faith that something of the care he had invested in creating this therapeutic haven might still permeate their psyche.

Patrick leaned on the windowsill, his face warmed by the autumnal sun and bathed in contentment at the course his professional life had taken until a new tear in the Saab's soft-top claimed his attention. Its paintwork faded and scratched and with repair bills mounting, it really was time to sell, and he sighed, anticipating no satisfaction at all in the once-a-decade process of changing his means of transport. He conjured images of lines of men in W.H. Smith, as still as statues, poring over *What Car, Exchange & Mart,* and *Auto Trader* as if they were porn magazines. His contempt was razor-edged, but, as always, the manufactured sense of his own superiority failed to deliver the required measure of reassurance. For one whose business was largely about helping people cope with change, Patrick found change remarkably difficult to manage in his own life.

He checked his watch. Twenty-five past eight, the exact time Nuala's bus leaves for sixth form college, the bus he reminded her of every morning as she dawdled and chattered her way through breakfast. 'Bus minus five!' he'd chirp, as if he was really not that bothered whether or not she caught it. And he remembered that today she would not be running for the bus, for she was in halls at Newcastle University, fresher year, probably still in bed, and quite possibly not alone.

Chasing the idea from his mind, he substituted a vision of the empty nest at the top of the cul-de-sac that he shared with Maggie. His thoughts climbed the stairs to Nuala's room. It remained 'Nuala's room' despite Maggie's suggestion that they should re-decorate and turn it into a guest room. It was home to Bruno, Rabbit, & Mole, no longer required in Nuala's new grown-up life and left scattered on the floor until retrieved by Patrick and arranged in a neat, harmonious line across the bedspread. He wandered through to their bedroom, with its unmade bed and army of shoes sprawled lazily underneath, almost incognito under a veil of dust. Every so often, Maggie made noises about getting a cleaning lady, but, to Patrick's relief, such intrusion into the narrow confines of their intimacy somehow never came to pass.

He recalled that morning's conflict; it was over the gasman, coming to service their troublesome central-heating boiler. A week ago Maggie had asked Patrick to be home to let him in as she had a corporate golf day arranged with clients and would be out until late. He had agreed, and, of course, had forgotten all about it until she reminded him as he prepared breakfast.

"... But I can't. I've got clients booked in!"

He registered the contempt in her stare, the exasperated sigh, and the way she strode from the kitchen leaving him standing by the worktop, half an eye on the toaster he had absent-mindedly neglected to switch on. He was still considering how to respond when her voice drifted back from the hall, as clinical and mechanical as the answering machine into which she was reciting her message.

"Mrs Chime here, I'm sorry to inform you I must cancel the boiler service arranged for this afternoon, I'm afraid my husband can't get his act together. I'll ring you later to book another time. Goodbye."

'O.T.T.,' he thought, but it provided sufficient impetus for a retaliatory strike and he ventured out into the hall.

"Was that really necessary?"

"You think not? Well, next time, *you* do it!" she snapped. "You know the trouble with you, Pat? You never bloody listen! You spend too much time living inside your own fucking head!"

Patrick's mouth gaped like a fish out of water but no sound emerged. If it had, it is unlikely Maggie would have heard, for she was already climbing the stairs to gather up her golf attire. And so, lacking the resolve to chase after her, stand toe to toe and slug it out, Patrick did the one other manly thing he could think of, grabbed jacket and car keys and stormed out of the house.

Patrick didn't need to puzzle long over the episode, he already knew which barbs carried most poison: '... my husband can't get his act together ... the trouble with you ... never bloody listen ... living inside your fucking head', all laced with that sneering tone of voice. What made these jibes all the more uncomfortable was his suspicion that they carried a sizeable measure of truth. It was becoming clear to Patrick that it wasn't only his car that needed serious attention, and he sighed once again, knowing only too well that some things in life are easier than others to repair. 'The M.O.T runs out in the New Year,' he reminded himself. 'I'll decide what to do then and just patch-up the soft-top for now. As for my marriage ...'

Patrick glanced at his watch, reached for the diary and prepared to face his first client of the day.

Meanwhile, back at the house, Maggie had locked up, set the alarm, and was out on the drive carefully arranging her golf clubs and shoes, and a small holdall containing towel, toilet bag, change of clothes and underwear, in the boot of her VW. Maggie was indeed setting off to play around, but as on previous occasions over recent months, she would not be setting foot on any golf course.

8

Chapter Three

THROUGHOUT THE SESSION, PATRICK observed Neil retreating deeper and deeper into himself until he sat like a leaden weight, chin on his chest, eyes offering no further contact. An armchair away, Patrick watched and waited. A minute passed but felt like more. Silence, it's such a rare commodity nowadays, as Patrick likes to tell new student counsellors, one that most new entrants to his profession find difficult. Most quickly learn to bite their tongues, some even take foolish pride in never being the one to break the silence, but few truly come to terms with either the lack of stimulation, or the delegation of responsibility, in allowing silence to run its course.

"I didn't wanna come today," Neil muttered at last, his voice drained of any semblance of enthusiasm.

Patrick nodded, allowing a further silence to elapse.

"So, why did you?" he enquired at last, when it became apparent more was needed.

"What, cancel at short notice and get a bill from you for half-fee?" Neil groused through half-open lips, stealing the briefest glance at his inquisitor before resuming his former pose.

"Is the money the only reason you decided to show up?" asked Patrick.

"I could ask you the same thing!" he muttered under his breath.

"Why don't you?" said Patrick, provocatively.

Neil just squirmed in his seat and did not rise to the challenge.

"Look, I know you're trying to help," he said at last, "but it just isn't getting any better."

"What's not getting any better?" asked Patrick.

Neil sighed in exasperation.

"The way I feel!"

"And what's wrong with the way you feel?"

"Christ, don't you listen?" spat Neil, seizing the chance to express some justifiable anger, "I've been telling you for weeks, I'm miserable, I'm fed up, everyone else's relationships work out, why don't mine?"

Pat's eyes widened ostentatiously.

"*Everyone* else's? Have you seen the divorce figures lately?"

Neil shifted uncomfortably, glanced at Patrick, looked away, then back at his close tormentor, and for a moment Patrick wondered if he'd pushed Neil too far. Early thirties, bit of a short-arse, prematurely balding, designer-suit but ill-fitting, and permanently anguished; it was never quite clear who Neil despised most, himself, or the world of successful men he aspired, and conspicuously failed, to join. Patrick's tease had stretched what little rapport they'd established to its limits. Grudgingly, Neil let out a snort, which soon dissolved into a laugh; a laugh that grew loud and prolonged, triggering a half-smile in Patrick, until he realised that Neil was not only laughing, but also crying. Patrick waited, wondering whether to speak, just as Neil slumped forward and began rocking to and fro, his arms wrapped around himself like a straitjacket, and his bitter lament squeezed out about between sobs.

"I just … want to know … when I'll feel better … can't bear, the thought … of … going on like this … not knowing; I just want to know … when I'll feel better!" This last almost a shriek.

"I know you do, Neil" replied Patrick, leaning forward, "and I realise you're very unhappy, and I wish I had a magic wand that would conjure up an answer, so I could tell you, 'Here Neil, such and such a date, this is when you'll feel better, this is when you'll be happy …' But I haven't fucking got one, have I? And what's more, you know I haven't, and that's why you didn't want to come here today and why inside you're so angry, because, like all the other significant people in your life, Neil, I'm a let-down. I'm a disappointment to you."

On hearing this, something gave inside Neil, his chest heaved, he gulped a lungful of air as if it was his last, and his sobs began again, but meatier now, closer to the bone.

Throughout Neil's torment, Patrick remained still, bound by the dutiful, helpless regard of a father paying silent witness to a son's pain. He thought he recognised Neil's tears; they were tears for what might have been; tears for the love a son expects will always be denied; tears for the love he doesn't believe he deserves and, should he ever stumble across it, most probably would not trust.

Minutes passed, and only when Neil had set about wiping his eyes and runny nose with his clenched fist, did Patrick reach out and nudge the box of tissues across the coffee table. Neil pulled out one, then another, and his chest gave another mighty heave before he spoke.

"I battle all the time, I keep telling myself to keep trying, to listen to what you say to me, to not give up on this; and then another part of me says, don't listen to you, don't keep coming here, you don't really care, all I mean to you is forty-five quid an hour for sitting there doing nothing. And that's why I nearly didn't come today."

Now it was Patrick's turn to sigh.

"This is the crux, isn't it, Neil? Can you believe that you really mean something to another human being? Do I really give a shit about you? Do I really want you to feel better? Because once you do, you won't need to come any more, and I'll lose what you see as my weekly supply of money for old rope."

For once, Neil was watching as well as listening.

"Well, do you? Do you give a shit?" he asked tentatively, and looked away before he could receive any answer, clenching his teeth so as not to cry again.

Patrick waited before responding,

"Well, what do you think?" he asked, softly.

"You always do that, turn stuff back to me," Neil complained.

"And if I told you whether or not I gave a shit, would you believe me?"

"You're doing it again, turning it all back to me!"

"Yes, it's my job, to make you think," Patrick said firmly, and felt a twinge of discomfort at the note of self-satisfaction he recognised in his own voice, as if he'd just made the telling

11

point in the argument.

"Some job!" Neil sneered, shaking his head.

"It pays," replied Patrick, tilting his head, coquettishly.

Neil responded like a flash, his laser stare locking onto Patrick's features in fearful search of a fond father, while Patrick's heart accelerated as a lifetime's doubt and hope hovered between the two men. Neither spoke, until Patrick saw Neil's eyes soften and fill.

"Same time next week, Neil?" asked Patrick, kindly, and with a tentative smile.

The younger man nodded.

"I'll be here," he whispered, and reached inside his jacket pocket for the money.

"Me too," said Patrick, leaning across to receive it.

Patrick sat at his desk in the corner of the reception room. He had already written the date and the words *Neil, In There, Disappointment, Anger, Trust,* and now sat back staring at the page. One of the things Patrick loved about therapy was the opportunity, indeed the necessity, to ponder the meanings of language. Since commencing his training in the days before management consultants turned the stuffy old Marriage Guidance Council into image-conscious Relate, he had heard his trainers and fellow students speak readily of 'going *into* therapy'. Interesting how no one ever speaks of going *into* counselling. People *have* counselling, but *enter* therapy. It is a distinction that used to irritate Patrick, seeing it as pretension on the part of those who clothe and elevate themselves in the title 'therapist', as if their customers, in buying time and thoughtful attention from a fellow human being, in addition to being re-branded as 'clients', must pass through some kind of portal, into a holy of holies where the therapist holds court. For much of his career he had stuck to the term 'counselling', more down to earth, less grandiose. But as years went by Patrick observed how the counselling profession too, seduced by business opportunities and society's spray-on counselling response to various traumas, had fallen in love with itself, and he was now much less enamoured of it. He gave a sigh. 'Whatever you choose to call it,' he thought to himself, 'there are times when it's not sufficient to simply come along and talk *about* your problems, those very problems have to be experienced and addressed first-hand in the therapeutic relationship. That's what Neil did this morning, and it was far from comfortable for him. Come to think of it, it wasn't too cosy for me either, for, until this morning, I can't say I much liked him.'

Patrick scribbled a large 'S' at the foot of the page, signifying, 'Take to supervision!', filed the sheet away in the buff folder and checked his diary ... *10:30 a.m. Grace.*

Out along the ring road, two cars were heading in opposite directions, each driven by a female occupant en route to a secret assignation. The black Volkswagen Passat travelled the faster of the two, its thirty-nine-year-old driver already aware of the first rush of anticipation stirring between her legs. Glancing at the rear-view mirror, nothing close behind, she then craned her neck to check her make-up and was pleased that, having long since come to terms with guilt, her eyes easily held her stare. She did not notice the silver Audi pass by on the other carriageway, driven by a woman of similar age and attractiveness, a woman also on a mission, a woman close to the edge.

13

Chapter Four

THE SESSION WITH NEIL served to take Patrick's mind off Maggie's verbal assault but irritation kicked in once more as he sat awaiting the arrival of his new client. The jibe that he 'never listened' was easy to deal with. Now, if she'd only charged him with being a 'poor listener', or stuck to the key issue by challenging him on why he'd forgotten that particular request; but in opting for exaggeration to stress her point Maggie had merely undermined her own case, enabling him to dispatch the accusation with a flurry, way beyond the boundary. Next up, 'the trouble with you …' A cheap shot, like a fast bowler sending down a bouncer at a tail-ender; intimidating, but hardly a tactic to be proud of. Patrick was warming to this post-match analysis and starting to feel a little better. Next up, '… spend too much time living inside your own fucking head'. Clean bowled, middle stump, no appeal necessary, or allowed. Patrick's undoing was what is referred to in his trade as 'attending to process over content'. Fascination with process, it's what made him a half-decent therapist, and such an infuriating husband.

The knock was so quiet he wondered if he might have missed an earlier one, but she said not. Patrick's antennae set to work: dark hair cut in a smart bob, cradled by raised collar of long camel coat (unbuttoned), limp handshake, cold hand, light make-up, black pencil skirt, good shoes, dark eyes, tentative smile.

"You must be Grace …"

"Grace...R-Reynolds, that's right." And he detected a tremor in her voice as she stumbled over the first syllable of her surname.

"I nearly said Darling!"

"I'm sorry …" said Patrick, thrown by such an inappropriate endearment, and at such an early stage in

14

proceedings.

"Darling … my maiden name, after my father's great heroine and namesake ever since he learned about her at primary school: Grace Darling, the lighthouse keeper's daughter up on the Northumberland coast? She rowed out with her father in a storm to save the lives of sailors shipwrecked on rocks a mile off shore. Well, my father was so impressed by the story he persuaded my mother to name me Grace."

Patrick could see she was gabbling but decided to go with the flow, at least until they had sat down.

"And how do you feel about being named after another man's daughter, albeit a famous heroine?" he asked, closing the office door and drawing her further inside.

"I like it, but I'm glad he drew the line at Grace, her middle name was 'Horsely'. Anyway, I haven't been a 'Darling' for sixteen years so I don't know what made me almost say it just now."

Patrick could hazard a guess, but said no more on the subject.

"Shall we go through?" he suggested, and led the way into the therapy room.

"That chair's mine, take whichever of the other two you prefer."

Grace chose the one nearest the coffee table, and closest to Patrick. She kept her coat on but drew it like curtains revealing a crisp white blouse, undone at the neck to just the correct degree, and a black fitted knee-length skirt. She crossed her legs, straightened her skirt and settled her hands in her lap in readiness for him to begin. And all the while three words revolved through Patrick's mind, 'classy, respectful, slender'.

Beginnings had always fascinated Patrick. Playing cricket for the school team, next man in, pad up, tighten the buckles, don't forget your box, don cap and gloves then march steadily out to the middle, nod to your partner at the other end, take careful guard, request confidently of the umpire, "middle-and-leg please, sir … thank you". Wander about the crease, give the pitch one or two suspicious prods with the bat, take an ostentatious look about you to appraise the gaps in their field, listen for the announcement: "Right arm over, two to come",

15

until all ritual delay dissolves to nothing and the demon fast bowler bears down, scenting blood.

Now, in his mid-forties, it was the drama of therapy that held him enthralled, and he stalked it with the stealth of an experienced hunter. His prey? Those moments when the therapeutic alliance rests upon a knife-edge, when rapport could tilt hope-wards, or plummet into despair. Despite long years plying his trade, he still loved the uncertainty of settling down to await a new client's arrival, with nothing more than a name in the diary and a week-old sense of a voice on the telephone, knowing that, somewhere out there, en route to his haven, a stranger was also contemplating this initial encounter. Some prospective clients try to explain in that first phone call why they are seeking help, but Patrick always tries to stop them. It detracts from the delicious uncertainty he feels on hearing that first knock at the door.

Having used the space to consider this refined and attractive woman sitting before him, Patrick was about to launch into his usual preamble about the boundaries of time, place, and the limits of confidentiality, when she wrong-footed him a second time.

"I think it's me who needs rescuing!" she blurted out.

Although somewhat taken aback, Patrick's response was smooth and unruffled.

"From what, or from whom?"

"From myself, I think. From the awful creature I've become."

"Tell me about her."

"The awful creature?"

"Mm-huh."

And for the next thirty minutes Grace Reynolds described in a relatively calm and measured manner, how this dutiful, responsible wife of sixteen years, mother of three bright, healthy children between nine and fourteen, who holds down a responsible job as a part-time optometrist, was currently, and for no justifiable reason, contemplating running away with the boy she used to sit next to at primary school.

Grace described her husband, David, a consultant gynaecologist, as a decent man, conscientious and safe, who, despite leaving the bulk of the parenting and domestic realm to her, remained a loyal and committed partner. He neither ran up debts nor drank to excess and had never once struck her, although of late, she had almost been pushing him to do so. Her female friends adored him, one in particular would do virtually anything to get on his list, but, as far as she was aware, David had never been unfaithful. It was not that he didn't find other women attractive, it was just that he realised how much trouble it would bring. Mr Reliable. She always knew where she was with David, and it was somewhere she no longer wanted to be.

"If David was a bastard, it would be so much easier," she stated.

"Easier … to feel justified in leaving him?" asked Patrick.

"Yes."

"So being unhappily married isn't reason enough to seek a divorce?"

Now it was Grace's turn to allow a pause as she turned this statement over and over in her mind.

"No, I suppose not," she replied at last.

"How come?" Patrick prompted.

Grace sighed.

"Well, there are others to think of: three innocent children who deserve better than a fractured family, not to mention my parents, they'd never forgive me. On the outside I strive to appear grown-up and independent of my parents, but underneath, I still seem to wear them like a vest. Staunch Baptists, they're big on duty. They believe in personal responsibility, and doing the right thing. 'A hedonist's best friend is the devil,' was one of my father's favourite sayings, and my mother told me time and again as I grew up, 'Happiness is no raison d'etre, Grace!'

"And what does happiness mean to *you*?" asked Patrick, a mite too eagerly, for he was already half-smitten, impressed not only by the look of this woman, but by her feel for metaphor and her ability to respond so readily to his interventions. For some moments she made no reply, yet looked all the while as if her lips were struggling to speak but the words kept eluding her. He watched as her agitation deepened and her eyes filled with fear. He saw the turmoil in

17

her throat, as she began swallowing, hard and repeatedly, to such extent that Patrick imagined that at any moment she would be violently sick, wave after wave of projectile vomit spewing forth over the coffee table, her fine clothes, his new carpet, the walls, and over him too. He contained this gruesome image, until, unable to bear the tension any longer, he offered up words to assuage her distress, delivered with all the compassion and tenderness he felt for her in that moment.

"Grace, I guess right now you cannot tell me what happiness means to you, but perhaps your body is showing me, and what I think I see, is that happiness means the earth to you, so much in fact, that it's almost too much for you to bear."

And with these words all the years of trying so hard to attend to her children's needs, her husband's, her parents', her patients', indeed everyone's needs but her own; all the years of not being understood by her husband, dissolved to nothing, and the effect was like the breaching of sandcastle walls as streams of tears cascaded down her cheeks.

Grace cried on and off for the remainder of the session, interspersed with pauses during which she provided further details of her upbringing and marriage. Patrick learned that her old-school friend was called Simon, he lived in Wiltshire and she had told David about him from the very first contact through Friends Reunited. At first David appeared unperturbed, but as the months went by he began making sarcastic remarks about the postman's bag being considerably heavier of late. Then, several weeks ago, unbeknown to Grace, David took the morning off work and discovered, stashed at the back of her wardrobe, a wad of letters from Simon, which he brandished on her return from her work. What protest she made about such invasion of her privacy, David brushed aside, quoting incriminating lines that he had clearly studied at length. These were love letters, he argued. Had they met up? Were they lovers? She considered lying but could not bring herself to do so, and duly confessed on both counts.

Since then, things had accelerated. Grace had driven down to London to meet Simon; David's threat, 'If you go, don't bother coming back,' ringing in her ears. She went nonetheless, and returned the following day, to find that David had rallied the children around him, making her, as indeed she now felt herself to be, the villain of the piece. Since then, the atmosphere at home was hell for all concerned, and it seemed obvious to Grace that she was entirely to blame for allowing herself to fall in love with a man she knew she should relinquish, a man who asked nothing of her but that she be herself, and the first man in her life with whom she had ever really dared let go. Simon made his living as a freelance journalist and travel writer and a favourite maxim he had picked up along the years was 'When in doubt, walk about!' In his last letter, he'd outlined his intention of undertaking a long-distance walk along the latter section of the pilgrim trail to Santiago di Compostella, in north-west Spain, and had invited Grace to join him for part of it. The possibility struck a chord with Grace; perhaps some time out would be beneficial, an opportunity to clear her head, explore her options, and discover whether a week ensconced with Simon would bring too much reality to bear upon her dreams. She broached the possibility with David. His reply was as sharp as his scalpel, 'Do what you want, Grace, just make up your mind one way or another and put us all out of our misery; but make no mistake, you may choose to leave this marriage, but the children remain with me.'

Over the past two months, David had transformed himself into a responsive and available father, so successfully that Grace no longer questioned why he had not done this before, but instead embraced her guilt, and in the face of his threat to amputate the fruit of her womb, had almost convinced herself that he was now more fit to raise them than she.

Patrick stole a glance at the clock, two minutes after time, how unlike him; in allowing himself to become absorbed in the content of Grace's story, he had overlooked his duty to monitor the process. He apologised for the oversight while acknowledging her need to have been allowed to get all this off her chest, for, apart from Simon, David, and, to some degree, the children, no one else knew anything of what had been going on. Patrick covered the basics of confidentiality and contract he had skipped at the beginning and chose to offer Grace a single thought: that someone else did know, someone with no vested interest in the outcome, someone detached from all those others, someone who will be here at the same time next week if she would like to make another appointment. Grace met his eyes briefly, forced a weak smile, and reached for her handbag.

"I know I've got to make a decision one way or another," she said, "but I just cannot face that right now, so perhaps this is one commitment I can manage," and promptly wrote out a cheque for both sessions.

From his window above the car park, Patrick's eyes followed Grace across the tarmac towards a silver Audi, where she slipped into the driver's seat and checked her features in the rear-view mirror. After fumbling in her handbag she dabbed her face with a tissue. At last, she straightened, re-adjusted the mirror, fastened her seat belt and gripped the steering wheel. Patrick heard the muffled sound of an engine revving, but instead of moving off, Grace glanced up at the window causing him to step back sharply into the room. By the time he dared peer out again she had gone.

Chapter Five

"DO YOU THINK HE suspects?"

"No."

"You sure?"

'So this is why he suggested a walk,' thought Maggie, 'rather than heading straight back to his hotel, as usual.'

"Look Gavin, what's up with you? Come on, out with it!"

"Nothing, I was just thinking about the leaves still left on the trees and wondering what sort of winter we'll have," he replied, a little too glibly to allay her suspicion.

"Gavin!" Maggie's command was laden with intent.

"All right. I was wondering about us, about where it's going," he confessed.

She sought to press him.

"Where do you want it to go?"

They continued along the towpath in silence, for once careless that their gentle pace and absorbed manner surely gave them away as lovers, each step adding weight to the question that hung unanswered in the cool afternoon air.

They had lunched at a small pub down by the lock, in accord with their practice of selecting out-of-the-way places, preferably frequented by neither one before. Their respective jobs involved travel over a wide area of the north, ensuring the locations were varied and their liaisons well planned. Spontaneity being the prime missing ingredient in their relationship, his suggestion of a post-lunch walk along the towpath saw her leap at the prospect of something so innocent and ordinary, but she now saw that his suggestion was neither spontaneous, nor innocent. Lunch had been good: humus, salad, warm pitta bread, and a half-bottle of decent white, but the silence now churned her stomach as she anticipated where this uneasy conversation might be leading, and she braced herself for the sentence she dreaded hearing. Reckless of any concern for appearances, he reached and took her hand, clasped it tightly and began caressing her fingers with his thumb. His palm was warm, his touch intent. Was this how it would end, she wondered, almost a year to the day since they first met? He stopped in his tracks and turned towards her, his eyes tracing every feature of her face.

"I've something to tell you."

'Here it comes,' she thought, 'keep steady girl, and whatever you do, don't cry.'

"I've left Vicky."

"You've done what?" She hadn't seen this coming. Perhaps she didn't know him at all.

"I moved out yesterday. I've taken a six-month lease on an apartment not far from here, down by the wharf. I want to show you. I pick up the keys on Saturday, until then I'm staying at the hotel."

"Jeezus," she whispered. "Have you told her about us?"

"No, this isn't just about us; it's about me. I can't go on living a lie any longer. I know we have to put on an act when we're out in public but I'm no longer prepared to go on living a lie at home." And there was something in his strong voice and fine words that made her realize just how precious he was. She took his face in her hands, gave his lips a slow, loving kiss and felt him shudder at her touch. Slipping her arms around him she held him close, drinking him in until, full to the brim, she stepped back and reached out her hand.

"Come on," she said, "take me to bed."

There is something wonderfully decadent about sex in the afternoon, quite unlike any other time of day. By the time they had finished it was after four, but for once neither had any concern for the hour as they lay in the gathering gloom while the late autumn sun sank beneath the rooftop of the old warehouse opposite the hotel.

"It feels different," she said, removing the cigarette from his hand and taking a long, slow drag before replacing it between his fingers.

"You don't smoke!" he accused.

"I used to. See, you don't know everything about me."

22

Gavin pulled a face.

"What feels different?" he asked.

"Making love with a free man."

"In what way?"

"Not sure, I haven't figured it out yet. It just does."

"Better, or worse?"

"Riskier."

"How come?"

She paused before replying,

"It's worth more."

He stubbed out his cigarette, turned towards her and held her close, softly stroking her bare back with his free hand.

It was six-thirty and already dark outside when he awoke to find her sitting on the bed in fresh underwear, pulling on her hold-up stockings.

"You showered?" he asked.

"Of course."

"I didn't hear you."

"You were out like a light. You look like a little boy when you're asleep, I couldn't bear to wake you."

His lips and eyes gave a smile, and it warmed her heart.

"Don't forget these," he said, reaching under the covers and retrieving the worn panties discarded during their lovemaking and throwing them at her with a wink. She stowed them in her carpetbag alongside her unused golf attire.

"The rules will be changing, won't they?" she asked, wistfully.

"The rules?"

She threw him a weary look,

"Our rules."

"Oh, yeah, see what you mean. Guess so."

"Means I'll be able to phone you at home."

"And visit me."

Now it was Maggie's turn to pause before responding.

"We'll see," she said at last, and immediately thought of another change to the balance of their affair, one that she was not yet prepared to voice aloud, 'I've now got more to lose than you.'

She handed him the laminated card containing the room

service menu, asked him to choose something light, and a slim-line tonic.

"And get dressed, you'll have to sign for it."

It was almost nine as she left the ring road, turning things over in her mind. She hadn't got the measure of this new development. No doubt Gavin, freed from the constraints of living with, and lying to, his wife, would soon start expecting more from her. How would she cope with his increased accessibility in contrast to her own, and how would the platform that had sustained their affair survive the detachment of one of its four legs? Their lovemaking had always taken place on neutral sheets in hotel bedrooms, the marks and scent of their bodies removed by anonymous hands and quickly laundered out of existence. What would it be like to steal away from his bed, leaving her scent and juices for him to savour? Rather than chase answers, she decided to allow them to unfold in the course of time.

As she drove through the suburbs, instead of second guessing the future, she found herself thinking back to their first meeting, at a hotel in Birmingham, inadvertently sharing the lift down to breakfast; he'd smiled and made small talk, all friendly enough, nothing untoward. Then, some thirty minutes later, brief-cased and be-suited, waiting for the lift to take her down to reception, its metal door slid open.

"Hi again!" he beamed.

'Nice smile,' she thought.

"Good breakfast?"

"Mmmm ... fry-up," he answered sheepishly, "wouldn't be allowed it at home!"

She smiled again. 'Married then,' she thought to herself.

"Tomato ketchup!"

"Pardon?"

"On your tie!"

He glanced down at his silk tie, then up at her, and his eyes laughed as he covered his mouth with his hand, like a small boy caught raiding the toffee jar.

"It's the only one I've brought with me," and he pulled a face. "Running repairs!" he said, and headed off down the corridor with the intent of a cub scout, key-card in hand.

"Oh, thanks!" he called out, before opening the door, and he saw that she stood watching him, and for a split second the corridor was filled with the searching stare of these two strangers, until he was taken aback by the sound of his own voice winging its way across the empty space towards her.

"Are you staying here?"

She stared back.

"Well, I don't work here!"

"Yes, well no, I mean, tonight … will you still be here tonight?"

"Mmm-huh, until tomorrow."

"Me too. Fancy a drink in the bar this evening? Seven o'clock?"

She smiled broadly, gave a cynical sigh and turned away before she blushed, just as the lift door closed in her face. She grimaced, as much in embarrassment as irritation and when she opened her eyes and glanced back to where he had stood, he was still there, grinning inanely. She frowned, shook her head, and strode off to find the stairs.

As she descended the four flights, she had no idea what her answer would be. Later in the day, during intervals between meetings with architects and clients, when touching up her make-up at a toilet mirror, she remembered, and fell to wondering. It was only later, back at the hotel as she lazed in a long bath, that she knew the answer.

There was no need to fret over what to wear; apart from her work suit, she had packed only a pair of jeans and new white linen shirt. He was seated at the far end of the bar facing the entrance, looking relaxed in grey moleskin jacket, white tee-shirt, blue jeans. His eyes lit up. 'Nice eyes, they really speak,' she thought, as she wandered across and he stood to greet her.

"Gavin Bell."

They shook hands.

"Maggie Chime."

And as the ridiculous juxtaposition dawned on them both, they let go, raised their hands to their mouths and began to giggle.

"Well, that's the ice broken" he said.

By the time they had eaten and the waiter had brought them

each a second cup of coffee, they understood without saying that they would most likely end up in bed, but each appreciated, again without needing to explain, that it would not happen tonight. The first requirement was that they must step back, take stock, and re-commit, for they were both were well aware that the stakes were already too high to settle for a one-night stand.

The car behind gave a polite toot; Maggie hadn't noticed the lights change. She hurriedly found first gear and pulled abruptly away and, by the time she found third, was already pushing thoughts of Gavin back into the safe compartments of her mind, and gathering herself for the arrival home.

Spotting the old Saab neatly backed onto the drive Maggie decided she was too tired to emulate the manoeuvre and instead drove straight in, parking alongside, nose to tail. Were she not feeling somewhat tense at the sudden memory of that morning's row, the symbolism of this parking arrangement might well have occurred to her, the two vehicles juxtaposed in a travesty of the position her and her lover's bodies had adopted with such reverential concentration, a few hours earlier.

"Hi," Patrick called out as she closed the front door behind her and she was glad of the confirmation that they were back on speaking terms. She found him in the back room downstairs, spread across the larger of the two sofas, feet up, thick walking socks that might well have been hers, jogging bottoms, sweatshirt, hair tousled, unshaven since the morning. She noticed the gas fire was on full and remembered the problem with the central-heating boiler.

"You look rough," she said, not unkindly. "Been asleep?"

"Nodded off," he said, stretching, "the front door woke me up."

"Sorry."

"No-no, it's all right. Did you have a good day?" he enquired, and made it sound like he hoped she had.

"It was all right. You know what those corporate golf things are like."

"Do I?"

She looked down at him. He was staring vacantly at the television, the sound turned off. He filled the silence with a weary sigh.

"You all right?" she asked, in a tone conveying as much suspicion as concern.

He raised his eyes in her general direction but from where he lay could see only her bottom half, so returned his gaze to the screen.

"Me? Yeah, three clients, two supervisees, long day's listening, I'm tired."

"Mmm, me too," she replied with what she hoped was at least a note of affection, for right now she was more interested in establishing common ground than division.

"I'll go and put your golf clubs in the garage," he said, hauling himself up from the sofa.

"Leave them," she said, "they'll be fine in the car 'til morning."

He pulled a face but chose not to object, and stood to face her.

"About this morning ... the gas man."

"I know," she interjected, "Don't worry about it."

And with that they trudged upstairs to bed.

Chapter Six

"WHAT HAVE YOU GOT today?" Maggie enquired, as he filled her glass with orange juice.

They each understood this to be a coded way of asking, "*Who* have you got today?" out of due regard for the sensitivities of Patrick's profession. For the very same reason, his answer would be delivered in the form of nicknames for his various clients, a device employed throughout the fourteen years of his private practice and most could be recalled by Maggie as well, if not better, than himself: there was his first ever client, *Mr Well-Shod,* a control freak and self-made businessman of sixty-five, so thrown by his wife's sudden decision to leave him that he turned up at his first session wearing odd shoes; and *Miss Stunning,* who, for sixteen sessions never wore the same outfit twice, then failed to show up for the seventeenth and Patrick never heard from her again – he said it was because she'd reached the end of her wardrobe; there was the *Young Fogey,* sadly old before his time, and the *Singing Nun,* the ex-novice who'd been abused by her father, and longed to be a singer but got panic attacks before auditions; there was *Your Honour,* the barrister who turned up for his first appointment straight from court sporting brilliant white tennis shoes beneath his pin-stripe trousers. Then of course, there were the couples: *Musetta and Marcello,* not strictly speaking a couple, she, the bountiful, estranged wife of a successful property developer, he, the young lover who had begun to tire of her gifts and charms, and who, when dragged along to her first session, sat downstairs in her car, stubbornly refusing to come in. She pleaded with Patrick to go down and fetch him and was most put out when he refused. There was *Jack Spratt and his wife,* and *The Tit-for-tats,* who all speak for themselves; and of course, *B.L.T.,* the couple who spent sixty pounds (Patrick charges more for couples) and an entire hour arguing over his loving preparation of, and her dismissive response to, a club sandwich. That was about as much as she knew of these people, although, in the early days, when Patrick was more open with her, she sensed, from his tone of voice, which of them was getting under his skin, those he worried over or found irritating, and the ones he really enjoyed. She knew, without being told, whenever he was due to see *Miss Stunning* for he could never decide which shirt to wear. For his part, Patrick enjoyed the fact that these nicknames enabled him to share something of his professional life with his wife, while preserving his clients' identities. Nowadays, of course, this device had become mere habit, of little more meaning than her informing him that she had a meeting down in London, or a site visit over in Manchester. Their professional worlds butted up uneasily against each other; Patrick had due regard, but little admiration, for his wife's work, and although Maggie still harboured an element of respect for his, she no longer held it in awe. At her company's 'do' last Christmas, she had introduced him to a male colleague, who expressed interest in what line of business Patrick was in. 'Oh, that's different' he'd remarked, 'and must be interesting.' 'Not really,' Maggie interjected, flirtatiously, 'we're all whores, darling; I sell carpet by the metre, he pedals attention by the minute, and I've got the better sales figures!' On the way home, he'd challenged her about it, said it made him feel cheap, his work was better than that. She laughed and told him he should put his fees up. They drove home in silence, and by the time he parked up on the drive she was asleep. In the morning, she was hung-over and he was still smarting. When at last he reminded her what she'd said, she apologised, blaming too much white wine.

"… No one," he replied. "I'm briefly calling at the office then driving over to see Beth at eleven, so I'll be home early. I've phoned the plumber by the way; he's coming after two this afternoon; I'll be back well before then."

"Oh right, good," she replied, careful not to show too much appreciation. She felt jealous of her husband's supervision sessions with Beth, who, at nearly seventy and having been married for forty years, was the woman her husband had chosen to confide in for an hour and a half, once a month for the past fourteen years. Maggie understood, of course, that ongoing supervision was a professional requirement, but what other profession gave it quite the same status? *DRIVER UNDER SUPERVISION* it says on the back of a bus and no passengers allowed on until the driver has passed muster. Whereas counsellors and psychotherapists, no matter how experienced or well qualified, are required to have monthly supervision until the day they retire. Maggie once asked Patrick to whom Beth goes for supervision of her supervision? She meant it as a joke but he recited the woman's name immediately. 'Christ, where does it all end?' she asked, half expecting him to answer 'God', or at least 'Freud', but Patrick just stared back, unflustered. She used to tease him about the measure of dependence built into such a system but ceased the day he informed her that her criticisms were simply born out of envy. He was right, although it wasn't supervision as such that she envied, but the prospect of being appreciated, understood and attended to by a wise and caring woman, old enough to be her mother.

"Oh well, enjoy it, I must rush," she said, gathering up her things, "business calls."

"Leave the breakfast things, I'll clear up," he called out, as she reached the front door.

"Ha-ha!" she cried cynically, and, unseen by him, stuck out her tongue. "See you tonight," she called, as the door slammed behind her.

Alone at the table, surrounded by the detritus of breakfast, Patrick felt a sadness descend. Breakfast was so half-hearted an affair these days: cereal bolted down, coffee and juice left half-drunk. It was different when Nuala was around; Nuala drew breakfast out until the last possible moment, spreading Marmite on one half of her toast, marmalade on the other, jabbering away with him all the while, or chattering down the phone to one of her school friends, who in a matter of minutes she would meet up with on the bus; and then her shock as she realised the time, shoved back the stool across the tiled floor and rushed for the door, often as not grabbing a half-slice of toast off his plate as she passed. Whereas Maggie ... Maggie

30

would be somewhere in the background, lurking by the kettle or toaster, one ear on the radio, or more likely upstairs in her study, sorting out her diary, or already on the telephone, confirming or re-scheduling some appointment. 'Maggie, come and sit down and eat!' he'd plead, but it seldom did any good and somewhere along the way he just accepted it. Only now, with Nuala gone, did he feel the draught around the table.

He picked up his mobile.

"Nuala?"

"Oh, hi, Dad, how goes?"

"Yeah, fine. And you?"

"Yeah, cool. Just on my way into Uni, got an early lecture on Fridays, what a bummer."

"Okay, won't keep you. Thought we might come up and see you on Sunday, maybe take you out for lunch."

"Umm, Sunday … yeah, well, look, can I phone you back later? Gotta go."

"Sure, okay, take care," he said hurriedly, adding, "love you!" just as the phone went dead. For a moment, Patrick felt the swell of gathering tears, but took a deep breath, stowed the breakfast things into the dishwasher, grabbed his wallet, diary, keys and chequebook, and left the house to itself.

At the office he found two answer-phone messages. The first was from a woman called Gina, requesting an appointment, she said she had been highly impressed by his directory entry and was prepared to wait. The other was from Jake Dean, a physiotherapist who had been given Patrick's name by a nurse colleague who had consulted Patrick a couple of years ago; he wanted an appointment as soon as possible and left a mobile number. Patrick tried Gina's number; it was engaged. He returned Jake's call but was diverted straight to voice mail, where he left details of his fees and an appointment for nine-thirty the following morning. Offering two Saturday morning slots was intended as a way of reducing the number of evenings Patrick saw clients. In the event, over the two years since their introduction, he found he enjoyed those Saturday appointments more than any other time of the week; somehow, his Saturday clients seemed more relaxed, more open than

31

when they saw him during, or at the end of, a working day. Of course, the thought had occurred to Patrick that the same might also be said of him, as he found it all too easy to skip off to work leaving Maggie to her Saturday lie-in. He was somewhat relieved that she had never questioned why, less than a year since the Saturday morning slot was instigated, he had slipped back into his former pattern of seeing clients on three evenings a week.

Patrick loved the journey over Strines Moor to Beth's farmhouse in the Peak District. The narrow road twisted, turned, climbed and swooped down through the rugged terrain, offering numerous vistas that took his breath away even after all these years; a bit like his consultations with Beth herself. Although semi-retired, Beth remained nobody's fool and he considered himself fortunate to have enjoyed her support, challenge and wisdom throughout the greater part of his career. When he first approached her he had baulked at her fees, but, a decade on, he marvelled at their good value, and not just because, unlike his own, hers had not kept pace with inflation.

It was a grey, overcast morning and he used the journey to consider which aspects of his current work he should present. Neil … most certainly, and of course, his ending with Sarah just a fortnight ago after more than three years hard struggle for them both. Having been sexually abused throughout her childhood, and having survived two suicide attempts, Sarah remained, at forty-nine, vulnerable and lonely, but no longer felt herself a victim. Yes, Neil and Sarah, that should suffice. Just then, an image of Grace Darling, (he'd forgotten her married name) popped into his mind, but he ushered it away.

He pulled up in the lane outside and at the gate a pair of ducks came to greet him as usual. He stepped around them and approached the left-hand of the two white-painted doors. He recalled the very first occasion when he'd knocked on the left-hand door only for Beth's face to appear at the right. The following month, he knocked on the right hand door and Beth opened the left. He couldn't decide whether she was toying with him, or in keeping with her psychodynamic background, unconsciously presenting the classical Kleinian dilemma of

32

good breast or bad? Either way, he'd guessed wrongly and felt a fool, but she warmed to him when he confessed his embarrassment, and he warmed to her when she told him that instead of feeling embarrassed, he might have told her to put a bloody sign on the door! His second dilemma had been over which seat to take? Beth had already claimed hers, leaving him the choice between an easy chair with thick arms or a huge, squidgy sofa. He opted for the sofa and immediately regretted it, feeling marooned in a vast lifeboat without rudder or paddle. On his next visit he dived into the armchair where he'd remained ever since.

As usual, Beth's coffee was weak but welcome nonetheless, and the fine bone china cup and the little macaroon biscuit placed, as always, in the saucer, reminded him of visits to his grandmother as a small boy, a not uncomfortable comparison, as he always cycled away from his grandma's feeling nurtured and at least an inch taller in the saddle.

He commenced with Sarah, and was surprised to find this took up the best part of an hour. They reviewed this long-term piece of work, which had tested him as much as anything he'd faced before. Sarah's despair arose from a deep slab of shame relating to a catalogue of losses: the sudden loss of her husband; the removal of a breast; the deaths of her cat, her brother, and her best friend; as well as being made redundant from the part-time job she valued; all these gouged out of her life during the eighteen months prior to contacting Patrick. She regularly cast Patrick in the guise of Saint Jerome, who would always be there and never lose faith in her. At other times, she saw him as an exasperated schoolmaster, who sooner or later would tire of her shortcomings and write her off as a lost cause. He'd relied heavily upon Beth's support to contain those powerful projections, and remain for Sarah something more realistic: a compassionate, thoughtful witness to her story. Just when he thought it might be appropriate to move on to discuss Neil, Beth brought him up short.

"Patrick, we've talked about what you must have meant to Sarah, and, without doubt, she'll never forget you. In a long career we see many hundreds of clients but only a small handful really change us as a therapist, and I think Sarah is one of those. So tell me, what mark has Sarah left on you?"

Patrick knew better than to chase an answer, as he would have done back in the early days when he was so keen to impress. Instead he allowed Beth's question to weave its way between the slatted walls of his consciousness to see what it triggered. He pictured the bouquet of flowers he'd presented to Sarah as she left his office for the very last time, something he had never considered doing for any client before, and the card, bearing the message, *To Sarah, A Decent Woman,* and felt a tightening in his chest. He visualised Nuala's face, staring down from the window of her room in halls the day he deposited her at university, so grown-up, so composed, waving her daddy goodbye; and he'd waved back, wondering what had become of the vulnerable little girl that used to run down the hallway and leap into his arms when he arrived home from work, who used to cry on his shoulder, and who he'd carry from the car after long journeys back from the cross-channel ferry, trying hard not to wake her. And he visualized that morning's breakfast table, sitting alone, surrounded by all the droppings and leavings, and a wave of tears swelled in his chest.

Beth was alive to his pain, and addressed it gently, "It's hard to say goodbye and let go," she said, "when you've been through such a lot together."

Patrick recognised the validity of her sentiment but was unsure precisely to whom it referred.

"I'm not good at letting go of things," he replied. "Should have dumped my car by now; and I miss Nuala dreadfully since she's gone off to university; it hurts to even think about it. I suppose that's why therapy has been such a suitable profession for me, providing a steady stream of temporary intimate attachments. It's like London tube trains, little need to mourn one's passing because there'll be another along any minute."

"An interesting image, Patrick, but some clients are more special to us than others, aren't they?" and she fixed him with that penetrative stare he knew so well. And as he looked into his supervisor's eyes, he wondered, just for a moment, whether he might be special to her, and feeling himself start to blush, he quickly brought the focus back to Sarah.

"Yes, Sarah was special."

"To me too," said Beth, "remember, almost every month for the past three years, I've sat here listening to your struggle to be there for her, and let me tell you Patrick, it's the best work you've ever done."

And he was suddenly eight years old again, and an inch taller in the saddle.

Only twenty-five minutes remained to talk about Neil. He gave Beth a succinct summary of Neil drawn from their seven sessions to date:

"Thirty-four years old, though seeming younger, despite his receding hair; Neil works at a call centre in Leeds and hates it; a bit of a loner, he struggles to make relationships with the opposite sex; women find him too serious, too intense, 'a bit creepy,' one said, and they soon drop him. Neil seethes with anger but doesn't know what to do with it. It leaks out from time to time but most of it he turns in on self. He originally went to his GP to get something for depression, but omitted to tell the doctor he was addicted to Internet porn." At this point, Beth thought she detected a trace of contempt in Patrick's voice and wondered whether it was in response to Neil's Internet habits, or something else, but decided to allow Patrick to complete his summary.

"The GP referred Neil to the practice counsellor, but he saw her only a couple of times and gave up on her."

"Do you know why?" asked Beth.

"I asked him at our first session and I remember he pulled a contemptuous face. Apparently all she did was keep asking how he felt, and every time he told her she just said, 'Hmm-huh.' 'Typical bloody counsellor,' according to Neil."

"Okay," said Beth, glancing at the clock, "so, why are you telling me about him now?"

"Because the work has started to move on, he's begun challenging me on whether I really give a damn or not, and whether it's worth persevering with therapy. He wants me to assure him that it is."

"And do you?" Beth asked, in that typically pointed fashion of hers, which he'd incorporated into his own style.

35

"No way, that's for him to decide," he said, a little too sharply to get under her radar.

"You don't like him much, do you, Patrick?"

The blow was like a punch to the solar plexus, and brought him up short.

"Is it that obvious?"

Beth saw no need to answer this; she knew what was required.

"What is about him you don't like, Patrick?"

Patrick understood the value of her question, but still visibly squirmed.

"Neil plays simultaneous projective identifications, dependence on the one hand, power on the other, the worst combination to work with."

Beth was unimpressed.

"Patrick, don't hide behind theory. I know the theory. Such clients are demanding of help yet resistant to whatever you try and do for them. But you've had lots of difficult clients, and you don't always dislike them."

'Got me,' thought Patrick. He'd already owned up in his case notes to his dislike of Neil, but had not seen fit to explore its origins. Beth's question was necessary, and one he found difficult to answer. After a lengthy pause, he blurted it out.

"I don't like his mouth. He's got weak wet lips, you know, like a toddler's; milky lips, always scoffing, milk and juice running down the chin, but he never gets full; in one end and out the other."

"You fear he might suck you dry, Patrick? And all your care and nourishment won't be sufficient to satisfy this pained and troubled young man?"

"Yeah. But he spits out whatever I give him, and then asks for more."

Beth smiled. She knew she'd got him, and could afford to treat him gently.

"I know how that hurts, Patrick, and even the most caring and concerned parent can feel utterly useless once the little brat learns the power of spitting parental love back in our face. It can easily become a battle. But such battles aren't really about food, are they Patrick, and Neil's attempts to get you to assure him that it's right to continue with therapy, aren't really about therapy, are they? Maybe what he's really worried about is what you really feel towards him, and whether you really *want* to continue working with him. It's quite hard, isn't it, to ask what you really mean to someone?"

Patrick said nothing, but noticed how his jaws had clenched in response to Beth's line of enquiry.

"I've noticed, Patrick, you're less tolerant of men's needs in this respect, and have a tendency to hold back some of your warmth with some male clients?"

"What do you mean?" Patrick asked, tamely.

"Well, I wonder if there are issues of gender, in this, and perhaps identification, that might be getting in the way between the two of you, creating a barrier for trust?"

"Neil does find trust difficult," Patrick argued, "and it's because deep down he doesn't really trust himself."

"I don't think you're hearing what I'm saying," countered Beth, "maybe the difficulty doesn't rest only with Neil?"

"How do you mean?"

Beth allowed the question to hang.

"You think about it," she said at last. "Our time is up for today. I'll see you next month."

Sometimes Beth could be infuriating.

Chapter Seven

ON HER WAY HOME Maggie called at a small shop selling gifts and greetings cards and chose a square Charles Rennie Mackintosh design embossed on superior, off-white, matt card. She paid the woman, wrote her message, *To your pied-a-terre ... x,* sealed the envelope and extracted from the zipped compartment of her handbag the card bearing Gavin's new address.

Her day had been fraught but had ended with confirmation that she had won the contract to carpet the new hotel being built on the site of an old brewery. She was mightily relieved, despite it being no more than she felt she deserved for the effort put into winning over the client. She made use of the post box across the road before calling at the off-licence a few doors along and picking up two bottles of champagne, one of which came straight from the chill cabinet; she placed it on the passenger seat, the other she stowed in a corner of the boot.

It was six o'clock, already dark, and the mature shrubs that lined their drive shivered in the hastening wind as she edged her new car in alongside Patrick's old Saab. The temperature had dropped sharply over the course of the day and the forecast for the weekend warned of gales and torrential rain and as the first drops dotted the windscreen Maggie felt glad to be home. Her hands full, she pressed the doorbell with her nose, but, with no response forthcoming, put down bottle, handbag and laptop, located her key and let herself in. She discovered Patrick upstairs soaking in the bath, a John Martyn CD blaring from the small machine in the bedroom.

She found him lying back in the water, eyes closed, head swaying to the rhythm of the music, quite unaware of her presence as she leaned against the door jamb. For once completely free to observe him, she had forgotten just how pale was his body, despite seeing it almost every day. His torso had thickened in his forties, and the fact that he could stand to lose a few pounds was evidenced by the way the crown of his belly breached the surface of the water like a small island. In the shallows, his penis dancing this way and that, creating little eddies above itself, such that it seemed to her a quite semi-detached thing, perhaps not unlike the wife she had become; a comparison she had little desire to pursue right now, for she knew it didn't always pay to enquire too deeply into things; you're likely to reach conclusions and then have to do something about them. She assumed that was why she had entered an affair rather than therapy; besides, with Patrick so prominent in his field, to whom could she possibly have confided?

Her eyes travelled up her husband's body until she regarded his face, eyes still closed, head floating from side to side on the tide of the song, lips mouthing the words. Like a small child engrossed in the delight of his own senses he remained oblivious to her presence, and for once, truly vulnerable. She was disturbed to realise how unsure she was of her feelings about his vulnerability. It wasn't always so. It was those glimpses of the relaxed, unselfconscious, young man that she had initially fallen in love with, but which had become so maddeningly elusive once he began training as a counsellor. She used to wonder if he let go elsewhere, with colleagues, friends, or a lover perhaps? Most likely with colleagues, for he had no real friends any more, having lost contact with those from schooldays and long since having dropped his cricketing pals and the colleagues from his previous career in the Probation Service. As for lovers, there was a bit of something with a neighbour way back in the early years of their marriage; it evolved out of a foursome, which, thanks to too much wine and hormones, became a little too close over a summer of long Saturday evenings. Far from a swingers' orgy, what began with smoochy dancing with the lights down low, developed into a little regulated partner-swapping, with much kissing and fumbling, but the clothes kept strictly on. But a torch was lit and for a while the other woman, Suzie, sought to carve a little niche for herself with Patrick, but Maggie was wise to it and let her know that she was trespassing on private property. Within a few months the other couple had moved away.

Maggie assumed there might have been some sort of fling with a fellow trainee back during Patrick's residential training courses with Relate, with a ratio of six women to every man there was no shortage of opportunity, but she never asked, and he never said; besides, she could see it was the work he was infatuated with, and any woman, however attractive, would have had to put up with coming a poor second.

Unaware that her gaze had shifted from Patrick's face to the wall above the bath, and had lost itself in a patterned tile, Maggie failed to register that the track had ended or that Patrick's eyes were now wide open, staring up at her.

"Christ!" he said, making her jump. "I could have been murdered in my bath; what a way to go, and to the strains of *Johnny Too Bad,* how appropriate. Hello, darling, I'd invite you in but there's not enough room."

"There was a time," she replied, gathering her composure, "of course, we were both slimmer then," she added, choosing to overlook the fact that she remained the same neat size ten as when first they met.

"That's generous of you," he said knowingly, and, impervious to any riposte, dunked his head under the water. She stared down into his distorted features as he held his breath for what must have been half a minute. He used to tease her like this when they first got together and he knew how she hated it; she always wanted to walk away but knew she must wait until he surfaced. A tiny bubble escaped from the corner of his mouth, then another, then nothing more as he held every fibre of his body still in order to eke out a few more precious seconds. When he finally broke the surface he looked across to the doorway. It stood empty.

He appeared downstairs wearing a towelling dressing gown, hair still damp, and found her in the kitchen dressed in jeans, vest, and spangled flip-flops, chopping a large onion. She did not look up.

"You okay?" he asked, tentatively.

She nodded and sniffed. He moved closer, taking up position just behind her.

"You crying?" he asked,

"It's the onions," she sniffed again, "they get to me," and her shoulders gave a heave.

"I thought that was my role in life," he replied, putting his hands on her shoulders.

Her body stiffened and she slammed the knife down on the board.

"Don't do that!" she snapped, and he let go at once.

"Sorry! Bit touchy are we? Bad day at the office?"

"It wasn't your hands," she said intently, "it's your words, Pat, I can't keep up with the verbal gymnastics; I get tired of chasing each other round in words and getting nowhere. I'm tired, okay? Just leave it that!"

A sticky silence followed, pierced only by her half-hearted attempts to chop the onions even smaller. Concerned she might have gone too far, she sought to strike a conciliatory note.

"As it happens, Pat, I've had a very good day, that ended with confirmation I've got the hotel contract, the culmination of a lot of hard work." And with that she planted a kiss on his cheek, informed him there was a bottle of champagne in the fridge that required opening, and set about attacking the remaining half of the onion.

In silence, he did as she asked, fetched two flutes from the cupboard and placed them on a small tray, took up the bottle, stripped the collar and cage from its neck, gripped the head of the cork and slowly twisted the bottle, drawing the cork with a muffled pop before tossing it casually into the sink. He poured two half glasses, topping up each in turn. Taking the tray in one hand he approached her like a waiter at a cocktail party.

"Madame?"

She shuffled the chopped onions into a neat pile at the centre of the board, before turning to face him with a sweet smile.

"Why thank you, kind sir," she replied, and gave a little curtsey before taking the glass and raising it to her lips.

"Madame … here's to you … very well done!" and he could not have sounded more genuine.

Peace restored, she felt relieved. Still more so when he told her to go on through to the lounge and relax as he would finish the food.

"Hot spicy prawns," she said, helpfully, "the prawns are in the freezer."

"Yeah, I know," he said, "go on, off with you, I'll see to this." And as she turned away his hand aimed a pat at her neat arse. He missed.

That night they made love and had sex, although it was never quite clear who was doing which at any one time. Nonetheless, it seemed to Patrick there was more to it than their usual well-choreographed pattern, something perhaps in the odd moments of stillness, when one or the other was a little more open, a little more aware, of what was being given, what was being received. He pondered this as he lay in the dark afterwards, and whether it was worth remarking upon. He was still considering it as he fell asleep.

Maggie lay in the dark, listening to the tap-tap-tap of rain upon the window, and the reassuring sound of Patrick's breath, rising and falling like a low, midnight tide caressing the shingles. She thought of his penis inside her just minutes before, a, for once, not unwelcome guest who appeared to regard and appreciate her, rather than just taking its fill in return for the earlier product of his lips and fingers. What was missing between herself and Patrick, she realised, was not orgasms, orgasms are easy, but what she had in abundance with Gavin, and possibly glimpsed an inkling of again just now: the realisation of what it is to play both guest and host, and willingly embrace whichever role is allotted in the moment, in body, as in heart and mind. Most men, Patrick once told her, see sex as a means to intimacy, whereas for most women, intimacy is a pre-requisite for sex. 'There's a recipe for frustration if ever there was one,' she'd replied. But when she was with Gavin, intimacy and lust were like tango dancers, each taking turns to forge ahead, but maintaining perfect contact throughout.

Her chest swelled as she drew a long, deep breath and her thoughts sailed away over rooftops, gardens, pavements, streets, and countless secret spaces of the heart, to the anonymous bed where her lover lay asleep, his last night in that anonymous hotel room, and she planted a kiss on the small of his neck and felt his flesh quiver. She imagined Gavin's wife, Vicky, lying awake, trying to piece together the shattered fragments of her marriage, *The bed's too big, the frying pan's too wide,* as the old Joni Mitchell song put it so acutely. 'Surely Vicky must realise a vital piece of the jigsaw is missing,' thought Maggie, before her thoughts left Vicky and retreated to that warm berth inside her that these past few months she had given so freely to Gavin, and into which, moments ago, her husband unloaded his own soft cargo, which now oozed and seeped into the Egyptian cotton sheet. She and Patrick were well practised at living together; they still fitted, but no longer well enough. And in her heart, Maggie knew as much, which is why the more meaningful wet patch was the one spreading slowly, relentlessly, across her pillow.

Chapter Eight

PATRICK PLACED THE MUG of tea upon Maggie's bedside table and gave her shoulder a gentle squeeze.

"Mmm, what's the time?" she drawled, without opening her eyes.

"Ten past eight," he whispered, "I'm setting off soon; got a new client at nine-thirty. Your tea's here."

"Mmm … Saturday," she groaned, "I'm having a lie in," and briefly opened her eyes and gave him a weak smile.

"Why don't you, you sound bushed. Get some rest. Don't forget we're at Sheffield tonight."

Maggie's eyes opened abruptly, "Sheffield?"

"The Lyceum, *La Bohème*, remember? I said I'd try and get tickets."

"But you didn't say you'd got them."

"Didn't I?"

"No, you apologised for the fact that we'd seen it twice before but said we could do with a good cry and you'd try and get two tickets and when I never heard any more I assumed you'd either forgotten all about it, or they'd sold out."

"Sorry, thought I'd said. Not great seats, way up in the gods, all they had left."

"Up in the gods?" she whispered to herself.

"Is it a problem?"

"No, course not. It'll be lovely. It will."

"Bring tissues, fetch lots," he quipped. "See you at lunchtime." He set off down the stairs.

"Okay … take care," she added, out of earshot, without knowing why. And as she listened to his car start up and drive away, she tried to remember whether or not he had actually informed her about the tickets.

Patrick arrived at the mill at nine-fifteen. A new-style Mini was parked near the car park gate, its driver made no move to acknowledge him, but Patrick sensed its occupant might be waiting for him. He opened up the office and checked the answer machine: just one message, from his eleven o'clock appointment, postponing due to car trouble. Patrick remembered Nuala; how was it left, was he supposed to phone her? A call this early on a Saturday wouldn't go down well, anyway, her phone would no doubt be switched off. He sent a text: *we'll pick u up Sunday at 12, x.* He had just finished when there was a knock, and a lean, well-tanned boyish face appeared around the door.

"Hi, I'm a little early, sorry!" the voice carried warmth and appeal, which impressed Patrick, despite the intrusion.

"That's okay," said Patrick, "but don't make it a habit, I won't always be ready," and just as the young man was about to retreat, Patrick's reassuring smile and proffered hand beckoned him into the room.

"Patrick Chime."

"Jake Dean."

Jake's grip was firm and carried conviction.

"Welcome Jake, let's go through."

Jake settled himself in the chair furthest from Patrick's and threw his coat onto its empty neighbour. His hair was streaked, brown on blond, or the other way round; an earring, leather-thong bracelet; gay, Patrick guessed. He dealt with the basics of boundaries and confidentiality to which Jake nodded readily, conveying what Patrick recognised as a touch of impatience.

"So, why are you here?" asked Patrick, cutting to the chase with gentle precision.

"I've been living a lie and can't go on any more." Jake's well-rehearsed opening gambit was delivered with confidence. "I've got to tell someone something that is going to ruin their life and I don't to how to do it. That's why I've come."

"A sort of rehearsal?" asked Patrick.

"Yeah. I think about it all the time, in the car, at work, and when I lie awake at night. I'm a physio at the General Hospital, and also work part-time at a sports injury clinic – it's worse at home because it's always in my head, the words chase themselves around, I re-arrange the sentence this way and that but it won't come out and I think my brain's going to explode."

"What is the sentence?" asked Patrick, with a rare directness so early in a first session. It was just what Jake needed.

"I'm gay," he replied, and his watery eyes looked beseechingly across at Patrick.

"Hmm. And who is the someone it's so hard to say that to?"

"Kia … my wife."

Patrick nodded but said nothing; he didn't need to, for Jake took up the slack.

"When we got married, I knew there was maybe ten per cent of me was attracted to men, but I thought it would diminish in time because Kia and I got on so well. Well, seven years and two kids later, that ten per cent is more like eighty, and I've been having a relationship for the last few months with a guy I met at the clinic who wants us to be together. I feel such a shit, I know I've got to tell Kia but I'm dreading it."

"What are you're so afraid of?"

"How she'll take it?"

"And what's your worst fear about that?"

"It'll destroy her."

"What will?"

Jake looked puzzled.

"What precisely do you imagine will destroy Kia?" repeated Patrick.

Jake looked nonplussed, prompting Patrick to continue.

"Is it the shock of the unexpected; the impending loss of you; the shattering of her idea of you; the impact on your children; the humiliation of having to explain to family and friends; the fear of having contacted H.I.V.? Or something else?"

"You don't spare the horses, do you?"

"Would you rather I pretended, Jake? I thought you were sick and tired of pretence?" And Patrick noticed the sharp edge to his own voice, and wondered momentarily what Beth would have made of it.

Jake hung his head and fiddled with his wristband before replying.

"I am sick of all the pretence, it just that it sounds so awful when you spell it all out like that."

"Jake," Patrick consciously injected an element of warmth into his voice, "I'm just trying to help you be more specific. Are you telling me that those possible consequences haven't occurred to you already?"

"No. Of course they have, I think about them all the time, it's just the first time I've heard them said out loud by somebody else. Michael, that's my friend, says she'll get over it and the sooner I tell her the better. But it's not that easy. I love Kia, that might sound ridiculous, but I do, and what I've done, and what I'm contemplating doing, is unforgivable."

"You want – forgiveness?" asked Patrick.

"I've no right to expect it, I know that."

"Who would you like forgiveness from, Jake?"

"From Kia, I suppose, who else?"

"Well, I imagine there's your own family, and Kia's family, but also your children, who are too young to fully comprehend, but they won't always be, and gay or straight, living with them or apart, you're still their father."

Jake looked sombre and lowered his head to avoid Patrick's gaze.

"I'm frightened Kia will tell me I can't see them any more."

"You think that's likely?"

"I don't know, she'll be devastated, I'm not sure what she'll do, but I can't imagine she'll ever forgive me."

"Some seek forgiveness from God," Patrick said, at which Jake scoffed and shook his head, "but sooner or later," he went on, "we have to decide whether we can forgive ourselves."

"Yeah, I've thought about that. I used to think my mum might have guessed, but she never came right out and asked. I sometimes wished she would. And then, when we got married, Mum seemed, well, so pleased. It would crease her up if she ended up losing contact with her grandchildren."

"What about your dad, Jake?"

"Him? He's been out of the picture for years; new wife, new life. He's not interested in me, or his grandchildren. He sends them money at birthdays and Christmas but hardly ever sees them. Look, I'm not ashamed of what I am; what I'm ashamed of is the deceit, and not just over this last year, but back at the beginning, I should have been more open with Kia then, I should have trusted her more."

"And you didn't trust her with your 'ten per cent' because…?"

"She'd have dropped me. She's so straight-up-and-down; she could never have accepted something like that. And if I'd found the courage to tell her then things wouldn't have got this far."

"And your two children wouldn't exist. Would you change that if you could?"

"Not now, of course not." Jake insisted, and went on to describe his relationship with the son and daughter, who clearly meant a lot to him.

"Okay," said Patrick at last, "the fact remains that you found someone, chose someone, you thought would never be able to understand or come to terms with that part of you that you found so hard to accept in yourself?"

"Yeah, but what woman could accept something like that?" Jake retorted.

Patrick chose not to get diverted into discussing the range of female attitudes towards homosexuality and bisexuality, or the myriad structures and patterns of marital life he had heard described within these walls over the years.

"What makes you think Kia doesn't already know," he asked instead, "or at least harbour suspicions? Are you that good an actor?"

"I try to be. It feels like an act all the time, especially in bed. Not that there's been much of that since the kids were born. I suppose you expect sex to tail off once kids come along; and it took a while for Kia to get over Billie's birth and the change to the pattern of our lives, and then, when she started to get interested again I was the one making the excuses."

"How often do you and Kia have sex these days?" asked Patrick casually, as if it was the most ordinary question in the world.

"It got down to maybe once a month, now it's stopped altogether; the last time was back in August. It was her birthday. Some present!" he sniggered. "We still cuddle up on the settee and in bed; that's when we're closest. I really do care about her, you know." There was urgency in his voice as his eyes filled with tears and he looked across beseechingly at Patrick.

"I believe you," said Patrick, and meant it.

"Do you ever wonder, Jake, about the possible explanations that run through Kia's mind when she lies awake, trying to figure out why the husband who cares about her so deeply can't, or won't, make love to her? She must have asked you what's wrong?" Patrick cursed himself for adding a second question on top of the first and thereby blurring the focus.

"Many times, many times."

"And how do you answer?"

"I used to say I was tired or that I was stressed at work; I had a new line manager for a while who I didn't get on with, but then he left and I couldn't use that excuse any more so I just said I didn't know, I couldn't explain.'"

"But you did know, and you could have explained, but were frightened of Kia's response?"

Jake sighed.

"It sounds pathetic, I've been a real chicken-shit."

"Well, I imagine it isn't the easiest thing in the world to tell a spouse, but you won't be the first man or woman who has had to do it; but then, you wouldn't be the first to go on living a lie. The choice is yours, Jake."

"There is no choice," Jake interjected fiercely, "I've got to tell her," and there was a steely determination in his voice.

"But you already knew that before you came here today?" Patrick suggested pointedly.

"Yes, but I wasn't doing anything about it, was I?"

"Are you really sure you're going to tell her?"

"Yes," Jake nodded, "I've got to."

"But first you had to own up to someone else?"

"Hmm. Apart from Michael, no one else knows. There's this nurse at work who saw me upset the other day, and I told her it was to do with my marriage but without going into any details and she gave me a card with your name and number."

"Okay," said Patrick with all the firmness and reassurance he could fit into that one small word. "Shall we talk about how and when?"

And they spent the next half-hour playing with options of

time, place, method, and the various 'what ifs?' that might follow. By the end of the session, Jake had not reached any definite conclusion as to the precise details but could see the value in writing it all down in a letter, whether or not he actually gave it to Kia; it would help him be clear about what he wanted to say and what he felt. He also heard Patrick's warning that Kia is bound to have a range of responses, but won't have them all at once, so will need time to adjust to the news. What Jake was clear about, was the need to make a commitment to the truth. He asked if he could come back in a week or so, once he'd broken the news.

"You've got it," assured Patrick, reaching for his diary.

When Patrick arrived home Maggie was in the kitchen, reading a magazine and drinking coffee.

"You're early?"

"My eleven o'clock cancelled, but it gave me the chance to catch up on some admin."

"Want a cup? It's only de-caff, I'm afraid."

Patrick hesitated.

"Oh, all right, go on then."

"Look, if you don't want it, say so, don't have it just to please me," replied Maggie. Feeling the nip in her voice, Patrick sought to strike a conciliatory note.

"No, sorry, I'd love a coffee. Thanks."

She emptied the remains of the cafetière into a small mug and placed it on the opposite side of the kitchen table. Patrick picked it up, wandered over to the window and stared out over the rear garden.

"Conifers need pruning, they've got way out of control," he said, wistfully.

"I'll phone the tree man," she replied.

"I'll do it," he replied, smartly.

"Don't you think they're too high for you and the stepladder?"

For some reason this stung Patrick.

"I meant, I'll make the phone call," he replied, curtly, without looking across at her.

"Please yourself. I was only trying to help."

And he felt that familiar pang of discomfort that, once again, he was the cause of her vexation.

"I'm sorry," he replied, "We're not communicating very well over jobs around the house these days, are we?"

"Well, I thought that was your line of work, Patrick."

"Communication or tree-felling?" and he looked straight at her.

"I suppose some skills are more useful than others," she said, wryly.

"There speaks the master saleswoman, still preening yourself after yesterday?" he asked with a forced smile.

"Certainly am. Good bonus coming my way."

"Well done, girl," he replied, and, putting aside the knowledge that he would never be able to make the same boast to her, moved across, bent his head and fleetingly kissed the top of her head. As he stepped away she looked up to catch his face, but he was no longer looking in her direction.

He removed his jacket and hung it on the rail in the hall alcove, before returning to the kitchen, opening the fridge and perusing the shelves.

"Lunch?" said Maggie.

"Is that an offer or a request?"

She sighed inwardly at this riposte, but opted not to bring to the boil the row that was clearly brewing,

"I'll have tzatziki please, if there's enough left, and some crackers. Or there's cheese, if you prefer."

"By the way," said Patrick cheerfully, after assembling the assorted items and cutlery on the table between them, "I've sent Nuala a text to say we'd pick her up tomorrow about twelve and take her out for lunch. That all right with you?"

Maggie's hand hovered for a second above the tub of tzatziki, before she ripped off the lid and drew a sharp intake of breath.

"No, it is not all right. I'd planned to go the gym tomorrow and I've booked a couple of treatments afterwards, you should have asked me first."

"Yes, I realise that," Patrick conceded, "but the same applies to you," he added for good measure.

Lunch progressed in silence, punctuated only by the clatter

of knives on china, the snapping of crackers and the grinding of teeth.

"You're right, I should have mentioned it," she replied at last.

"It's no problem, I'll go on my own," he said, trying to sound as neutral as possible.

"Now I feel guilty," she murmured.

"Guilt, that's the …"

"… price we charge ourselves for doing what we really want," she interjected. "I've heard it a hundred times Pat, and even if it's true it doesn't make it any less uncomfortable."

Patrick was tempted to pursue the point, just as he'd do with a client, and ask, 'Just what is so uncomfortable, the thought that you might care more about your workout or manicure than you do about your daughter?' But he stowed the thought away and plunged the knife into the brie, gouging a thin runny wedge and smearing it across his remaining water biscuit with such force that the cracker shattered, casting crumbs across plate and table-top. He collected the larger pieces and awkwardly set about reattaching them to the piece still in his hand before giving it all up as a lost cause.

"It's all right," he said, at last, coming to her rescue. "It's my fault as much as yours. I'll explain. I'm sure she won't mind."

"Thank you," replied Maggie, gratefully.

'At least, not as much as I do,' he thought, as they finished their lunch in silence.

Chapter Nine

THE FINAL WARNING BELL sounded in the Circle Bar as the late arrivals vied to place orders for interval drinks and Patrick and Maggie drained their glasses and made for the auditorium. While Patrick fumbled in his jacket pocket for the tickets, Maggie noticed a woman staring at him intently, looking as if she was about to speak but then turned away just as Patrick met her gaze. Maggie had the distinct sensation of being a gooseberry and it was only the usher's hand reaching for Patrick's tickets that dissolved the tension. The woman headed towards a seat in the front row, whereas Patrick and Maggie climbed towards the rear of the circle.

"Client?" Maggie asked, once they'd settled.

"New one," confirmed Patrick.

"Was that the husband?"

Patrick hadn't noticed the man with Grace, and he craned across the rows of heads to gain a glimpse.

"It never gets any bloody easier, does it?" whispered Maggie.

The performance was by a Russian company, sung in Italian; Patrick had established that much before booking; what he hadn't counted on was the electronic English supra-titles suspended high above the stage. Patrick was aghast, like a television screen in a hospital waiting room, no matter what drivel was showing, it proved impossible to prevent his eyes being drawn to the screen. On both previous occasions they had seen *Bohème* one lead singer had outclassed the other and this Rodolfo's voice now seemed almost drowned out by the orchestra. Mimi, thankfully, was excellent, and her first aria, *Mi Chiamano Mimi,* held him so enthralled he barely noticed Maggie's hand slip from his. As Mimi's pure voice poured forth from the rear of the stage, Patrick's eyes scanned the illuminated libretto, *But when the thaw comes, the first warmth of the sun is mine.* His attention was caught by a stifled choke in Maggie's throat and a heave in her chest as she fought to retain her composure, a sensation he recognised only too well in himself from previous occasions at this particular opera, and, reassuringly, he reached across and reclaimed her hand.

As was customary, Patrick drove home, for it was recognised that Maggie spent more than enough hours at the wheel in the course of her working week not to wish to add to them at weekends. They were both aware it had been the poorest of the three *Bohèmes* they had seen over the years, and as they exited the car park Patrick wasted no time in pulling it to shreds. Poor acting, amateurish choreography, lack of humour, unimaginative sets … the list went on, only Mimi and Marcello he deemed worthy of praise.

"Please," said Maggie, wearily, "will you please stop going on and on about it."

"I'm sorry, I didn't realise I was 'going on and on'!"

"Well you were. You can be so critical when it comes to other people, you don't always see the good that's there, I know it wasn't a great performance overall, but Mimi's was, and all your criticism just serves to obscure that fact and spoil any pleasure in it."

They continued the journey in silence, each nursing their own disappointment.

"Did you notice your client didn't stay to the end?" Maggie said at last as they left the dual carriageway and neared home.

"Really?"

"Yes, she left her seat just as the second act was about to begin. He followed her at the end of the nightclub scene. No doubt you'll hear all about it in due course."

Patrick made no reply; he was too busy wondering about Grace Darling.

It felt strange driving up to see their daughter on his own, almost improper, and yet he felt freer without Maggie beside him, as the constant tension between the two women in his life left him feeling both powerless and responsible, a recipe for stress if ever there was one.

He parked outside the hall of residence and sat listening to the midday news before trying her mobile number.

"Not quite ready, Dad, give me a minute, I'll be right down."

Ten minutes later Nuala appeared and made towards the Saab's rear door, before realising the front seat was vacant, whereupon she slung her bag onto the floor and climbed in.

"Where's Mum?" she asked casually, fastening her seatbelt.

"She's exhausted love, hard week, couldn't face four hours in the car."

"So, where're we going then?" Nuala asked readily, and Patrick was greatly relieved he was not called upon to mount any further defence of her mother's affections.

"Your choice, I did wonder about a look at the sea, or, if you prefer, we could find a café bar down by Gateshead Quays?

"No, everyone takes their parents there; the sea sounds great."

Patrick steered the Saab eastwards from the city and followed the river out towards Tynemouth where they took in the covered flea market in the Victorian railway station and Nuala perused a second-hand biography of John Ruskin by Joan Abse, which Patrick was happy to pay for, not least because it was a book he had much enjoyed reading himself.

"I cried at the end," he said as if that provided an added incentive for her to finish it.

"You're proud of that, aren't you?" she said provocatively, and he felt embarrassed at being sussed so accurately by one so young.

"It's all right, Dad, I still love you. Look, can we walk before lunch?" she asked, suddenly, linking her arm in his.

"Sure, but if we leave it too long we might struggle to find a table."

"Please, Dad, I want to see the sea."

In a loft apartment bedroom, a hundred miles south, Maggie glanced around at the walls.

"It's a bit bare," she said, "I was going to buy you flowers, but guessed you wouldn't have a vase, so decided to make do with the champagne. Then on the way over I called at a garden centre and found the orchid, and it came in its own vase, clever, hmm?"

"It's lovely, thanks," replied Gavin, regarding it on the chest of drawers in the corner of the bedroom. "I didn't think I could bring much with me. Maybe I'll fetch some pictures and stuff later when things have calmed down a bit, or perhaps I'll just start anew."

"'Start anew,'" she echoed, "there's a thought. Could you really take nothing from your past, just start completely afresh?"

"Dunno. It has some appeal, travelling light, less clutter, let go a lot of the stuff you pick up along the way. People are like Velcro, stuff sticks to us all the time, we get used to it being there even though much of it's no real use, and it's too much trouble to pick off all the bits one by one. Better ditch the coat every few years and move on."

"But that's easier for men, isn't it?"

"How should I know? I've never been a woman." Gavin pulled a face, as if to lighten the tone.

"Well, you make it sound easy," and it was hard to tell whether she was critical or envious.

"Actually, I think most people find it easier just to stay put," he replied.

Maggie turned her head to look up at him, but the angle was too steep, and she lowered her cheek once more upon his bare chest and continued stroking his belly with her thumb.

"*I* don't feel very comfortable," she said, softly.

"Want me to move?"

"No!" and she pinched him gently. "Lying here with you is wonderful, timeless, but also unbearable, like I'm lying here waiting for something to happen, for Vicky to come pounding at the door, or a policeman, or …"

"Your husband?"

"No, Pat doesn't know this exists, he thinks I'm at the gym."

"I've just realised," said Gavin, "Vicky knows I've got a flat somewhere in town but doesn't know the address; no one at my work knows I've moved; your husband thinks you're at

56

the gym. Not a soul knows where we are!" and he sounded chuffed at the very idea.

"The landlord?" asked Maggie.

"The letting agent!" he sighed. "She knows I'm here. Oh well, another illusion goes bust."

"Another illusion?"

"Yeah, like the illusion I'd finally agree to go through I.V.F. with Vicky and eventually we'd succeed in starting a family; the illusion I've enough love in me to satisfy a child, or for that matter, Vicky. And the illusion I'd one day play in goal for York City!"

"Don't put yourself down like that, Gavin," she said sharply.

"Listen don't knock it, York City might be crap, but they're my crap."

"I wasn't referring to your choice of football team."

"You don't choose a football team, darling, they choose you."

There was a pause, each uncertain whether they wished to pursue the matter of his self-esteem.

"Anyway, what's so bad about being a goalie?" he said at last. "Not everyone can be a striker or midfield genius. Goalies are one-offs, they're like drummers in rock bands, a bit crazy, they dive head first at rushing boots and take great pleasure in spoiling things."

"Spoiling things?"

"Of course. The goalkeeper's job is to foil attacks, to dive through the air, tip a rocket shot over the bar and spoil what would have been goal of the season," and he grinned, boyishly.

"Do you really enjoy spoiling things, Gavin? Were you a teenage vandal?"

Gavin gave a mock frown.

"Delving into my past eh? You've been married to Pat too long, some of it's rubbing off."

"Gavin, don't!"

And he realised he was out of line.

"Sorry, Maggie."

"I was being serious, Gavin, I'm interested."

"All right, I confess … I carved my name on my school

57

desk," he said in hushed tones.

"That doesn't count, everyone does that!"

"I tore up my dad's photograph and smashed his precious collection of LP's when he left my mum!" And the way he blurted it out brought them both up short.

"Hurt that much?" she asked, biting her lip.

"Angry that much," and he looked away before she could see his pain.

"No," he said, gathering himself together, "I don't take pleasure in spoiling things for other people, unless they've got it coming, like when a hypocritical politician gets exposed in the press."

"Yes, but people in the public eye are easy targets, aren't they, we can all sit back and take pops at them through our TV screens."

"Who cares?"

"Well clearly you don't."

"Not about them."

"So, what do you really care about, Gavin?"

"I care about being straight with people, and never pretending to be more than you are. I cared about my mum, especially when my dad left, when I saw what a hard time she had of it. And I care about you."

"Why?"

"Because you love me, and because you are like me."

Maggie allowed this last comment to hang in the room for some moments before giving in to the temptation to know more.

"Are we really so alike?"

"Yes. From the word go, we were equal, we found something special in each other and we wanted to savour it without rocking the boat. We both earn good money, much more than our spouses; and we've each made too many concessions in our marriages. It's because we're equal, I find it easier to care for you; I don't feel obligated, or responsible for you, the way I do with Vicky."

She hung on these words, they felt like a gift, and she wished to reciprocate.

"Pat says me earning more doesn't bother him, but I'm not

sure. Men usually do mind, don't they?"

Gavin said nothing.

"I think for too long I sort of put Pat on a pedestal. Pat's one of the wisest people I've ever met but he increasingly pisses me off with the way he uses that understanding. I've seen how cynical he's become about people and their motivations; perhaps he's different with his clients, but that's how he comes across to me, always so cynical. And I find it hard to believe the extent to which I've accommodated his lack of interest in friends. I know what he means when he says social chat and banter is shallow, but it's also fun, and he and I never have any fun any more."

"That was what my dad said," Gavin interjected.

"What?"

"When I met up with him again at my mum's funeral, I asked him why he left me and Mum, and that's just what he said, that he couldn't remember the last time he and Mum had any fun together. He said he knew it was selfish but the longer he stayed the more shrivelled up he became inside. I told him he did it because he didn't give a damn about who he hurt."

"What did he say to that?"

"He told me he cried when he saw what I'd done to his record collection. I told him it was less than he deserved. He said he wasn't crying over a pile of broken vinyl; he was crying because he realised how much he'd hurt me. I don't know why, but I believed him." Gavin took a huge breath, "Something changed after that. I think I stopped hating him."

"Really?"

"Yeah. You were talking about easy targets; well, I began to see that's what my dad was for me when he left us. I'd seen him as entirely in the wrong and Mum as the innocent party; well, now I've been married, I realise things aren't always so simple."

There was a pause, as Maggie mulled over what she wanted to ask.

"Do you know what you really want from life, Gavin?" and she hoped it didn't sound too much like she was fishing for commitment.

"There are a lot of do-gooders out there," he answered,

"spending their energy trying to improve the world. Well, I'm sorry, Maggie, but I'm just not made that way. I'd rather other people got on with their lives and I'd appreciate it if they'd allow me to do the same."

"Makes you sound like a loner?"

"Not at all, I enjoy good company, fun and friendship, and being desired, and that's what I get from you, and give back in good measure, I hope. I just don't believe in trying to make people happy, it doesn't work, and all you're really doing is trying to control them."

"Control them?"

"Yeah, isn't that what all those counsellors and therapists really do, want us to believe that we can't make a decision, or cope with a bereavement or a divorce, without paying some know-all to hold our hand and explain what's happening to us, which is only common sense anyway, and we'd see it for ourselves if we only stopped being so dependent on them and gave it five minutes serious thought."

"Why are you getting at Pat?"

"I didn't realise I was, but if the cap fits..."

"Let's leave Pat out of things, shall we?"

"Suits me."

But she wasn't yet ready to drop her inquiry into Gavin's heart and mind.

"So, you revel in freedom and independence, Gavin? But isn't that just selfish?"

"It would be if I didn't allow others to do the same, but I do," he said, hurriedly.

"Do you think Vicky would agree?"

"Not if you asked her right now. But isn't that what I've done by leaving her? Instead of encouraging her to believe I still want what she does so that we end up hating each other and neither of us being happy, I'm giving her the chance to find someone who wants the same things as her."

"You'll be telling me next that you left her in order to make her happy."

"I left her to set myself free, it just so happens that it also sets her free, even if she can't yet see it."

Maggie hauled herself onto the pillow and looked him in the

eye.

"Listen, Gavin, it was a big thing for me to come here today."

"Because Pat wanted you to go with him to visit your daughter?"

"Yes, but more than that …"

"What?" he asked. "… What?"

She looked more vulnerable then he'd ever seen her. Her lips quivered, parted, and closed again, as if the words were not yet ready to be born.

"Maggie, what is it?" he asked, eager to know.

"But when the thaw comes," she said, "the first warmth of the sun is mine," and slow tears trickled down her cheeks.

"I don't understand," her lover said, and leaned forward to catch a salty tear in his lips.

"Neither do I," she whispered.

Two figures on an isolated bench on the promenade, overlooking a brooding, grey slate sea. The young woman, slumped in her seat, hands shoved down inside coat pockets; her male companion turned towards her, trying to engage her attention.

"Nuala, you should have phoned us."

"Dad, don't, please don't!" she sighs.

The sea breeze whips her hair across her face and as she moves to sweep it back inside her coat collar, he seizes her hand in his, while the fingers of his other hand gently caress her hair.

"Nuala, I just don't know what to say. I'm so sorry."

At last she makes eye contact and her tears well up.

"It's me that should be saying sorry, it was the last thing I meant to happen. It was the last night before I came away, I was out with the gang, we ended up at Simone's and her parents were away, and, well, Sam and I had both agreed it was over between us and it was just like, you know, for old times' sake, a way of saying goodbye, I suppose. We were both a bit drunk, and well, the thing just came off. I know I should have gone to the doctor and got something but I was getting ready to go off to Uni and I just thought it would be all right. I wanted you to know but I didn't want to have to tell you!"

Her confession took such an effort that she collapsed into him, and they sat for some minutes, his arm enveloping her, too late to save her from the tidal wave that had swept her from her little dinghy and beached her in his arms.

"Dad, don't tell Mum. Please!"

"Nuala, I've got to! Or you have, she's your mother, she's got to know."

"Dad, I couldn't bear it if you told her. Please, Dad, please, I'm begging you, Dad please don't tell her. I really don't know what I'd do if she found out."

"Nuala, this is crazy, I don't understand what you're so afraid of. What do you think she's going to do or say? Sure she'll be upset, any mother would, I'm upset, but it's not the end of the world, it really isn't."

"Dad, you don't see how it is between her and me; you just don't see and I can't explain it to you. I wish to God I'd never told you!" and she broke away from his embrace and began gathering up her bag.

Patrick let out a huge sigh of frustration; he wasn't prepared for any of this.

"Don't say that Nuala love, please don't say that, I'm glad you chose to tell me. I'd hate to think of you having to go through all this on your own."

"I'm not alone!" she said emphatically, "My friend Jackie knows, and I've been to see a counsellor at Uni."

Patrick squirmed at discovering he was third down the line.

"Did they help?" he asked, the greater part of him hoping she'd say yes.

"Yeah, Jackie's been really supportive and the counsellor's good."

He sighed and nodded.

"I guess you must have been thinking about what you might do?"

"I'm not keeping it, I know that," she said quickly, "but I don't feel good about it, and I don't want Mum to know, or Sam," she said defiantly, "so don't you *dare* go anywhere near him! I may decide to tell him at some point, and I will tell Mum, but not until it's all over, and in my own time, all right,

Dad? Promise me?"

"Christ, Nuala, you don't know what you're asking."

"Maybe not, but I'm still asking. Promise me, Dad, please?"

Patrick nodded, and immediately wondered what he was letting himself in for.

"Listen, Nuala, I'll be here when the time comes, if you want, I'll be here, I'd like to be, if that's what you want?"

"Thanks, Dad, I'll let you know, I promise."

After a poignant goodbye at the hall of residence, in which he didn't know if he was bidding farewell to a woman or a little girl, Patrick drove south along the A1 and was twice flashed for hogging the middle lane. He pulled into some services for petrol and to purchase some mineral water, for his mouth was parched and he was finding it hard to swallow. Before setting off again he rang Beth, and told her something had come up and that he needed to see her soon, next week, if possible.

"Friday week at a quarter to nine, is that soon enough?" she asked, "you see I'm going down to visit my granddaughter's tomorrow for a week or so, she's expecting. Can you get across here that early?"

"I'll be there," said Patrick, just as he was disturbed by the rat-a-tat-tat of a coin beating upon his side window, and a man's face appeared, wagging his finger and mouthing something about the phone and the forecourt. Patrick thanked Beth, switched off the phone and told the finger to fuck off.

Patrick was dreading arriving home and having to fend off Maggie's questions. In the event, it was easier than he'd expected, for he found her in her study at the computer and she seemed satisfied with his brief, sanitized summary of his time with their daughter. Similarly, Maggie was relieved to find Patrick content with just a perfunctory exchange of pleasantries as to her afternoon's exertions at the gym, after which they reconvened downstairs to watch television, a pursuit that enabled them each to keep their secrets intact.

Chapter Ten

PATRICK SLEPT IN FITS and starts, waking finally at five forty-five and, for a blessed few seconds, knew only tiredness and the relief that he didn't have to get up just yet. Then memory kicked in. He listened to the gentle rhythms of Maggie's breath, grateful to postpone the moment when he would have to begin not-telling her all over again. 'That's the thing about secrets,' he thought, 'they absorb such a lot of energy.'

It was a long time since he had held a real secret from Maggie, a concrete, emphatic, no-nonsense secret, like his mad fling with their neighbour Suzie, way back in time. He was surprised how quickly Maggie had found out about that, as if she possessed a sixth sense about such things, although it deserted her during the time of his 'almost-affair' with Leah during the course of his Relate training; but then, that wasn't conducted under Maggie's nose. Until now, he regarded these as the sum total of the secrets he had kept from his wife. Of course, he realised how practised he was at keeping less concrete things from her; he hid much of what he thought and felt when they were alone together, a whole host of observations, thoughts and feelings revolved inside like articles of clothing in a tumble dryer, fleeting shapes flitting past the glass but the door stayed firmly locked. 'But doesn't everyone do that,' he told himself, 'filter their part in conversations, while conducting silent running commentaries on the interaction of the moment?' He liked to think so; it would help dispel the growing discomfort that, the longer he worked as a therapist, the more he became an onlooker, monitoring all his social interactions and slave to the constant obsession with process. Patrick's inner world was growing increasingly constipated and he knew of no available enema to loosen him up.

*   *   *

With Maggie flying off to Holland to visit her company's head office for a two-day round of strategy meetings regarding a new Europe-zone product launch (how Patrick loved the language of business, it amused him almost as much as the psychobabble of his own profession) he was able to speak openly on the phone to Nuala each evening. On Monday he found her cheery as she prattled on about her course. On Tuesday, she informed him she had been given a date at a clinic; in Leeds, as she did not want her time in Newcastle peppered by reminders. He asked when it was to be and she hesitated before replying.

"You've not told Mum, have you?"

"No."

"It's Tuesday of next week; I have to be there by nine in the morning," she added.

"I'll come and get you on the Monday evening," he suggested eagerly, "you can stay here that night."

"No, Dad, No! I don't want that. I've already checked and I can get an early train."

"Are you sure? I'll meet you at Leeds station, I'll drive you there, if that's what you want."

"Thanks, Dad, thanks. I mean, for everything," she said, and promptly failed to keep a grip on the tears inside.

"Sorry, Dad. Gotta go."

"Wait, love. Bye! And take care!" he urged, but the connection was already closed. That night Patrick broke with his long-held practice of not drinking alone.

By the time of her return on Wednesday evening, Patrick was now a fully-fledged accomplice in the deceit of Maggie, and had already begun reaping the rewards of complicity. The sense of being the chosen one, preferred over Maggie to bear their daughter's confidence, was a familiar position, given the array of secrets lodged with him down the years by clients whose partners, parents or lovers, know nothing of his existence, let alone what is being told him by their loved one in the privacy of his therapy room. But when it's your own flesh and blood doing the choosing, he realised, the rewards are all the more precious. His thoughts turned to the booby prize of

65

being the one excluded. He had listened many times to the anguish of clients who discover their spouse has been having an affair: they say it is rarely the adultery itself, but the deceit that inflicts the deepest cuts. And the lacerating questions that always remain, no matter how often they are posed and answered: 'When, why, how often? Was he/she better at it than me?' Patrick empathizes with the hurt and anger that prompts such interrogations, but, sooner or later, always challenges the questioner: 'Okay, what if you received detailed written answers to all of your questions, how would you know whether to believe them? Or if you were shown video-recordings of the lovers' every conversation, of their every romp in a hotel room or the backseats of a car … would the pain of exclusion be any the less?' Because Patrick knew that's what extra-marital affairs do, exclude the other spouse, banish them beyond the pale of trust and intimacy, and you can't rebuild trust with a bucket load of facts, or restore intimacy on a torrent of disclosure. And remembering such noble sentiments born from the long experience of plying his trade, Patrick suddenly felt truly sorry for Maggie, amputated by her daughter and betrayed by her spouse.

Chapter Eleven

TWELVE MINUTES AFTER NEIL'S scheduled appointment time and with no word received, Patrick leafed through the notes of their seven sessions to date: fifteen minutes early on the first occasion, ten minutes late for the second, more or less on time ever since. At that moment the outer door swung open and Neil strode in.

"Reading your notes? I hope they're mine, I may be late but it's still my session you're getting paid for!"

Patrick stared back, expecting an apology for the late arrival, or perhaps a smile that might lessen the jibe, but neither was forthcoming as Neil marched on through to the therapy room. By the time Patrick joined him there, Neil was already seated and ready to begin.

Patrick settled himself and looked across to meet the gaze of his client, which, as usual, was taking refuge in some fascinating spot upon the carpet. A minute passed in perfect silence, possibly two. Patrick became aware that at some point his eyes must have abandoned their dutiful watch upon his client and were now focused upon the right hand of the two Degas prints upon the wall. *L'Absinthe*, a couple side by side in a Paris bar, each staring blankly into space; a study of isolation if ever there was one, and a perfect match for what was happening here in the room. He forced himself to look back at Neil, still no change.

"They were," Patrick said at last, having quite run out of patience.

Neil immediately glanced up, and his look was quizzical.

"The case notes ... they *were* yours!" Patrick reiterated, and immediately regretted the extra emphasis, after all, it wasn't his style to try to convince clients of his trustworthiness rather than allow it to develop, or not, of its own accord. Or was this what Beth meant by showing more warm concern for his male clients? In the event, Neil merely shrugged as if, despite what he'd said on arrival, he really didn't care either way whose notes they were. But for once Neil returned Patrick's gaze, rather than return to staring at the floor.

"Did you think I wasn't coming?" Neil asked at last.

"I didn't know what to think," replied Patrick.

"Did you think I wasn't coming?" Neil repeated, with a noticeable touch of irritation.

"I guess it would have surprised me if you hadn't shown up at all," answered Patrick.

"So, you expected me to come?"

"All right, yes, that's fair comment," replied Patrick, suddenly aware that Neil was now conducting an interview.

"And what made you expect that I would come?"

'This is clearly going to be the way of things for a while,' thought Patrick; 'stay with it,' he urged himself.

"Because Neil, towards the end of our last session, for a few fleeting moments, I thought we made a real connection."

"And how many sessions had we had by then, Patrick? Six? Seven, was it?" Neil asked, rather theatrically. "Now let me work that out, I make that … three hundred and fifteen pounds for one fleeting moment of connection."

"So what are you saying," asked Patrick, "that it isn't worth it?"

Neil stared right back, ran his tongue across his lips and surprised them both by spitting the question back with all the sharp intent of a peashooter, and it landed right between Patrick's eyes,

"You tell me?"

"Whether what we're doing here is worth your money? It's a good question, Neil."

"Which as usual, you're not going to answer?" replied Neil, relieved for once to be on the offensive in their weekly game of cat and mouse.

"I can't answer for you, Neil. I can only answer for myself, as to whether I think you're worth my time and effort. It's for you to decide whether your investment in me is worthwhile."

"I knew you'd say something like that."

"Does that mean I'm living up, or down, to your

68

expectations?"

"It's not fucking funny!" snapped Neil.

"No, you're right, it's not, and I apologise for making light of it; that quip was wrong of me."

"I'd like an answer. Do you think I'm worth your time and effort?"

Neil was clearly not going to let this go.

"All right," replied Patrick, "but I'm allowed more than one word, okay?"

"You're the boss!"

Patrick squinted and frowned, "That's not funny either, Neil!"

Neil allowed a tentative grin.

"Listen Neil, forty-five pounds an hour is a significant amount of money, to me too, and I believe I earn my fees. Whether someone comes here three times or thirty-three, I want them to leave here after their final session feeling that their time with me was worthwhile. Given that many of my referrals come via personal recommendation it doesn't benefit me to go on seeing someone who I don't really think I can help."

"Should I take that as a 'yes' then?" said Neil.

Patrick grinned.

"Okay, it's a 'yes'. So much for my question, now what about yours? Is coming here worth *your* time, money and effort?"

Neil lowered his gaze and spoke into his chest.

"But don't you see, that's what I want from you, some confirmation that I'll get better, and my life won't always be like this."

And something in Neil's words, or the desperate, forsaken look upon his face, got beneath Patrick's defences and brought a lump to his throat. Patrick did not resist, or seek to dispel the emotion with words, and this time Patrick did not need to look away for stimulation. Besides, he knew the left hand of the two Degas prints, *Au Café,* intimately; indeed, he was living it out in that very moment, as, just like one of the two female characters depicted, he maintained close intimate regard of his troubled companion, and was content that it was so. At last,

Patrick took a deep breath and shuddered as he exhaled. Sensing this movement, Neil looked across and his eyes widened on seeing the feeling etched in the older man's face.

"That's my hope, too," whispered Patrick.

Neil visibly softened, as if Patrick's words carried meaning for him.

"But why can't I just accept that?" he replied, "Why do I always need you to convince me to keep going on?"

Patrick inhaled deeply before replying.

"I'm not sure, Neil, but I realise that you do look to me for reassurance, and one of the things you struggle with is having to accept that I just don't work that way. I will not promise more than I can deliver, for the simple reason that I don't want to let you down. You see, I don't know how *my* life will turn out, let alone yours. Hope and faith are on the menu here, guaranteed outcomes are not."

"Yeah," Neil gave a resigned sigh, "coming here's not like taking your boots to the menders, is it?"

"Hey, that's my line!"

"You said it at the end of my first session. See, I do listen, most of the time."

Patrick smiled, warmly.

"There's something I want to tell you," added Neil.

Patrick waited.

"Since Kate, that girl I went out with, told me she found me creepy, I've more or less given up looking for a relationship."

Patrick nodded, allowing Neil to go on.

"I've hardly gone out since, I come home from work, bolt down something to eat and plug myself into the Internet."

"The porn site you told me about: Red-something?"

"RedSky."

"Does it help?"

"For a bit; the anticipation is usually better than the event."

"Tell me about the anticipation, what's it like?"

Neil thought for a moment before replying.

"It's like when I was a kid, before going fishing with my brother, getting ready, hoping to catch a big carp, imagining the float disappearing and the electric tug on the line that shoots right up the rod, along your arm and into your heart.

70

Know what I mean?"

"I guess so … I've never fished."

"Well, that's what it's like, you log on, post a message on some thread in response to a woman's picture, and wait to see if she'll reply. Or if you feel really brave you start a thread of your own; that's the real risk, of it slipping down the board and no one posting a pic, or even a comment."

"Neil, the folk who use this site and contribute to these threads, they're all anonymous, yes?"

"Yeah, people use nicknames, so you never know who anyone really is but you learn about their characters from their comments and pictures."

"So if everything is anonymous, then the risk isn't really being found out? So what is at stake, Neil, rejection? Nobody wanting what you're offering?"

"Yeah," Neil took a deep breath.

"Okay, so tell me, Neil, what is it you offer there?"

Neil thought long and hard before replying.

"A few of the men who post just slag off the women, but most of them are all right, some have got a wicked sense of humour."

"And what about you Neil, what are you like when you post?"

Neil frowned, and thought for a moment.

"Polite, respectful. I'm always complimentary about the women who post pics of themselves, even when they're, you know, not so hot. I don't want to put them off. I know what it's like to be sneered at."

"Do unto others … is that it?"

"Exactly."

"Neil, you said that for the most part, the event doesn't live up to the anticipation, but there must be occasions when the experience is good or you wouldn't keep logging on, so what's it like when it all works out?"

"It's fun, sometimes you get a playful conversation going with a woman who enjoys flirting with you; she responds to what you say, and her pics become more and more revealing. It's the older women I prefer, they've got more about them. I bet you think the whole thing's pathetic, don't you?"

71

"Did I say so?"

Neil flashed Patrick a look that made him regret his knee-jerk response.

"I'm sorry Neil. No, I don't think it's pathetic. I think it sounds like it could be fun and anonymity always frees people up, a bit like a masked ball. Like I said, I'm no fisherman, but I've heard that anglers always say how quickly the hours flit by, even when they're not catching anything. But I imagine there must be times when the hours you spend there leave you frustrated, or perhaps sad, because everyone can only be there by pretending, hiding behind their nicknames or masks, it that so?"

"Most posters blur the faces in their pics, but even those that don't still use nicks," Neil confirmed.

"So no one ever says, look, this is me, this is who I really am?"

"No, I suppose not," and Neil looked solemn, as if Patrick's description of the shallowness of the porn site struck a chord of guilt or shame in the young man. Without thinking, Patrick sought to alleviate the damage.

"But I wonder, Neil, is that so very different from the outside world? How often in our everyday exchanges with colleagues, family, friends, lovers, do we really say, look, this is me, this is who I really am, this is what I really think! You ever considered that?"

"What you are you getting at?" asked Neil, with a mixture of curiosity and irritation.

Spurred on by Beth's encouragement to give more help to his male clients, Patrick took the plunge.

"I suppose what I'm saying, Neil, is that all of us hide and conceal to a large extent, whether it's behind our roles, our uniforms, our British reserve, manners, shyness, protocol, deceit, fashion, or simple anonymity, so it's odd that you choose to beat yourself up as if you're the only one who's ever done so. Remember when you told me everybody else's relationships always work out but yours, and I challenged your perception? Well, maybe you need challenging again about being unduly hard on yourself when it comes to apportioning guilt and shame, or even success for that matter."

Neil squirmed.

"Yeah, but that just lets me off the hook."

"Come on, Neil, I thought you were the angler, now you sound like the fish, what's more, a fish who deserves to be hooked. Are you really that bad, or that dangerous?"

"I'm not dangerous."

"Okay, so tell me about bad."

"I've already told you, I told you about being adopted, and how it all changed when they found they could have a child of their own. Do I have to go over it all again?"

"Only if you want to?"

And reluctantly, Neil described in greater detail the increasingly toxic relationship with his adoptive father after the two boys had been playing on a frozen pond and their own younger son fell through and drowned; and the repeated comments about his birth mother not being able to cope with him, and the bullying he endured at secondary school, until the last grains of enthusiasm Neil held for his childhood dissolved to nothing.

"Okay," said Patrick, noticing the hour and the need to begin summing up. "You grew up in a family where there was a well of unhappiness and much of it got funnelled into you. And somehow, Neil, you got stuck with it, and here you are in your thirties feeling like you'll never be able to shake it off and you've almost convinced yourself it's what you deserve, so that whenever somebody offers you back something good about yourself, you don't let it in, you scoff and sneer and argue your way back onto the hook."

"I don't enjoy being like this you know!" Neil snapped back, clearly riled by this indictment of his own character.

"Yes, I know that, Neil. There's far more misery than happiness in this for you, but the fact remains, you cling to the status quo, and whenever I give you the chance to let yourself off the hook, I watch you bite down on it all the harder."

"So what's the answer, sell the computer?"

"I think the answer, if you want to put it that way, is to get to the nub of why you don't believe you deserve to be let off the hook."

"You're the expert, you tell me!"

"No, Neil. I've got ideas about that, educated guesses if you like, but simply telling you isn't what it will take; you have to be able to see it and feel it for yourself. My job is to try and help that to happen."

"Can you do that?"

"I'm trying, it depends … partly on me, but also on you."

"What do you mean?"

"Time's up for today, Neil. You think about it."

Neil looked sombre as he drew the neatly folded notes from his jacket pocket, and tossed them down on the coffee table.

For once the case notes didn't flow and Patrick had the niggling feeling that he'd somehow missed the point in the session with Neil, but, for the life of him, he couldn't see what it was. He had only just finished writing them up when Grace arrived on the dot.

"Welcome," said Patrick, his typical opening gambit for second and subsequent sessions. Then, again typically, he waited.

Grace looked composed in a smart tweed suit and brown opaque tights, but her eyes looked nervous, and once she'd realised the floor was hers, she seized the moment.

"At the theatre on Saturday, that was so awkward, I'm really, really sorry, and I hope I didn't embarrass you by my presence, or spoil your and your wife's enjoyment."

Patrick noted the assumption that the woman he was with was his wife, but found greater interest in another aspect of Grace's statement.

"Hmm, the unexpected often does feel a bit awkward, Grace, but I'm intrigued as to why you feel a need to apologise?"

"Well, I imagine you like to leave work behind when you're out socially. I know how strongly David feels about that, it can ruin his evening if we bump into a patient."

"Do you apologise to him on such occasions?"

"Um, well, yes, I probably do, not that it's my fault, but I probably do still say I'm sorry, I don't know what else to say."

"Well there's always, 'Oh Shit!'" Patrick suggested.

"I don't swear, at least very rarely … my upbringing!" and

she pulled a face. "Why, is that what you felt?"

"No," he replied emphatically, "I was just surprised to see you standing in front of me and it took me a second or two to adjust. But I'm still intrigued as to why you feel the need to apologise, any more than I. Surely my presence was as much a potential source of awkwardness or embarrassment for you, as yours was for me, so what made you feel you were the one in the wrong? You couldn't have known I'd be at the opera that evening, you didn't intentionally intrude upon my social life, so why the guilt, and why take responsibility for my feelings?"

Grace felt pushed into a corner and tried to gather her thoughts before offering any meaningful reply, but any coherent answer kept eluding her as she stumbled again and again over his use of the word 'intrude'. She felt like a little girl being told off by her father for having got it wrong, first by intruding into Patrick's social life, then by apologising for having done so. Her instinct was to apologise yet again, but it was obvious this would only get her into more trouble. In the event, she did the only thing that made any sense; she started to cry.

"I knew I shouldn't have put mascara on," she joked, in a vain attempt to lighten the mood, as she reached into her handbag for a tissue and began dabbing at her eyes.

Patrick addressed the tears and teased out the response to his challenge and the little-girl-in-the-wrong feelings it had triggered in Grace. He tried to get beneath the guilt and self-reproach to the anger he sensed must lurk deep inside, but although Grace could contemplate the possibility of its existence, she was nowhere near as in touch with her anger as with her acute sense of responsibility for the discomfort of others. Patrick switched his angle of approach.

"So, tell me about *your* evening, Grace, did bumping into me spoil your or your partner's enjoyment?"

"That was my husband, David. As soon as we sat down, he asked who you were. I can't imagine he thought you were Simon, he knows Simon lives hundreds of miles away, but I could tell he was suspicious from his tone of voice."

"How did you answer?"

"I don't tell lies, and even if I did I wouldn't be any good at it. I just said you were a counsellor I'm seeing, and then the curtain went up. The evening did get spoiled but not by that. It was my birthday and David insisted on us going, even though I didn't really feel in any mood to celebrate, but he knows how I love Puccini. It became a little easier once the lights went down and we didn't have to talk or look at each other. Then something happened, towards the end of the first Act when Mimi was singing her aria, *Mi Chiamano Mimi*. She was standing apart from Rodolfo at the back of the stage and her voice was like the finest filigree, so light and strong, and she sang, *Ma quando vien lo sgelo il primo sole é mio –"*

"Which means?" interjected Patrick.

"But when the thaw comes …" and Grace swallowed hard to hold back the gathering ranks of tears, "but when the thaw comes … the first warmth of the sun shall be mine!" And in completing the translation, the damn broke and Grace's sobs filled the space between them.

For a while, Patrick said nothing, just remained in close attendance to the raw, pained heart of this beautiful woman, and tried not to ponder the strange coincidences of time and place, and the line in the libretto that had touched not only his client but also his wife. Then, like a master chef he turned down the heat and gave a gentle stir.

"Powerful stuff, Grace," he said softly, "I often think the magic of opera gets lost in translation, but it seems that it's the translation of that line that holds the meaning for you, is that so?"

Grace nodded, gradually composing herself, glad of the chance to explain to one who might understand.

"It's like the breaking of a shell," she explained, "they call her Mimi, but that's not who she really is. Mimi apologises for her status as a poor seamstress, but dreams that one day, one day the thaw will come, and she will feel the warm spring sunshine on her face, and then, she will …" at which point Grace's voice tailed off.

"Bloom?" Patrick offered tentatively, and wondered whether he should have been more patient and let her find the word herself.

She looked up at him, nodded, and spoke softly.

"Yes, exactly. Bloom," and Grace's eyes filled once more with tears, but quieter, less urgent this time, for she now knew she was no longer alone.

Chapter Twelve

PATRICK SPENT THE AFTERNOON with two supervisees, one of whom had done sterling work with a couple whose toddler had been killed eight months ago in a road accident right outside their front gate. Each had been pottering in the garden assuming the other was watching over her. Rather than bringing them together, their grief was driving them apart, one bearing all the guilt, the other all the bitterness and laying the blame, if not at the feet of spouse or God, then certainly at the manufacturers and drivers of 4 × 4s, the type of vehicle that struck their daughter. At first there appeared little for Patrick to do but listen, and support the counsellor in what she was already doing so well, i.e. hearing both sides, addressing and appreciating both the anger and guilt, and holding the tension between the two as she tried to facilitate the slow, painful process of each partner learning to own their rightful share of *both* sets of feelings rather than continuing to project one lot on to their partner. But as the discussion ensued Patrick sensed another defence was at work in the counselling, besides the splitting of anger-guilt between the couple. He tentatively voiced as much, and by so doing, helped the supervisee identify the fear that was preventing her deeper engagement with the well of grief: the anxiety that something similar might befall her own daughter of similar age. Her face coloured up, tears welled, as valuable insight was gained that she could now take back into that work. Then, just as she was gathering up her things at the very end of the supervision she blurted out that she, too, drove a 4 × 4, a fact she had carefully concealed from the clients by no longer parking in the counselling centre's car park. Patrick made the observation that the couple were not the only ones labouring under a yoke of guilt, or living in fear of the destructive power of rage.

His final appointment of the day was a difficult supervision session with a male counsellor who had felt the need to give one of his female clients a hug at the end of what had clearly been a highly emotional session. Patrick established the fact that the hug had been offered by the counsellor rather than requested by the client, and when he raised the question of whose needs were being met by the embrace, found his supervisee far more concerned with self-justification than self-examination. He attempted to justify the hug to Patrick in terms of what the client needed. Patrick was having none of this, and challenged him hard over the extent to which a counsellor is there to fulfil a client's unmet needs, but no consensus was reached by the end of the session. As they parted, Patrick urged him to give the appropriateness of the gesture more thought before their next meeting.

Patrick wrote up his notes, stashed the supervisees' files in the drawer and realised he had the beginnings of a headache. He nursed it all the way home and was less than enthused when Maggie announced there was a movie on at their local cinema that she'd read good reviews of and wanted to see. He'd rather have sat at home listening to music but took a paracetamol and agreed to go.

Patrick often thinks of marital therapists like himself as conduits for a couple's communication. Of course, conduits are not always therapists. It was a British film directed by Ken Loach, *Ae Fond Kiss,* set in Glasgow, concerning a young man called Casim, a second generation Pakistani Muslim, betrothed to a girl of his parents' choosing, who embarks upon a clandestine relationship with Roisin, an Irish Catholic schoolteacher. Discussing the movie in the bar afterwards, Maggie was clearly moved by the plight of Roisin, so unacceptable to her lover's Asian family and to her own rigidly orthodox parish priest. Patrick, on the other hand, was impressed by the portrayal of the Muslim family's pain at their son's betrayal of the values they held dear, and the resultant shame for the family within their community. Their discussion grew more and more heated, with Maggie insisting that Patrick see it her way, while he gamely stuck to his point. They were heading for a major row, but he wasn't prepared to give ground by simply dismissing a well of painful feelings that derive from cultural values different to one's own. He was endeavouring to explain this point of view when Maggie pushed her drink to one side, slopping the contents on the table, grabbed her handbag and announced she'd had enough and wanted to go home.

Patrick lay in bed, listening to the turning leaves of Maggie's novel, and mulling over her reaction to the film. He did what he always did when baffled by something: strip it down, take it apart and inspect the pieces. In the movie, Roisin longed for things she wasn't allowed: her Asian lover and the approval/permission of her priest to continue teaching at her Catholic school where he was Chair of Governors. On both counts what stood in her way was a moralising, judgemental establishment and Roisin felt let down by what she saw as her lover's lack of conviction in the face of it. If Casim really loved her, Roisin (and Maggie) believed, he should stand up to his family and be prepared to pay the price. In the bar, Maggie had accused Patrick of being on the side of Casim's parents, which he knew was not the case, but, unlike Maggie, he could at least feel compassion for their distress in the face of their eldest son's disregard for values they held dear, but the more Patrick tried to make the distinction between advocating someone's point of view and simply trying to understand and appreciate it, the more irritated Maggie became. Round and round it went in his mind, but, despite his best efforts, Patrick couldn't get to the bottom of why the film had affected Maggie so strongly. He realised she saw most things more black and white than he, and was generally the more decisive of the two. Perhaps that was it, the oscillation on the part of the young male lead, feeling torn both ways, unable to make a clear commitment in one direction or the other? But why would that annoy Maggie so? Patrick couldn't deny that these were elements of his own character; is that what she found so irritating? He could ask her, but she was absorbed in her book, it was late, and anyway, he didn't have the energy to withstand any more flak. So instead, he turned over, closed his eyes and turned his thoughts to Nuala.

His secret felt no better now than when he first gave his word on the bench up at Tynemouth. Lying in bed, a mere breath away from his wife, it occurred to him that he had an alternative: he could seize the moment to tell Maggie everything and pledge her not to say anything to Nuala until their daughter chose to come clean of her own accord. It would ask a great deal of Maggie; she would have to contain the feelings of rejection, tolerate the complicity between her husband and daughter, and hold a weighty secret; what's more, she'd have to trust Patrick to continue shouldering the support of their daughter on her behalf. The possibility of repairing the schism with Maggie held some appeal, but at what risk? He couldn't be sure how she would react to his confession and he could well end up with both his wife and his daughter feeling betrayed. And so, having flirted with the prospect of change, and having successfully talked himself out of it, Patrick closed his eyes and went to sleep.

Maggie became aware of staring at the page with no conscious recollection of the paragraph she had just read. She placed the book on the bedside table and turned on to her side away from the husband who was already gently snoring. She pictured Gavin asleep in his new apartment, an empty space beside him, and imagined lifting his duvet and snuggling in alongside. When she first learned Gavin had left Vicky she wondered what difference it would make to their affair; fearing it might upset the careful balance and undermine what they had created and maintained so successfully for the past year. Gavin might begin wanting more than she could give; or worse, now he had his freedom, might find he has little need of her after all. Able now to phone, or text, at will, she had embraced such newfound liberty with enthusiasm. Gavin striking out for what he wanted had made her realise that she, too, has choices; she could have so much more of Gavin if she only dare reach out for it. She could make up more excuses, more visits to the gym, conjure up more nights away through work; all that had worked well enough in the past, surely she could manage a little more inventiveness, a little more deceit? But Maggie held little enthusiasm for all the slinking around. How enraged she had felt in the film, when Casim was driving Roisin around town and he forced her to duck down in the front seat lest she was spotted by one of his relatives. She wanted to shake Casim, tell him to be a man and stand up and be counted, just like Roisin had tried to do with the priest who had the power to have her sacked from her teaching post at the Catholic school, and just like Gavin had done in leaving his marriage. And in that moment Maggie saw just why the film had got under her skin; the skin of an outwardly dutiful wife and part-time lover, afraid to face the consequences of stepping into the light and announcing, 'This is me, this is who I am and this is what I want!' She imagined turning over, shaking Pat awake, and telling him she was leaving him, but knew straight away it was too soon, too vast a step. She imagined a lesser confession, 'I've been seeing somebody, and I thought you should know.' What would he do? He wouldn't dare hit her; more likely utter some expletives, storm out, slam the door and end up asleep downstairs. No, all that rage and judgement would come, but not at once. At first he'd be all at sea, capsized, and try to right himself by interrogating her ... who, what, where, when, why? Yes, that's it, he'd interrogate her, and he'd be so good at it; he wouldn't insult her, not yet, that would mean conceding the moral high ground and he'd be reluctant to relinquish that. Yes, he'd interrogate her, politely, systematically, penetratingly, and try as she might to hold onto her treasure, she would be forced to hand bits of it over, little jewels of truth and semi-truth, prised from her grasp, one by one, until he had taken possession of what had for the past eleven months been solely hers. Maggie knew she wasn't yet ready for that, and so, just like Casim, her spirits faltered, and she doused the light.

Chapter Thirteen

PATRICK BEGAN TO DOUBT himself as he drove down the winding, leafy avenue a second time. He had expected the clinic to be more prominent, attached to a hospital perhaps, certainly altogether more institutional than the Edwardian villa he eventually came across set back from the road in its own small grounds. He followed the *Visitors Parking* arrow, backed the Saab into the angle between two hedges and checked his watch: ten minutes before the time she was told to report. He surveyed the scene: three other cars stood parked, each as far away from the others as the space would allow: a shabby white Fiesta with one female occupant; a new Renault Laguna with a middle-aged woman at the wheel alongside a younger female passenger; and a Ford Ka, that appeared to contain two young women. Apart from an initial enquiry as to how Nuala felt (which he instantly regretted) the fifteen-minute journey had been conducted mostly in silence, punctuated by his occasional remarks about how the city of Leeds differed from his beloved Sheffield. Believing that the situation now called for something more, Patrick fingered the steering wheel trying to think of something meaningful to say and grew impatient with his lack of inspiration. In the event, Nuala paved the way.

"Dad ..."

"Nuala, are you sure this is what you want ...?" he blurted out.

"Dad, don't, please!" she pleaded, gathering up the bag that had nestled in her lap all the way from Newcastle, and reached for the door handle.

"Dad, thanks for bringing me; my friend Jackie is driving down from Uni to pick me up, I'll be all right, I'll ring you tomorrow, okay?"

"Nuala!" he called, as she stepped from the car.

"Thanks, Dad," she cut him short, trotted away and

disappeared into the building.

It was as if her decisiveness had broken the spell cast over the entire car park, as first the Ka passenger and then the Fiesta driver vacated their vehicles and followed Nuala up the stone ramp and through the doorway. Only the Laguna retained its human cargo, and Patrick watched as the two female occupants embraced. At last the younger one appeared to pull back and make to get out, but her mother, for Patrick assumed, indeed wanted, it to be her mother, held fast and reached to touch her daughter's cheek. At last they alighted and the mother fetched a small bag from the boot, which the daughter reached for, but the mother would not leave go and the two women linked arms and wandered slowly across the asphalt. At the foot of the ramp the daughter turned abruptly, wrenched the bag from her mother's grasp and planted a fleeting kiss on her cheek before running up the slope and disappearing inside. For a few moments the mother stood alone, staring after her departed baby, before lowering her head and retracing her steps towards the car. On reaching the driver's door, something made her look across to where Patrick sat, watching all the while. He held the woman's gaze until he recognised something so penetrative, so accusatory, that he felt compelled to lower his eyes and stare down into his lap until he heard the Renault's engine bursting into life. When he raised his head again his was the only remaining vehicle. His chest and throat were full of tears, not the healing tears of sadness, but the bitter tears of shame, for the mother's stark, judgemental gaze had brought home to Patrick the fact that he was the one male witness to these joyless deliveries. Where were these missing men? Perhaps, like Sam, having deposited their sperm, they remained blissfully unaware of what incredible feats of endurance and ultimate penetration they had got up to in their absence? Or had they been told to stay away, this being women's business? Or were they just doing what men so often do in the face of vulnerability, leave it to their women? And with this final thought the phalanx of Patrick's anger drove away his shame and his words were spat out at a world that was neither aware nor listening.

"Why the fuck don't we teach our boys to take

responsibility for their sperm!"

He fired the engine, turned out the drive and sped away down the avenue, hitting each of the speed bumps far harder than was wise.

Realising he would be in no condition to listen to clients, Patrick had already cleared his diary for the rest of the day, but had failed to give any thought to how he would fill the time. Finding himself boxed into the wrong lane he ended up heading south on the M1 rather than west on the M62 as intended; it meant a few extra miles, but what the hell, he had all day. He considered going straight home but ruled it out; too close, too many reminders. Several times he had to tell himself to slow down; fifteen years since his last speeding ticket, he had no wish to spoil the run now. He left the motorway at junction 39 and pulled up outside a farm shop, intending to find something wholesome for dinner. It wasn't open; it felt like lunchtime but his watch showed it was not yet ten. He telephoned Maggie.

"Hello," her voice was clipped and short, he could tell she was heavily in work mode.

"Hi Maggie, how are you? Where are you?"

"I'm driving! What is it, Pat?"

"I was just wondering what you might like for dinner tonight?"

"What?"

"I'm at a farm shop and I was just wondering what to get."

"What? There's plenty of stuff in the freezer, for God's sake!"

He flinched.

"Okay, it doesn't matter, it's not open yet anyway."

"Pat, are you all right? Look, I really can't talk now. I'm on my way to a site-meeting; I'll see you tonight." And with that she hung up.

At the roundabout at the top of the hill he turned left and drove through Bretton village and into the Yorkshire Sculpture Park where he parked up and checked his watch. Five past ten; he tried imagining what was happening to Nuala but succeeded only in summoning the emetic reek of hospitals he knew so well from his enforced confinement when his tonsils had been removed as a boy. He left the car and wandered off alone. A damp Tuesday in November meant that the park was much quieter than last time he was here, a bright Sunday afternoon a year or two ago. He wandered anticlockwise to avoid a couple approaching from the other direction. He passed the three steel prize-fighters away to his left, jostling each other around an invisible grass ring; flat metallic giants, as tall as a double-decker bus, their entire bodies dotted with perforations as if victim to a monstrous, marauding hole-punch machine. He'd seen them several times over the years, but for the first time wondered why there were *three* pugilists in the ring? The path veered downhill, past a bronze male figure sitting on a bench, shamelessly displaying his sad genitals to the world; his face looked empty, as if he had nothing left to offer but his nakedness. Through the trees, two bronze water buffalo faced each other like duellists, while further along a rampant cast-iron hare shadow-boxed atop a tall spire; on another day, it would have made Patrick smile. A little way across the field stood a muscle-bound bronze bull with an impelling scrotal sac that appeared to hold two full-sized rugby balls. Everywhere Patrick looked, stark visions of masculinity, redundant, yet defiant, in the autumn of their lives.

Patrick ducked beneath the spreading canopy of a Cedar of Lebanon and leaned back against its trunk. The compacted soil beneath his feet appeared dry and firm and instinctively his hand reached up and felt the cool wetness in his hair from the persistent drizzle he'd failed to notice as he'd ambled along. Since his father disappeared from his life when Patrick was just a small boy, he'd stood in awe of men muscle-pumped on testosterone, men who swaggered, brawled and rejoiced in intimidating others. He'd always admired men who did the decent thing, men like the tennis champion Bjorn Borg, who'd harnessed his aggression, played fair, was generous in defeat and magnanimous in victory, and who never lost control. But now, when he contemplated the works of men, he felt mostly sadness or anger: Penetration Man, with his so-called precision bombing of Belgrade, Kabul, Baghdad and Fallujah; Insurgent Man, lobbing mortars into street markets or detonating his suicide vest on a rush-hour bus; Hijack Man, drilling civilian aeroplanes into crowded buildings; Drive-by Man, laughing as he fills some rival drug dealer's gut with lead; Road-rage Man, foot to the boards, out of my way, you fucker; Rapacious Man, knickers off, ram-it-in, take that you bitch! And in that moment, more than anything in the world, Patrick wanted to grip Sam by the throat, slam him up against this tree so hard his feet dangled off the ground, and scream at him, 'Do you know what you've done? Do you have any … fucking … idea … what you've done?'

Patrick hated feeling like this, as bitter, vengeful, and violent as the men he despised and condemned; but worst of all, utterly impotent.

Chapter Fourteen

"I RANG NUALA TODAY," said Maggie.

Patrick gave a jolt but managed to keep his eyes trained upon his plate.

"How was she?" he asked, as his fork twice tried, and failed, to spear the last remaining garlic mushroom.

"I don't know, her phone was switched off; she's probably out of credit. Suppose I'd better send her a cheque."

"I'll do it."

"No, it's my turn, you've done your bit."

"How do you mean?"

"Going up there, taking her out for lunch. I'll send her a cheque for a hundred and a note saying not to blow it all on booze and dope."

Patrick, closed his eyes, shook his head, abandoned both fork and mushroom and began clearing the plates.

"What?" she asked, pointedly.

"What, what?" he replied, grabbing a tea towel and moving to open the oven door.

"Don't start that. And what's with the look?"

"Salmon *en croute*, all right?" he said, ignoring her question and placing the baking tray in the centre of the table.

"Fine, a little elaborate for mid-week. What's up?"

"I've had a quiet day, I felt like cooking, that's all."

"Are you sure you're all right? You sound … flat."

'Oh, that's good,' thought Patrick, 'a leaf out of my own book.' But just as Maggie's empathy began to bite she broke the silence and offered them both a means of escape.

"Oh, and what's with the phone call this morning? I'm driving around the middle of Harrogate searching in vain for a parking space and there's you on the phone wanting to know what I'd like for dinner."

"Yeah, dumb wasn't it?" he conceded with a forced smile

and slid a salmon parcel onto her plate. "Oh, green beans! Almost forgot!" and he fetched the dish from the microwave, added a knob of butter and spooned a portion onto each of their plates.

"Looks good," she said, approvingly, as she carefully scraped away the butter to the side of her plate, and Patrick's heart rate appreciably slowed.

That night, at Patrick's instigation, they had sex. She found him rather more attentive than usual, to her face and neck, as if it was really her he was seeking to enter and not just her body, so much so that she felt uncomfortable, and gently but firmly, pressed on his shoulders, guiding him down until his face nestled between her legs, and commenced something less challenging for them both.

"Why do you call me Pat?" he asked after both were done and had been lying on their backs for some minutes in the dark.

She half-turned her head towards him, then let it sink back into the pillow.

"I just do."

"You're the only one who does."

"Does it matter?" she asked, in a tone that suggested it should not.

"Names are important."

"Of course they are, but does it bother you?"

"Not until now," he replied, enigmatically.

"I've always called you Pat," she said, justifying herself.

"No you haven't."

"I have, always!" She was indignant now.

"No, the first time you called me 'Pat' was when we first had sex."

"But that was only two days after we met!"

"I know, but I noticed the change, you called me Pat, when we were making love that very first time."

Maggie was incredulous.

"I can't believe we're having this conversation. Are you really telling me that after twenty years together you've never liked me calling you Pat?"

"I didn't say that. I said that it matters, and I wondered why you chose to use it that first time, and why you've continued doing so ever since, when nobody else ever does?"

"Pat …" she let out an exasperated sigh, "look I … I just did it, all right? Unlike you I don't have to analyse everything little thing I do or say, okay?"

"Okay."

Patrick backed off, and a long half-minute passed in silence.

"Pat, don't do this, don't sulk on me. Do you mind telling me what the point of this is?"

"I don't know. I was just thinking out loud that's all, about who I am and who we are, and names came into it. I didn't mean to go on about it. It's all right. Go to sleep."

She turned on to her side, away from him.

"Goodnight," she whispered, as an afterthought.

Patrick replied in kind and then lay in the dark, mulling it over.

He had lied. He knew very well what it was all about. That very first time he had entered her and she whispered "Pat, Pat," over and over, he'd felt claimed by it, as if it signified her taking possession of him, thereby transforming him from the stiff, shy Patrick he knew himself to be, into someone more easy-going and acceptable. 'Pat,' such an approachable little word; off-pat; pat-hand, pat-on-the-back. It surprised him hearing her utter the name that first time, but he'd liked the sound of it; and the context helped overcome his twinge of discomfort at its androgynous nature. Strange how no one else has ever called him it, before or since; perhaps because he always introduces himself as 'Patrick,' thereby ensuring that 'Pat' remained firmly a feature of Maggie's terrain. Then he remembered an instance from their early years together, having dinner at their all-too-close neighbours, Suzie had suddenly addressed him as 'Pat' and he noticed Maggie's reaction. Nothing was said, but within days, Maggie had extinguished any proprietorial designs emanating from that quarter.

Patrick fell to thinking of his sister, Rose, who, within a year of their mother's death, had begun calling herself Roisin; had left her husband, bought and sold a flat in Putney, packed in her teaching job and moved to a cottage in a small town in Donegal, from where she sent a postcard, commencing, *Dear*

Padraig (just teasing!) He was not amused. Way back when Maggie was pregnant with Nuala, his mother, Brigid, had asked about names, 'If you're blessed with a boy,' she suggested, 'what about Cormac?' It had led to the worst ever row between Patrick and his mother. Cormac means 'son of a charioteer' and was the forename of an ancient king of Ireland, but was also his father's name, a drunkard who'd treated their mother badly, and Patrick would have no son of his named after him. What's more, he couldn't see why his mother would wish for such a thing, when her husband had been more fond of the bottle than of her, and ended up in prison after nearly killing a man in a bar-room brawl. He died in gaol, beaten to death by another inmate. Patrick was just three at the time and understood only that his father was a bad lot and had had to go away. His sister Roisin told him the truth when he was seven. After his father's death, his mother took the children and their grandmother across to England to begin a new life. It was the 1960s and the Irish were unpopular in England, so their mother adopted anglicised versions of their first names and dropped the 'O' from O'Donnell. Within two years she had married an Englishman, Robert Chime, who willingly gave his name to the children, thereby ensuring their Irish heritage was consigned to the past. Patrick got on well with his step-dad but, when Patrick was fifteen, his mother discovered that Robert had been having an affair, living at the other woman's house when he was meant to be working away, and she kicked him out, and forbade him to see the children. She stubbornly refused to divorce him, until in her late forties, when for no apparent reason, she changed her mind, gave Robert his freedom and, for some reason Patrick never understood, began expressing a yearning to return to Donegal. She might have gone too, but for the impending arrival of her one and only grandchild, for there'd been no signs of any offspring emanating from Roisin's marriage. Patrick was relieved it had turned out to be a girl, and chose an Irish name as a sop to his mother. He settled on Nuala. It was the cause of the one and only major row he'd ever had with his daughter, the day he saw she'd changed it to Nula on all her school exercise books. She couldn't understand why he'd hit the roof. 'It sounds like Nula, why shouldn't I

91

spell it Nula?' she protested. Maggie was no help, her mother still insists on calling her Margaret to this day. More to the point, Patrick couldn't explain why it upset him so much. 'It's spelt Nuala,' he just kept repeating, as if she was deaf. He thought he'd lost that battle until a few months later he saw she'd recovered all her books and reverted to the old spelling. Nothing more was ever said. Patrick turned over, pulled the covers tight about him, and smiled to himself as he thought about her name. It means 'fair-shouldered and exceptionally lovely'.

'Don't know about exceptionally lovely', Maggie joked shortly after giving birth, 'but I can vouch for those shoulders.'

'Fair-shouldered and exceptionally lovely, she still is,' thought Patrick, and he hoped to God she was all right.

92

Chapter Fifteen

"IT'S ME."

"Hey, Maggie, I've so missed you."

"Me too."

And something in her voice made Gavin ask if she was okay?

"I think Pat suspects."

Silence.

"Say something, Gavin."

"… What makes you think he knows?"

"He doesn't *know*, I said I think he suspects!"

"You sound worried."

"Yes. No. Oh, I don't know; it's the uncertainty that's getting to me. Whenever there's a lull in conversation, I'm bracing myself for him to ask me if something's going on. I'm relieved when he doesn't and the next minute I'm wishing he would. Does that sound crazy?"

"And if he did … ask you?"

Silence.

"Well? Maggie?"

"Gavin, can I see you?" The need in her voice was palpable.

"This afternoon, at the flat, I'll be home by four."

Home. She was struck by Gavin's rapid adoption of the term, for in the days of her French gîte holidays with Pat, when Nuala was small, whenever Maggie referred to any gîte as 'home,' Pat would challenge her of the word, and Nuala, as always, would side with her father, adopting that precocious tone that Maggie found so irritating, 'It's not *our* home, Mummy, this is just somewhere we're staying!' What do you do when home has become simply somewhere you're staying? Maggie was pleased Gavin was able to choose where to call home; it made it seem possible that one day she might do the same.

"One more thing, what would you like for breakfast?"

"Don't joke, Gavin, you don't know how I long to wake up alongside you."

"You have, three times, you see, I keep count."

"In hotel rooms, Gavin; it's not the same."

"So, bring your toothbrush; bring a suitcase!"

"If only it were that easy."

"It is."

"I'll be there at four," she said, and hung up.

"Dad?"

"Oh Nuala! How are you?"

"Back in halls. I'm OK."

"Good." He paused, anxious not to rush in, "Er, how did it go?"

"It? You can say the word you know, I'd rather you did. Or is Mum there?

"No, she's not back from work yet," and he hesitated, unsure which word to use. Pregnancies are terminated; foetuses aborted. He decided to err on the side of caution.

"The termination; how was it?"

"You'll be pleased to know the abortion was a success."

"If we're going to quibble over words, Nuala, I take issue with the idea of me being pleased. At best, I'll admit to feeling some relief mixed with a large measure of sadness and concern for what you've been through, or rather what you're going through, because it's not over yet. You've now got to live with it."

"Thanks for that, you sound just like a counsellor."

"Do I? I feel more like a dad."

"What's that like? Bit of a let down, eh?"

Her question triggered a bolt of anger, rifling from within.

"No!" he shouted down the phone, so loud he shocked himself, "Nuala, don't ever, ever, allow yourself to think I'm disappointed to have you as my daughter. It's me, I always feel I should be able to do more, to protect you, to put things right, I know it's crazy, I'm always telling my clients they expect too much of themselves and here I am doing the very same thing. It's just that it's different when it's your own flesh and blood."

94

"Dad, I'm sorry." Nuala said, sniffing away the tears.

"No, I'm sorry. I don't know why I'm shouting at you."

"I'm sorry," she repeated, desperate for it to be heard.

"There's no need to apologise, Nuala. I love you."

"I know, Dad. Thanks," she muttered, through her snuffles.

"When do you think we might see you?" he asked. "Why not come home this weekend for some TLC?"

"I will, Dad," she said, regaining some composure, "But not this weekend, maybe the weekend after? I'll give you both a ring on Sunday."

"Okay. How are you off for money?"

"Oh, I got a text from Mum, it said, 'cheque in post'. I replied, but thank her again for me."

"Tell her yourself, she'll be home soon, I'll get her to ring you."

"Dad, don't push it, please."

"Okay, okay, I'm sorry. You take care now."

"I will."

"Love you."

And he thought he heard her start to snuffle again just before the phone went dead.

Patrick had already availed himself of a gin and tonic and was a good three-quarters of the way through a bottle of his favourite Penfolds Bin 389, and this, coupled with the volume of his new Leonard Cohen album meant he did not hear Maggie's car ease onto the drive, or the sound of the front door closing behind her.

"Mind if I turn that down?"

She was standing in the doorway as he opened his eyes.

"Fancy a drink?" he replied, ignoring her question.

"Yes," she said, and walked across and reduced the volume several degrees.

"Too much!" he protested, and she raised it back up a notch.

He set off for the kitchen, returning with a second bottle and another glass to find her cross-legged on the carpet, leaning back against the armchair. He filled her glass with the remaining wine, drew the cork from the second bottle and topped up his own. He placed hers on the floor beside her before taking his seat on the sofa opposite, somewhat unsteadily.

"Are you drunk?" she asked.

"Getting there."

"Still sober enough to talk?" she persisted.

"Yes," he said, "I'll start. Where have you been? It's late. You didn't phone, and your mobile was switched off."

They both glanced at the clock; it showed a little after ten-thirty.

"I know I didn't phone and I should have. I'm sorry." She took a sip of wine and placed the glass carefully on the carpet, a little further away than before.

"Patrick, I'm seeing someone."

He stared at her.

"You called me Patrick."

"I said I'm seeing someone."

"I heard you the first time. A therapist?"

Maggie stared back impassively.

"No, I didn't think that was what you meant," he said, raising his glass and taking a sizeable gulp. "You're seeing someone," he repeated calmly, taking the words in and letting them slosh around for a turn or two, and he wished for a spittoon. In the event, he swallowed them down, and spoke with a superficial calm.

"This is where I get irate, right? And demand to know what's going on, who the hell he is, what he's got that I haven't, and then we shout and bawl until you storm off to bed and I end up sleeping on the sofa? Isn't that how these scenes unfold?"

"If you must," she replied.

"Well, you may like to know that I don't feel like ranting and raging tonight."

"Me neither."

"What's going on?" he asked, as gently as he could, more for his own well-being than hers.

"I'm not really sure I can answer that," she replied, "But I have been seeing someone."

"That's the third time you've said that. How long?"

She paused before answering,

"Some months."

"How many?"

She lowered her eyes, took a deep breath, raised her head and looked straight into his eyes.

"Ten. Eleven. We met by chance almost year ago."

Now it was Patrick's turn to look away.

"Did you not suspect something might be going on?"

"No. I did not suspect something might be going on." It helped to repeat her words; they were like a handrail down the side of a dark steep gorge and he was fearful of losing his footing. "Look, I'm not stupid, I know things haven't been right for some time, but … well, let's just say I've tried not to think about it."

"That's not like you, Pat."

"It is when I feel impotent to do anything about a situation."

"So I make you feel impotent? Is that it?"

"I didn't say that."

"No, you didn't, I'm sorry," and her apology was genuine, which made it all the harder for him to accept.

Silence.

She raised her glass once more to her lips but lowered it again without drinking.

"I suppose that's where you've been tonight, with your someone?" he asked, and was tempted to also inquire about last Sunday at the gym, and numerous other occasions when she had been late home from work or required to stay away overnight, but he managed to refrain. The time for anger and recrimination would come, but not yet. He would savour it, like an ace of trumps, for when he really needed it. For now the moral high ground was his, why concede it by chucking rocks down on a sitting target.

"Yes," she said softly.

Her calmness annoyed him. She seemed so unruffled, and just for a moment he visualised throwing his wine over her and then calmly taking himself off to bed, but stayed his hand.

"Look, Maggie, I'm not sure I can do this right now," he said at last, and swallowed hard.

"Hmm, I picked the wrong time, eh?"

He made no response other than to haul himself to his feet

and plonk his glass down upon the coffee table. Slops of red wine bloodied the pale carpet and he stared down at her, questioningly.

"What made you decide to tell me?"

"Do you remember that promise we made to each other way back at the very beginning, how we would always be straight with each other, no deceit?"

"That's because we knew there'd come a time for lies," he answered, "there always does."

"You know, Pat, you've become so damned cynical and I hate it. I really hate it. I'm not entirely sure why I told you. I think perhaps because I didn't like the cynical liar in myself. The secrecy was a thrill at first; it was forbidden, it was mine, and I kept it in a watertight compartment where I could cherish it, and keep it safe by thinking of it as completely separate to you and me. That way no one got hurt; but things don't stay still, despite our best intentions. It may sound odd but, lately, I felt the secrecy was coming between us, and over the past week or so I've been half-expecting you to ask me outright. In the end I just got tired of waiting. Deceit is tiring, and even more corrosive than the actual infidelity."

"Careful, you're sounding like me," he sneered.

"After all these years you'd expect some of it to rub off," she replied, staring up at him, her eyes soft with tears. "Pat, we have to talk."

"Yes, I know. But not now, I'm tired, I'm going to bed," and he hauled himself to his feet like a weary old man, and as he left the room called out 'goodnight' without looking back.

For once, Patrick left his clothes strewn on the floor by his side of the bed, and pulled the covers over his head like he did when he was a small boy still scared of the dark. His head was spinning and he regretted the gin and tonic, for he knew that on the rare occasion he began an evening with one it usually meant he would end the night drunk. The last sound he heard before falling asleep was the opening and closing of kitchen cupboards as Maggie set about removing the red wine spills from the pale carpet.

He awoke around three to take a pee, and again a little after five when his concentration was claimed by the rise and fall of Maggie's breathing until he could bear it no longer, and rather than smother her face with his pillow, he quietly extricated himself from the covers, put on a bath robe and wandered off downstairs.

Kneeling on the floor by the front room window, he folded his arms and leant on the windowsill just as he did as child, staring out at a world of fragments, trying to piece them together. The glow of the streetlamp cast an amber haze over their front garden, illuminating the shapes of their two cars, side by side on the drive, and he imagined each in turn, parked there in isolation. It was easier to visualise the old Saab, for to see Maggie's new VW standing alone posed too many uncertainties that he had no desire to address until forced to.

He considered his alternatives: He could place the knowledge of Maggie's infidelity in a pocket at the back of his wallet and allow her to carry on as before, the guilt and deceit replaced by a new compact of complicity. Such arrangements work for some couples, but he doubted his need of her was so great that he could accommodate the resultant damage to his self-esteem. He could perhaps, via some heroic gesture, see to it that all hell broke loose and the affair was brought to a sudden and dramatic end? Messy, but appealing. He knew it was a common outcome where extra-marital affairs are concerned; the affair as transitional object; its discovery injecting a massive stimulant of anger and passion into an otherwise becalmed marriage, and after the initial period of finger-wagging, breast-beating and general air of crisis, the couple adjust to the new reality and begin talking properly for the first time in years. And if there's sufficient glow in the embers, new life is breathed into their marriage and they almost begin courting again. Anyway, that's the theory, he told himself, and it sometimes works.

Far from ready for such decisive action, Patrick sought to consider things from Maggie's perspective. He tried to work out what had made her decide to tell him. 'She can't be considering ending the affair' – he noted the stark reality of his first use of the word. 'If she'd wanted to end it she'd have done so, why create extra problems for herself by confessing all to me now? Perhaps, as she'd implied, she needed to expiate her guilt. That makes sense, but is unlikely to be the whole story, for in coming clean now she's relinquished a large measure of control over the affair. What if she's in love, and wants more of her 'someone' and therefore wants out of our marriage? Then why didn't she say as much last night? Breaking me in gently, I suppose.' He racked his brain to remember her exact words – 'Patrick, I'm seeing someone,' not 'I've been seeing someone,' – 'present tense, on-going, continuing. She'd called it a thrill ... exciting. Well, you'd expect that; so what? Thrills are temporary and excitement wanes, but cherish; she said *cherish;* cherish is for keeps; it goes deep. It's obvious,' he decided, 'this someone is significant and has to be reckoned with; she was telling me that much for sure. But maybe she was also putting me to the test; do I care so little I'll just shrug, or is there enough passion in me to stand up and fight for her? It's plausible, but right now, any passion seems well out of reach, she and her someone have cornered the market. Besides, if she'd said she'd *been* seeing someone, it would have fitted better with that hypothesis, providing not only a threat, but also some hope. So, conclusion: she's letting me down in stages: first, she tells me she's having an affair; next she'll confess that she loves him; followed swiftly by the third and final act, when she informs me she's had enough of our marriage and wants out. That's it, sorted.' And Patrick let out a sigh, but wasn't sure whether it was borne of sadness, relief, or anticipation of the ordeal to come.

At seven, he took her up a mug of tea, left it on her bedside table and got straight into the shower. When he emerged, she was sitting up in bed, staring at him.

"Are you all right?" she enquired.

He gave a weak, cynical smile, and continued towelling his hair.

"Pat?"

"Yes, I'm all right. Whatever that means."

"We need to talk."

"Yes, you said so last night," he replied, "and since you're the one calling the shots, when do you suggest?"

She ignored the provocation, and then remembered her diary.

"Oh God it's Thursday," she groaned, "I'm down in London tonight!"

She seemed genuinely to have forgotten. 'Maybe she's not so in control after all,' he thought. And then he twigged, lowered the towel and stared directly at her.

"On my own! Pat, I promise."

And something made him believe her.

"Tomorrow night, then?"

"Tomorrow night," he replied.

Chapter Sixteen

THE GATES WERE JUST opening as Patrick drove past at eight-thirty. This was no modern-day expensive garden centre with cafeteria and extensive gift section, just two poly tunnels of plants grown from cutting or seed by the ageing hippy woman who lived in a cottage on the site. He stopped the car and walked back to enquire if she was open.

"No," she said, "I've run out of milk and I was just going to the shop."

Patrick pulled a face and turned towards the car.

"But if there's something specific you want?"

"A flowering shrub," replied Patrick, "something that won't need tending."

"Come on," she said, and led him over to the open beds behind the second tunnel from where she selected a none-too promising looking specimen. "Here, try this azalea," she said, lifting it up and offering it to Patrick to inspect.

"Go on, it won't bite."

Patrick was more worried about getting soil on his jacket or trousers, and held it away from his body.

"Don't know much about plants, do you?"

"How did you guess?" replied Patrick.

"It may look nothing more than a bunch of twigs now, but just you wait."

He paid her and stowed it in the boot of his car.

Neil was five minutes early, and Patrick was barely ready to receive him. Instead of asking Neil to take a seat in reception, Patrick found himself leading him directly through to the therapy room where Neil plonked himself down, the heel of his left foot tapping rapidly on the carpet. As usual, no eye contact offered.

"What's up?" asked Patrick directly.

Neil's head gave a sudden shiver, his only reply.

"Come on, Neil, what is it, what's happened?"

"What makes you think something's happened?" the younger man snapped back.

"You want to come over here and take a look at what I see?" asked Patrick.

Neil's foot stopped tapping, and he spoke without raising his eyes.

"I've had a shit week"

"In what way?"

"I asked a girl at work out for a drink. She said 'no', but it was the way she said it, as if I was an idiot to even imagine she'd go out with me."

"Did she say that?" asked Patrick.

Neil flashed a look at his interrogator.

"Look, you weren't there, I saw her face, all right?" and the emphasis poured into those last two words defied Patrick to contradict him.

"All right," said Patrick, content to give ground. "So, the week started badly, you took a risk, it backfired, and you were left feeling … what, hurt, angry?"

'Christ, I'm now putting words in his mouth; stop trying so hard!' Patrick silently rebuked himself.

"Humiliated."

"Hmm, that's a horrible feeling," Patrick said slowly, allowing a pause before continuing.

"What made you choose her?"

"What?"

"What made you choose *her*? You work in a call-centre in Leeds, right? There must be lots of young women there. What made you choose her?"

"I can see the back of her head from where I sit. She's got long blonde hair, beautiful hair, dead straight, like that weather girl on Look North, Lisa, know the one?"

"I've seen her."

"Well, I stare at this girl's hair every day, I lose myself in it. And we happened to be on a break at the same time and she was standing alone over by the water dispenser, so I went across and asked her out.

"Just like that?"

"I said, 'Hi, do you fancy going out for a proper drink sometime?'"

"And?"

"She turned around, pulled a face, shook her head, and said, 'Err, no. No thanks,' and walked away."

"Leaving you … feeling like shit?"

"Yeah."

"So what did you do?"

"Went to the bog, sat there, thought about walking out and going home."

"What stopped you?"

"I need the money, and my Mum would only go off on one."

"So, you realised you couldn't just walk out of the job, and there you were, sitting in the bog feeling like shit. So what happened?"

"Thought about a wank. Thought it might make me feel better."

"Did it?"

Neil shook his head.

"Someone came in. Wouldn't have been able to get it up anyway."

"That usually a problem?"

"Leave it out!" Neil said sharply, "It was being at work, too exposed."

"So you wanted to run away, but you couldn't. You wanted the comfort of a wank but you couldn't do that either, so you stuffed away your humiliation, went back to your desk and dealt with more irate customers?"

Neil nodded, and hung his head. Neither man recognised the potential of the metaphor.

"Hmm, a real bad day," observed Patrick, "and this was, when, Monday?"

"Last Friday, the day after being here."

Patrick wondered why Neil had needed to mention the link to his session, as if somehow pointing a finger of responsibility his way? He might have teased this out, but chose instead to continue the narrative of Neil's lousy week.

104

"Okay, that was Friday, what else has happened?"

"I spent the whole weekend in my room, on the computer."

"The show-tell-hide site?"

Neil glanced across quizzically.

"Well, isn't that what people do there? Someone shows a pic; someone else tells them what they'd like to do to it; and all the while everyone hides behind their aliases?"

"Nicknames, 'nicks' to be precise," insisted Neil, glad of the chance to correct the clever-dick therapist who had just summed up his pornographic cyber-world so succinctly and dismissively.

"Sorry, nicks," repeated Patrick, aware that he had deservedly been put in his place.

"What's yours?" Patrick asked spontaneously, prompted by a genuine desire to be less judgemental, endeavouring to summon up the warmth that Beth suggested he too often held back from male clients, in order to get alongside Neil and appreciate more of what his alternative existence meant to him.

But the question had made Neil freeze, his eyes now staring hard and disbelieving at Patrick, who realised straightaway that he had made a serious error. 'Spontaneous responses, along with therapist's self-disclosure,' as Patrick was fond of telling his more inexperienced supervisees, 'constitute high-risk interventions; they're sometimes necessary, but can be dangerous,' and he strove at once to make amends.

"Neil, I'm sorry, I hadn't realised what I was asking. What I was trying to do was appreciate and understand what this website, this alternative existence where you spend so much of your spare time and which you feel so ambivalent about, really means to you. That was why I asked your nickname; I should have realised it was as big a challenge as if someone on that website had asked you to post your real identity. I didn't intend putting you on the spot, and I'm sorry."

Neil looked tearful, angry, or both. He bit his lip, lowered his eyes, began picking at his nails and his foot resumed its earlier tapping. Patrick's heart was thumping. 'This could go one of two ways,' he thought, 'and I fear he'll do a runner.'

"Degas," Neil's whisper was barely audible and Patrick was grateful he didn't need to ask him to repeat it.

"After the artist?

"Yeah."

"Tell me why you chose him?" asked Patrick softly, concerned to build on the breakthrough but careful not to exert undue pressure.

"You've got one of his pictures up there on the wall. I noticed it the first time I came. It's called, *L'Absinthe,* or *The Absinthe Drinkers.* It's good, but it's not one of my favourites; the characters look too sad, they're cut off from each other."

Patrick resisted the temptation to point out that *both* pictures on the wall were by Degas, or indeed ask if 'sad,' and 'cut off' summed up how Neil felt about himself. That much was obvious. Anyway, Patrick had no wish to interrupt the flow.

"Degas is famous for his ballet paintings," Neil went on, "of rehearsal classes and behind the scenes stuff more than the actual performance itself. He was fascinated by the small details of preparation, like a dancer tying her shoes or practising by the rail. He painted horses and jockeys at the racecourse but had no real interest in the race itself, only the anticipation before the off, as the riders circled down at the start."

"Yes, I've seen one or two of those, they're good," enthused Patrick.

"They're all right. But what I love best are his paintings of women. Like a dedicated voyeur, he captures their most intimate moments, combing their hair, bathing in a tub, drying their feet; even doing everyday stuff like trying on a hat, or even ironing in a laundry. The paintings are incredibly beautiful; the women aren't slim and rich like models or film stars, what's beautiful is the way he looks at them. A biography I read claimed that Degas was a misogynist. I don't believe it; no one who hated women could paint them with such loving attention."

There was a pause, and it seemed that Neil had come to the end of his treatise on Degas and Patrick knew he must make some response. He opted to put his trust in immediacy.

"Neil, I've never heard you talk like that before. Such feeling and sophistication in what you were saying about what you find in Degas' art. I found it really moving to sit here

106

listening to you; I think I can see why you adopted him for your nickname; is Degas in some way like you?"

"I can't paint."

Patrick smiled.

"Me neither. But I didn't mean that. Perhaps in the way you and he look at the world? You talk about him being interested in what's on the edge of things rather than the central event; the time before the race, the dancer backstage tying her shoes, or resting in the interval? Is that like you, in some way always on the edge of things?"

"Suppose so. At home, school, at work, and when I'm out in bars, I always feel like an outsider, looking in. I don't want it to be like that, it just happens. But Degas notices what's going on away from the main attraction, and he values it."

"Yes, I think I see what you mean," Patrick said slowly, "you've expressed it very well, and taught me something, not only about Degas, but also about you." However, what he failed to add, was that Neil's description of being an edge person, always on the outside looking in, made Patrick aware that he and his client had more in common than he'd thought.

"Tell me about the other Degas, Neil, the one on the website."

"Degas prefers older women to the plastic bimbos," Neil explained. "He likes the ones who don't shove everything in your face. He likes the ones who talk, as well as just post pics."

"Does Degas converse with them? You know, chat?"

"Thank you, but I know what the word means!"

Patrick winced.

"Sorry Neil."

Neil frowned, but chose to continue.

"Yeah, it's great when that happens, it's like a real conversation between just the two of you, and sometimes you get the feeling you've really met."

Keenly aware of the parallels with his own occupation, in particular, the therapeutic alliance between himself and Neil, Patrick might easily have said something to that effect, but decided to let the moment pass. He soon regretted it, for without warning Neil launched a stunning verbal assault on all that had gone before.

"But it's just a fucking charade, isn't it, a fucking waste of time!"

"Whoa! Where did that come from?" asked Patrick, taken aback.

"It's like coming here, it's not real is it, just a load of sad people like me escaping from the real world? That's what Graham said."

"Graham? That's your Mum's partner, right?"

Neil pulled a face.

"You don't like him?"

"Me and Mum were on our own for seven years after my adoptive dad walked out, until I was in my early twenties, that's when she met Graham."

"And he now lives with you and your mum?"

"He's still got a place of his own, but he stays over at ours most weekends. He and I had a bust-up on Sunday afternoon, about me being there all weekend (he began mimicking Graham's voice) '… moping around, locked in your room, spending all day and night on the computer, wasting your life, your mother's too soft, if I had my way I'd kick you out!' Blah, blah blah! He's a stiff, and I don't know what she sees in him."

"And how did you deal with his onslaught?"

"Told him it was my room and my computer!"

Neil bowed his head and looked uncomfortable.

Gently, Patrick pressed him.

"What is it Neil?"

Neil gave a sigh.

"Graham said, 'It's your room, but it's your mother's house, and her electricity – it's time you grew up, and moved out, or at least paid her proper board and lodging!'"

Patrick looked quizzical. Neil noticed, and taking it as a look of judgement, sought to defend his position.

"I give her twenty-five quid a week. I know it's not a lot, but I don't earn all that much and it costs me a lot more than that to come here and …" Neil broke off in mid-sentence and shook his head, as if he'd had more than enough of being called to account.

Patrick waited, but Neil showed no sign of continuing.

"Is that it then, the shitty week?" asked Patrick, eager to try and maintain the momentum.

"No, not quite." Neil sighed, "I spent a lot of time on RedSky, and I fell out with a woman there. Her name's 'Moll', her nick, that is. I always look to see if she's posting, and that night she was; she lives in the States, so it was late and for a while it was just her and me, and it was going great and then I posted a pic, of myself, and she got upset, she called it a 'dick bomb' and said I'd abused the thread and was just like all the rest."

"Her words hurt?" asked Patrick.

Neil grunted and hung his head like a beaten boxer.

"I guess all of that qualifies as a pretty shitty week, then Neil. There was a lot of rejection, a heap of criticism and contempt that came your way. But one thing stands out, you might well have turned all this in on yourself, but you didn't, you chose to honour our appointment today and come here and tell me about it. And, you've opened up to me today far more than ever before, and I feel closer to you as result, and feel I know you a lot better."

"Yeah, but so what?" replied Neil, with a shrug.

"Yeah, so what?" echoed Patrick, striving hard to contain his exasperation with Neil's dismissiveness. "Look, Neil, earlier today, when you talked about the website being a fucking charade, you said it was like coming here. Well come on then, what's the fucking charade in here?"

"I dunno," replied Neil, off-handedly.

"Yes you do. Come on, Neil, the word 'fucking' implies that you're angry about what you see as a charade, and if you're angry about something it only proves how important it is to you, so come on, what's the fucking charade in here?"

Silence.

Patrick wasn't about to let this go.

"Apart from the guessing game," Patrick went on, "the word 'charade' means an absurd pretence. So come on, Neil, what's the absurd pretence in here?"

"That you really care!" Neil said quietly, through gritted teeth.

Bull's eye.

Disturbed by the enormity of his accusation, Neil

immediately scanned Patrick's face to gauge the response. Patrick looked solemn, but Neil had started something he now felt compelled to finish.

"Sometimes, I think you really do care," he continued, "then other times I think it's all just an act, because if you and I met outside in the real world, on a train or in a bar, you wouldn't want to know me. You wouldn't even pass the time of day with someone like me … would you?"

Unperturbed by the accusation, Patrick responded calmly and purposefully.

"Neil, you're saying that we're different, and because of those differences I wouldn't want to be your friend. And because of that you can't believe I really care about you, is that it?" asked Patrick.

Neil's head registered the tiniest nod, but his eyes no longer offered any contact.

"Well, you're right, Neil, I don't want to be your friend. And let's remember something else, you didn't come across me in a bar, on a train, or even on some porn site chat room, you approached me here, in a setting where I'm not available to be anyone's friend, or lover, or partner, or parent, I'm here simply as a therapist, trying to provide an honest, professional service."

Patrick could have kicked himself, why did he need to add that last phrase, as if trying to justify himself?

Neil made no reply to this proclamation, just remained slumped in the chair, head bowed, until eventually letting out a sigh.

Patrick took up the slack.

"What does this relationship really mean, Neil, what does it add up to? Isn't this the question we keep coming back to all the time, what is it really worth?"

"Forty-five quid!" replied Neil, reaching in his shirt pocket for the carefully folded notes he'd placed there before leaving home, and this time he deposited them gently on the adjacent coffee table, nudging them tentatively in Patrick's direction.

"But is it worth it?" asked Patrick.

"You tell me," replied Neil, "But you won't will you?"

Patrick smiled, weakly.

Patrick completed his notes on the session and scribbled a large 'S' as a prompt to take to supervision the following morning. This was what his work was all about, those edge of the seat moments that occasionally bubble to the surface within the therapeutic hour. But Patrick was troubled, troubled by his response to Neil's accusation about the charade of therapy. He'd intended to address it openly but ended up feeling that he'd been unhelpfully defensive in arguing for the honesty and professionalism of his own service. Nevertheless, there was some degree of comfort that not once during the hour had the parlous state of Patrick's own marriage entered his head. Just then the office door opened and Grace's face appeared.

"Sorry, I did knock."

From the far desk, Patrick apologised and beckoned her inside. Grace assumed her usual seat, crossing her finely trousered legs. He noticed she wore less make-up today, looking tired around the eyes. It was Patrick who broke the silence.

"This feels different, on both previous occasions you just launched in."

"I was nervous. I chatter when I'm nervous."

"And today you're not?"

"No. Tired, confused, a downright mess, but not nervous."

"You want to talk about it?"

"That's why I'm here."

And for most of the session Grace went on to explain in great detail how she and David had stayed up half the night arguing and agonising over their wounded marriage such that she now felt quite wrung out. David had been out for the evening with a friend, a fellow consultant from the hospital, and had evidently confided in him about their marital problems. It seems the friend's advice was to tell David to wear his heart on his sleeve and let Grace know how much he loved her, for David returned around eleven, poured a large whisky and began pleading with her not to leave him. Having spent much of her marriage longing to see her husband's elusive and vulnerable inner core, now it was laid at her feet Grace didn't know what on earth to do with it. She was like a boxer caught on the ropes, and when at last she managed to break free and head off to bed, David soon followed, and took her with a new and desperate hunger, his mouth swarming all over her body. She longed for sufficient willpower, or hate, to be able to cast him off. Instead she bit her lip and made it bruise. Once he'd emptied his vulnerability into her, she lay still in the dark until becoming aware of a sound, close by, yet far off; it was the muffled, whimpering of a puppy locked out in the rain, heart-wrenching in intensity and emanating not from outside, but from the husband lying spent upon her chest. He gave a choking noise, his body lurched and he began weeping uncontrollably. Instinctively, her arms gathered him to her breast and she hushed and soothed him as she would a small child. They lay like that until a knock at the bedroom door brought them to their senses.

"Are you all right?"

It was a plaintive cry from their youngest, alarmed by the strange sounds emanating through the bedroom wall. Grace gently coaxed the boy back to bed remaining by his side until he was safely asleep. By the time she returned, all was still. She climbed back into bed, careful not to touch his prostrate form, closed her eyes and prayed that he was asleep, but his arm reached out across her chest and lay there like a fallen bough. Frozen, pinned, claimed by a man of whom she'd had more than enough, her thoughts fled to Simon, who yesterday had set off on his pilgrim's trail. Her intention had been to fly out to join him in a few days' time, and she experienced a sinking feeling, for she now knew the extent of her family's need of her. She opened her eyes; the darkness seemed to extend for ever, beyond the bedroom walls, beyond the children's schooling, beyond the mortgage, an impenetrable darkness, world without end. Seeing no way out, she closed her eyes and prayed that, when morning came, she would not awake.

David roused her with a cup of tea and barely concealed impatience as he sat on the side of the bed waiting for her to come to. She sat up slowly and took the cup from him; his next words were like an ice-cold shower.

"Grace, let's go together to see that counsellor of yours, for

my sake and the children's; I'm begging you, Grace, please …
will you give this marriage one last chance?"

Grace opened her mouth but no words came, and she closed
her eyes, shook her head and her tea slopped into the saucer,
splashing on the duvet. David took the cup from her grasp and
asked her to at least consider his proposal.

Having told her tale, Grace looked done in, like a rag doll
who'd had the stuffing ripped out of her, and, having listened
patiently for so long, Patrick now felt an urge to gather her up
and rock her gently into the loving arms of sleep. Indeed, back
in his early days as a raw trainee, he might well have moved
his chair closer and reached out a comforting hand, but he was
wiser now, and knew the danger of counsellors and therapists
feeding their own repressed desires at their clients' expense.
Patrick knew how, despite their conscious intent, would-be
rescuers all too often turn into new persecutors, and he would
have none of it. And so Patrick inhaled deeply, let out an
extravagant sigh, but remained firmly lodged in his seat.

"Phew, I can see why you're tired, Grace. What was your
answer?"

"I said I'd think about it, and talk to you."

"Do you want us to do that now?" 'Hmm, *us,* not a term I
am used to using,' he thought to himself.

"I can't honestly say I *want* to," Grace replied, "but David
will be expecting an answer when he gets home tonight, and I
owe him that much. So what do you think?"

Resisting the opportunity to explore the prevalence of
obligation over desire within Grace's relationship with David,
Patrick instead addressed Grace's question directly.

"To be frank, Grace, it's more to do with what *you* think,
although before you decide, I need to say a few things.
Although I do have plenty of experience in marital and couple
therapy, it might be wiser for you and David to see someone
other than myself, someone new, who would be able to make a
fresh start with you both, without any preconceptions."

"I wouldn't want that!" Grace retorted, "No. I'm not
prepared to do that."

"Very well, but there are implications you need to be aware

of if the two of you are to be seen by me. At the moment, I'm your therapist, not David's, and my obligation, apart from to my professional code of ethics, is to you, not him. But should you decide to forego this individual work in favour of couple therapy, then my accountability would be to you both, rather than just to you. That doesn't mean I'd be striving to keep your marriage intact, nor, of course, would I be encouraging you two to part; whether you remain together or split up is your responsibility, not mine. But if, for example, the three of us agreed to work together for say, eight sessions of couple therapy, and after the third of those, you decided you didn't like the way it was going, you might want to resume your individual sessions with me. Well, that wouldn't be possible unless David were to agree. Do you understand what I'm saying?"

"Sounds like you're saying much the same as what David told me a few weeks ago – I can't have my cake and eat it?"

Patrick laughed.

"Spot on, Grace! And you've put it far more succinctly than I. But there's one important difference between what David told you then and what I'm saying to you now: David has a preference as to what you ultimately decide to do about your marriage."

"And you don't, do you?" and as she heard herself answering her own question, Grace was distinctly aware of her regret that it was so.

"No, that's right," confirmed Patrick, conscious that in giving the answer required by his profession, he was far from speaking the whole truth.

By the end of that session, Grace had come to no definite conclusion as to how to proceed. Two days ago Simon had flown to Bilbao to commence his walk and, she had been hoping to join him in a week's time in the cathedral city of Leon, but after last night her dreams and plans lay strewn and forlorn as wet confetti. She handed over her pre-written cheque, booked another session for the following Thursday and promised to inform Patrick by Monday whether or not David would be accompanying her.

*   *   *

Patrick endeavoured to write up his notes on the session but the page stubbornly remained blank. He had no clear notion why this was so, just an awareness of gripping the pen more tightly than usual.

Chapter Seventeen

AT 7.15 P.M., IN a London hotel room, Maggie finished leaving her voice message then sent a text to Gavin: *Have told Pat! Call me, x.*

On his way home, Patrick stopped at the service station and purchased a large packet of kettle crisps, the first since January when he made his resolution to shed a few pounds; it hadn't worked. He flirted with buying some panatelas, the first in fifteen years, but realised this was only a mental ploy to make the purchase of the crisps more excusable.

He went straight upstairs and took a shower to wash away the day. The heating system was again functioning reliably and he came down in a towelling robe and checked the answer phone. The small screen showed a red number '2': the first was from Nuala, 'Hi, Dad, Mum, all's well. Am out tonight so don't phone me back. Thinking of coming home the weekend after next. Speak soon. Love you.' The second was from Maggie, 'Hi, thought you'd be home by now. Hope you're okay. Felt a bit wobbly driving down the motorway. I hope you're okay. Oh, I already said that didn't I? Christ, I hate these things! Pat, I'm sorry, about everything … oh God, I didn't mean it to sound like that. I'm gabbling, I'm sorry, I'll try you later.' He felt a certain satisfaction on hearing Maggie's struggle and considered playing it again, but realised *schadenfreude* would only give way to empathy.

He uncorked a bottle of his favourite red wine, leaving just four from the two cases they'd ordered back in the summer. His earnings being considerably less than half Maggie's, she took care of the larger bills, leaving him to buy most of the food, drink and treats, and he realised that should they split up he would have to source a cheaper tipple. Pushing such thoughts from his mind, he pulled the most recent Blue Nile

116

CD from the rack only to find the disk missing. No doubt in her car, he groaned, then located one of their older albums, a one-time favourite of Nuala's; he placed it in the slot, settled himself on the floor and leaned back against the sofa. As he reached for his glass he realised he'd left the crisps on the Saab's passenger seat. 'Fuck it,' he thought, 'the floor's the safest place to be.'

"Pat? Pat? Are you there? Pick up the phone. Pat, pick up the phone, please!"

A far-off sound made him stir. He was halfway down the second bottle and must have dozed off. Blue Nile had given way to Bob Dylan's *Desire,* its second track, *Isis,* left on permanent repeat. He had taught Maggie the lyrics back in '87 and they'd sung along in mock Dylan voices side by side after making love, he on air-harmonica, Maggie air-violin, between verses. He reached for the remote and forwarded to the next track.

"How did he take it?" asked Gavin.

"Quietly," replied Maggie.

"And did he really suspect?"

"I'm not sure. I think he'd closed his eyes. Strange, it's not like him."

"What did he say?"

"He asked how long it had been going on."

"Did you tell him?"

"Gavin! What's with the twenty questions?"

Gavin was indeed eager for knowledge. He was not altogether sorry that their secret had been spilled, but recognised the bolt of uncertainty Maggie's confession had injected into their situation; a jealous husband with wounded pride spells danger, and puts pressure on a straying partner to feel contrite.

"I'm worried you'll go back to him," he blurted out.

"I haven't left him," she replied, the word 'yet' rolled enticingly around her tongue but did not stray beyond her lips.

"No, but you've allowed yourself to fall in love with me, as I've fallen in love with you, and I don't want to lose you

Maggie, I really don't want to lose you!"

And this would-be goalkeeper, spreading himself at her feet in a desperate attempt to prevent her slipping through his grasp, made Maggie's eyes fill with tears. She swallowed hard, lowered the phone and pressed it so hard to her breast that it hurt.

Chapter Eighteen

PATRICK SWITCHED OFF THE ignition and set about a final organising of his thoughts before presenting himself before Beth's scrutiny. Feeling wary of examination was not his usual approach to supervision, but he felt particularly vulnerable today and was concerned to retain a measure of control. It was the news of Nuala's pregnancy that had triggered the booking of this extra session; he'd start with that, and, if time allowed, present a case. He oscillated between Neil and Grace before settling on the former. He recognised a twinge of guilt at continuing to leave Grace outside the monitoring light of Beth's gaze but felt in no mood to do anything about it. As he locked the car he also resolved not to say anything about the state of his marriage until it became clearer what course things were going to take.

He settled himself in the usual armchair and took a sip of coffee before launching in.

"On Tuesday, I drove Nuala, my eighteen-year-old daughter to a clinic in Leeds where she had an abortion."

Patrick studied Beth's face, he thought he saw her wince, but then her features softened and she took on that knowing tenderness he valued so highly. She seemed genuinely concerned, enquiring patiently and tenderly, first after Nuala's feelings, then Patrick's, and finally Maggie's.

"Maggie doesn't know," he confessed, in response to the latter line of enquiry.

Beth's eyes narrowed.

"How come?"

Patrick drew a deep breath,

"Nuala broke the news when I travelled on my own up to Tyneside to take her for lunch. She begged me, literally begged me, not to tell her mother. I told her that was unfair, an impossible thing to ask, but she insisted. I tried persuading her,

119

I really tried, but she got so terribly upset and ended up saying she wished to God she hadn't told me. I thought she was going to run off there and then. I didn't know what to do. She was so distraught. I knew it was wrong to keep it from Maggie, but it would have been wrong whatever I'd done. I was there and Maggie wasn't; this was my child and I was worried what she might do if I refused. And so, reluctantly, I put my daughter's needs first."

"That's quite a secret to have held. I imagine it must have weighed heavily?"

"Yes. And no. Driving home down the A1 I was aware it had created a barrier between Maggie and me, even though she won't have known what it was. But as the days went by I began to feel it gave me a special responsibility, and I had to do my best to care for Nuala on behalf of us both. I still felt attacks of guilt, and late one night came close to telling Maggie, but I chickened out. There was too much chance of ending up with both my wife and my daughter feeling betrayed."

"What if the boot had been on the other foot," asked Beth, "and you'd discovered that Nuala and Maggie had kept that same secret from you?"

"Oh, that would never have happened," he asserted, "Nuala would never have told Maggie before me, they've not got a good enough relationship. I've agonised over that for years. I used to try and address it with each of them. They're each as stubborn as the other, but because Maggie was the adult I always saw the responsibility as resting more with her. Anyway, my attempts to resolve things between them never got anywhere, and, to be honest, I don't think I've ever really understood why things are the way they are."

"I see," said Beth, "but that wasn't what I asked."

Patrick looked puzzled.

"I didn't ask *if* you thought it possible the boot might have been on the other foot, I asked, what if it *had* been?"

Patrick was stony-faced.

"I'd be devastated, furious."

"Who with?"

"With Maggie, of course."

"Hmm-huh. Not with Nuala?"

Beth's prompt slipped beneath Patrick's radar; his insides began to churn, his hands gripped the arms of the chair, his face creased up and, before he could prevent them, tears welled and spilled gently down his cheeks; shed over an innocent darling daughter, who had fucked so drunkenly, and so carelessly, for old times' sake.

Beth bided her time, nursing her compassion for a grieving father, and an unfortunate young woman.

"A little operation ..." she said softly, once Patrick's tears had subsided. "That's what someone said to me once, with kind intent, a long, long time ago. A little operation, but it isn't necessarily accomplished quite so neatly and simply."

Patrick swallowed hard, looked across and saw the tears in his supervisor's eyes, and touched by their presence, breathed deeply before replying.

"No, it isn't."

Beth realised more was needed and rose to the task.

"It feels like you have more than your own grief to bear over this, Patrick. There's the sadness, of course, the loss of innocence, and the loss of what might have been; but there's also Maggie's share of all that sadness, which you are holding as long as she remains kept in the dark. For all I know, you're also bearing some of Nuala's loss, until she can face it herself. You said she's seeing the University Counsellor; and no doubt doing her grieving there rather than with you. What concerns me, though, is what her mother is being left to carry in all this."

And for the second time that morning this wise old woman's words left Patrick puzzled, and it showed in his face.

"The anger," Beth explained, "sooner or later, I imagine Maggie will find out, and then the anger, and the right to it, will be hers; and you, Nuala, or both, will be its target. And perhaps what's so unfair about that, is that although Maggie will be the one expressing the anger, it won't all belong to her."

Patrick grasped the essence of Beth's meaning and found it a sobering hypothesis, one that added a further layer to his guilt. For unbeknown to Beth, Maggie had already confessed *her* secret, placing herself in the dock ready to be pilloried; yet he had not seen fit to reciprocate. But if he'd done so, it would have been by way of retaliation, and he couldn't bring himself to use their daughter's predicament to punish his wife for her infidelity.

Patrick had gone as far with the topic as he was willing, or able, and they took a few minutes to wind down before moving on to look at Patrick's casework. He updated Beth on Neil and his newly revealed alter ego, Degas, and the stuttering progress of the younger man's developing trust in the therapeutic alliance. Beth responded with interest to the Degas material until Patrick cut it short and moved on to the case of Jake, who had sought counselling to find the impetus to at last own up to his double life.

"Secrets have been quite a theme today," said Beth, as she followed Patrick to the door.

'If you only knew,' thought Patrick, as he made his way towards the car. It was only as he drew away that he realised he'd forgotten to ask if Beth's new great-grandchild had arrived safe and sound.

On the journey back Patrick stopped at Hathersage and purchased a spade from a small hardware store. He drove slowly along the side of Ladybower reservoir, where two villages had been submerged by the building of a dam. The resulting series of reservoirs had been used as a practice site for Barnes Wallis's bouncing bombs during the second World War. He rejected the location, too open, too exposed, and bearing too many associations of death and destruction. He drove on across the empty stretches of Strines Moor and, halfway across, parked up by a gate, removed the bush and spade from the boot, wandered down a track, crossed a stile, down through a wood, and emerged not far from the water's edge. There was no ceremony, he simply chose a spot and dug hurriedly, planted the shrub, ferried a few spadefuls of water from the reservoir, and stood back. It looked like nothing at all; 'Just how it should be,' he thought, 'something and nothing, a small sacrifice to mark a spot on this earth, it will suffice.' And he felt better for the gesture, despite having created yet another secret, but this time one that could do no one any harm. Without further ado, he turned away and trudged back up to the car.

As he drove through the south Pennine hills back towards his office, Patrick reflected on what his professional life had taught him about secrets in relationships. He recalled his distaste for surprise parties, which always seemed to him such a cruel joke to play on anyone. Many years back he had booked a surprise city break in Rome for himself and Maggie some three months in advance, but within a fortnight he'd realised the unfairness of keeping all the anticipation to himself and felt compelled to tell her. She was delighted, but chided him for spoiling what she said would have been a wonderful surprise; he realised then how very different they were. He recalled lines from a talk he'd given to a group of counsellors on secrets: 'A secret borne by lovers creates a powerful intimacy; but those knowing looks across a crowded room' – like the ones he shared with Leah during the latter part of his Relate training – 'mean nothing without the presence of oblivious bystanders. Exclusion is the true cost of intimacy, and the intimates always leave someone else to pay the price.' And as he drove his thoughts turned to the pact he had entered with Nuala, and although he could not admit to actually enjoying nursing it, he recognised the secret had created a special bond between himself and Nuala, a bond that depended for its very existence upon Maggie's exclusion. And following that morning's supervision, he began to see that being chosen to share their daughter's precious secret had boosted his own self-esteem in relation to the wife who had been increasingly leaving him behind.

At a small roundabout he crossed the Barnsley-Manchester road, thick with trans-Pennine lorries, and recalled the morning nineteen years ago when Maggie informed him she was pregnant. She had known for well over a week, but had kept the knowledge to herself until deciding where she stood with the something or nothing in her womb. He'd been shocked by the news, but revealed his genuine delight, and was glad that she appeared to feel the same. Sam, of course, knew nothing of what his sperm had got up to in his absence, or what fate had since befallen its wondrous achievement. He was relieved to be back on the quiet B-road. 'Secrets are about responsibility, and power,' he told himself, 'extra-marital affairs being a typical example; the lovers almost certainly aware of the existence of each other's marriages, even discussing them over illicit drinks in out of the way country pubs or anonymous hotel rooms: "You see, my wife doesn't understand me; I can't tell her about us, it would hurt her too much." – "Look, I want you to know, he and I don't make love any more." And a rarely felt contempt rose up in Patrick for such clandestine lovers, who screw behind the world's back and justify their actions with strings of faulty logic. Suddenly he had to slam on the brakes – a hairpin loomed up ahead and he was approaching much too fast, the Saab skidded violently, but somehow stayed on the road and came to a halt, sideways on. He let go of the wheel, took several deep breaths, and set off again, more slowly this time, but the accelerator of his mind remained pressed to the boards. 'Lambaste the duplicity of lovers all I might, there's no escaping the fact that Nuala and I are traitors and conspirators, and, as the parent, the lion's share of responsibility rests with me.' He tried taking issue with his conscience, pursued the tack that his crime wasn't so awful, that Maggie's betrayal of him was far worse; after all, hadn't his motives at least been honourable, to protect a child from unbearable distress? He argued that it wasn't he who'd conducted an affair behind his spouse's back; it wasn't he who'd become practised at lying about his whereabouts; and it wasn't he who had chosen to abort a new life because it didn't fit in with his plans for his own. But no sooner had he finished making the case for the defence, he realised such pleas of mitigation were worthless; for Patrick Chime, long-time liberal and therapist, could not allow himself to condemn a young woman for choosing an abortion. What's more, however justifiable the anger he felt towards Maggie, he realised that his wife's confession, albeit made in order to alleviate her own guilt, also served to point a crooked finger at his own.

Chapter Nineteen

PATRICK CALLED BY HIS office and checked the answer machine. The first message was from Jake.

'… I told Kia last night after the girls were asleep. She took it very calmly, she was tearful when we talked about what might happen in the future, but I went to sleep hopeful we might sort it all out amicably. Then this morning she was like a different person and insisted I have to tell the kids first thing on Saturday, pack my things and get out of their lives once and for all. So, I shan't be able to keep our appointment. I know it had to be done but I feel like shit. I'm going to stay at my mum's for a few days, until I decide whether to move in with Michael. I'll probably give you a ring, once I get settled. Bye'

'I wonder,' thought Patrick, that 'Bye' sounded final. He paled at the enormity of what the message contained. Kia's shock, and then anger, was understandable, as was the wish to eradicate from her life, and that of her children, the husband who had so humiliated her. But what will those children make of it? 'It had to be done but I feel like shit …'

'Sums it all up really,' thought Patrick, and Jake's words made him aware of another reason he'd acquiesced when Nuala had leaned on him so heavily on the bench overlooking the sea up in Tynemouth, and why he hadn't admitted his own betrayal to Maggie since she confessed hers: he didn't want to be seen as a shit.

The second message was from the male supervisee Patrick had challenged over his inappropriate hugging of a female client. His tone was smug as he informed Patrick his services were no longer required; he said he had found a new supervisor, one more in keeping with his own principles and way of working.

"Well, I hope you'll be very happy together," sneered Patrick aloud, grateful for the temporary distraction from his own shortcomings.

He spent the next couple of hours attending to a small pile of admin chores with as little enthusiasm as ever. Eventually, he locked up and made a detour through town, stopping for petrol and a lengthy browse through a store selling cheap CDs. For once he found little of interest, but it filled some time and diverted his thoughts from the evening ahead.

Maggie's car was already on the drive when Patrick arrived home. He reversed carefully alongside and wondered how much longer he would be carrying out this particular manoeuvre.

"There's soup, and I'll make a risotto afterwards," she said, in lieu of a welcome-home kiss.

"Soup? I'm not really hungry."

"No? Please yourself," she replied, and headed back towards the kitchen. "Tea? Drink?" she called over her shoulder.

"No thanks. I'm going to get changed," and he headed upstairs thinking how the conversation mirrored reality as they prepared to mull over what was left on the menu of their marriage. He decided to shave, a ritual that always made him feel better and delayed a little longer the inevitable confrontation. Donning jeans, tee shirt and the tatty but comfortable moccasins, splattered with olive oil from some ancient culinary disaster, which he knew Maggie detested, he made his way downstairs and found her at the breakfast bar, finishing her soup.

"I will have some tea," he said, "want some?"

"It's in the pot, and yes, please, I will."

"Cup or a mug?"

"Doesn't matter."

He took a china cup and saucer from the cupboard and a mug for himself. He gave the distinction no thought, but long ago it had been his mother's practice to always serve your guests the best and make do for yourself. He placed the drinks on the breakfast bar and made to remove her empty soup bowl.

"Leave that," she protested, "I'll do it later."

Patrick ignored her plea and stowed bowl and spoon in the

dishwasher before taking his seat on the opposite side of the bar.

"First clear the pitch and mark out the goals," he said.

"What?" she sounded puzzled.

"Men and women," he replied, "we're different, haven't you noticed? Your lot just launch straight into deep and meaningful conversations, whereas we first need to mark out the pitch and agree the rules." He folded his arms and leaned forward. "So, we're agreed we need to talk and the object of this discussion is …?" He stared at her intently.

"Pat, must it be like this?"

"Like what?"

She hung her head, "Like two boxers squaring up at the weigh-in."

'Good analogy,' he thought, genuinely impressed. "Okay," he said, "But can we first set some limits, I really don't want this to go on all night."

"Can't you relate to anyone other than by appointment? Can't we just … *talk*?" The aching tenderness injected into this simple word was delivered straight from the heart, and if Patrick had dared allow it to register, it would have carved through his composure as keenly as any butcher's blade.

"All right," he replied positively, feeling that he'd had the better of the opening skirmish and could afford to relent a little, "… let's talk!" and he stared across at her expectantly.

She was staring back at him and he noticed her chin start to tremble.

"Pat, this is why, this is why I can't go on like this any more. It's not doing either of us any good."

"And is this also why you decided to have an affair?"

"I didn't decide!"

Patrick cocked his head to one side and raised his eyebrows cynically.

"I didn't, Pat. I didn't decide to go out and have an affair just like that."

"No, course not," he replied, "you just happened to meet someone."

"Yes, Pat, I *met* someone." And the oceans of meaning she instilled into that tiny word brought his-game playing up short.

"Who is he?" Patrick asked without rancour, until a mischievous voice inside made him add, "I presume it is a he?"

Maggie paused before replying and, when she did so, sidestepped the jibe.

"We met when I was down in Birmingham on business. He was staying at the same hotel."

"Convenient," sneered Patrick, and the tired look she gave him made him immediately regret it.

"I'm sorry. Go on," he encouraged.

"Look Pat, you've got every right to be angry, I know that, every right. And if you want to give me a hard time, then I can't stop you. But I thought that tonight we needed to really talk and not just bitch and fight."

"I'm listening."

"Having met him, – his name's Gavin by the way – yes, I decided to have an affair. It was my way of dealing with things."

Gavin. He mulled the name over in his mind a few times, to see what it attracted. Nothing much.

"Things?"

"Yes Pat, things … you, me, our marriage, Nuala growing up and leaving home. I don't think we've been properly happy for years. We've been together, we've been comfortable, but we've been growing more and more apart without the cracks ever really showing."

"There's a crack, a crack, in everything, that's how the light gets in."

"What?"

"Line from a Leonard Cohen song, one of my favourites."

"Pat," she said softly, leaning forward towards him, her hands tightly clenched under the breakfast bar, "Pat," she paused and ran her tongue tentatively around her lips before swallowing hard, "I think this marriage has run its course, don't you?"

"It only takes one to end a marriage Maggie, it takes two to make it work," he said, reciting the saying he'd used down the years with countless clients.

"I know that," she replied, "but do you *really* still want to make it work, Pat, do you?"

And her stare was so intent, so penetrating that he was forced to look away.

"No, that's what I thought," and she shook her head. "Pat, you know I'm right, you're just not prepared to be the one to bring it to an end."

"And you are, is that what you're telling me?" Now it was her turn to be put on the spot.

"Yes, I think so."

"You *think* so?"

"Look, Pat," she said, getting exasperated. "Look, this isn't easy for me either. I'm not certain about the future or what's going to happen. All I know is, I'm in love with someone else…"

"Gavin." Patrick offered helpfully, "I presume you mean Gavin."

"Fuck you, Pat!" she snapped, "Fuck you!" and she began to cry.

First knockdown to him, and he immediately felt bad. He sat frozen, watching his wife's lonely tears, tears her Gavin can do nothing whatever about. He considered reaching out across the breakfast bar but stopped himself. Her head was bowed and her face covered by one hand while the other was hidden from view; there was simply nothing for him to get hold of. He could, of course, have got off his stool, walked around to where she sat and put his arms around her. But that was a march too far.

"I'm sorry, Maggie," he said at last, "Look, I'm no good at this."

"Me neither," she snuffled, dabbing her eyes with a napkin.

He decided to come clean, at least about the matter in hand.

"It's just that it's painful, hearing your wife say she's in love with someone else."

"Well I am."

"Yeah. Right," and he took a deep breath and exhaled loudly. "What are you going to do?"

She shook her head.

"I'm not sure, all I know is that I've not felt like this in a very long time, in fact I'm not sure I've ever felt like this before. I was just a girl when you and I met, I'm a woman now,

129

pushing forty, and I can't carry on any longer creeping around like a petty thief. I want to feel free to …" she paused, "… to see where it goes with Gavin; to give it a chance, and I can't do that while I'm living here with you; it's not fair to anyone involved."

Patrick's antennae picked up on the 'anyone'.

"So … he's married, too?"

Maggie nodded.

"They separated quite recently, no children. I don't want to move in with him, at least not yet. I think I need time on my own. I realise there'll be a lot to sort out, but I'd rather not rush into solicitors and divorce proceedings and so forth. I just think I need to find somewhere to stay on my own for a while and see how things go. This is your home as much as mine, you stay here as long as you want, thankfully money's not a huge problem, and we'll sort out my share of the house if and when we need to."

He registered the 'if' but thought it safest to make no comment, lest she correct herself.

"How soon … how soon do you intend going?"

"Oh God, I don't know. Now we've talked about it, it makes sense for me to get round to some estate agents tomorrow and see what there is to let."

"Whereabouts will you look?"

"I don't know, around, not on the doorstep, obviously."

"Obviously."

"Pat, I am sorry it's worked out like this."

"Me too." He straightened his back and plonked his hands on the edge of the breakfast bar, "Is that it then, are we done?"

Maggie looked deep into him and her eyes welled again but this time she held back the tears. He returned the stare, as the need for self-protection jostled with the compassion he felt towards the wife who had been brave enough to say she'd had enough of him, and each impulse perfectly negated the other.

"I guess so," he said softly, answering his own question, and the legs of his stool scraped on the tiles as he left the ring and wandered through to the front room.

"I think I'll go and have a bath," she called out after him, but he made no response.

The warm soapy water lapped soothingly about her neck as she endeavoured to keep everything but her head submerged. It had been painful, of course, but she felt it had gone reasonably well; she'd managed to say what she'd wanted; there'd been no screaming or shouting and Patrick had no real argument to put forward. Perhaps it was asking too much of him to expect a less spiky, less combative response, after all, she was the one disrupting his settled existence. She wondered whether she really was the more unhappily married of the two, or merely the one more willing to do something about it? 'Yes, I want more than this,' she said to herself, 'I don't want to grow old in a passionless marriage; it's time to move on and start afresh.' This statement of intent reminded her instantly of Gavin. She realised he must be wondering what was going on; she'd hardly spoken to him all week. But she knew this wasn't just about Gavin, this was about hauling herself out of the status quo, taking charge, renewing her life, re-writing her script, as Patrick would say, and so far she'd managed it without recourse to any therapist. She hauled herself out of the bath, wrapped herself in a towel and felt relieved at the initial result of her evening's work.

Downstairs, Patrick lay sprawled on the sofa, staring through the open curtains into the yellow ochre glow of the street lamp. His felt his groin, wiggled his toes, flexed his knees, tensed the muscles in his loins, breathed deep within his abdomen, felt his chest rise and swell, rotated his jaw, twitched his nose and raised his eyebrows. Everything intact and in working order, he was still in one piece, and likened himself to a man opening his eyes to find the café, in which he'd been quietly eating lunch, blown to smithereens and the floor littered with human remains; yet he remains at his table, covered in dust and bemused to find himself unscathed.

'Must be numb,' he told himself, 'still in shock, can't have registered the enormity of it all.' He was relieved by her words about the house; the prospect of having to move out immediately he found terrifying. He still had the twin stations of his life: house and office, the base camp where he slept and the summit where he soared. 'It will do, it'll have to. I'll be all right. After all, what's the alternative?'

He heard the swish of the door brushing against the carpet, and realised he never had got round to sanding down that bottom edge.

Maggie was in her dressing gown.

"Can I come in?" she asked, "Or would you rather be left alone?"

He swung his legs off the sofa and sat up, "No, come in, if you want." And she produced from behind her back a bottle and two glasses,

"I couldn't find the corkscrew," she said.

"It's here, I forgot to put it back."

"Will you?" she asked handing him the bottle.

He fondly examined the label.

"Not many left," he said wistfully.

"You want me to put it back?"

He shook his head.

"We'd better savour it then," she said, with a half-smile that matched his own.

He did the honours while she settled on the floor and leaned back against the sofa, her back brushing the side of his leg.

"Music?" she enquired.

"Careful, I might think you're trying to seduce me."

"And we can't have that, in the circumstances," she said by way of riposte, and was relieved to hear his stifled laugh.

"There's Dylan or Blue Nile or something, still in the machine," he proffered.

"Schubert, actually, I was listening to it earlier, will that do?"

"Go ahead," he said, and she reached for the remote.

"Pat ... are you okay?" she enquired, half turning her head in his direction, but she could not quite see his face. He reached down and gave her shoulder a reassuring pat.

"Good," she whispered.

They sat in silence for much of the first movement. Patrick was first to speak. It felt, he suggested, a little like being on a first date, neither one sure what to say for fear of how it might be received. Maggie seemed amused by this analogy, until he

132

pointed out that on a first date, there is at least the possibility that the parties might be heading in the same direction.

"Whereas …" He left it to her to complete the sentence.

Maggie ignored the bait.

"Do you ever wonder about the direction you're going?" she asked.

"I will be doing now."

"No, seriously, Pat, you must have done, given what you do for a living?"

"Sometimes. I try not to dwell on it."

"Why's that?"

"Because if you can't do anything about something, what's the point of agonising over it?"

"But that sounds terrible, like you've given up."

"Not at all, it's just a matter of not beating yourself up trying to change things that are beyond you."

"Pat, this is your life for God's sake!"

"I'm sorry, I thought I was talking about our marriage."

She paused before replying.

"So you've been unhappy too?"

"Yes."

"You don't know what a relief it is to hear you say that. Why couldn't you have said it before?"

"You never asked."

"You could have said."

"Would it have made any difference?"

"I'd have felt less alone."

"Hmm. But would it really have changed anything? We've been growing into increasingly different people, maybe it was inevitable."

"How do you see the difference, Pat?"

"I'm not sure this is a good idea, going into all this now, it feels too much like marital therapy without a therapist."

"And we can't allow that can we, it might start a trend and you'd be out of a job!"

And he began to laugh, a stuttering laugh at first, then deeper, from way down inside, and as he placed his hand upon her shoulder, she reached up and used it to swing herself around, and kneeling on the floor before him, she opened her arms and he slipped into them, lay his head on her breast, where she held him close, offering gentle hushes and 'there-there's as he wept all the way through to the end of Schubert's second movement.

Chapter Twenty

PATRICK AWOKE AROUND THREE to find Maggie snuggled into him, the pair like two spoons in a neatly kept cutlery drawer. When he woke again just before eight, the space behind him was empty and he heard the shower running. He considered joining her there, less out of lust, more that he recognised there were unlikely to be many further opportunities to do so. It even occurred that he might already have had his final taste of her; 'If I'd realised as much at the time,' he considered, 'I might have offered something apt as I pulled out of her, like, "When we first tried this the challenge was combining our bodies, now its our heads that can't get it together!" On second thoughts, perhaps "Thanks for the ride" might have been kinder.' He pulled the duvet tight about him; somehow, a quick thrash in the shower didn't tally with his sentimental notion of a last, intimate embrace.

While Maggie was out doing the rounds of estate agents, he took a call from Nuala.

"Oh, hi, Dad, shouldn't you be at work?"

"No, my client's wife put the kybosh on him coming."

"Therapy, the great threat to a marriage, eh?"

"In their case it's a bit late for that."

"Well, anyway, no offence but it was Mum I really wanted to talk to, is she there?"

He was taken aback, not only by her words but her apparent cheeriness at the prospect of communion with her mother.

"Sorry, she's in town. Shopping," he added, as an afterthought.

"Thought you had the groceries delivered these days?"

"We usually do. She's looking at clothes, I imagine."

"Dad, I've decided to tell her. I thought I'd get it over with before coming home next weekend."

Stony silence.

"Dad, you still there? Say something?"

"I don't know what to say … um, yes, good," he stuttered, aware that he failed to sound in the least encouraging. "I'm just wondering how she'll react, not just to news of the abortion, but to being kept in the dark when I've known about it all along. I imagine we'll both get it in the neck, so brace yourself."

"Are you trying to put me off? You were the one urging me to tell her!"

"No, of course not. I'm just saying that she'll be hurt; so be sensitive, make allowances for her initial response, whatever it might be. I'm sorry to sound so parental but …"

"You're a parent, right?"

"Right."

"Look, Dad, I'll phone back later this afternoon, I don't want to try her on her mobile, it's not the sort of thing a mother wants to hear when she's queuing at the check-out, is it?"

He laughed weakly; glad she was well enough to see the funny side.

"Nuala, would you rather I told her? I will?" he blurted out, in one last vain attempt to shield his little girl, or at least retain some measure of control.

"No, Dad, I'll do it, it's important, and don't worry, I know I put you in an impossible position, I'll make sure she hears that. I'm sure she won't divorce you for it."

"I've got to go," he said abruptly, "I'll speak to you later, love." And as he hung up, marvelled at the combination of maturity and innocence in one so young.

He glanced at his watch, eleven forty-five, Maggie said she didn't know how long she'd be gone; probably back sometime mid-afternoon. He envisaged the scene: she arrives clutching sheaves of details on apartments to rent and he wonders how much interest it is appropriate to show in his soon-to-be-estranged wife's new life. Mustn't throw too much cold water by pointing out the roughness of a particular district or baulking at an exorbitant rent; but neither was it appropriate to gush over the photographs, 'Wow, that kitchen looks well-equipped, and what a lovely bedroom, darling … you'll be just fine in there!' And then the phone will ring, 'Mum, I've something to tell you ...' And he will listen to Maggie's responses, inserting for himself his daughter's lines, before the call ends and Maggie summons him into the dock.

"Jeezus," Patrick said aloud. "I'm out of here!"

He grabbed the newspaper and scoured the sports pages, looking for the day's football fixtures; Sheffield Wednesday ... at home! It didn't matter who they were playing. As a boy he had been a regular supporter but interest faded when he went away to university. The last time he visited Hillsborough was back in 2000, when he talked Maggie and Nuala into giving it a try. Maggie said she'd be taking along a book to read and he believed her, although it never actually emerged from her handbag. Patrick prayed for plenty of goals in order to secure a ten-year-old daughter's interest. His prayers were answered in that three were delivered; what he hadn't planned on was all of them being scored by Leeds United. Nuala never wanted to go again. There was never going to be any point asking Maggie.

The match programme informed him of his old team's recent fortunes. Having sunk to the depths of the third division of English football, they had climbed back up to the second tier where they had clung on and survived last season; and were now enjoying a good run which had seen them haul themselves clear of the relegation zone. Cardiff, today's visitors, topped the league, which created a buzz of expectancy inside the ground but did little to enthuse Patrick. The home team enjoyed a decent share of possession, and both sides had chances, but the match finished scoreless.

As he queued in the traffic he pondered his responses to the game. Despite being grateful for the distraction, he'd been less than comfortable in his surroundings. When the Owls had had a near miss, his heart failed to propel him from his seat like those around him, and when their keeper parried a powerful Cardiff shot in the closing moments, rather than sharing the home fans' elation he felt only mild relief. It was different when he was a boy; back then he was partisan; he and Sheffield Wednesday were one, blue-and-white striped, through and through. Now, he'd turned into a disinterested observer of events, appreciative of the aesthetics but lacking any real commitment to the cause. What had happened? He'd grown older, of course, but not like these around him; they'd kept the flame, they'd remained attached and committed in a way he had not. For them it still mattered, they would live and die as Wednesday supporters, regardless of how their team fared. Apart from death, it was the one real certainty in their lives; such attachment, such loyalty, the very antithesis of this day and age. He wondered if it might do him good to buy a season ticket, to stoke the embers and see what ignites? Perhaps it might enable him to get off the fence and once again become an involved and committed member of the human race? For his training and years of working with Relate had produced the very reverse of partisanship: 'The refusal to take sides, and the ability to tolerate and embrace ambivalence', as his first Relate trainer described it, 'is not only a prime requirement of a marital therapist, but a pressing need of humanity, for if more of us could develop that ability, the world would be a safer and more harmonious place.' But what that trainer didn't explain to Patrick and his fellow students was the price they would eventually come to pay in terms of the inability to wholly and passionately commit to any single cause, body, or individual. And that is why, deep down, Patrick knew he wouldn't buy that season ticket; it would be wasted on him.

He arrived back at the house around six and Maggie's car was on the drive. As he stepped into the hall the eerie silence informed him that Nuala had already rung. He found her seated on a stool in the kitchen, an overnight bag at her feet like a sheep dog awaiting its master's bidding.

"Where have you been?" she asked coolly, her voice full of intent.

"Does it matter? Football," he added quickly.

"Why didn't you tell me?"

He was tempted to say, 'Because you were out looking at apartments,' but her tone of voice carried menace, so he answered obediently.

"She begged me not to."

"I know, she told me. Oh yes, she was keen to get you off

the hook. She may well have pleaded with you, Pat, but that wasn't what I asked. I asked why *you* chose not to tell me, why *you* decided to put your daughter before your wife, because that's what you always do, isn't it, Pat, put her first?" And these last three words were spat between gritted teeth.

Patrick stared impassively, it was time to own up to the truth, Maggie deserved that much.

"You're right. On this occasion I put her needs above yours."

"You always do, Pat, you always do. Just why is that, Pat? You tell me, why?

"You tell me," he snapped back, "I imagine you've got your own ideas to explain it?"

"Don't try that with me, Pat, it might work with your clients, but it won't wash with me. It's a straight question; I want a straight answer. So come on, you tell me, I want to hear it."

"Because she's easier to love than you; she gives more back." He swallowed hard. There, he'd said it, unrehearsed, spontaneous, and it shocked him how light he felt on hearing his own words, or was it just the clank of his chains, breaking apart? He'd have done better to leave it there, but couldn't resist another comment. "And once that was established," he added, "It inevitably reinforced itself."

It was what she needed.

"And that suited you, didn't it, Pat, to take the easy way out, to fawn over an impressionable young girl rather than learn to love a grown woman."

"Not just a young girl, *our* daughter," he objected, still on the ropes but at least now making a fight of it.

"Do you think I need reminding of that?"

"Yes, I do actually," he said defiantly.

"You bastard, you bastard! You place her above me, you fawn over her and make me into the baddie, you take her side in everything, and you cut me out at a time when you should have stood alongside me and shown her that we were not for splitting."

"Fine words, Maggie, but aren't you overlooking one key fact? At the time you accuse me of not standing loyally, side-by-side with my wife, my wife was lying side-by-side with Gavin in a secret love nest, and enjoying it so much she couldn't even be arsed to go visit her own daughter!"

"Fuck you, you bastard, fuck you!" and she snatched up her bag and stormed out the kitchen.

"Don't wait up!" he heard her shout just before the front door slammed.

A calm descended on Patrick. The explosion of anger had lanced the boil, at least for the time being, and he was relieved it was she who had thrown in the towel. It felt like a victory, although he wasn't quite sure what he'd won. He considered phoning Nuala but rejected the idea; why stir up more emotional upheaval before it's necessary? Instead, he breathed a huge sigh, uncorked the penultimate bottle and settled down for the evening, in the comforting presence of his treasured red, and the reassuring lyrics of Leonard Cohen. They felt like his only friends.

Across in Leeds, in his riverside apartment, after a comforting form of love, Gavin lay back and cradled Maggie's head in the crook of his arm. It had been a sober, tearful coupling on her part, intended to drive the demon of self-doubt from her mind. For Gavin's part, it was his way of showing support; he was glad to offer it, and she'd appreciated the effort, even though they both knew it hadn't really worked. After some minutes wondering whether to raise the subject, Gavin enquired about her relationship with Nuala, and immediately regretted it, for Maggie instantly welled up, began swallowing, hard and repeatedly, unable to speak. Gavin shifted, wrapped his arms around her and held her close, lovingly stroking her back without any of the pressure of desire.

On Sunday afternoon, Patrick took a walk to escape the reminders of Maggie's absence. As he approached the house on his return, a car he did not recognise pulled away from the road outside. Back inside, he discovered a scribbled note left on the breakfast bar, un-addressed and unsigned, *Came for more clothes and work things. Staying at Gavin's.* It said all there was to say; he screwed it up and tossed it at the bin. He missed.

Chapter Twenty-One

THE EARLY PART OF the week passed without incident, Patrick was pleasantly surprised by how calm he felt, not only on waking alone, but as he set about his daily tasks. Only each evening, at home alone, did a grating discomfort kick in. With so much happening in his own life he felt no interest in catching the News, and the television, like the car radio, remained switched off. His worst time came when, unable to postpone the moment any longer, he slipped into bed and pulled the covers tight around him, pining not for Maggie, whom he assumed would be luxuriating in Gavin's embrace, but for his own absent someone to tuck him up, whisper 'there-there' and tell him he will be a very fine soldier when he grows up; only then would he be able to go to sleep safe in the knowledge that, when he awoke, he would find himself intact. But Patrick's someone failed to materialise and sleep proved elusive as through the long night he was assailed by anxious thoughts about his own survival. Several times an urgent groundswell in the pit of his belly sent him rushing from bed to toilet, but when he sat nothing came of it, and he climbed back into bed and tried in vain to recall his mother's face. He remembered her putting him and his sister to bed, she was always tired and the bedtime stories rare, and the 'goodnight's cursory. As the younger sibling he enjoyed much the easier ride of the two; the only thing his mother asking of him was that he didn't go the way of his father. Each night, after she switched off the light and left the room, his sister's voice would drift down from the top bunk, cruelly mimicking their mother's broad Donegal tongue, 'Mind you don't go to the bad, son, like your father!'

He awoke around four and lay there until it was almost time to get up, only then would sleep tamely offer itself up. He thought about phoning Rose-Roisin, for that was how he now tended to think of her, although he dare not address her as such. The first time he called her 'Rose' after her name-change she tore him off a strip, leaving him wary of calling her anything at all. He looked up her number and then realised it must be two years since they'd last met and almost a year since they last spoke. He closed the address book. So much for family ties.

On Tuesday morning a postcard arrived from Newcastle, on its front, a monochrome photograph of the 1950s football legend, Jackie Milburn, clad in the black-and-white Magpie stripes of Newcastle United, thick Brylcreemed hair, arms folded across his chest. On the back, *Isn't he handsome? Arriving Friday, Leeds Station, 18:08?* He didn't know what to make of it, which troubled him; Nuala was usually such an effective communicator. He stood the card upon the mantelpiece where he could regard it from time to time, and sent a text, *Good looking chap, sure he's not a little old for you? 18:08 I'll be there! Dad x.*

At the office, he picked up an answer-phone message left late the previous day. The voice was male: 'My name is David Reynolds – you've been treating my wife, Grace. I believe she has made a provisional appointment for us to see you together this coming Thursday morning at her usual time, 10.30? Well, I'm simply ringing to confirm.' Patrick played it through a second time, the voice sounded confident and precise. He smiled at the medic's use of the term 'treating' then pondered why David had opted to make the call himself rather than let his wife attend to it? Perhaps he wanted to convey how un-phased he was by the prospect of a stranger peering through his net curtains and beneath his duvet, or was it simply his way of wresting control from Grace?

On Wednesday morning, Patrick returned a call from another male voice, this time a stranger, looking for marital counselling for himself and his wife, 'We've run into a bit of a sticky patch,' he added and Patrick smiled, as if the road surface was responsible for the condition of their relationship rather than the cause having anything to do with themselves. He was glad of the opportunity to refuse and offer instead the name of one of his supervisees who saw couples, thereby underpinning his conviction that he remained fit to cope with the remainder of his work.

The daytime calmness endorsed this self-confidence, waning only as each afternoon wore on and dusk set in. With no word from Maggie, he placed her daily post in a neat pile on the breakfast bar, and it soon became apparent how much more of the home mail was addressed to her. He resolved to do nothing about informing Nuala of her mother's departure until she arrived on Friday, or until he heard from Maggie and they could discuss what was to be said, and by whom. Suddenly he buckled, unable to remember whether he'd actually informed Maggie of Nuala's plans to come home this weekend. He racked his brain but to no avail. He thought of sending her a text, but realised that if he had already informed her, his text would appear foolish, or worse, just a flimsy excuse to make contact. 'Fuck it,' he thought, 'if she can't keep in touch with her own daughter, it's her look out.'

He walked the quarter mile to the service station and came back clutching a six-pack of beers. He awoke downstairs at a quarter to one and hauled himself off to bed. He awoke at seven with a foul head and took an age to find the paracetamol, which at least provided an outlet for some rage.

Neil was five minutes late for his Thursday morning appointment and bore a sluggish, uninterested air that Patrick found irritating, although he tried not to let it show. Patrick's head still ached, and the thought ran through his mind, 'If you can't be arsed, Neil, why should I?'

The first twenty minutes contained nothing much to speak of, some silences, a bit of fidgeting and several false trails leading nowhere in particular.

"Look, what's going on here, Neil?" Patrick said at last, having grown decidedly bored with proceedings.

"You tell me, you're the expert."

'Here we go again,' thought Patrick, and gave an audible sigh, which Neil pounced on.

"See, I knew you'd get fed up with me, everyone does. You're just like all the rest!"

Patrick felt exposed and regretted allowing the sigh to

escape; to have stifled it would have maintained the uneasy truce, yet the sigh was genuine, it was what he felt, tired and fed up with this young man's determination to sabotage any progress here. He took a deep breath and went for it.

"Yeah, that's right, Neil, sometimes I get fed up, fed up with the way you always go back to rubbishing what you do here. I'm fed up with the way you seek comfort in old familiar scripts like 'no-one-loves-me-because-I'm-crap', or 'I-can't-love-anyone-because-the-whole-world's-crap!' I get fed up with the way you rubbish any trust that grows here; the way you stuff it in a bag, tie a knot in its neck and dump it in the river, and you're right, I get bloody fed up having to stand by watching something with real potential being drowned at birth!"

It was hard to tell who was more surprised by this outburst; it wasn't just the words that shocked both men, but the passion with which they were uttered. The tirade had left Patrick unhinged, for he realised his closing metaphor applied as much to recent events in his own life as his client's. However, now was neither the time, nor the place, to follow up that particular thread. Neil, for his part, was astonished, not simply by the show of anger from this older man whose living was made at Neil's expense, for Neil was accustomed to being on the receiving end of anger, whether from Graham, who would like nothing more than to see the back of his partner's indolent son, or from the bullies back at school. But this was different, Patrick's anger carried passion and conviction, and there was the unmistakable sense that what Patrick really wanted was *not* for Neil to get up and clear off for good, but for him to use this relationship more fully, and for that to happen, Neil would have to start trusting it more.

"Can I ask *you* some questions?" Neil enquired, sitting up in his chair.

"You're free to say what you want here, just as I'm free to answer or not, as I see fit."

"How did I know you'd add that last bit?"

"Because you're getting to know me?"

It was a casual response on Patrick's part; of such seemingly low risk that he wasn't prepared for the speed of the

144

strike as Neil saw his float bob beneath the surface of the water.

"No! Don't you see, that's just it, I *don't* know you; I don't know anything about you, whereas you know so much about me. It's all so unequal here, I feel like a specimen on a slide and you peer down the microscope hiding behind a surgical mask."

"I can see why you say that, Neil, but it's only true to a certain extent, I've shown you quite a bit of who I am, here in this relationship."

"Quite a bit? No!" he shouted, "Glimpses that's all; just frustrating glimpses. Don't get me wrong; if it weren't for those I'd have stopped coming long ago. But you're the stranger here."

"An intimate stranger, I'd like to think?" suggested Patrick, echoing the title of one of the books on therapy on the shelf above his desk in reception.

"Intimate? That means coming close, yeah? Showing who you really are?"

Patrick nodded, but sensed another morsel of bait being prepared.

"Well, I'd like to do something about the balance of intimacy in here, because I find it a little too one-sided, okay?" Neil allowed a moment for Patrick to object, and when he failed to do so, took a deep breath.

"Right, back to my questions: how old are you?"

"Forty-two."

"Married?"

"Yes."

"How long?"

"Nearly twenty years."

"Your wife a therapist?"

"No."

"What does she do?"

"Sales director. Carpets and flooring."

"Pretty?"

Patrick's face froze. He stared hard into Neil's eyes. Neil did not flinch.

"Pretty?" he asked again, with a touch more volume.

Patrick nodded.

"Kids?"

"One."

"Boy?"

"Girl."

"How old?"

"Look, I don't like this, what's it to you how old she is?"

"I'm not trying to get off with her if that's what you're thinking. I just want to know who I've been talking to all these weeks."

"Eighteen, away at university."

Neil nodded.

"Thanks."

"That it?" asked Patrick.

"Not quite. Are you happy?"

"What?"

"You heard. Are you and your wife happy?"

Patrick stared at his interrogator and tried to remember what this was all about, 'trust, trust, trust,' he repeated to himself.

"We've been married a long time and, like any marriage, we've had our ups and downs; I think I can safely say that the present time is not the easiest, or happiest, that we've had together."

Neil looked sombre, but relieved.

"It's good to hear that, no offence mind, it's just that you always seem so together, as if everything in your garden is rosy."

"And that makes it hard for you, does it Neil, the thought that my life might be free from trouble or care?"

Neil gave a tiny nod.

"And now you know it isn't?"

"I feel a bit better about you. Don't worry, I won't tell anyone."

Patrick gave a nervous smile, as did Neil. And as the tension began to drain from Patrick, he briefly closed his eyes and shook his head, and thus failed to notice that Neil had stopped grinning and was now staring directly into him.

"What?" asked Patrick, once he'd registered the ashen look on his client's face.

"I've one more question. Have you ever been to a prostitute?"

"No, Neil, I haven't. Have you? Is that what you've been trying to tell me?"

Neil was once more looking down, and his head gave the mere hint of a nod.

"It's why I came here in the first place, but couldn't bring myself to tell you, then the last couple of sessions I've been trying to tell you but couldn't find a way."

"Ashamed?"

"It's nothing to be proud of."

"Does anyone else know?"

"No."

"Don't worry, I won't tell anyone," he said with a half-smile.

"Your supervisor?"

"Hmm, yes, sorry, but she doesn't know who you are Neil, and never will."

"All right, you've convinced me."

"Have I, Neil?"

"I said so, didn't I?"

"Yes, you did. I'm sorry if it sounded like I didn't believe you."

"Well, you didn't, did you, or you wouldn't have asked."

At this Patrick felt duly exposed and chastised, and for a few moments fell silent, nursing his wounds.

"Do you want to tell me about it, Neil?"

"Get off on getting your clients to tell you about that sort of stuff, do you?"

Stung again, Patrick just stared back at Neil.

"I'm sorry," the younger man said, "I didn't mean that."

"If you didn't mean it, why did you say it?"

"Look I said I'm sorry, can't we just leave it at that?"

Patrick gave a nod but said nothing more.

And Neil went on to describe his parallel relationship with Connie, the older woman he visited at her home in Barnsley, on average once a week, spending seventy-five pounds for the pleasure of being received with a version of desire. He had been making these visits for almost a year.

"What do you find there, Neil" Patrick enquired, hoping his voice sounded free from any hint of salacious interest.

"What do you think?"

"Is that all?"

"Sometimes."

"And other times?"

"I'm not sure. There are times, moments, when you almost forget that you're paying someone to desire you, or act as if they do. That's when it's best; then it feels real. But the trouble is it's like a drug, when you come down off a high you feel the worst of all."

"And is that when it's worse with Connie, after those moments when you forgot she's only doing it because you're paying her?"

"Yeah, it's when I start the car, glance in the mirror and the truth of it stares me in the face, and I hate myself for believing, and I hate her for pretending. And I sink really low, because I imagine I'll be doing this for the rest of my life, paying someone to want me."

Patrick stole a glance at the clock, damn, two minutes left. Not enough time to explore this any further. For Patrick knew that it needed exploring, for there was meat here, amongst the bone and gristle of Neil's fumblings with a prostitute. More than that, there were implications for Neil's other relationships, and the lack of them; and the relationship he paid to have here with him, joined in order to shed the habit of Connie, and yet, in coming here, Neil seemed only to have encountered more of the same struggle.

The session came to a natural end at that point without Patrick having to call time, the two men leaning on the ropes like a pair of prize-fighters who, on hearing the final bell, know they've been through one hell of a scrap and, for a precious moment, neither wants the judges' verdict to divide them. The spell was broken by Patrick asking, 'Same time next week?' and Neil placing three neatly folded notes on the coffee table, an act that now bore an added poignancy for both men.

Patrick's pen remained unused as he sat mulling over the session. The knock was loud and bold, and he knew at once

148

that it had not issued from Grace. He opened the door to be met by a towering, be-suited man; a senior partner in a firm of solicitors Patrick would have guessed, if he hadn't known that Grace was married to a consultant gynaecologist. Grace cut a slight figure, loitering behind him. Patrick shepherded them through to the therapy room, where David promptly occupied the seat that had hitherto been the preserve of his wife. Grace stood aghast between the three chairs, while Patrick looked on helplessly.

"What? Am I in the wrong seat?" David asked, to neither one in particular. "Do you want me to move?"

Grace's reply was to plonk herself down in the second chair in the manner of a truculent adolescent, whereupon Patrick assumed his usual seat and attempted to make himself appear more comfortable than he felt.

"Before we begin I'd like to establish one or two facts, ground-rules, that kind of thing ..." Patrick's words claimed the arena with a quiet authority that satisfied both partners' need for the situation to be safely held, and he didn't wait for their permission before continuing, "Firstly, you are both here of your own accord rather than under duress?"

David leaped in.

"I asked Grace if we could attend together, on the basis that she appears to have a measure of confidence in your expertise. Grace?"

Patrick detected the first sign of anxiety in David's voice as he said his wife's name and looked across to where she sat so impassively. Grace's nod provided the minimum confirmation and Patrick resumed his introduction.

"As you're both aware, up to now Grace has been coming here on her own, and it's important we establish the boundaries of what's been said in those earlier sessions ..."

Grace cut in.

"There's nothing I've said here previously that I haven't already told David, or which I'm not prepared for him to hear."

David stared across at her.

"Good," answered Patrick, "So I won't be holding secrets between you. What is said in this room is extremely private. I will, from time to time, discuss my work with my supervisor,

Beth Clarke, who lives in Derbyshire, and who, like me, is obliged to respect your privacy. The only other proviso being that should I hear anything from you that suggests a risk of serious illegality or abuse to a child or other vulnerable person, I might have to break confidentiality, but would first seek your consent, and even without it, would inform you of what I intended to do. I'm sorry if that all sounds rather heavy, but it is an important formality. Is that all right with you both?"

Grace nodded, as did David, who added an audible sigh.

"Let's get on with it then, shall we?" offered Patrick, by way of response, "What have you come here today hoping to say, or to hear?"

Grace continued to stare impassively at some fixed point on the carpet midway between the three chairs. David looked first to his wife, then to Patrick, before clearing his throat.

"I would like to assure Grace that I deeply regret the way things have developed between us over the years, such that it has reached this sorry and uncertain state of affairs, forgive the pun, unintentional." He turned to look at Grace, "Grace, I want this marriage to work, I have no wish to see our family disrupted any further, or to have our children suffer the experience of a broken home." He then interlocked his hands, placed them in his lap and crossed one leg over the other.

'A timely pause, to good effect,' thought Patrick, who noted that it seemed to cut no ice with Grace who remained transfixed by her spot on the carpet.

David continued his opening address.

"... I realise I have been at fault, been too absorbed in my work, and have left far too much of the domestic responsibilities to my wife ..."

David was again addressing his remarks to Patrick, and although he shot his wife a brief glance, Grace offered no response, and he quickly turned back to Patrick before continuing his statement. 'I was right,' thought Patrick, 'he would have made a good barrister.'

"... But I am confident that the situation has changed as I am now extremely involved and playing a full and active part in the welfare and upbringing of our children." David paused again, just long enough for some confirmation of that fact from his wife, and for it to become apparent that no such endorsement would be forthcoming.

Patrick seized the opening.

"David, I sensed you looking to Grace just then; what was it you were looking for, was it some confirmation from Grace, of the recent changes in yourself as a parent that you were speaking about?"

"Well, yes, a little confirmation would have been nice to hear."

Grace flashed her husband a withering look before spitting out her response.

"But that's not all you want, is it, David? You want me to fawn over you, to congratulate you on your conversion to a reasonably attentive and responsive father after years of delegation and neglect?"

"Do you have to be so negative, Grace?" David sighed. "I'd hoped that coming here was a chance to be constructive, to use the opportunity to learn more about what's gone wrong and to try to put it right, for the sake of the children, if not ourselves."

Patrick waited a second or two in order for Grace to reply to David's challenge, and when none was forthcoming, he took up the slack himself.

"David, have you always seen it as yourself holding the positives, and Grace holding the negatives, in the relationship?"

David looked relieved to be able to address their problems with a fellow professional rather than continue such an unrewarding conversation with his wife.

"I've never really thought about it like that until these last few months; it's certainly like that now as you can see. Before all this blew up, I suppose Grace would get sort of … low, you know, perhaps a little depressed from time to time, whereas I…"

"Sod off to the golf course," muttered Grace, without troubling to look up.

David's face reddened and Patrick remembered Grace's comment about always being so apologetic and not being a person who swore, and, although he knew he shouldn't, he couldn't help but feel proud of her.

David's response to his wife's accusation was to look appealingly across to his fellow professional, but found that Patrick's attention was focused elsewhere. Sensing David's stare, Patrick drew back from Grace to take in the couple, and addressed them both.

"It appears that rather than getting low or depressed, Grace is now getting angry." said Patrick, "Is that a new thing, Grace? And what it's like for you, David, being on the receiving end of Grace's anger?"

And for the first time since they arrived, the two spouses really looked at one another.

Patrick went on to explore with them the patterns of relating that had developed through the early years of their marriage; the division of labour that somehow evolved without ever being negotiated, but which Grace had come to resent and had felt so helpless to do anything about. Her rebellion manifested itself in the bedroom, where she increasingly failed to respond to David's advances with anything resembling enthusiasm. It seemed David could tolerate even this as long as Grace didn't mope around the house. There was clearly something in the demeanour of a depressed, dissatisfied woman that rang loud bells for David, for his response to Grace's obvious unhappiness was one of growing discomfort followed by a hasty retreat to work or golf course. To the outside world, everything appeared normal, the children availed themselves of the ample opportunities provided by David's income, and were well sustained by their mother's seemingly endless supply of emotional nourishment. But month by month, year by year, this loyal wife and mother's tolerance had been leaking away until she was running on memory and duty alone, and then, out of the blue, she received a contact from Friends Reunited.

Patrick saw another opening.

"But Grace hasn't been the only adult in this family with emotional needs; I'm wondering how and where yours were met, David?"

Patrick's question left David baffled and he offered no reply. The session was drawing to a close and Patrick could allow the silence to stretch no further.

"It's an important question, David, and there are other key

152

questions that might also need addressing: such as why anger and despair was split between you both so rigidly and for so long, with each of you carrying the other's rightful share along with your own. Such as, what's left in this relationship other than your children and a heap of hurt, resentment and uncertainty? Is there any hope left, or any semblance of fondness or desire upon which to build? The pain here between you today was palpable, and it's a pain held by each of you, but I don't yet know whether you can dare reach out to each other's distress? May I suggest you think on these questions and that we meet again a week from now to see where you've got with them. What do you say?"

David looked first to Patrick, then to Grace, then back to Patrick.

"I'll come back, will you, Grace?"

Grace stared, not down at the carpet, but into Patrick's eyes, as if looking for direction.

Patrick met her gaze, but said nothing.

"We need to pay you," Grace said at last, reaching into her handbag.

"Grace?" David eyes were now pleading.

"Twenty-two fifty each," she informed him.

"Thirty each actually," said Patrick, "I'm sorry, Grace, I thought I'd explained at your last session, I charge sixty pounds for couple therapy; it's harder work."

"You're telling me," Grace replied, tossing a twenty and a ten in the lap of the husband who bore a look as if to say, 'Has it really come to this?'

David tried to wave away his wife's contribution, but Grace would have none of it.

"Just pay Patrick and make the appointment, David," she told him firmly.

David took out his wallet and produced a further thirty pounds of his own.

"Shall we say the same time next week?" asked Patrick.

"I've a meeting at work next Thursday morning," said David.

"That's a problem then," said Patrick, clearly offering no solution to it.

"I'll get out of it, we'll be here," said David, proffering the clutch of notes to Patrick, who at that precise moment was looking hard at Grace and wondering what was going through her mind.

154

Chapter Twenty-Two

IN THE SNOW AND ice, the journey across the moors was treacherous and Patrick parked up outside Beth's cottage almost fifteen minutes after his session should have begun. He hated being late, it made him cross, and this, coupled with one of her ducks taking a peck at his ankle as he passed, made for a less than harmonious beginning as Beth welcomed him inside. A simple, 'Sorry I'm late,' was insufficient for Patrick, who felt compelled to describe the hairy journey in considerable detail. By the time he took a sip of coffee, it was not only weak, but also lukewarm.

"Sorry, right out of biscuits," Beth apologised.

"That's okay," answered Patrick, who couldn't resist feeling punished. He knew this was nonsense but what was not a figment of his imagination was the racing of his heart. He was more nervous than at any time since the very first occasion he presented himself before Beth's penetrative stare, and, having resolved at last to tell her about his marital problems, he now truly understood how Neil could complain of feeling like a specimen under a microscope.

"How are you?" Beth asked, and Patrick immediately wished that she hadn't.

"Still a bit shaky, and my throat's dry," he replied, taking advantage of the platform provided by his prolonged description of the treacherous roads to sidestep the more personal nature of the enquiry. "You know, I'm not as confident driving through snow as I once was."

"Yes," she smiled, "I could say the same about walking!" and the moment of shared humour around their vulnerabilities helped ease the tension in his stomach. "Would you like a glass of water? I know I make lousy coffee, my husband's always telling me so."

And Patrick realised he could have come here for another

five years and still not found the nerve to tell her that her coffee was crap.

"Thank you, that would be nice."

Beth hauled herself out of the chair, and he registered her pronounced limp as she headed off to the kitchen. She returned moments later with a tall glass in a hand that bore a noticeable tremor as she handed it over. He knew Beth's facial expressions like the back of his hand, but it was the first time he was conscious of observing the movements of her body so closely. Normally she beckoned him into the sitting room ahead of her, and followed him to the front door as he left, thus he had no sense of how long she'd carried such a severe limp. Her hair had turned from grey to white over the years but that hadn't concerned him, for her mind was as sharp as ever and he'd imagined she would go on indefinitely.

"I noticed you're limping," he ventured.

"Yes, some days worse than others. I'm due to have a have a hip replacement and can't say I'm looking forward to it, but most of my friends have had at least one, and one old dear is bouncing around on her third; they all assure me I'll be fine but most of them don't share my fear of hospitals. When I was a little girl all the important people in my life who went into hospital never came out. The truth is I've put it off far too long. Of course, sitting in one place so still and long doesn't help, so I've got a lot to think about. I only see six supervisees these days, and four or five clients, and the pain has made me realise I can't go on for ever. But until I've had the op I really don't know how much longer I shall *want* to go on. I should like to stop while I'm ahead, if you know what I mean. My husband has promised to take me to New Zealand for a long holiday, when I'm back on my feet again, so I suppose I'm saying you might need to start thinking about finding another supervisor, at least on a temporary basis, or perhaps permanently if this might be a suitable time for a change."

Patrick was stunned and struggled to know what to say. He realised some words of compassion for his mentor's discomfort, her fear of hospitals and growing realisation of her own mortality were in order, but could see no further than his own impending loss, of the woman who had taught him so much and whose challenges, support and encouragement over the years had helped turn him into what he hoped was a fine foot soldier in his chosen profession.

"Phew," he whispered, aware of the thin ice beneath him.

Instinctively, he summoned up the small boy within, eager to assist his grandma to go on being there for him.

"Thank you for telling me, I hope you'll be all right. I heard an article on the news a few weeks ago about some new technique for hip replacement where they need only make a small incision and you're discharged within a couple of days."

"Really? Well, I don't suppose it has reached rural Derbyshire yet. Anyway, Shall we crack on?"

And they did.

Patrick resisted the temptation to aim a kick at the still disgruntled duck that followed him to Beth's gate. He threw his briefcase onto the back seat, slammed the door and settled himself in the driver's seat. The tyres skidded on the slush as he drove off, his foot treading angrily on the accelerator. He cared about Beth, and was sorry for her, and was cross with himself for not being more charitable, but he'd paid good money today and felt he'd not obtained what he'd really wanted and he drove away feeling cheated. He wished he could close his eyes and open them to find himself back home, snug and safe in bed, the covers pulled tightly around him. The moor roads were only marginally better than on the way across and he drove gingerly. He was relieved to spot the isolated outline of the Strines Inn up ahead and soon pulled over into the empty car park. A log fire burned in the grate and he received a warm welcome from the woman behind the bar.

"Ah, a customer! You deserve a medal, or at least a drink, what can I get you?"

"Just a coffee please, black and strong, espresso if you've got it."

"Just filter, I'm afraid. But I can make it strong. Are the roads easing?"

"Barely!"

"Which way you heading?"

"North, into Yorkshire, I passed by here a couple of hours

ago, it was worse then. I should have taken the motorway but it's a lot more miles, anyway, motorways are boring, and hell when congested."

"When aren't they in this country?" she retorted. "A friend and I were touring central Spain, early last summer, hardly saw another car for much of the time and we weren't on back roads either. I've heard Ireland's much the same, although I've never been. There ..." she handed him the cup and saucer and he settled at a small table in front of the fire and drew back into himself. She recognised the signals and knew not to engage him any further.

The reference to Ireland struck a chord in Patrick. He had never been back since being brought to England at the age of three. Patrick knew the first requirement of any good therapist is curiosity; it's what every client has a right to expect; curiosity about what is being said and not said; about what they long to change in their lives and why they will resist that change at all costs. Patrick prided himself on retaining his curiosity after so many years listening to the woes of others. But Patrick had his own blind spots, those aspects of the world he deemed unworthy of interest: finances and pensions, politics, sociology, statistics, working out at the gym, joining any club, the honours system, nationality, fashion, most television programmes, D.I.Y., celebrities, the inner workings of the human body, and of course, Ireland. Back in the years of 'the troubles' he showed a passing interest in events in Northern Ireland, sufficient to endorse his opinion that there was nothing to be gained by crossing the Irish Sea. Then, as the ceasefires took hold and the Celtic tiger found its roar, he responded with disdain to the plethora of 'plastic paddies' and the rash of makeovers that turned down-at-heel inner-city English boozers into instant-Irish theme pubs. To Patrick, Ireland was simply, 'somewhere over there' and no matter how often its symbols and images called 'It's behind you!', like the character in the pantomime, he never quite managed to see it.

Patrick pushed aside thoughts of Ireland along with his empty coffee cup. The bar-woman had clearly been aware of him, for she was there at once, retrieving his cup and enquiring if he'd like another.

"No, I'll be awash," he replied, and she turned away. "Wait," he said, "I'll have a brandy, an Armagnac if you have it?"

"We do indeed," she called from the bar. "Small one, large?"

"Just a single, thanks."

It tasted good and he felt a rare decadence, sipping brandy on Friday lunchtime in this isolated inn, miles from anywhere, with a good dusting of snow outside. Then, warmed by the fire and the Armagnac, he felt a sudden stab of aloneness, both in his chosen profession, and in his personal life. He tried to shrug it off by focusing on that morning's supervision, which had been far from satisfactory. The news of the impending loss of Beth, whether temporary or permanent, had thrown him, and that was on top of the anxiety he felt about the apparent break-up of his marriage and the impending arrival of Nuala for the weekend. He had intended telling Beth about his marriage problems but the realisation that she might soon be retiring put paid to that. Instead, he'd told her for the first time about Grace, but it had not gone well, with Beth prodding away at him unhelpfully. Beth said she was finding it hard to get in, as if he were keeping her out, protecting the work from her observations. He'd begun to wish he'd opened with Neil instead, but somehow they never quite reached a stage where he could easily let Grace go and move on. By the end, he felt frustrated, exhausted, and strangely resentful as he handed her the cheque. He raised his glass and took another sip, its warm energy burned his throat, and he wanted more than anything to lie down, curl up, and forget about everything. He put his hand to his face, which was flushed from the heat of the fire. He caught sight of the woman behind the bar, eyeing him as she polished glasses. A decade older than himself, heavily built, but with a warm strength about her, he imagined her sliding the bolts on the heavy front door, topping up his glass, pouring one for herself, then taking him and the bottle upstairs to a vast iron bed of feather and down, where, an hour later, his passion spent, she would cradle him in her loving arms. At which point in his reverie, the latch clamoured and the front door gave way to two pairs of grey-haired walkers, with loud sticks, matching coats and rucksacks, who approached the bar leaving a trail of melting snow as they commandeered the space. The husbands noisily perused the beer pumps while their wives scanned the blackboard and stole envious glances towards his table by the fire. Patrick rose, tossed a five-pound note onto the table and left without draining his glass.

Chapter Twenty-Three

PATRICK HEADED BACK TO his office where he remained until it was time to set off for Leeds to meet Nuala's train. There is a measure of innocence in ignorance, and having received no word from Maggie all week, he felt relatively nonchalant about her whereabouts or intentions. The train was on time and he spotted Nuala as she approached the ticket gate; what he hadn't noticed until she was wrapped in his arms, was that behind her, loitered a young man, waiting be introduced.

"Dad, this is Jack. Jack, meet my Dad,"

"Pleased to meet you, Mr Chime!" an outstretched hand was proffered at her dumbstruck father.

"Dad!" Nuala's voice jerked him into action.

"I'm sorry, forgive me, um, let's start again, I'm Patrick, how are you, Jack?"

"Well, actually, my real name's John, John Milburn, but my mates call me Jackie, or 'Wor Jack' after ..."

"... the 'Toon' footballer, Jackie Milburn," Nuala beamed, "he even looks like him, don't you petal?" and the two youngsters giggled and gushed in mock Geordie-speak, leaving Patrick utterly bemused.

Nuala and Jack piled into the back seat as Patrick stowed their bags in the boot. Thick traffic meant it took the best part of an hour to reach the house, during which time the youngsters provided most of the chatter allowing Patrick the role of quiet chauffeur. It gave him valuable time to adjust to the unforeseen circumstances.

"Did you tell your mum you were coming home this weekend?" Patrick enquired at last, as they left the ring road.

"Err, yeah, why?" came Nuala's puzzled response from the back seat.

"She's been away all week, we haven't had much chance to talk," he said defensively. "I don't know what plans you've got for the weekend, I thought we'd eat in tonight, Spag Bol, fancy it?"

"Sounds great," replied Jack, on behalf of them both.

"Thought I'd take Jack off to town tomorrow night and show him off to my girlfriends," announced Nuala, "Steph and Josie are home this weekend, too."

And as he swung the Saab into the cul-de-sac, Patrick received his second shock of the evening, as he made out the shape of Maggie's car parked on the drive.

"Oh, she's here," said Patrick, failing to conceal his surprise. "Does your mother know you were bringing Jack?"

"Of course. You know, you two really ought to talk more," Nuala joked, "Jack, you wouldn't believe my Dad used to train Relate counsellors!"

They poured out of the back seat and Nuala led Jack towards the front door, while Patrick retrieved their bags from the boot.

"Oh, sorry, Dad, afraid I lost my key!"

"What, again? How many is that, do you know how much they cost?" he grumbled, putting down the bags and reaching in his pocket for his own.

"Sorry!" Nuala pulled a face.

"Here, let me get the bags," cried Jack, swiftly gathering them up.

'Good man, first point on the board,' thought Patrick, as he unlocked the door to find Maggie standing on the other side, poised to greet them.

"Special delivery," Patrick announced cheerily as their eyes met for the briefest of moments, "One much loved daughter and Wor Jackie Milburn, the finest number nine ever to grace St James' Park."

"What?" Maggie seemed suitably perplexed.

"Nuala, I'll leave you to explain," said Patrick, "the chef has a Bolognese sauce to create."

"I've done the food," said Maggie, abruptly, "Lasagne, just about to go in the oven."

Patrick was undone, and sorely tempted to ask whether she'd had the gall to use the mince he'd bought yesterday from the farm shop, but thought better of it.

"Right! Lasagne it is," he proclaimed, and clapped his hands rather loudly, "Now who's for drinks?"

"Coffee for me," said Nuala, "Jackie will have a lager, and please, Dad, not one of your old-fashioned real ales!"

'Point lost there,' thought Patrick.

"And what about you, darling?" he said, staring hard at Maggie. "What can I get you?"

"I'll have coffee too, I'll see to it," said Maggie.

"Nuala, why don't you take Jack up and show him the spare room, while we get the drinks sorted," Patrick said, in one last attempt to regain control.

The youngsters bounded upstairs, leaving Patrick staring at the wife who showed no inclination to suspend her coffee-making to give him her attention. He opened the fridge, retrieved a can of lager, and scanned the shelves in vain for the mince.

"Maggie?"

She continued ignoring him.

"Maggie!" he snapped, as if she were a dog refusing to come to heel.

"Spare room, eh?" she jibed, "there's a modern father for you."

"What? I can't fucking believe this," he hissed, "you waltz in here unannounced after a week shacked up with your lover, hijack my mince, and have the gall to criticize me for not being prepared to allow my eighteen-year-old daughter to fuck her boyfriend under my roof."

"*Our* roof, and she's nineteen, last Thursday, perhaps you forgot? Oh and by the way, you hijack aircraft, not mince!"

If he'd had a carving knife in his hand he'd have felt tempted to run her through, but then, if he hadn't been so shocked to learn that he'd missed his daughter's birthday, he might have seen the funny side of his minced beef melodrama. Instead, he snapped open Jack's can of lager and wrenched the top off a bottle of Black Sheep Ale, an appropriate choice given how Maggie's remarks had left him feeling.

"Perhaps you're right," he whispered as he poured the beers, "then *you* could have slept in the spare room!"

"I'd intended to," she said, as calm as you like.

163

The sound of two pairs of feet bouncing down the stairs brought about a cessation of hostilities.

"Your mother's coffee won't be long," Patrick announced, "here's your lager, Jack."

"Thanks, Mr Chime, I mean, Patrick."

"Nuala, come here," Patrick held out his arm and she readily nestled into it. "I'm really, really sorry I forgot your birthday!"

"Oh, that explains why the card was in Mum's writing. Thanks for the cheque by the way," and she cast her mother a sheepish glance, "much appreciated!"

Maggie gave a weak smile and handed her daughter a mug of black coffee.

By the time the lasagne was out of the oven the men had polished off a further two beers and the women had seen off half a bottle of Sauvignon Blanc. At the table the food and drink worked its magic and the conversation flowed almost as easily as the wine. The uninitiated might not have noticed the minimal amount of communication between the older couple, or the fact that it was only the younger pair who touched: a pat on the shoulder here, a playful punch on the arm there, and a considerable amount of fondling under the table.

They undressed in silence, and as Maggie climbed into her familiar side of the bed, she made to reach for her book, which of course, was lodged elsewhere. Its absence shocked her, far more than Patrick's lack of contact all week, his forgetting of Nuala's birthday, or the charade they had maintained so successfully without one word of negotiation since her return that afternoon. She switched off her bedside lamp and stared into the dark.

Patrick lay on his back puzzling at the evening's events. Jack seemed a nice enough lad; Patrick could take to him for sure, but it would have all been so different if Nuala hadn't brought him along. In the car, the two of them would have talked. Car journeys are good for that, clear boundaries of time and place, just like therapy, but without the pressure of maintaining eye contact. He would have asked how she was, and gently, sensitively, let her know that he and her mother were going through a difficult time, and assured her that the cause had nothing to do with her. There would have been tears, of course, and on arriving home, a loving hug, but it would have been all right, and more grown-up and justifiable than the play-acting that had gone on all evening downstairs. Who knows, it might even have shaken some sense into Maggie. That last was a cheap shot, he realised, for deep down he knew that Maggie had talked sense last weekend when she described their marriage as having run its course. He was tempted to reach out to her, but in the dark it was hard to predict on which part of her anatomy his hand might land. In the event, the sound of a door gently opening, quiet footsteps along the landing, then another door opening and closing, stayed his hand. The direction of the footsteps indicated it was Nuala going walkabout rather than Jack, and Patrick felt relieved; he would have had to deduct at least five points were it the other way round.

"Sounds like there's a spare room after all," he whispered in the general direction of the body lying next to him, "you should give Gavin a ring, we could have a really interesting house-party."

"Pat ... you know, you really ought to see someone," she said softly, turning over away from him and pulling the covers tight about her.

"You mean a lover?"

"A shrink!"

Across the landing, in the spare bedroom, Nuala snuck into bed alongside Jack, and found him wearing tee shirt and shorts.

"What's with these!" she asked.

"Well, it's your parents' house," he whispered, tamely.

"Not for much longer, the way things are going," she said, with a sigh.

"They're not getting on, are they, even I could see that? I like your dad though; he's cool, in an un-cool sort of way. I don't think I'd let my daughter's boyfriend sleep in her bed under my roof."

"You haven't got a daughter, or your own roof."

"No, I've got you though."

"You haven't got me, Jack, we're just passing this way together for a while, that's all."

It was a line she'd heard her father use and she liked the veneer of independence it bestowed on the speaker. It was also an extremely good cover up.

"You know that poem, of John Donne's?" she asked, "'No man is an island ...?' well, my dad says, we're all tiny islands floating like duckweed in a vast pond, and every now and then another tiny island floats by and we brush against each other and maybe stick together for a moment or a lifetime, but we must never forget that we are separate people."

"That's bleak."

"Is it? I think it's beautiful."

And in a vain attempt to prove that John Donne was mistaken, Jack put his arms around her and drew her nakedness towards him.

"Well, we hoofed it through Act 1, got any ideas for Act 2?" Patrick asked, once he saw that Maggie's eyes were open.

She stretched and yawned before replying.

"I'm in town today, got two apartments to look at, one for the second time and one that's owned by someone I know through work."

"So, you've told people at work, then?" he observed.

"I've told a person at work, someone I trust, not 'people'," she insisted.

"It's happening then, it's becoming formalised."

"Seems that way."

He shrugged, and pulled a face.

"What does that mean?" she challenged.

"What?"

"That shrug, that look, as if you think this is all some aberration of mine, that this has got nothing at all to do with you. Let me remind you that throughout all of this, you've not given me one single reason why you think I should stay, not one."

"Would it make any difference if I did?"

"Don't play games, Pat, you had the chance last week to make the case for continuing this marriage, and you fell silent.

166

You just don't like the fact that I'm the one who's taking action."

Patrick did not appreciate being summed up so concisely and accurately by one untutored in the art of psychodynamic analysis.

"Look, Pat," Maggie continued, "I don't want to fight, it's pointless. I can appreciate you're still angry but don't you see we're just hurting each other in order to score cheap points?"

"Okay, so what do we say to our two houseguests, or to Nuala at least? Should I take Jack off to football while you tell her, or do you want to take Jack to cast an eye over some apartments while I do the deed?"

"Pat ..." her voice now full of tears, "Please, don't! I can't go on like this. I really can't."

"So, what do you suggest?" he said in a voice drained of all vulnerability or tenderness. It was sufficient to lance the boil, and Maggie leapt from the bed, and for the first time in many a long year, Patrick Chime saw his wife wearing a nightie. She grabbed Patrick's dressing gown from the back of the door, swept across the landing and returned a few moments later leading Nuala by the hand and gestured her to sit on the foot of their bed, while perching herself on top of the duvet a marked distance apart from Patrick, and took a deep breath.

"Nuala, there's no right time or any easy way to say this, but there's something we've got to tell you, and for various reasons it seems I'm the one who has to do it. I wasn't working away last week; I was staying away. I was staying away because your dad and I have not been happy together for some time, and recently it's all come to a head, and what's triggered it is that I've been seeing somebody, and it just seems best if your dad and I have some time apart, at least for a while, so that I can think, so we can both think, about the future."

Nuala's mouth was open, but made no sound, her eyes darting to and fro between she who spoke and he whose silence shouted all the louder.

"Dad?" the word struck him like meteor, a shower of questions exploding from the impact and not one could he answer.

Nuala glanced at her mother whose face was flushed, and

then back to her father who looked simply beaten.

"Dad?" This time her question sounded more accusing than beseeching, but reaped no better reward.

Nuala claimed the space abandoned by her parents.

"I'm not stupid, you know, even Jackie could see things weren't right with you two; I just hadn't realised it had got to this stage. You know, Mum, I used to joke with Josie that you couldn't wait for me to leave home so you could too. Spot on, eh?"

"Nuala," Patrick interceded sharply. "Nuala, it's not that simple, whatever's happened in this marriage was made by us both, we each share the responsibility. It's not fair to simply blame your mother."

Maggie appreciated her husband's fine words, whether or not he actually meant them. Nuala, however, did not, and leapt from the bed, slammed the door and retreated to the spare room and the reassuring embrace of her Jackie.

Neither parent moved. Maggie gave a loud sigh, and the thought occurred to Patrick that he had been part of an opera whose second act had just closed abruptly, leaving him wishing he were a member of the audience rather than one of the cast. Life was so much easier when there were clients to enact the scenes on your behalf.

After half-hearted stabs at breakfast the two couples parted company, the youngsters heading off to see Josie, leaving the older couple to reflect on the likelihood that news of their impending split would soon begin seeping through the neighbourhood. Nuala's cursory goodbye was laced with venom, which Maggie felt more keenly than Patrick, who at least recognised the hurt underneath.

"Will you two be back before going into town tonight?" Maggie asked as she and Patrick jostled to see them to the door.

"Doubt it," said Nuala curtly, "Dad's given us a key so don't wait up." Only Jack's sympathetic smile conveyed any sadness and compassion. Patrick found it rather touching.

"Do you want another coffee?" Patrick asked after closing the front door.

"There must have been a better way," Maggie replied, to an altogether different question.

"Let's not post-mortem it," said Patrick, "there's no point. A hundred and sixty-thousand couples divorce each year, and most of them have kids, I don't imagine many of them think they break the news all that well."

"Maybe so, but it was still awful. Do you think it'll be easier for her being away at Uni, rather than living at home and watching us squabble every night?" asked Maggie, searching for anything salvageable amongst the shards and splinters of their fractured family.

"You're not here every night," he reminded her, pointedly. "Besides, I read an article recently, about parents splitting up just as their offspring leave for university; it likened the kid's experience to a diver bouncing on a springboard, and just as the kid places their full weight on the board, it snaps off underneath them."

"Thanks for that, Pat," she said sarcastically, "you know, you really are a great help! Look, clearly I'm going to have to be the bad guy in all this, so I can't see any point in my coming back here tonight, they won't be home until the early hours and I'd rather not have a slanging match when she comes home drunk at two a.m. I'll drive over after breakfast and see her before she leaves."

Patrick stood at the front door staring at his wife's back as she walked over to the car.

"Take care," he called out, for no apparent reason.

It was only as she opened the driver's door, that she allowed herself to glance back, looking for the tender smile that was not forthcoming.

Sunday morning, early, and Patrick was already downstairs in the kitchen making a mug of tea when Nuala appeared and snuck up for a wordless cuddle.

"Tea?" he said at last.

She shook her head,

"Water, lots."

"Bad head, eh?"

She nodded.

169

"I heard you come in."

"Did we wake you?"

"No, couldn't sleep. Your mum didn't stay here last night." And he felt an immediate stab of guilt at telling her.

"I know. Her car wasn't on the drive. With her lover, eh?"

"Nuala, I'm sorry; this has taken over everything. How have *you* been?"

"I don't know why I'm so upset about it," she replied, ignoring his oblique reference to the abortion, which anyway, she was glad to put behind her, "I can't see it's going to affect me all that much. What will happen to the house?"

"Nothing for the time being. I'll be staying here and when the time comes for it to be sold, I imagine we'll simply halve the equity."

"That simple, eh?"

He didn't know what to say, so said nothing.

"Then what will you do?"

"Don't know, haven't really thought about it. My work is obviously around here so I can't see any point in moving far away. I suppose I'll buy a small weaver's cottage or something, I don't see myself in a modern loft apartment, do you? Rest assured, I'll make sure there's a spare room, so you can always visit." 'Visit.' Even though he could see it was the appropriate term, it sounded so very different to, 'come home'.

She cast him a withering look that only added to the guilt he already felt.

"Dad ... there must be there something you can do? You counsel couples all the time, can't you see what's wrong and do something about it?"

And Patrick was suddenly reminded of the little girl who looked up into her father's eyes and believed he could do anything in the whole wide world.

"Nuala, years ago, I used to think the same thing. And you know what, all that knowledge about relationships, all that theory, doesn't make a scrap of difference; you can't prevent people from growing and changing and you can't make someone love you when they've grown out of it. Your mum's right, our marriage has run its course, it's just that she's woken up to that rather earlier than me, and been brave enough to do

170

something about it."

"No!" she shouted, "You sound like you're on her side! Why can't you just be angry like any normal husband?"

"I have been, I've been twisting the knife this past couple of weeks; I'm not proud of it and it hasn't got me anywhere. Deep down, although it may not seem like it to you now, your mother and I still care about each other."

She flashed him a disbelieving glance.

"It's true, Nuala, people don't stop caring about each other just because they don't live together any more."

"I don't understand," she shook her head and looked away out of the kitchen window into the still-dark garden.

"Nuala, I'll let you into a secret; when it comes to relationships, none of us really understands anything, and anyone who tells you different is a fool. Look, you studied Hamlet at A level; remember the line … *There are more things in heaven and earth, Horatio, than are dreamt of in your philosophy?* Well the same applies to marriage and relationship theory."

She frowned, shook her head, and planted a fleeting kiss on his cheek.

"Fraud!" she said, pulling a face, but before the jibe could register, added, "Paracetomol?"

"Bathroom cabinet."

"Thanks, Dad. Train's at one."

"You and your mother need to talk, without me around," he announced firmly, as she headed off upstairs carrying two large tumblers of water. But she pretended she hadn't heard.

"Your mum's calling by after breakfast, make sure you're in," he called after her. "I'll be going for a walk, I need some fresh air. Talk to her!"

A weary, "Okay" drifted down from upstairs.

Patrick would have preferred them both to see the kids off at the station, but that would have involved taking two cars and undermined the display of togetherness. It made more sense for Maggie to be the one to drop them off, as the station was more or less on route to Gavin's.

As the three of them got out at the station and loitered on

the edge of goodbyes, Maggie stepped forward, pressed a hug upon each young person and was saddened to find that Nuala's body felt the stiffer of the two. She climbed back in behind the wheel, stole a glance at their backs, and drove back the way she came. Despite having signed a six-month agreement on a flat that would be hers from tomorrow, it did not feel right to move into her new life direct from Gavin's apartment. And, for some reason she could not explain, she felt the need to leave home one last time. And so it was, that a couple of hours after he'd stood at the door and waved goodbye to his three houseguests, Patrick opened the last remaining bottle of his favourite red, fetched two glasses and carried them upstairs on a small tray. There is something so illicit about sex in the afternoon, especially when it's with your estranged wife.

Chapter Twenty-Four

MAGGIE WAS ALREADY UP and about, unplugging computer leads in her study. She'd decided to leave Patrick the PC but needed to take her printer. Patrick was idling in the bedroom, getting dressed for work: smoke-grey needle cord suit, blue shirt, no tie. As he bent to fasten his shoelaces he noticed he had on odd socks; his marriage was unravelling and it felt like he too was coming apart at the seams. He set off for his sock drawer and having resolved the faulty combination, for once tied his shoelaces in a double bow.

He reflected on the previous afternoon's coupling. The well-choreographed moves were as familiar as ever, but something felt different. He wondered if it was the knowledge that she was no longer his that gave the procedure that strange new twist of ... what? Lust? More like surprise, akin to a letter from the taxman containing a small but unexpected rebate. He wondered if she'd felt it too, and regretted not asking her. Afterwards they'd shared a pizza and watched a DVD of *Groundhog Day*, and although he'd enjoyed the movie more than Maggie, for a while it almost felt like they were teenagers again, and he'd wondered, fleetingly, whether it was not too late to begin again.

"Cute film, corny ending," she'd said, as the credits rolled and she gave a yawn. "May I stay tonight, spare room?"

"Sure," he replied, "but no need to go that far," and was touched that she'd felt the need to ask. He made no move on her, and none was sought. She was asleep in no time, gentle snores, like a cat's purr, lulling away his fears, and he fell asleep trying to recall how many years it was since their last cat died.

Dispensing with breakfast, he was ready to leave for work and found her still sorting through files of papers in her study; it occurred to him that it would not be *her* study much longer.

Their goodbyes were cursory, not out of any undercurrent of hostility, but to diminish the poignancy of parting.

At the office, Patrick opened the diary and cursed himself for having booked in a new client who had rung a fortnight ago requesting a Monday morning appointment. Gina ... somebody, for once he had omitted to note down the surname, and gave a silent wish that her husband had not just left her. He felt little enthusiasm for setting out on a new journey of therapy, whatever its focus, and certainly no desire for any new marital work, but it was too late to cancel. 'You should see someone,' Maggie's words had been ringing inside his head like a persistent telephone.

"Maybe I should see someone," he whispered aloud, trying his best to reframe them as a gift rather than an indictment, and immediately felt that give in his chest informing him that her observation was not only accurate but a source of considerable anxiety. But who could he approach? Most practitioners within a twenty-mile radius were either supervised by himself or one of his supervisees, had been trained by him, or knew him personally. He reached for the directory of the British Association for Counselling & Psychotherapy and leafed through its pages. It gets fatter every year, and he stopped buying it several years ago, so some of the entries were probably out of date. He told himself he really should get a computer installed at work and go online. He perused the ranks of foot soldiers, 'waging a vain war on real life and unhappiness,' he thought cynically. Not keen to trust himself to a complete stranger, he closed the book and placed it back on the shelf.

He picked up his address book and began perusing the names of various colleagues and acquaintances, and was struck by how many he no longer met up with, the entire book having become little more than a Christmas card list. 'Strange,' he thought, 'how you can have such access to the most intimate corners of other people's lives, yet feel so alone in your own.' One-sided intimacy, that was what Neil had called therapy a while back and Patrick had sought to contest the point. Today, he would have offered up no argument. Under 'W' he recognised a name, Sally Winters. Sal. By now she must be in her early fifties; he recalled that she lived somewhere between Bradford and Skipton. Back in the nineties, they had occasionally run courses together for Relate, although he hadn't spoken to her for at least three years, and it must be five since they last met. He picked up the phone and promised to hang up if it went straight to answer-phone.

"Sal Winters."

Her voice was warm, friendly and efficient, just what he wanted to hear.

"Sal, it's Patrick Chime."

"Patrick! Hello!" She sounded pleased to hear from him. "How are you doing? Long time no-hear."

"Yes. I know. I let things go too readily sometimes, sorry."

"Still the old attachment ambivalence, can't bring yourself to edit the address book but neither can you be arsed to give old friends a ring?" She laughed, "I'm only teasing, it takes two to keep in touch … it's good to hear from you, Patrick. What's up?"

Patrick hesitated for a moment, unsure whether to stall or blurt it out. In the end, he elected to steer a course between the two.

"Well, yes, something is up, and I could do with talking to someone, someone I trust, not as a therapist, but as a friend. And I thought of you?"

"Well, I'm glad you're not looking for a therapist because I don't do it any more, besides, I think I'd have struggled having you as a client; being beholden doesn't come easy to the likes of you, Patrick."

"The likes of me?"

"Don't worry, I'm the same; I don't like being one-down, and I recognise the same trait in you. Do you want to talk now, or shall we meet up sometime?"

"I can't talk now, and I'd rather not talk on the phone. I've a new client arriving in ten minutes, but I'm free after that until late this afternoon? I know it's short notice."

"Um … I could meet you for lunch? How about Salts Mill, over at Saltaire? I've a hair appointment at two-thirty, but it's only a short drive from there,' she said. 'Meet you in the

Hockney gallery, around twelve?"

It turned out Gina's husband hadn't left her; Gina hadn't even got a husband, but she did have man trouble, big time. She was a high-flying manager in an NHS Trust, with a history of falling for married men, who always promise to leave their wives but somehow never do. She was in her late thirties and starting to seriously question the course her personal life had taken. Already nearly two years into a relationship with the current object of desire, she was dreading Christmas when he would be ensconced with wife and children up in the Lake District, while she awaited the surreptitious phone calls he'll slip out to make on Christmas Eve, and again, if she's lucky, on Boxing Day. For the past fortnight, she had carried Patrick's number in her phone, but it took news of her lover's Christmas *en famille* to sting her into making the call.

"Gina, what do you want from coming here?" asked Patrick, after she had outlined her story.

"Until recently, I'd have said I want help to find a way to get him to make a real commitment," and she gave a deep sigh, which served to draw his attention to her not-unbecoming breasts, prominent beneath her cashmere sweater. "But it's not going to happen, he's been kidding me and I've been kidding myself. I'm here because I've been wasting my life and it's time I looked at why I keep falling for guys I can't have. Is that something you can help me with?" And as she asked the question she looked across at him intently, and he saw that the penetrating look from her dark green eyes was every bit as appealing as her breasts, and he knew at once why men fell for her. It was not lost on Patrick that he didn't feel quite as married today as yesterday, but a sexual relationship with a client still remained strictly off-limits. Besides, he guessed that Gina's fundamental issues would be found to lie, not as she supposed, in her relationships with men, but in her deep-seated attitudes towards the wives and mothers, whose power she unconsciously feared and envied, and at whom she struck back by trying to steal their men. He could refer her to a female colleague, who might be better placed to help her face up to all that, but she probably wouldn't go. He realised that if he took her on himself, he'd almost certainly have to put up with, and confront, considerable erotic transference, at a time in his life when his own need to be loved and desired had never been less fulfilled. He sighed, made the spontaneous decision to up his fees to fifty pounds from January 1st, reached for his diary and booked Gina's next appointment.

It was well over a year since Patrick had visited Salts Mill, the last time being with Maggie and her mother, when she last came to stay. It had been a fraught visit, with Patrick uncomfortable in the role of peacekeeper between two highly tetchy women; perhaps that was why he had not been back since. Unbeknown to him, Maggie had paid two subsequence visits, once to buy a card and present for her lover's birthday, the second time quite recently, to meet Gavin for lunch before spending the afternoon at his nearby hotel.

Patrick parked in the small car park just up the road from Salts Mill and wandered down past Saltaire village shops. The street had a reassuring feel to it, reminiscent of England of the 1950s and 60s before branded stores made each high street look the same. Yet many of these shops were aimed at visitors rather than locals, indeed Saltaire had latterly been listed as a World Heritage Site, a fact which made Patrick smile, but he found it an attractive place to wander, or perhaps it was the prospect of meeting Sal again that made him so warmly disposed to his surroundings. It was two minutes to twelve as he eased open the vast wooden door of the 1853 Gallery, and felt the welcome rush of light, colour, opera music and the heady fragrance of lilies flood his senses. He peered down both aisles between the rows of David Hockney originals suspended from the original pipe-work of the mill. No sign of Sal. Then he remembered, she was always late; it was one of the things that had got her into trouble as a Relate trainer, her sessions with groups of trainees always running over schedule. "Who cares about time," she'd say, "it's passion and learning that's important, not the ticking of the bloody clock."

He purchased a postcard of Salts Mill for Nuala, and then wandered off down one of the aisles, pausing before a huge collage of a nude Marilyn Monroe look-alike made up of

177

postcard-sized snaps of her body parts. The portrait seemed not unlike himself: exposed, in pieces, and more than a little excited. He felt a hand on the small of his back.

"Not one of his better pieces," she whispered.

He turned and greeted her warmly, kissing her on both cheeks.

"You look well," he offered, without really considering whether indeed it was so.

"Do I? Good, I've been looking after myself more these days. Doing a lot of swimming and bodywork after years of neglect, so it's no chips for me, I'm afraid. But never mind, let's go and have lunch, the salads here are excellent.

They placed their orders and Patrick asked the question that had been on his mind since making the phone call.

"Sal, you said you don't practice any more, how come?" Patrick asked, suddenly aware that she really did look extremely well.

"I guess things are all bound up together," she answered, "everything always is, isn't it? I discovered Matthew was having an affair, with his secretary, would you believe? What a cliché. That's what I told him, and that I thought he might have been capable of something more original. I was trying to make out I was cool and aloof, I suppose. I wasn't. Soon enough I did 'angry', and 'how could you!' and he told me very clearly how he could, when his own wife had long been more interested in delving into the hearts and minds of complete strangers than seeing what might be going on inside her own husband. 'Pockets of intimacy' that's what he sneeringly called them, my precious hours with my clients, locked up in the consulting room in the annexe, where he must never enter. Of course, he said all this to justify his own behaviour, but that didn't alter the fact that it was true. I'm not the kind of wife who can turn a blind eye and pretend an affair isn't happening, and I realised that even if I forgave him and he agreed to put it all behind him, and we carried on as before, there would probably be a next time. So, I had a choice, divorce him, or change myself? I opted for the latter; I stopped doing therapy, knuckled down to getting my old body in order and started wooing and supporting my husband, who, after all, earns five times what I did. Oh, I insisted he sack her, of course, and he made me a director of the firm, so I now pop in whenever I like just to keep an eye on him; it keeps him on his toes. All in all, it works. Sometimes in life, Patrick, you have to make sacrifices to get what you want."

Their bowls of Salade Niçoise arrived, they were overflowing, and one would have sufficed between them.

"Do you miss it, therapy?" he asked, eager to know.

"No more than he misses his secretary. Eighteen years, that's long enough tending to the unhappiness of strangers and neglecting your own, isn't it?"

Patrick stared hard, but made no reply.

"Anyway, enough of me," she said, picking up her fork, "you said something was up, so come on, tell Auntie Sal all about it."

By the time the waitress came to take their order for coffee, Patrick had said far more about Maggie's affair than he'd really intended, mentioning Gavin by name, how they had met, and his sense of the clandestine meetings the lovers had manufactured throughout the past year, as well as much detailed reporting of his own conversations with Maggie since the affair was revealed. He felt surprisingly vulnerable telling Sal about it. Whenever he and Maggie had spoken of the affair he'd drawn the comforting cloak of moral superiority about his neck, but in Sal's presence this device deserted him and his cuckold status was laid bare. He finally got around to mentioning his complicity in the secrecy surrounding Nuala's recent 'spot of trouble', as he put it, before lowering his voice to mouth the 'A' word. Sal listened patiently to all this, never once needing to rush in with penetrating questions or soothing platitudes, and he appreciated her all the more for that. He'd always imagined her to be a far better therapist than he, for she didn't have such a large ego to feed, which he guessed was why she'd been able to let it go. Or perhaps Sal's ego was simply more flexible; for, when the need arose, she was able to detach it from her therapist-self and re-invest it in Sal, the wife and woman. Patrick might currently be tired of seeing clients, but, as yet, harboured no wish to jettison the role of therapist. It was what was keeping him afloat.

"I'm sorry to hear of all your troubles, Patrick, sounds like all three of you have had a tough time of late. Have you told anyone about this; your supervisor? Are you still seeing Beth?"

Patrick nodded.

"Beth knows about Nuala, I had to tell her, but she doesn't know about me and Maggie, you're the first person I've told."

"She needs to know, Patrick, you know that. And maybe *you* should see someone, someone you can trust, where you can take all the feelings and get a perspective on what's happening inside you."

It was not really what Patrick wanted to hear, but it was why he'd come, and he knew she was right.

"Here," she reached in her handbag for a pen and scribbled something down on his unused paper napkin. Folding it neatly, she handed it to him as if it were a portion of wedding cake to take home as a treat for a poorly child.

"He's good, he was my supervisor for the last two years before I packed in. Give him a ring. Look, I must go, come on, you can walk me to the car."

"Business must be good," remarked Patrick as he watched her settle behind the wheel of a new silver-grey Mercedes sports car.

"Benefits in kind, I negotiated it. I call it my silver-bonus; after twenty-five years of marriage I decided I deserved nothing less!" and her smile was that of one who had found contentment. "Don't leave it another two years, Patrick."

He smiled and waved as she drove off.

Patrick fumbled in his pocket for his car keys and the paper napkin fell to the ground. He stooped to retrieve it but the breeze sent it prancing across the tarmac. He pondered whether he could be arsed chasing after it. It settled against a kerb and he resolved to make one more attempt, if it eluded him again, the wind could have it. He lunged forward and the breeze whipped up into his face but the flimsy napkin was secure under the sole of his boot.

Patrick sat at the wheel fingering the scuffed tissue bearing a shoeprint over a name inscribed in blue ink that had bled into the paper, *Michael Underwood,* under which was scrawled a row of figures, the first part of which he identified as the York area phone code. He folded it neatly, inserted it into the back of his wallet, took out the postcard he'd purchased at the gallery and scribbled a message across the back, *Hope you're all right after the weekend. Love Dad, x.* and underneath, *PS – I like him, you've good taste!* It was only after dropping it into the pillar-box he realised he'd omitted to affix a stamp.

Chapter Twenty-Five

BACK AT THE OFFICE, Patrick had what turned out to be his final session with Margaret, a woman in her late forties, whose husband was no longer interested in sex since her mastectomy two years previously. Margaret had tried talking to him about the situation but to no avail. In their last session she'd persuaded Patrick, against his better judgement, to write to her husband, inviting him to come with his wife to address the impact of the cancer on their marriage. Patrick received no reply. Margaret explained that she'd been at home the morning his letter arrived. Her husband had opened it but made no comment. Yesterday, her patience evaporated and she queried his response to the letter; he replied, "I burned it!" Margaret could muster no word of reply, but took herself to bed and cried herself to sleep. Margaret said that as a result of her husband's response, she saw no point in continuing with the counselling. Patrick did his best to persuade her to stay but she would not be swayed, thanked Patrick for his time, paid him in cash, and he accompanied her to the door and wished her well.

The atmosphere left behind was palpable and rather than go to his desk and write up his case-notes, he returned to the therapy room, sank into Margaret's chair and wallowed in the aura of helplessness that enveloped him like an old overcoat. He soon became aware of another feeling, anger, a bright red gash of it festering inside, emanating, he reasoned, from Margaret, and, almost certainly, from her husband. Patrick cursed himself for not having done more to bring it out. He had been too gentle, too protective, too fearful of inflicting further wounds. "Shit," said Patrick aloud. He hauled himself from the chair, attended to his notes, put away the folder in the 'closed cases' drawer and sent Nuala a text explaining the Salts Mill postcard fiasco.

It was half-past five on Monday, no one else to see, and

nothing more to do. He leaned across his desk to peruse the car park; pencils of rain bounced off the roofs of the few remaining cars and he cursed himself for still not having got the soft top patched up. He thought about the wallet in his jacket pocket, pressing against his chest, and recalled his previous experience of therapy. He'd paid £1200 for the best part of a year back in the mid-90s. Too often he could think of nothing to talk about as he sat across the room from the woman whose woodenness prevented him feeling he was really welcome in her home. She was as learned as he was evasive, and it was hard to know which of the two found the sessions more frustrating. At their final session she accused him of endlessly putting her to the test, and he accused her of repeatedly failing it. However, he did learn something useful, the significance of the journey to and from. On one occasion, he'd sobbed for most of the long drive home, tears so profuse he'd had to pull over to the side of the road. In the following session he tried telling her of this, and although his tears were analysed, it was with emotional disinterest, and they remained outside in the car, waiting to accompany him home.

He picked up the telephone, dialled the number, and, fully expecting a recorded voice, rehearsed the message he would leave.

"Hello, Mitchell Underwood."

The voice was alive.

"Hello, is that Michael Underwood?" Patrick asked nervously, buying a few precious seconds.

"No, this is *Mitchell* Underwood, is that who you're looking for?"

Patrick quickly examined the scrawny napkin, spread out on the jotter. *Mitchell*. 'Shit!'

"Yes, I'm sorry, I read it wrongly. Someone gave me your name."

"It's all right, you're not the first person to do that; people don't expect Mitchell to be a first name. What can I do for you?"

It seemed Mitchell had already begun doing it, for his simple question triggered a lump in Patrick's throat and he had to gather himself to speak coherently.

"I was given your name by a friend, she's retired now, Sal Winters, I believe you were her supervisor?"

"Go on."

"Well, I think perhaps I could do with talking to someone professionally, if you've got the space."

"Are you phoning as a potential supervisee, or as a client?"

'How astute,' Patrick thought, 'to couch it like that, and make me own the word.'

"Client," he replied, solemnly.

"What's your name?"

"Patrick Chime."

"Hmm. I've heard of you. It's all right, nothing untoward," he added hurriedly and with a note of warmth, "We're in the same profession, I believe?"

"Yes, is that going to be a problem?"

"Not necessarily, as long as we're careful with our boundaries. My supervisor is Sissie Jacobs, she lives up in the Thirsk area, and it is with her that I discuss my case-work."

Patrick grimaced at hearing himself reduced to a piece of 'case-work'.

"I've heard of her," he replied, "our paths haven't crossed."

"Fine," Mitchell replied. "Ah, hold on, I've just remembered something … I've recently taken on a new supervisee, who I believe was previously one of yours. He told me he'd informed you of the change, but I think I should mention it now in case you have any feelings about me as a result, as I gather you and he ended rather abruptly."

"I can guess who you mean. No, he didn't tell me the name of his new supervisor, and yes, I do have feelings about him, but not about you, and I really don't need to say, or hear, any more on that score."

"Good. Okay, let's see … you'll need to know my fees, £55 per fifty-minute hour."

Patrick grimaced, not at the money, even though it was a little steep for the provinces, but at the ridiculous notion of a fifty-minute hour. 'Why not call it a fifty-minute session if that's the way you work,' he thought, but kept the criticism to himself.

"Is that all right, Patrick?"

"Yes."

"Well then, let me see when I have a space."

Patrick listened to the turning pages of a diary.

"Tuesday evening, that's tomorrow, at seven o'clock, I've had a cancellation. I could see you then for an initial assessment, but if we set up an ongoing contract we'll need to look ahead and find a different slot."

"Fair enough," said Patrick, scowling at not only being reduced to a piece of case-work, but a slot for a fifty-minute hour. The rapport was deteriorating badly. They exchanged addresses and Mitchell gave directions to his home.

"I'll see you tomorrow then, at seven; should you arrive early ... oh, I was going to say my usual bit about waiting outside until seven, but I don't need to tell you that, do I?"

"No," said Patrick wearily, and hung up the phone, conscious of how far he had already retreated from the encounter.

On the way home Patrick stopped at the service station and picked up a four-pack of beers and a packet of panatellas. He fought back the sense of urgency to see whether Maggie's car was on the drive. It was not. He put the beers in the fridge then spotted the note left on the breakfast bar, *I'll call you later in the week – take care of yourself, x.*

He read it again, examining every word and letter exacting every ounce of meaning he could find, then screwed it up and tossed it in the bin along with the panatellas.

He went upstairs but on reaching the landing had forgotten what he'd come for. He wandered through to their bedroom and opened Maggie's wardrobe. Its rail stood two-thirds vacant, a handful of summer dresses and skirts hung on one side. He rifled through her chest of drawers, the top two usually contained her underwear and the third her stockings and tights; all were empty. The bottom two remained full of summery vests, swimwear and shorts. He went to look in her jewellery box; it was gone. She had taken her toilet bag although several bottles still sat upon the bathroom shelf and he shook them to measure their contents. As he did so he caught sight of himself in the bathroom mirror and was struck by how old he appeared. His hand reached for the radiator and was surprised to find it warm.

He went back downstairs and checked the answer-phone, just one message, from Nuala, saying she hoped he was all right and thanking him for making Jack feel so welcome. He went downstairs, lit the gas fire, poured a beer, and settled down to lose himself in BBC News 24, and the pictures of Iraqi civilians cleaning up the debris after a suicide bomb had destroyed a market place and over thirty lives; Westminster mutterings about more government sleaze; a mini tornado ripping the roofs off a row of houses in London, and the likely frontrunners for the position of next England coach. Patrick turned it off and stared at the blank screen. The news often appeared to him like rumours from a far-off land; tonight it came from a different planet.

Chapter Twenty-Six

PATRICK TURNED INTO A dimly lit side road of substantial Edwardian terraces and scanned the thresholds for house numbers. He located his destination at the far end, bearing one of the smarter facades, butting up to some railings beyond which a grassy bank swept down towards the river. Through the railings he caught the reflections of a line of towpath lamps, tickling the black water. The rain had ceased and a riverside stroll seemed more appealing than his purpose here. He'd arrived, as intended, a little early, so he turned off the John Martyn CD and regarded the house-front. It looked freshly painted, cream or buttermilk, and white, with a large black '49' on one side of the stone gatepost. A woman emerged from the basement steps, fumbled in her shoulder bag before climbing into a silver hatchback and heading off down the road. Ten to seven. He checked his wallet, damn, only a twenty and a ten. He reached for his chequebook and wrote out a cheque for fifty-five pounds, folded it in three, and buried it in the top pocket of his jacket. He realised he was dressed almost entirely in black: jacket, jeans, Chelsea boots, and was thankful he'd opted for a grey long-sleeved sweatshirt rather than his black one. 'Sod it,' he thought, 'he can make of it what he will.'

He locked the car, climbed the steps, made for the illuminated doorbell and gave a firm, confident press. Footsteps sounded an approach and the black panelled door swung open revealing a wiry, gnomic figure, hair and beard speckled grey, beige cardigan, brown cord trousers and leather brogues, looking much like a refugee from the cover of a 1950s knitting pattern. The voice that emerged was surprisingly deep and rich with a hint of accent that Patrick had not picked up on the phone, and which might have been Canadian.

"Patrick? Pleased to meet you, I'm Mitchell."

They shook hands, the other man's palm far rougher than

his own, which struck an ambivalent chord in Patrick. He seemed like a man at home in the outdoors, a trout angler used to tying his own flies, the proud owner of a workbench and socket set, a man who knew how to fix things. Fifty-five, perhaps sixty, Patrick estimated, and was glad of the age gap. Mitchell led the way along the hall and down some stairs to the basement where his study-cum-therapy room was located.

"It can be a bit dark during daylight hours but it's secluded from the rest of the house, and there's a loo through there at the back, if you need it," Mitchell explained, reassuringly.

There were two forms of seating: a large, squishy three-seater sofa over by the bay window, of the kind that'd make you want to kick off your shoes at the day's end and lie back with a stiff gin and tonic, your lover nestling in the crook of your arm; adjacent to that, a leather swivel armchair, its seat squashed flat under a much-corduroyed shine.

"Yours, I take it?" gestured Patrick.

Mitchell smiled.

Patrick settled himself at the end of the sofa closest to Mitchell's chair, crossed and uncrossed his legs until he achieved a respectable degree of comfort, at least on the outside. His right forearm rested along the sofa arm, his hand clutching the round, springy edge as if it was a mother's breast. Mitchell's elbows rested on the arms of his chair, his chin cradled by interlocked fingers, and the two men eyed each other like poker players awaiting the river card.

"Shall I start?" enquired Patrick, respectfully.

Mitchell allowed a small frown.

"Well, I was going to say a few words, you know, about boundaries, confidentiality, etcetera?"

"Yes, I do know, and I'll take those as read," Patrick cut in.

Mitchell gave a wry smile and an affirmative tilt of the head.

The two men then sat in perfect silence for the best part of a minute, Patrick staring at the older man's features, and slowly adjusting to the experience of being, for the second time in his life, in therapy.

Maggie unpacked the new tablecloth and spread it upon the

small round IKEA table in the open-plan kitchen-diner-living space. She placed the new pie dish in the oven, uncorked the bottle of Chablis and placed it back in the door of the fridge. She looked around at the light, tidy apartment, with its laminate floors and clean lines; no wooden tea-chests, no cardboard boxes piled high against a wall with marker pen identities scrawled on the sides, *Bedding, Towels, Kitchen, Books, Nuala, Study, Ours*. 'It's amazing how light a single person can travel,' she thought, and went off to her new bedroom to change out of her work suit before she dissolved into tears.

"So," said Mitchell, after twenty-five minutes listening to Patrick's story, "That's what has been happening to you of late, but I'm wondering why you're here, and more specifically, what you want from me?"

"With all that going on," Patrick replied, "I need to make sure I'm still fit to practice."

"Surely that's what your supervisor is for?"

Silence.

"... Your supervisor is aware of all this, I presume?" Mitchell added.

"Most of it. Not all, not yet," Patrick confessed, "I haven't told her about Maggie moving out. I wanted to come here first."

"Okay, so you're here. Now what?"

More silence. Mitchell let him stew.

Patrick lowered his eyes,

"I feel," he said at last, "... like I'm coming apart at the seams ... and I don't know what to do about it."

Mitchell nodded and stared into Patrick's eyes before responding,

"Patrick ..." Mitchell let the name float in thin air for what seemed an age, long enough to have Patrick hanging on his next word, "... I thought just then ... you looked, and sounded, for the first time since we began ... really vulnerable, I'd say, almost frightened?"

Mitchell's voice was velvet-deep, and his words delivered with a measured solemnity that reminded Patrick of listening to Alistair Cooke's *Letters from America* on Radio 4, which he did avidly throughout his teenage years. And for some inexplicable reason, the experience of sitting in this unfamiliar room, hearing Mitchell's voice reaching out to his feelings, gouged a great swathe of emotion from somewhere deep inside, and Patrick's chest shuddered and gave a heave as a half-strangled cry escaped from his throat. The cry was deep and guttural, heralding the first of a series of waves of sobbing, each lasting up to a minute before receding and allowing a temporary calm, before the onrush of the next wave cut short the brief period of respite. Patrick had never experienced emotion on this scale before, emanating from un-charted depths of his being. The entire deluge lasted some fifteen minutes, during which neither man spoke a word, although through the brief interludes of calm Patrick emitted the sighs and groans of a man pushed far beyond what he imagined to be his limits. The second and third waves were the most intense, the subsequent ones somewhat reduced in power as fear gave way to exhaustion, and, somewhere between the fifth and sixth, it became hard to distinguish Patrick's tears from his laughter. The seventh proved to be the last and shortest, and as it receded, Patrick's hand released its vice-like grip on the arm of the sofa, and he fell backwards, the stiffness in his spine and shoulders relented, allowing the back of his neck to nestle deep into the soft cushion. Patrick closed his eyes, and, as the tension ebbed from his body, the only sound was the stuttering of his own breath, punctuating the silent basement.

A sudden creak of leather made him look up. Mitchell was now sitting forward, forearms on knees, hands clasped rather than interlocked, and Patrick saw the whiteness under Mitchell's nails, and for the first time noticed the rimless spectacles that covered his grey glistening eyes. Mitchell's mouth opened and the tip of his tongue ran a coat of saliva across his lips, as Patrick waited to hear, for the first time in forty years, a father's words.

"It's over, Patrick … it's over for now … and it's all right … it *is* all right." And this strong, gentle voice seemed the most beautiful of sounds, and the simple reassurance of the words made Patrick cry once more, but softly now, for these were tears of acceptance, tears of relief, and of gratitude for survival.

Mitchell stole a glance at the clock on the wall.

"That's a heavy load you've been dragging around, Patrick. I imagine it's been there a long, long time. Talking of which, we're almost out of time for today. You're going to be leaving here very soon and you'll need to take good care on the way home. You've come a long way this evening in a short space of time; you've put yourself through the mangle. You've a long journey ahead. It's dark and cold out there, but remember, you're no longer in this alone. Let's make another appointment."

'Shit!' thought Patrick, who had to explain with embarrassment that he'd forgotten to bring his diary.

"I will phone you early tomorrow morning then, before my first client, so we can book another session," said Mitchell, "and when next we meet we can talk about a contract, okay?" and he handed Patrick a business card confirming his contact details.

Patrick nodded, took the card and hauled himself to his feet.

"Just one more thing ..." Mitchell's words jolted Patrick into remembering his status, and he reached into his front pocket, extracted the neatly folded cheque and handed it over to this intimate stranger.

About the same time as Patrick locked the car and stepped, exhausted, through his front door, a buzzer sounded in Maggie's new apartment and she rushed across and pressed the button of the intercom.

"Hello?"

"I'm really sorry I'm so late, something came up, I tried phoning you from the car but ..."

The buzzer cut in and Gavin heard the outer door unlock.

"Is it spoiled?" he asked nervously, as he stepped inside.

"Fish pie, home made. It's rather dried up," she replied.

It was plainly obvious to Gavin that she'd been crying; just as it was obvious to Maggie he had something to tell her.

"What is it?" she asked.

He looked away.

"Gavin?"

"Vicky's pregnant."

191

Maggie blinked hard, felt her leg buckle and she reached instinctively for the back of the closest chair.

"Is that where you've been?"

"She rang to tell me the news and I went across to see her. I had to."

"Jesus, Gavin. When did this happen?"

"I don't know. I told her way back in the spring that I wasn't sure about going ahead with IVF treatment, and after that sex virtually stopped."

"Virtually?"

"A couple of times at most, in those last months, it must have been the last time, not long before I moved out. It was stupid, I don't why I did it, for old times' sake, I suppose. I just can't get my head round it."

"What is she going to do?"

"She wants to keep it of course, it's what she's always wanted."

"And what about you?"

"It's not up to me, is it? She's a woman, it's her body, her pregnancy."

"That's not what I asked, Gavin."

"I don't know. Well, I do, I suppose I'd rather she had a termination, but that's not going to happen; all she really longs for is to be a mother. I don't know, I can't think straight, it's all happened so fast. This afternoon I assumed Vicky was no longer a part of my life, one last Christmas card, which she'd no doubt tear up, and that would be it. Now, she's going to be the mother of my child, and at the very least, I'm going to have a financial responsibility for the next eighteen years, and probably a whole lot more besides. I just can't get my head round it."

"Will you go back to her?"

"Don't be silly!" And she saw how Gavin's eyes shrank from her stare.

And that is how Maggie came to spend the second evening of her post-Patrick life, not dining by candlelight, nor proudly showing her lover around her new apartment, or even freely shagging the night away, but taking part in a reluctant, maternal coupling, culminating with him crying in her arms.

Chapter Twenty-Seven

PATRICK OPENED HIS EYES. The clock on Maggie's bedside table showed four-thirty and he realised he had been dreaming, disturbed by rain lashing the bedroom window as the gale ripped through the tree-lined cul-de-sac. He peeked through the curtains and saw lines of Christmas lights swaying alarmingly in the branches of the garden opposite, while a jovial Santa gazed down from an upstairs window, smug and warm inside. As he wandered through to the bathroom, Patrick noticed the stiffness in his joints and as he stood over the bowl watching the lazy stream of urine, the dream came back to him: a gaggle of monochrome figures assembling at his gate, men and women dressed in rags and blankets, their eyes trained on his window. As he peeks through the curtains, they spot him at once and their eyes burn with need and wild arms beckon him outside. The house is a small end-terrace with a barren front garden in which nothing grows but coarse grass and dandelions, and an abandoned fridge whose door hangs off its hinges. Patrick leaves the house and approaches the small crowd shuffling expectantly beyond the gate He hears a distant rattle that might be small arms fire, and a deep rumbling that could be an artillery shell, and the line of refugees (for that is what he now realises they are) snatch nervous looks over their shoulders before crowding in upon his gate. He steps forward to address them, like a nervous political candidate who already knows his cause is lost.

"I'd like to help you," he stutters, "but I don't have the wherewithal. I'm sorry, but you will have to look to yourselves; there's nothing more I can do."

The crowd leans forward, hanging on his every word, but although Patrick's words are mouthed, not a syllable emerges from his lips. He tries again, but no one can lip-read, or if they can, they clearly do not believe him, and, sensing he has room to spare, they press harder on his gate.

"Go tell your leaders," he pleads, "ask them to help you!" But again, no sound emerges.

Patrick tried to recall what happened next, but that last vain plea must have been the moment he awoke. Shaking away the last stubborn drips, he flushed the loo and returned to bed, but before climbing back in, snatched another glimpse through the window. His car sat alone on the drive, no one at his gate, only Santa's smug face beaming down from the house opposite with electricity to burn. Patrick climbed back into bed, pulled the covers up to his neck and realised he was lying, just as when he awoke, on Maggie's side of the mattress. The dream had disturbed him and he pushed it away by recalling the date and counting the days until Christmas. He had yet to buy any cards, and realising he would have to sign them *from Patrick*, wondered whether to forego the ritual altogether. Then he remembered Nuala, who was bound to be coming home at some stage. Perhaps he would just get a Christmas tree for the porch.

Way across town and beyond, Maggie lay listening to the wind howling outside, and her lover's gentle snores in bed beside her, another life away. She told herself that sooner or later he would move back in with Vicky, for, despite his protestations about not being cut out to be a father, he could not let this opportunity pass by; there was far too much at stake. She was just glad he had not gone back there last night, and she snuggled up and wrapped her arm around him, while she still could.

For once, Patrick overslept. He gathered up the post from the mat as he headed down to make a cup of tea: one bill, two junk, and two Christmas cards, one of which was from Nuala, the first she had ever had to post and, interestingly, addressed to them both and signed *Nuala and Jack*. Underneath, a scrawled note, *Hope you don't mind, Jack's invited me to his parents' farm up near Hexham for Christmas. I'll ring you both to arrange when I might see you. Love N.*

Perhaps he wouldn't bother with the tree.

He heard the phone ringing as he emerged from the shower, and got there as the answer-machine clicked in so he left the receiver on the hook and listened through the speaker.

"Hello, it's Mitchell, with a message for Patrick. I can see you tomorrow, that's Thursday evening at seven, or the following Thursday at the same time; after that there'll be a two-week break as I shall be away over Christmas. Please confirm by the end of today, whether you require tomorrow's appointment, and/or next week's, or whether you would rather wait until the New Year. It's your call. Bye."

Patrick felt sheepish not picking up the phone, but was relieved not to have to engage so soon with the man who had seen him at his most naked.

Maggie threw on a robe, saw Gavin off to work then phoned in sick. She poured another coffee, plugged in the laptop and played with creating a small insert, the kind that people with a penchant for the pseudo-intimacy of round robins like to slip inside their Christmas cards, although this one was not full of kids' tallies of A-levels and swimming certificates.

It is with a mixture of sadness and relief that we are letting you know that we have decided to live apart. As from now, Pat remains at the old address ~ Maggie's new address is ... We hope everyone will keep in touch.

"I'll have to phone Pat," she said, and wondered why she'd needed to speak the words aloud.

Chapter Twenty-Eight

THEY'D ARRANGED TO MEET up after work, at a Leeds wine bar she'd once visited with Gavin, but Maggie realised it was a bad choice the moment she arrived; the office Christmas party season was in full swing, and although she'd taken a table in the far corner the noise from the bar was deafening. Patrick arrived and greeted her with a brief kiss on the cheek as if they were business acquaintances about to do a bit of catching up, which in a way they were, but first, the preliminary rituals had to be got out of the way. They delivered their brief lies and quickly unified around a shared contempt for the leery crowd at the bar.

"Look, this is awful," he pronounced, "Shall we go somewhere else?"

"Yes, I'm sorry," she replied, and thought about inviting him back to her place.

"There's a Café Rouge, not far from here," he said, "we could try that; I could stand to eat something, what about you?"

Maggie was too busy reflecting on the missed opportunity to consider whether or not she was hungry.

"I'll share yours," she answered, "let's go."

They perused the menu and he was comforted that it appeared to have changed little since the last time he'd eaten there, and he tried to remember how long ago that was.

"*Confit de Canard*," he said to the petite waitress. "Maggie?"

Maggie would have preferred to talk rather than eat, for whenever she ate with Patrick, the business of eating seemed to command the arena rather than act as an accompaniment to their conversation. When she watched him eat, she saw a different part of him, a hungry, greedy self, engrossed in his own satisfaction, only rarely troubling to look across at his companion. It had often puzzled her, yet she had never felt able to ask about it. She now wondered whether it was just when he ate with *her*? Despite these misgivings, she couldn't bring herself to make him eat alone.

"Just a mixed salad," she said at last, settling for something she could idly pick at with a fork.

"*Du vin?*" asked the young girl.

"Yes," he said, "bring a bottle of Côtes de Gascogne with the cork and a jug of tap water."

"Funny how you do that," said Maggie, once the waitress had departed, "always ask me what I'd like to eat but assume sole responsibility for ordering the wine."

"Are we going to have a row about this?" he asked.

"I wasn't complaining. I quite like it, I just realised how odd it is."

"Aren't all couples odd," he replied, "each with their own idiosyncratic ways of relating?"

"Do you think so?"

"Yes, of course, because two people living together as a unit for decades is such an odd thing, I know it makes sense for the raising of kids, but as a couple, it's quite bizarre, sleeping in the same bed, sharing the same bathroom, eating together, going places together, sending joint Christmas cards, greeting each other with the same daily rituals of hello and goodbye, recognising each other by the way you put on your clothes, clear your throat, fart or make love, growing simultaneously ever more together and apart. And all this you take for granted, when you're in the everyday thick of it, it's only when it's no longer there that you really notice it."

"Yes, and I guess that's what I meant about ordering the food and drink. But ..."

"But what?"

"Well, I was going to say, that I've been thinking about those kind of things quite a lot over the last few years, about what we're each like as persons, and how we relate to one another, the patterns and habits and so forth. And I came to realise that a lot of it wasn't all that suitable any more, it no longer fitted with who I am and what I really want. But it's only when the other person isn't around any more, that some of those things that had come to irritate, well, you start to

197

remember them with a certain … fondness."

She looked at him.

He stared back at her.

"I keep waking up on your side of the bed," he confessed.

She peered deep into his eyes.

"I'm sorry," she said.

"What for?"

"I don't mean sorry. I think I mean, I'm sad. I'm sad that it's worked out this way."

"Hmm," he replied. "How's the apartment?"

"It's fine. You must come and see it. Come for coffee at the weekend, Sunday morning?" she blurted out, but, before he had time to turn down her invitation, added, "Here, I've something to show you," and removed from her bag a small cream-coloured card and presented it to him.

"I thought it could go inside the Christmas cards. What do you think?" She seemed eager for his approval.

He reached across to take it from her and thought about touching her fingers as he did so, but the moment passed. He appraised the message, printed in a delicate brown font that mimicked real handwriting.

"Yet again, you're a few steps ahead of me. I'd thought if I ignored Christmas it just might go away."

"Well, that's one option," she said, giving a mock frown.

"No, I'm grateful. It's a good way of informing people, I just wonder how they'll respond."

"What do you mean?"

"Well, don't you think it might be a bit of shock, Jingle Bells on the outside, marital break-up on the inner."

"I don't usually send musical cards with flashing lights, credit me with a little more sensitivity."

"I know, I was teasing," and he hated the fact that he had to explain that to her. "But don't you think people will read this and think that if we're getting on well enough to concoct a harmonious message like this then what are we doing splitting up in the first place?"

"You think people would rather we just slagged each other off?"

"God yes! Most folk can't tolerate ambivalence and find it

totally bemusing when others do."

"Would you rather we were like that," she asked, "fighting and rubbishing each other?"

"No, like I told Nuala, you don't stop caring about someone just because they don't live with you any more."

And he saw her eyes well up, and, for once, discarded his therapeutic training and addressed, not the tears, but the little cards.

"I think they're excellent, Maggie, thank you, well done." And seeing the approval in his eyes, she reached into her bag, brought out a podgy little envelope and a folded sheet of paper on which was a list of all their joint friends and acquaintances.

"Would you like to get some cards and send them off with one of these inside?" and she handed him the envelope, which he placed in his jacket pocket.

"And this is for you," she added, handing him a small white card bearing her name and new address in purple font. "Come and see me Sunday morning, for coffee."

He examined it somewhat enviously, how comforting to know who and where you are, and then he wondered how long it would be before she ditched the name Chime. He secreted the card in his wallet, but before he could think of what to say about it, the waitress arrived with their plates.

Chapter Twenty-Nine

PATRICK ARRIVED AT HIS office early and in full working mindset. The answer machine showed one message but when he played it back, heard nothing but silence. The post proved more informative, a large brown envelope and three smaller ones, the first of which contained a letter from the landlord giving notice of a significant hike in rent from the first of April next year, while the other two contained Christmas cards, one of which was also from the landlord, 'How sensitive not to include it along with the rent increase,' thought Patrick, as he ripped it up and tossed it in the bin. The second was from Sarah, the woman he had seen weekly for three years of the most challenging therapy work he had ever undertaken; it read, *Thank you for restoring me to Life – A Happy Christmas to you and your family.* The message brought him up short, for he understood the significance of the capital 'L'. In the early days of therapy, just a few weeks after a suicide attempt, Sarah had talked long and hard about the challenge, indeed the fear, of surviving; the thought of actually 'living' seemed way beyond her the day she edged her way tentatively into his therapy room, But that was all so long ago. He looked again at the card and read again its warm message to him and his family; if she only knew. He wondered how come he could mean so much to strangers, yet so little to his wife, and had a sneaky suspicion that the answer had more to do with him than with Maggie, but now was not the time to go there. He placed the card on his desk and picked up the large brown envelope. It was unstamped, and marked, *For the Personal Attention of PATRICK CHIME.* Inside was another sealed envelope along with a loose handwritten note.

Dear Patrick,

Forgive me for dumping this on you; I hope that you will understand. Enclosed is a letter.

I would be grateful if you would open and read it out at the beginning of our session today, for I shall not be attending. The letter explains everything, or at least tries to. I don't know how David will react to its contents, perhaps that's something you can help him with.

Rest assured, I am all right, (or at least think I am) and I <u>will</u> return to see you, either with David, or alone.

Thank you for being there, I'm sorry to put you in this position but I really don't know what else to do.

Grace.

Patrick re-read the note and could hear Grace's voice as if she was there beside him reading it aloud. He was still pondering its implications when the door opened and Neil wandered in, and, without acknowledging Patrick, strode straight on through into the therapy room. Patrick left Grace's note on his desk and followed on, only to discover Neil ensconced in Patrick's chair, clearly ready to begin. Patrick hesitated for a moment, before assuming the chair normally occupied by his client.

"Welcome. Things look any different from over there?" Patrick asked, after a short silence.

"I could ask you the same thing."

"And my answer would be 'yes' and 'no.'"

"Now why doesn't that surprise me?" said Neil, sarcastically.

"Because you're getting to know me?" asked Patrick.

"Yes, and no. 'Yes' because I'm getting used to the way you work, I see the patterns in how you do this therapy stuff, and 'No' because I really don't know you at all."

"You seem uptight, a bit jumpy today, Neil, are you upset, angry? Or are you on something?"

Neil flashed Patrick a fierce look.

"Don't try to change the subject," he snapped.

"I'm not. In here, the subject never changes; and the

201

subject, Neil, is you."

Patrick felt pleased with this response, and it appeared to stall Neil momentarily.

"Okay, the subject is me, and that includes my relationships, or lack of them, right?" Neil asked.

"Right."

"And if I want to talk about my relationship with you?"

"Go ahead, but don't expect a strip show, with me pouring out another list of facts about myself. If you want to talk about our relationship, that's fine, but remember, that involves looking at what this relationship means to you, and the part you play in it."

"Why do I feel ticked off?" asked Neil.

"Good question, why do you?"

"Because you sound like a bloody schoolteacher."

"Yes, I know I can be a bit teacher-like, but is your feeling ticked off all down to me? Anyway, what do you imagine you were being ticked off for?"

"Pinching your chair!"

Patrick grinned.

"What's funny?"

"Is that why you did it," asked Patrick, "to see if it would wind me up enough to punish you?"

"Not really. I've thought about doing it before but never felt brave enough."

"Well, today you found the courage. But I'm still intrigued by your motivation? You couldn't have known for sure what my reaction would be, and yet you took the risk, so there must have been some possible gain you were seeking, hmm?"

Neil looked down, a sure sign that Patrick's words had struck a chord.

"I often wonder," said Neil, sheepishly, "what it might be like to be you, to sit in this chair, to do your job … to live your life," and he blushed.

"You seem embarrassed," said Patrick, gently. "Is it hard to admit having those thoughts about me?"

"Suppose so. Not very grown-up is it?"

"I'm not so sure. I like to think my job is pretty grown-up, yet it involves me wondering all the time what it might be like to sit in the client's chair and live their life."

"Yeah, but you only do that because it's your job."

"Yes, it is my job, but I also do it because I'm interested in what people are really like underneath, and what makes them tick. Maybe we share the same curiosity?"

"Yeah, but with me it's more than curiosity. When I say, I wonder what it's like to sit in this chair and be you, I mean I wish I *was* you."

"Because ...?"

"Because your life is so much better than mine," Neil asserted.

"How do you know?"

Neil's eyes flashed like daggers.

"Bollocks! You wanna swap?"

"No, Neil, I don't want to swap lives with you, but not because it's you, or because of the way your life is at the moment. I don't want to swap lives with anybody, however attractive their life might appear, because I'm me, and I want to stay me, happy, sad, warts and all. And I know that's easy to say when everything is rosy, but for me it remains true, whether my life is going well or badly."

"So I shouldn't waste my time fantasizing then?"

"I didn't say that, Neil. I answered your question about whether I wanted to swap lives with you. Now you're asking me a different question, whether I think it's wrong to fantasize about being someone else. And I'll answer you straight. No, I don't think it's wrong; in fact I think it's a very common, indeed a necessary, part of growing up. In adolescence we often model ourselves on someone we admire. Mostly, we grow out of it, but we take things from the people we look up to and we try to integrate them into ourselves. It happened to me, way back, as a newly qualified trainer of counsellors, I got a shock one day when I heard myself challenging a difficult student in a group by employing the exact tone of voice and hand gesture that one of my own trainers had used with me, and I felt embarrassed to realise how much I'd hero-worshipped him. It happens in therapy too."

Patrick paused, looking deep into Neil for a response.

"Go on," said the younger man.

Patrick took up the cue.

"Neil, we see things through filters of our own making. What we imagine is so wonderful or enviable about someone else, in reality might not be so desirable at all. Similarly, our perception of ourselves can be distorted. And because, generally speaking, you know very little about the details of my private life, you see me through the filter of your own projections, it's called transference, to give it a name. So I don't think wanting to be someone else is wrong, but I do think it's rather sad, because it amounts to living a life based on distortions of reality."

"So I'm a sad bastard then?"

Patrick laughed, "You really do want me to kick you today, don't you?"

"I was being sarcastic."

"Were you?"

Silence.

"Let's dispense with the apology, Neil. Something made you use that expression; I imagine part of you really does feel that you're a sad bastard. That's why you're here, isn't it, because you feel your life is crap and you're hooked on porn and prostitution and you can't shake them off? You look around and everyone else seems to be having fun and half the time you blame yourself, and the other half of the time you blame the world. And you look at me and think to yourself, 'Lucky bastard, what's he got that I haven't? I'd trade places with him any day.' Does it go something like that, Neil?"

"Something like that," Neil concurred.

There was a long pause, with Neil staring down at his hands, fingers picking at his nails, as Patrick tried to absorb what had passed between them. Patrick felt unsure whether to speak, or indeed what he might say. It was Neil who broke the silence.

"I've killed him."

"Who?" Patrick asked gently, careful not to rush in.

"Degas."

"How come?"

"He wasn't any good. It didn't get me anywhere, so I killed him."

"How did you do it, in temper?"

"Not really, I just got fed up with it all and pressed a switch, *Delete Account,* gone."

"But what made you do it, Neil; something must have happened?"

"It's all just a waste of time, an illusion, it's not real, there are moments when you think it's real but most of the time you're chasing something that isn't there. So I killed him."

"Big step."

"Maybe."

"Why maybe?"

"In the cyber-world there's always reincarnation. I can bring him back to life anytime I want, that's the problem."

"Why is that a problem?"

Neil grimaced and fidgeted.

"If I couldn't, it would be easier to live with, there'd be no temptation, but I can just open another account in his name anytime I want. That's the trouble."

"You mean trusting yourself not to go back on the step you've taken?"

"Yeah, it would be easier if it was final, no going back, no return ticket."

"No choices to have to make, no commitments to have to honour?"

"Hmm."

"So killing Degas off was a huge step because, having made it, you've laid yourself open to the possibility of back-tracking, and then, you'd feel … what?"

"A fucking useless sad bastard."

"Like I said, big step," confirmed Patrick.

Neil took a huge sigh, looked down into his own lap as Patrick watched and waited. Neither man seemed to know what more to say.

"You can have your chair back," Neil said at last.

"Sure you don't want to keep it till the end of the session?" queried Patrick.

"No."

"Why not?"

"It doesn't work."

*   *   *

Patrick's notes were not his usual couple of paragraphs, but a list of words scattered about the page: *Chair, Envy, Swap, Identity, Murder, Revenge, Relief, Temptation, Trust, Desire, Fantasy, Reality, Disillusionment, Anger* and at their centre, a single name in capitals, *NEIL*. He sat back staring at the sheet, as if there was something he was not seeing. He failed to notice the time and it took a bold knock on the door to wrest his attention from his previous client.

The two men greeted each other but David showed no inclination to step across the threshold.

"It is ten thirty-five and Grace isn't here yet," David explained. "She went into work early this morning and said she'd meet me here. I didn't want you to think we'd reneged on the appointment. Shall I'll go back and wait for her downstairs?"

"No, David, you'd better come in."

"Are you sure?"

"Yes. You go through and take a seat and I'll be with you in just a second."

David settled himself in the same chair as last week and Patrick arrived carrying various items. He placed the pen, diary and receipt book down on the coffee table, then took his seat and arranged an envelope and sheet of paper on his knee before looking across at David.

"Normally," Patrick began, "when I'm working with a couple and one of them turns up alone, I don't see them as it would undermine my working alliance with the couple. But as with all rules, David, there are exceptions. Grace has informed me she won't be coming today, and I can tell you more about that if you wish to proceed alone. Do you?"

"I haven't come here just to walk away again. If you've something to tell me, I'd like to hear it," said David.

"When I arrived here this morning I found an unstamped envelope addressed to me. In it, was this other sealed envelope," Patrick held it up, feeling suddenly self-conscious at being a puppet in Grace's hands, "along with this note of explanation," which he then proceeded to read aloud.

David listened attentively to Grace's covering letter to

206

Patrick, his only response to these dramatics being to stroke his brow. Patrick then picked up the sealed envelope and held it close to his chest.

"Clearly, the envelope came addressed to me, so I cannot simply hand it to you, David, but I can of course do what Grace has asked and read it to you, but first I need to ask if that is your wish? After all, I don't know what it might contain."

David sighed, impatiently.

"Read the damn thing, will you; let's get it over with."

Patrick tore open the envelope, removed two sheets of close handwriting and read aloud.

Dear David,

I'm sorry for being so manipulative; it feels strange, for despite all the hurt I have caused you of late, deceit does not come easily to me. I lied last night when I told you I was calling in at work before our session with Patrick today. In fact, as you read this I will be at the airport, boarding a plane to Spain, to meet up with Simon and undertake part of the pilgrim's trail to Santiago di Compostella.

I feel I am handling this very badly, like an adolescent girl running away without telling her parents. Not that I've had much experience of running away, or for that matter, being an adolescent girl, as my own adolescence rather passed me by.

As you know from a previous conversation (although conversation is far too polite a term for what was in fact an ugly and painful exchange) I was thinking of getting away to try and clear my mind and see what I should do about everything, because I realise my chaotic behaviour is putting you and the children through hell. I can assure you it is not doing much for my own state of mind either.

I shall be away for six days and I realise I am leaving the parenting responsibilities entirely with you. I have noticed how well you have adjusted to taking on more of that role in recent weeks, and you are indeed proving a much better father than I had thought possible. Perhaps I might have shown more appreciation of these changes if I didn't harbour so much resentment for the years of being taken for granted and left to shoulder virtually all responsibility for the home and our

207

children.

I know I am behaving unreasonably, and it must seem as if, these last few months, I have quite gone off the rails. I regularly tell myself I must be mad, or, at least, undergoing some kind of mid-life crisis (or 'nervous breakdown', as you prefer to call it). But, you see, I don't much care if that is the case, as this rebellion, against so many of the expectations I've tried to live up to throughout my life, feels the most important thing in the world to me right now, and I know I have to see it through and discover what it means, and where it leads.

Believe me, David, I do realise how selfish this must sound, (and indeed is) as well as all the hurt and upset I am inflicting upon you and the children, and the responsibility I am asking you to hold while I'm going through this journey, adventure, misadventure, nightmare, or whatever you care to call it. I can have no complaint if on my return you have come to your own conclusions about our marriage and its future.

I can offer you no ray of hope, other than the fact that I <u>shall</u> *return next week, and that I do still care about you and the family we made together, even though it may not appear so to you now. You will no doubt argue that if I truly cared, then I would not be treating you and the children like this. I cannot deny that what I am doing is causing others pain, but that is truly not my motivation.*

I have dumped this not only on you, but on Patrick too, who knew nothing of what this letter contained. I am not up in a plane laughing at what I have left you both with; rather I am praying (that's rich, for latterly I've even rebelled against my own maker) that Patrick will help you with your feelings just as he has helped me with mine.

Patrick, more than anyone, seems to sense how deep these issues of selfishness, happiness, duty and responsibility reside within me, but even he does not realise how close to the edge I have been. I had even begun thinking that the world might be a better place without me, (at which point Patrick felt his own tears well up and had to swallow hard to contain them), *but I seem to have got past that of late, and have chosen, for now, the path of rebellion rather than obedience – or, for that matter, oblivion.*

Grace.

Patrick lowered the letter, allowing it to rest upon his knee as if it were now too heavy to hold. He wanted to let out a sigh; he wanted to say, 'Phew, fucking hell!' He would have liked to rush from the room and set off at speed for the airport, find Grace at the check-in desk, take hold of her hands and ...? But he knew he must attend to David's feelings before his own, and he swallowed hard and looked across at Grace's abandoned husband, who was now leaning forward, head in hands.

"David, I barely know what to say. You only had a few seconds between learning of this letter's existence and hearing its contents. Is it what you feared, or expected?"

David removed his hands from his face and slumped back in the chair; he looked crumpled, beaten.

"Not quite," he said at last. "I imagined it would be the verdict, the final judgement, announcing the end of our marriage, Grace's way of telling me it's all over and that she wants a divorce. Whereas it's neither one thing nor the other and the agony just goes on." He shook his head and exhaled deeply, "Do you think she'll come back?"

"Her letter said so. Doesn't Grace normally keep her word?"

"Apart from her vow of fidelity which she broke earlier this year, and not turning up here today, I'd have to say that she does."

"Well, no one's perfect, David." And Patrick winced, realising he'd spoken as Grace's advocate rather than attending to David's distress.

"No. You're right, none of us are perfect," David replied, clearly referring to himself and allowing Patrick to breath a silent sigh of relief.

"So, where does the letter leave you, David?"

"Still not knowing where I am."

"I know how hard that is."

"Do you?" asked David, sharply.

209

"Yes," Patrick replied firmly, returning the other man's gaze.

Silence.

"What am I going to do?" David asked, plaintively.

"As Grace hinted in her letter, David, you have options; they may be limited, but you do have options."

"Such as?"

"Well, as she said, you could use the time to come to your own decision about your marriage. Or, you could hold on, do your best to contain all the anxiety and uncertainty, and wait to see where you both are on Grace's return, then sit down together and talk it through, by yourselves, or, if you prefer, here with me."

"I think I'd like to talk now, if you've got the time?"

"Well we don't have Grace, but we do have plenty of time."

"I didn't think it would ever come to this, sitting in front of someone like you, with my marriage falling apart."

"Which bit is such a shock, your marriage becoming so unstable, or having to seek help from someone like me?"

"Both. Grace has always been so reliable, so steadfast, I could always count on her to keep her end up, if you know what I mean, with the children and the house, and ..."

"With you?"

Silence.

"You look sad, David."

David gave a sniff, reached for the tissues and buried his face in one, trying desperately to snuffle back the tears, but try as he might they kept welling over and behind the flimsy tissue his face flushed red, as if in shame. Patrick looked on, feeling real compassion for this man, who in his chosen profession was accustomed to knowing precisely what to do to remedy female complaints, who wielded his scalpel and laser with delicacy and precision, but who lacked any tool with which to remedy either his wife's unhappiness, or the disappointment lodged in his own heart.

"I am sad," he sighed, blowing his nose like trumpet, "and so damned helpless. I've known for a long time that Grace's feelings for me have changed, far longer than just this past year. A man can tell, when his wife doesn't hold him, or gather him into her the way she once did. You notice such things, but you don't say anything because you don't know what to say, and because you're afraid of what she might say if you did find words to talk about it. Every now and then, when you feel brave, you ask if she's all right. She answers that she's just tired, and so, one day, you stop asking. And you tell yourself it's just a phase she's going through, it's to do with being a mother, with her hormones, you tell yourself to give it time and it will probably pass. And when it doesn't, you tell yourself to focus on the elements that still seem to function: the children, the house, the dinner parties, the plentiful holidays, the golf club and so forth, and when that doesn't work you get your head down and throw yourself into your work because that's the one place left where you feel really effective, where you're any good as a man, and where you feel you can hold your head up because there you're needed and you amount to something. Do you understand?"

'Better than you realise,' thought Patrick.

"Yes, and it sounds very lonely," he replied.

And it took just that one word to pierce what was left of David's defences like a dart thudding into the bull's-eye. 'Lonely,' a word summing up David's inner life over the past decade and way beyond; a feeling, a condition, which he'd never diagnosed, never voiced, not even to himself, but which he now saw described the very heart of him, as accurately and precisely as any incision from his scalpel. And as Patrick watched the stream of David's tears, he knew that this one-word diagnosis applied every bit as much to himself as to his client.

David pulled one last tissue from the box, blew his nose and regained some composure, before reaching for his wallet and paying Patrick his fee.

"Hopefully," said Patrick, "I'll see you both, same time, next week. And if not, perhaps you'll let me know," and he handed David a receipt.

"I imagine at least one of us will be here," replied David.

They shook hands as they reached the outer door, "and, thank you," added David, as he gave Patrick's hand an extra firm squeeze. David stepped out into the hallway then swung round abruptly, just as Patrick was closing the door.

"Oh, may I have my letter?"

Patrick hesitated.

"Ah, err, I'm … afraid not, David."

"Why not? It's addressed to me!"

"It begins 'Dear David,' that's true, but the letter was sent to me, and I was simply asked to read it, not to hand it over."

"What's the difference?" David said accusingly.

Patrick ignored this question.

"I will hold the letter," Patrick stated firmly, "until I receive express permission from Grace to give it to you."

"Give me the letter!" demanded David.

"I'm sorry, David, that's how it has to be."

David reddened. He was a man not accustomed to being disobeyed.

"Damn the pair of you!" he shouted, turned on his heel and stormed off along the landing.

Patrick sat at his desk, heart pounding, pen poised over an empty page, unable to write a word. Instead, he stared out of the window up at the slate-grey sky, and imagined a woman, a beautiful, elusive woman, in a silver aircraft way beyond the clouds, an empty seat beside her.

Chapter Thirty

"YOU CONFIRMED BY EMAIL," said Mitchell, once they'd taken their seats, "Would you prefer I contacted you by that means rather than leave a message on your answer machine?"

"No, the phone is okay. I was at home when you rang, I just didn't want to speak at that precise moment," replied Patrick.

"Hmm. The telephone is an intrusive beast," observed Mitchell, "perhaps you hadn't made up your mind at that stage about whether you wanted to proceed with therapy?"

"It wasn't that, I just didn't feel like engaging with you again so soon."

"After being so exposed."

Patrick gave a weak smile, "I suppose it comes to us all," he replied, "how was it for you, Mitchell?"

"Do you mean here with you the other evening?" Mitchell asked, taken aback by having the spotlight turned in his direction.

"No, when you were in therapy."

"Hard going at first. Painful. Enlightening. How about you?"

'This is turning into a game of ping-pong,' thought Patrick.

"I found most of the forty sessions of my training therapy deeply frustrating," he replied.

"Frustrating?"

"It's old news, Mitchell, I don't need to talk about it."

Mitchell nodded, before asking, "And the other night, here with me?"

"Exhausting. Scary."

"Why scary?"

"Like you said, it's exposing, I was born a Catholic."

"And the anxiety about being exposed?" Mitchell's inquiry seemed laden with seductive intent. Patrick met it straight on.

"What you'll think of me."

213

"That matters, does it?"

"Seems to," replied Patrick, rather hurriedly, as if keen to close down that particular line of enquiry. He took a deep breath and leaned forward earnestly.

"Look, Mitchell, something made it feel safe for me to let go here with you the other evening, otherwise I wouldn't have come back again today. There's something I haven't voiced to anyone, and I need to talk about it, but with someone who might understand, and the way I see it that needs to be another therapist, and for now you seem to fit the bill. But I don't want you to just sit there nodding, I want to know how you see things too, or whether it's just me, am I making sense?"

Mitchell continued to stare intently, fingertips touching, brushing his lips.

"Well, why not say a little more and let's see if I catch on?"

Patrick stared hard into Mitchell's eyes.

"Do you ever feel impotent, Mitchell?"

Mitchell stared back hard but made no reply.

"Do you ever feel that there's all this stuff going on out there, wrong things, bad things, people being abused, cheated, conned and terrorised; not only in places like Iraq, but here in Britain, on the streets and in people's homes, and the terrorists aren't just Jihadist suicide bombers, they're our own guided missiles and cluster bombs, they're the crack-head burglars, the con-men who fleece old folk, the boozed-up bullies who go home from the pub and beat up wives and kids. And what allows them all to do these things is that they feel no shred of empathy with the distress of their victims. My wife watches *Crimewatch,* you know, that TV programme about real crimes? She'll watch it in bed while I try to lose myself in a book, but I can't help listening in, and I get drawn into the stories, of rape, robbery and murder, described by the victims or re-enacted dramatically on the screen. And at the end of the programme, the presenter smiles reassuringly and tells you not to worry, because the world really is a very safe place after all. At which point Maggie turns off the light and goes to sleep!"

"Whereas you?" asked Mitchell.

"Lie awake, stirred up by all this dreadful stuff out there and there's sweet fuck all I can do about it other than sit in my therapist's chair, listening to the occasional bit of fall-out."

"What would you like to do about it?" asked Mitchell.

Patrick drew a large intake of breath.

"I've been having this recurring dream. I see this plane, although sometimes it's a train or car, hurtling out of control. It's going to crash and I'm standing watching and can see what's happening. I open my mouth to shout a warning, but no sound emerges, and the plane crashes. I feel so impotent. I wake up feeling awful. It's obvious the dream is about helplessness, powerlessness and responsibility. I could join a political party, but what's the point, there's little between them any more, their main concern is spin in the service of self-preservation. Direct action is more effective, but when I listen to apologists for some anti-this or anti-that pressure group, it seems obvious that most of them are just making themselves feel superior by pointing the finger of blame elsewhere. Anyway, I'm too much of a fence-sitter, so I stare at the news and shrug my shoulders. And when, every once in a while, I hear the story of some mad gunman running amok in a school or restaurant, I shiver, not just at the awful damage and grief he inflicts, but because some part of me understands where he's coming from. I spend so much time trying to understand others, rather than judge them, but every now and then anger rises up inside; more than anger, rage, a dark rage that fills me up and frightens me."

"You're frightened of … what you could do? You mean violence?" asked Mitchell.

Patrick nodded.

"Does it ever leak out, or erupt, Patrick?"

"Something always blocks it, and it slinks away, back down inside, and I'm left feeling helpless and upset."

"What do you think blocks it, Patrick?"

Patrick heaved a sigh and looked up at the ceiling.

"All the usual stuff I suppose, years of conditioning by home, church and school. And fear."

"Fear?"

"Of what I could become, someone capable of inflicting the same monstrous damage I find so upsetting when I see it done by others."

215

"And then … you'd hate yourself?"

Patrick nodded and lowered his gaze to the floor.

At this point, Mitchell embarked upon a lengthy monologue about anger and rage being a defensive response to an earlier feeling, usually hurt or fear, and hypothesized that when Patrick observes great swathes of damage being inflicted out there in society, his identification with the pain of the victim is an echo of an earlier hurt of his own.

"And what do you think your own childhood wound might be, Patrick, that lies beneath your rage?"

Patrick recognised the pause as a prompt for him to fill the space, but he had already disengaged from Mitchell's treatise on anger and rage and its origins in early life experience, and had barely heard Mitchell's question. He'd been thinking about himself. Not the fear of becoming a monster, he knew there was little real risk of that. No, he'd moved on to thinking about being an outsider, an edge person like Degas, sitting at the margins paying attention to the stories of others, their tales of battle-scarred encounters with love and loss, squeezing out every morsel of painful learning such stories have to offer, but failing to engage at a personal level with the political and social struggles of mankind. And he felt a swathe of contempt for what he had become. And so, neatly sidestepping Mitchell's enquiry about his past, Patrick spoke instead of his present.

"Since Nuala, went off to university, and still more since Maggie left, I've become aware of a gaping hole in my life. I think it's been there a long time but I've only recently come to realise it. Being married, having a family to come home to, made me feel connected, although more with Nuala than with Maggie. I can imagine no longer being part of Maggie's life, but the thought of losing Nuala would be devastating. Maggie and I are like two plastic ducks in a bath, we bob about, give each other passing nods, occasionally bump into each other with some bit of our anatomy, but it's mostly all done from habit and memory, there's no real life in it any more. But as long as we were together, there was at least the semblance of connection. Now Maggie's moved out and Nuala's away at university … I see how disconnected I really am. Over the years I've let go my friends because their conversations seemed so banal; I resigned from the golf club because I couldn't bear the stuffy pretentiousness and ritualised sexism; I don't go to football any more because Relate saw to it that I'm too well trained in seeing both sides of every argument to allow myself the freedom and passion of being partisan. I work alone, and have no real interest in networking because the counselling profession seems like an adolescent that's fallen in love with itself, and I've little time for all that preening and posturing. Most days I see no one other than my clients and supervisees, and apart from the diminishing amount of contact with Nuala, these are the only meaningful connections I have with anyone on the planet."

"Hmm …" said Mitchell, buying a few moments to think after such an outpouring. "Tell me about those connections you make through your work, Patrick."

"They're the moments of drama, when you see someone on the edge, clinging to their defences and, at the same time, daring themselves to let go and face up to something, you know?"

"Like here the other night, and here again now?" asked Mitchell.

Patrick stared back, eyes wide and wondering.

"Yes. And my tears the other night weren't just about my marriage ending, I had them inside me years ago when I first had therapy, but the therapist worked only from the neck-up, and the tears stayed inside, except occasionally on the long drive home after each session, when they'd seep out, but never there in the sessions with her."

"Those moments you were referring to, Patrick, those dramatic moments of therapy that you find so compelling … they're what has been filling the hole in you, that you just described?"

"Yes," said Patrick, sombrely.

"Hmm. Those essential, life-giving moments of drama and intimacy," Mitchell summed up, "that are absent from other parts of your life, and which you seem only able to find in the therapy room."

"Sounds like a character flaw when you put it like that."

"How would you put it?"

"Exactly like that," said Patrick and grimaced. "And then I feel bad because it's dishonest and because therapy isn't enough, it's like I'm sitting on the sidelines like Degas, mixing colours while Rome burns."

"Don't you mean Nero, fiddling away?"

"No, I don't, I mean exactly what I said!" snapped Patrick, but comforted himself with the fact that Mitchell clearly had felt a need to flaunt his supposedly superior general knowledge.

Mitchell, aware that his hand had been duly slapped, said nothing.

"Look, Mitchell, We both know that most of us come into this profession not simply to help others, but to meet unconscious needs in ourselves, but when you sit there hour after hour, week after week, year after year, listening in from behind a screen that allows you to see more than others, sometimes more in a single hour than a client's nearest and dearest see in years of proximity, all that listening in to the pain of strangers does something to you. And one day you wake up to the fact that you don't know who you are any more unless you're sitting in front of a client.

"And that realisation leaves you feeling …?"

"Like a fraud" answered Patrick, with intent.

"A fraud?"

"Yes. For feeding off the hearts of others rather than sharing my own heart on equal terms. My clients pay me, and I know I try to do a good job, and for the most part do, but lately it's begun to feel all wrong, like I should be paying them for the opportunity they provide me to indulge in hour-long pockets of what amounts to one-sided intimacy."

Mitchell shifted in his chair, heaved a great sigh and sat up straight.

"Listen, Patrick," and he made a small stabbing gesture with his finger, "there's a heap of pain out there in the world, a vast heap of pain, and no one can go on hearing it, year after year without it getting to them. We all have to learn how to take good care of ourselves in order to avoid burn-out."

"I'm not talking about fucking burn-out, Mitchell, I'm

talking about cop-out!" Patrick snapped at the hand that seemed to have stopped feeding him and was now patting him on the head. "Don't you see? I'm talking about the insidious effect of sitting in that chair so long it grows into your skin and you no longer know where it ends and you begin!"

"You're really beating yourself up, aren't you?" and the superior tone and accusatory edge in Mitchell's voice were not lost on Patrick. "Your wife's just left you," Mitchell went on, "you're missing your daughter who has recently undergone the trauma of a termination, after doing what all children should do, namely leave home and parents in order to make her own life. And, instead of simply bearing all that grief and loss, you're now putting yourself and your chosen profession through the mangle. Well, it's your right to do so, Patrick, but be careful you don't squeeze out the very things that make you who are."

"Such as?"

"Oh, I dare say the fascination with what makes others tick; an inquiring mind; a willingness to hear and bear witness to other people's misery and pain; an ability to step back and reflect rather than rush in brandishing potted solutions that come to nothing; and a willingness to create of yourself a crucible, in which a client's fear and anguish are transformed in dramatic moments that are, well … little short of alchemy."

Patrick listened to these fine phrases, lifted straight from the book on therapy that Mitchell was currently writing, this poetic vision of therapy coupled with an analysis of Patrick's character, flowing from the lips of this would-be father who, two nights ago, was there for Patrick in a way no man had been before. And Patrick shrank inside, for in saying the unsayable about the true cost of being a therapist, it seemed that he had only raised Mitchell's own defences; and all Mitchell's hymn of praise to their mutual profession achieved was to draw from Patrick the thick bile of contempt. And Patrick realised that Mitchell had taken him as far as he could, far more in these two sessions than in the forty of his previous therapy, but, as soon as this fifty-minute hour was up, he would hand over the cheque, vacate his seat on Mitchell's vast sofa and depart his basement crucible for the final time.

Driving back through the December dark, Patrick was crying, not loudly, not angrily, but quietly, accompanied by occasional shudders deep in his chest that made his hands grip the steering wheel ever more tightly. His tears were not for the loss of Mitchell, they were more primitive than that, older than Mitchell's long and impressive career, almost as old as Patrick himself; they were the tears of disappointment that once again a father turned out to have feet of clay. He drove fast, way above the limit, in his desire to put distance between himself and his boy-place on Mitchell's sofa. Drunk on vitriol, several times he overtook quite recklessly; he was home in no time.

The search engine took precisely 0.07 seconds to locate the website for Neil's favoured porn site. Signing up was simple and immediate, the only requirement being an email address and credit card to make the $25 payment for one year's membership. Like a client, about to knock on Patrick's door, wondering whether to walk away with his or her secrets intact, or plunge headlong into an uncertain, intimate exposure, Patrick's finger hovered over the SUBMIT PAYMENT button, and then struck like a cobra. He poured a second stiff shot of Armagnac, took a deep breath, logged in, and in no time at all was browsing the Explicit Photo-Bulletin Board. Thread titles jostled like supporters outside a football ground, the tame and polite rubbing shoulders with the wild and aggressive: *Let me see your breasts ~ Hotel window/Balcony shots ~ Flashing in Public ~ Shaved Pussies ~ Hairy Pussies ~ Naked but for Pantyhose ~ Women in uniforms ~ DD breasts and above ~ Small breasts drizzled in Cum ~ 40+ ladies ~ Blowjobs, eyes at camera ~ Show what U wear under that business suit? ~ Naked at the computer.*

Patrick clicked on the *Hotel Window/Balcony* thread that revealed fourteen posts, half of which were photographs of several different women clearly enjoying making public exhibits of themselves. In one, the woman stood naked, legs apart, back to the tiny balcony, smiling at the camera as builders worked on the roof of a building in the background. On another, departing somewhat from the thread title, a woman perched on a barstool, mini-skirted legs parted to reveal a knickerless crotch. Patrick clicked on the *40+ ladies* thread, by far the fullest with some sixty posts to date, presenting an array of greater and lesser bodies, posing with various degrees of nudity, self-consciousness and sexual intent. He read each message posted in response, mostly single sentences amounting to little more than 'Wow, don't stop, show more!' From there he moved onto the threads specialising in small drizzled breasts, blowjob eyes, and naked but for pantyhose, this latter producing the first stirrings of arousal in Patrick. He checked the time and, to his surprise, fifty minutes had gone and his glass was empty. He replenished it, clicked *REGISTER* and when asked what *USERNAME* he was entering, without thinking, typed in the word *Degas*. In seconds, the screen informed him that Degas was now active and he was free to commence posting. Degas returned to the pantyhose thread and posted two appreciative replies to photos of different women, the second of which received a *Thank you, Degas, x* along with another photo and a message asking him what he liked most about her body. Degas typed his reply, more fulsome and appreciative than the poster might have expected. Only as he hit *POST MESSAGE* did it occur to him that *Hot-Glenda* might well not be Glenda at all, but Glenda's husband or boyfriend, and that Glenda, if that is indeed her name, might not even be aware that her naked charms were being displayed in cyberspace for an anonymous world to pore over.

He took a deep breath and hit the button: *START NEW THREAD*. What to call it? He settled on *Please post for Degas,* poured another brandy and continued browsing the board. Within a few minutes his thread indicated a response had been posted. He opened it to find a professional quality photograph of 'Sandi' a well-tanned, pear-shaped blonde of around 50, sprawled on a sheepskin rug in front of a fake-coal fire, wearing only fishnets tights, her heavily made up eyes trained on the camera lens. And, underneath, ran the following message:

Degas, dear heart, missed you, where have you been lately?
Patrick froze, heart pounding, before typing his reply.
Been busy, too busy – good to see you, Sandi.

221

Sandi's response came soon enough: another photo, this time of her standing alone, an elbow leaning on the mantelpiece, mimicking the pose and manner of a Victorian gentleman, albeit in a black lace, open crotch, body stocking, which made him laugh aloud. By the time he'd sent an innocuous but appreciative reply, there was another post, this time from *Moll,* whose photograph revealed a voluptuous, less than youthful, pale-skinned body, sporting dark red nails and black glossy bra and panties. Less staged than Sandi's photographs, and of poorer technical quality, the image somehow exerted a greater pull; or perhaps it was that the face, blurred above the lips, offered no accusatory stare for him to defend against. The photo carried no accompanying message.

Patrick typed a response.

Welcome to Degas' thread, sweet glossy Moll ... you're lovely, and indeed most welcome!

He hit the button and took a sip from his glass. Her next photo showed her kneeling forward on the floor in the same bra from which an ocean of cleavage sucked at the lens. This time, a brief message accompanied the pic, *Still lurking then, Degas? You've been quiet. I thought I might have driven you away the other night?*

I'm here, and they are lovely, he replied, *a soft Degas kiss for my sweet glossy visitor, place it where you will, and may it bring a moment's tender comfort in the long, cold night, x*

My, Degas, aren't you in mellow mood this evening? Her response was almost immediate and accompanied by another photo, this time bra removed, hands cupping her ample breasts.

After last time, Degas, I swore I'd never post for you again. Glad to see you've softened up, you know, words can hurt, even here.

I'm sorry, Moll, Degas replied, *I don't always say what I really mean and it comes across all wrong. Anyway, I'd been drinking. Thanks for giving me another chance.*

A few moments later another photo was posted, this time Moll's head thrown back, her fingers squeezing hard on her nipples. He read the message.

Look, Degas, it's just harmless fun here, you shouldn't take it so serious, but neither should you think that we women who post pics don't have feelings, because we do ... drunk or not, they're your words and pictures, Degas, and you gotta learn to take responsibility for their impact. If I want a picture of your dick splashed all over my thread I'll ask for it, ok? Here's one more for you, kid. Gotta run, see you around, x.

He scrolled down to reveal Moll's next photo, sitting cross-legged and naked but for hold-up stockings and a wide-brimmed black felt hat pulled down to hide her face, her tuft of red pubic hair peeking out at the camera. And as he stared, and re-read her comment, tears of frustration welled up inside and he knew not whether they belonged to Neil, Degas, or himself. He heard Beth's voice calling from somewhere far off, 'Stay with the pain,' gently, firmly, encouraging him to pick away at Moll's message; and he did so, until he was left with just the contradictory injunctions: ... *you shouldn't take it so serious*, and *you gotta learn to take responsibility*. A classic double-bind if ever there was one, and a recipe for madness. He chewed over her use of the word 'kid', which was how her words left him feeling: young, crass, and chastised.

"Fuck it!" he cussed, spitting the words at the screen, "how come my feelings don't matter?"

The appeal bore a whiney quality that he did not recognise, and he wondered where it had come from. Too tired, to enquire further into that now, he slumped back in the chair, clicked *LOG OUT*, shut down the computer and waited till the screen went black. He then gathered up bottle and glass and retreated downstairs, where, opting for aural stimulation over visual, he fell asleep listening to Leonard Cohen's erotic masterpiece, *Chelsea Hotel No.2*, left on 'repeat play'. It seemed a lot more rewarding.

Chapter Thirty-One

PATRICK OVERSLEPT, WHICH MEANT he had to hurry to the office in time for his first supervisee of the day, but also ensured that he was spared having time to reflect upon the events of the night before. He arrived just ahead of his first appointment. It was one of those rare days when he got by listening largely on willpower alone. His skills may have appeared smooth but he knew that, for once, his heart wasn't in them, and he was more than relieved when at last he was able to lock up and head for home.

He spent the evening flicking through old photo albums, and a carrier bag of loose photographs; windows on better days. He marvelled at how together his little family appeared when Nuala was tiny, a clenched fist of a family beaming up at the lens; although once Nuala had reached the toddler stage, he noticed how they revealed an absence of physical contact between his wife and daughter. There it was, in photo after photo, always a slither of daylight between them, as if each were afraid of something contagious.

He was surprised how youthful he looked back in his twenties, and how little Maggie's body had changed over the years; only three years younger than him, the difference now looked more like ten. 'Perhaps, like Sal, I should get myself in shape,' and he shuddered at the thought of joining a gym. At the bottom of the bag, an old infant school photo of Nuala made him well up, while more recent ones filled him with envy. Her life was just beginning. His felt marooned.

In the morning he shopped and returned home to prepare two large dishes, and portioned up the results up for the freezer, for the simple reason that it felt purposeful. He idled the afternoon away watching sport on TV. Afterwards, he drank, until he fell asleep on the sofa.

Sunday morning, he felt energised and gathered together Nuala's Christmas present, wrapping paper, scissors and sticky tape, and stowed the bag in the boot of the car and noticed that his car was filthy, its number plate so mud-splattered to be almost illegible. This close to Christmas, the service station was busier than usual and the lull in the weather meant there was a queue for the car wash. He hadn't time to wait, besides, his old soft top would only spring more leaks. He ran a wet paper towel over the lights and number plate and filled up with petrol. He went across to pay and examined two black plastic baskets stuffed with bunches of flowers but the colours were gaudy and he passed them over and instead made a detour to the hypermarket where he purchased a bunch of lilies and a tall glass vase.

Maggie greeted him warmly, and he was glad to see her, but neither initiated any touch. As he stepped across the threshold he presented the flowers and vase, almost apologetically, explaining that she didn't seem to have taken any vases when she left. She smiled and thanked him, making no reference to the two new glass vases of lilies already ensconced, one in the open plan lounge-kitchen-diner, the other tucked away in her bedroom. She didn't need to, for as he followed her through from the small hallway, Patrick's eyes immediately fell on the former, containing five fine stems rather than the three he had just purchased.

"Oh well," he said, giving a resigned shrug.

"Pat, they're lovely," she said reassuringly, "A girl can't have too many lilies."

He was struck by her use of the term, 'girl', he liked it; it seemed to imply such faith in the future.

"I'll put them in water for now and find a place for them later. Coffee?" she asked.

No response. He was too busy mulling over the companion term, 'boy', and how removed it felt from the middle-aged man he now was, and he realised how much he envied her.

"Pat? Coffee?" she asked again.

"Sorry … yes, love some."

"Your usual espresso, or can I tempt you with a cappuccino? I've bought a new machine."

Patrick was taken aback. He was the one who had insisted on purchasing a Gaggia coffee maker, and who endeavoured, in vain, to create that elusive perfect espresso, whereas she'd always been content with the results of any old cafetière. This contraption was of pink metal; it looked chic, and expensive.

"Yes, why not?" he replied, keen to see her use it and aware of her eagerness to demonstrate her newfound prowess.

"Put some music on if you like, there's only a handful of CDs I'm afraid, mostly classical."

He regarded the portable CD player in the corner; it looked cheap.

"I'll get something better in due course," she called across as he sifted through the few CDs.

He saw this statement, along with the expensive new coffee maker, as proof of her commitment to this new life and it produced mixed feelings in him; he enjoyed the evidence of her valuing herself, but her words indicated there was little likelihood of any reversal in the direction she had taken. He put on a classical CD, the Rodriguez Guitar Concerto, knowing it was one of her favourites, and settled on one of the two small leather sofas that sat facing each other.

"The flat was already furnished," she called, from across the room, "which means I can afford the odd coffee machine and two new cups. Like them?" she asked, handing him a cup and saucer with Picasso's signature scrawled around the side alongside a thumbnail print of *Child With A Dove*. He hoped his smile concealed his discomfort at the thought that his were not the first male lips to drink from it. 'It's a bit sad,' he thought to himself, 'when you depend upon a dose of jealousy to fan the flames of desire.' He watched her settle herself on the sofa opposite, her boyish body slender and petite, in white vest, black linen shirt and trousers, and he realised that if he was meeting her now for the very first time, he'd perhaps have fancied her more than ever, but assumed that she was out of his league. He noticed her cup also bore Picasso's signature, but her print was of *The Old Guitarist*.

"It's nice," he said, taking another sip and looking around.

"It's simple, and it's not got much character, I know, and the noise from the other apartments is a bit of a pain, but it's bright and airy. It will do for now."

He was tempted to be say, 'I meant the coffee,' or even, '… your body!' but felt too unsure of his ground to bowl that kind of googly.

"And how's Gavin?"

She took two slow sips from her cappuccino.

"I'm not sure. He's going through a lot of change, in his work, and … well … let's just say he's going through a difficult time."

Silence.

"Froth."

"What?"

"On your top lip."

"Oh sorry, I mean, thanks," and uncharacteristically, she wiped it off on the back of her hand then looked about uncertainly for a tissue. He produced one from his jacket pocket, handed it across and as she snatched it from his fingers he saw her tears well up. Conscious of his attention, she hurriedly placed the cup and saucer on the coffee table, splashing a trail of milky froth across the polished beech veneer.

"Oh shit," she spluttered, and ran from the room.

She returned to find Patrick mopping up the spill with a J-cloth he'd located in the cupboard under the sink.

"Pat, hold me … please?" She stood before him, shoulders drooping, and he put his arms around her and stroked her back much as a parent might comfort a young child.

"What is it?" he said at last, once she'd stopped crying and her head lay still upon his shoulder.

She raised her head to look at him.

"Let's sit down," she said.

They squeezed together on one of the sofas, and he held her hand as she told him about Gavin's wife announcing her pregnancy after years of failing to conceive, and how the news had cast doubts over her own relationship with Gavin.

"You sure she's not making it up just to get him back, or to spite you?" he asked.

"The thought had crossed my mind, but Gavin doesn't think she'd use it as a ploy, it means too much to her for that."

Patrick raised his eyebrows, cynically.

"Anyway," Maggie went on, "she doesn't know about me. Well, she may suspect he's been seeing someone, but he hasn't told her. Besides, he didn't leave her because of me." And she realised, as she heard herself speak the words, how desperately she wished he had.

"What's he going to do?"

"I don't know. He doesn't know. He says he's not going back to her, but ..." Her words were strangled as she lost her composure once again.

"You think he might," he said gently.

She covered her face in her hands to stifle her tears.

"You love him?" His delivery implied that the question was at least part rhetorical.

"Hmm," she nodded.

"I'm sorry."

"What for, it's not your fault."

"I know. I'm just sorry you're so sad," he whispered.

"It's the price we pay for loving someone," she said.

"I'm sure that's another of mine that I'll have spouted somewhere along the line."

"You've spouted a lot of things at me over the years, Pat. You see I do listen. I think a lot about what you say, the way you talk about life, relationships and so forth. At first it all seemed so new and profound, hearing a man talk like that; you really made me think about things. I was almost in awe of you when you underwent your counsellor training and started coming up with that kind of stuff. I tried to take it all on board, but it soon became threatening, I was afraid you'd turn the spotlight on me and start analysing all my faults. I'd always thought you were cleverer than me to begin with so when you began all that deep psychodynamic stuff in your training I imagined it was only a matter of time before you'd become bored with my world of sales meetings, product launches, and carpet tiles. And you did, didn't you?"

"Yes," he admitted, with no trace of anger or apology.

"Then as time went on I got fed up with your know-all insights into relationships, when you didn't seem to want to see what was going on under your own nose. You didn't seem to see or care that you and I were drifting apart, and for all your theorising and pithy quotations on the human condition you didn't seem to want to do a thing about it."

"It wasn't a case of not wanting to," he replied, "you were getting more and more confident, and increasingly successful out there in a way I certainly couldn't match, and, to be honest, it seemed you no longer needed me the way you once did."

"You're right, I didn't need you as much, but that didn't mean I didn't still want you."

He seemed flustered by this for a moment.

"Well, anyway," he replied, glossing over her distinction, "I didn't have a clue what to do about it, apart from throwing myself into work. And the kind of work I do provided a plentiful supply of the excitement and intimacy that was missing between us."

"But look at what I saw, Pat. You always had time for your clients, you'd sit there at the dinner table when we had friends round, and you'd be thinking about your bloody clients, I knew you were. It was only Nuala who could get through to you, only her you had eyes for, only her who could snap you out of your therapist mode; you'd laugh and play with her in a way you never did with me. And if it wasn't Nuala, it was all those intimate connections you enjoyed with the other students in your Relate training, nearly all of them women; and of course, there were always your clients, your ever present clients, so needy, so demanding and oh-so bloody fascinating. I just couldn't compete with them."

Patrick threw back his head, closed his eyes and let out a huge sigh.

"What?" she asked, urgently.

He shook his head.

"Maggie, this isn't doing any good. If we were going to have this conversation we should have done it years ago, and I'm still not sure anything would have turned out very different."

"I thought you believed in talking?"

"I do, but it doesn't necessarily change anything."

"What do you want to change?" she threw the question at his feet.

229

He looked away and shook his head.

"I don't know any more," he replied.

"Then what's the point of it all?" she asked, beseechingly.

"Of what?"

"Of talking, if it can't change anything?"

It was a good question, one he had to ponder before attempting an answer.

"I suppose the point of talking," he said, wearily, "is to try to build bridges, to make contact across the spaces that divide us, it's how we find out who we are and what is real for each of us. It's how we discover that we're maybe not as alone as we thought," and Patrick realised his words sounded like they came straight from a marriage counsellor training manual or some self-help guide to better communication, but he didn't know how else to say it. "But sometimes," he added, "talking helps us discover the exact opposite, that people aren't who we think they are, and that includes ourselves." Yes, that felt more real.

"But don't you see, Pat, that's why I want to talk with you now, not to change the past, I know there is no going back, certainly not to the time we started drifting apart. Nor do I think me moving back in would be a good thing, despite how alone I feel in this apartment much of the time, and the fact that I well up with tears umpteen times each day, and cry myself to sleep at night. I've got to go through this, Pat, not only to see where things go with Gavin, but to find out more about myself, and what I want from the rest of my life."

He thought that last sentence made her sound bold, and he realised he quite admired her. He even considered telling her so but guessed it would only sound patronising. In the event, he played safe.

"Maggie, I didn't imagine you invited me round here this morning to see if we could get back together; I assumed you want to be with Gavin. But despite everything I know to the contrary, I still beat myself up for not being able to make things right ... between us, between you and Nuala, and for that matter between you and your mother, and when I fail, I feel awful, a shutter comes down and I back off. I know there are no magic wands, but there's a childish part of me that still

230

wishes I could wave one and put everything right, because I can't just ignore what I feel about you."

That last phrase was issued without thinking, and he felt immediately anxious, as if the words were an untrained puppy that squeezed out through a gap in the fence, and he was scared it'd run out into the road. It did, and Maggie promptly reached out and grabbed it by the collar.

"And what do you feel about me, Pat?" her question was slow and deliberate.

He paused, took a deep breath and stared into her face.

"I'm not sure any more, I'm really not sure." He guessed it was the last thing she wanted to hear, but he knew it was the only answer he could safely vouch for.

Wearily, she closed her eyes and shook her head.

"Oh for fuck's sake, Pat, I told you that you should see someone."

"I have."

She looked at him hard.

"And? Or shouldn't I ask?"

Silence. He looked sad.

"I'm sorry," she said, tenderly.

"I went twice this week, and saw someone I thought was someone else. It happens all the time." She leaned into him and rested her head against his chest so that he had to extricate his left arm in order to embrace her, and they sat like that for some time in perfect silence.

"I must go," he said at last.

And despite longing to lie in his arms and be made love to, she knew she would not ask him to stay; just as she knew that he would not offer that part of himself to her again. At least not today.

At the front door, she kissed him lightly on the cheek, held the lapels of his jacket and patted them down needlessly; it was a gesture he'd last received from his mother on the morning of his marriage, a gesture he found deeply unsettling, then, and now.

"Take care," she said.

"And you."

And he drove away without looking up at her window. If he

had, he might have noticed the tiny movement of the slatted wooden blinds before she finally shut out the low winter sun. He drove home even slower than his usual tempo, and it was only as he reversed onto the drive that he remembered Nuala's present and wrapping paper, still in the boot of the car. He sent a text the moment he got inside. *Forgot to give u Nuala's present ... an iPod, was going to leave it so u could add to parcel and send, x.*

The reply was immediate and took him by surprise. *Post it. – Just spoke to her. Am still off work so going up to see her first thing tomorrow x.*

Just then he heard the letterbox rattle; he found an envelope on the mat. It had been addressed with the wrong house number and his neighbour must have realised the error. It contained a Christmas card from Rose-Roisin, bearing a striking photograph of Croagh Patrick, Ireland's holy mountain, rising through the mist. Patrick fetched the unopened presentation bottle of Paddy she had sent him last Christmas, poured a small measure and surprised himself by locating her number and lifting the phone.

"Rose, it's Patrick!"

"Padraig! It's good to hear your voice, so you got my message?"

"Message?"

"I left a message on your machine, you know how I hate those things."

"No, I've been out, I just got your Christmas card and thought I'd phone."

"I posted it before receiving yours with the news about you and Maggie, I'm really sorry Padraig. How are you? Are you both okay?"

He would have preferred to tell her how her voice had changed, and how much more Irish she sounded than he recalled from their previous conversation.

"Yes, I've just got back from where she's living." ''Living' ... what a powerful, confident word,' he thought to himself, so much more established than merely 'staying'. "We're okay, Rose, I think ... we're not fighting, anyway."

"Good, that's good, though if it does come to blows, be sure to keep your guard up, little brother!"

"I will," he smiled. "Nuala's well, she's away at university up in Newcastle."

"I know, she writes me every now and then, which is more than I can say for her father. I got a card from her just this week, with a real nice letter inside, not one of those round-robin things. I gather there's a new boyfriend on the scene, and she told me about her spot of trouble, and that you'd been very supportive, but she didn't tell me about you and Maggie. I presume she knows? You go easy on her, she's a real go-it-alone one that niece of mine; I like that, but it's not always for the best. Are you still there, Padraig, you've gone awful quiet?"

"I never could get a word in with you, Rose."

"Listen, Padraig, you start calling me Roisin, or I'll go on calling you Padraig, deal?"

"Deal, Roisin!"

"That's my little brother. Now, Patrick, when are you coming across to the holy ground? What about a Donegal Christmas?"

"Roisin, I haven't even thought about Christmas. Nuala's going …"

"… To her young man's parents, I know. And Maggie's at her new address, on her own?"

"Maybe, I don't know."

"So that leaves you. So, when are you coming?"

"Roisin …" Patrick groaned.

"I know, I know, you need time to think about it. Jeezus, you're a one, you never could do spontaneous could you, little brother? Now, when you've thought about it long enough to see what a good idea it is, you give me a ring, let me know which day you're coming and I'll meet you at Derry airport. You can fly direct from Stansted for a pittance, Manchester for a bit more. Okay? You call me now, don't go leaving it another year!"

"I'll call you, Roisin," he promised, and realised he probably meant it.

And that night, for the first time since Maggie moved out,

Patrick climbed into bed and did not curl up on her side of the mattress, but lay back in the middle of the bed, gazing at the ceiling and pondering the likelihood of picking up a seat on a flight to Derry just before Christmas. And whether, tomorrow morning, he should telephone Sheffield Wednesday and enquire what price a season ticket for the remaining fixtures.

Chapter Thirty-Two

EN ROUTE TO HIS office and his second appointment with Gina, Patrick called at the post-office and sent the parcel off to Nuala 'special delivery'.

The answer-machine indicated one new message but when played back revealed nothing but silence. Gina arrived several minutes early and Patrick asked her to take a seat on the sofa in the reception area as he busied himself at his desk at the far end of the room. He could feel her eyes scrutinizing the surroundings, and taking him in too. He stole a sideways glance and at once regretted it, for he took in not only an expanse of opaque-stockinged thigh visible below her short black skirt, but also a smile that indicated she had registered his look. With still four minutes remaining until the time of her appointment he stowed his papers in the desk drawer, pushed back his chair and stood to face her.

"Shall we begin?"

Gina smiled again, and remained still just long enough for him to have to wait for her.

To his surprise, she settled herself this time in the chair furthest from Patrick's, although its angle meant it was more or less directly facing his. More predictably, she crossed her legs, allowing him yet another clear view of her thighs. Her slender legs pulled in his gaze like two powerful magnets, but he forced himself to keep his eyes trained on her face. Gina's own eyes were like dark saucers, and her lips gave the impression of sucking on a sweet, but Patrick guessed it was only her tongue, probing the inside of her mouth, sliding against her soft fleshy cheeks, its tip slipping between her lips, 'Get a grip, Patrick!' he told himself, 'she's toying with you. Look at her eyes, look at her eyes!' And he did, but the bombardment of sensual communication continued as his peripheral vision caught the movement of her high-heeled ankle boot, its pointed toe circling enticingly. 'For Christ's sake, keep your eyes on her face!' he scolded inwardly, 'and get to work!' He wondered, momentarily, whether to address the flirting that was so clearly in evidence, but it was still early in the session, and Gina would no doubt only act all innocent and turn it back on him. He decided for now to ride it out.

"So Gina, you've come a second time, does it feel any different?" He was oblivious to the pun but Gina was not; her lips parted and then closed, and her eyes betrayed a glimmer of a smile.

"Ye-es," she mouthed the word ultra-slowly then made him wait for the elaboration, "less of a step into the unknown: wondering whether this is the right place, wondering what it will be like inside, what *you* will be like? In fact, this time, I was quite looking forward to coming. Is that a good thing, do you think, Patrick, to look forward to coming?"

This time the wordplay was not lost on Patrick, nor the sense of being a mouse toyed with by a feline huntress.

"That remains to be seen," he replied enigmatically, aware that his response was yet another move in the game.

Gina, however, respected him rather more for this reply, indicating that he might not be quite so easily winnable, after all.

"Where do we start?" she asked, innocently. "I've already told you the basic problem."

"Yes, you keep falling for married men," he reiterated, and immediately wondered what had compelled him to fill the gap and state what they both already knew to be the case. 'Trying to impress her that I'm on the ball; watch your step, Patrick,' he told himself.

"I don't set out with that intention," she said, "I just happen to meet someone, a mutual attraction develops and by the time I find out he's got a wife and kids, something's already started."

"Makes you sound like an innocent victim of circumstance. Is that really how you see it?" he asked pointedly.

"In the early stages, yes. But I don't see myself as entirely innocent. When I discovered the present one was married, I remember thinking, oh no, not again, and knew I should have done a runner."

"What stopped you?"

"He did."

"How?"

"By being so sensitive and considerate. We had met for lunch, and while we were perusing the menu he said he was sorry but he had something important to tell me, and that he realised it might make things difficult for me. He said he quite understood if it meant I wanted to call a halt there and then and say goodbye, but he had to take that risk, because he already liked and respected me too much to let me think he was single, when he wasn't."

"And you said …"

"Oh!" She mouthed the word dramatically, making it round, soft, and laden with understanding.

"He asked if I wanted him to call me a taxi, and I said, we might as well eat now we're here. And so we did. After lunch we parted, without kissing or making any further arrangement, we just shook hands and two days later I received a little card, saying simply, *Lunch with you was the highlight of my week. A delight. Thank you.* A few days later flowers arrived, and the following day he called me; that was two years ago, the rest is history."

"Smooth operator," commented Patrick.

"You think so?" she asked, eyes wide.

"Yes," said Patrick, suddenly wondering if his comment had been applied to the right object.

"You see, I trusted him," Gina went on, "he made me believe I was special, that I was the highlight, not only of his week, but of his life, and it was only a matter of time before we'd be together. Pathetic isn't it? Well, over the past few months it's become increasingly apparent he has no intention of leaving his wife, even though he insists it's only a matter of time. I just don't believe him any more, but I'm in too deep, and I don't want to admit that another long relationship has been a total waste."

"So you've been in this situation before? How did the previous one end?"

"He was my dentist, it went on for almost a year until his

wife found out and he swilled me away with the mouthwash."

Patrick ignored the quip.

"So men dump you, is that the pattern?"

And for the first time, he thought he saw Gina's chin wobble, he found it half-convincing.

"… And that leaves you feeling …?"

"Like a piece of shit wiped off someone's boot."

It was a powerful metaphor, and he was tempted to ask if it evoked echoes of an earlier experience, back in the past, but chose not to go down that particular avenue; too early, he decided, and it would only lead to a neat and superficial interpretation, whose only profit would be to illuminate his cleverness.

"So, tell me what happens to the piece of shit."

"She dries up, hides herself away in her work and vows to do without men, until everything gets on top of her and she ends up going to her doctor and getting a prescription for Prozac, which she takes until the depression starts to lift, her libido kicks in again and the whole merry-go-round starts up again."

"And she feels?" he asked, staying with her use of the third person.

"Tired! Tired of the whole fucking game."

Patrick's mind was racing, pondering Gina's effective use of the third person to create a certain distance and allow a more honest perspective on herself, and her juxtaposition of the swearword and sporting metaphor. Is fucking always a game in this woman's world, or was this merely a device to convey her anger, and if so, with whom or what is she angry?

"Games," he said, "are playful, but they can also be bloody and have casualties."

He thought perhaps he saw her eyes glisten.

"I'm worried," she said, "that if I go on like this, I'll end up a lonely old hag, because people such as Max, that's the current specimen, won't be interested in me any more when I've lost my looks and figure, and by then everyone else will be happily married."

After responding to her fear of aging and being left on the shelf, Patrick returned to her use of the term 'specimen' and told her he was intrigued by its echoes of a fish caught on a line by means of deception, and yet she appeared to be the one who gets hooked, secreted away for a time in the keep-net, before ultimately being released and discarded.

At this, the first small tears slipped their moorings only to be gathered in by the application of one his tissues to prevent her mascara and eyeliner running, an endeavour: so carefully and precisely carried out that Patrick was for the very first time truly convinced of her vulnerability.

"Hmm. It's not a good place to be is it," he said, not unkindly, "and from what you're saying, Gina, the future looks even worse."

There was no trace of condemnation in his voice. Even though it was plain she was no innocent victim in these affairs, hers was *not* a good place to be, and unless she assumed control of what was driving her, her future did appear bleak.

"You said," he added, "that when you're older, you'll be less attractive to the more errant married men, by which time all the decent ones will be happily married. But the divorce figures suggest there are unattached men around, how come you only seem to meet married ones?"

"I don't know," she said, dismissively, back in her role as Miss Innocent. "Maybe that's something we need to look at," and she cast him a come hither look.

They spent the rest of the time putting in place some other pieces of the jigsaw such as her dismissive regard for women, which included her female friends, relegated in status once she gets involved with a new man, as if the males of the species are the one true currency.

"But you're a woman," Patrick stated, "so what does that say about your own value and status? Maybe that's something you might think about between now and next time?"

He checked the clock, perfect.

"As I said last time, Gina, there'll be a gap now for the Christmas holiday period. It means our next appointment will be on Monday the 7th of January." Gina uncrossed her legs and reached down for her handbag, a manoeuvre that instantly drew Patrick's eyes to the shape of her breasts. He corrected himself by reaching for next year's diary.

"Unless, that is," he added, perusing the pages, "you could come on Wednesday the 2nd?"

"Yes, although that would be my first day back at work and I might have to work late, so could it be early evening?" she said with a smile.

"Wednesday the 2nd, at six, how would that be?"

"Oh, you couldn't make it six-thirty, could you, getting through town in the rush-hour traffic, you know how it is?"

"I'm afraid not," he answered, for no good reason other than he needed to satisfy himself that he was immune to her charms.

"Oh well, six it is," she said, "I'll be strict with myself and leave at five, I realise how important it is to come on time."

Patrick remained tight-lipped, for, although he didn't realise it, this time Gina was the one oblivious to the innuendo.

She gathered up her handbag and looked across to him.

"Thank you, thank you so much, Patrick. I can't say I feel in great shape to face work after coming here," and she immediately apologised, "I didn't mean to suggest you haven't been helpful, I meant …"

"I understand," he interjected, a little too reassuringly.

Gina just looked at him and smiled.

"Is a cheque all right, I haven't had a chance to get to the bank?"

"A cheque will be fine."

And she leaned forward on the coffee table to write it out, using an elegant black fountain pen that perfectly complimented her long red nails and the heavy silver rings adorning her slender fingers.

'It's a cliché,' thought Patrick, 'but my God it works.'

Patrick stood at the window, watching Gina stride across the car park towards the black Mazda sports coupé parked over in the far corner. A window-cleaner up a ladder attending to the far bank of windows clocked her at once, his gaze fixing her like a laser beam, he dropped his cloth, causing Patrick to wonder how many accidents Gina's presence might have triggered as she went so innocently about her way. Patrick's gaze caught up again just as she reached her car, and he savoured the distant glimpse of her skirt riding up high as she climbed into the driver's seat. As the car moved off he reminded himself that its driver was a troubled and unhappy woman, bent on presenting the world with the only thing she thought it really valued about her. And here were two men confirming just that.

He settled at his desk and wrote all this down in his notes. He added a large 'S' at the foot of the page before filing the sheet away in its new buff folder. He checked the first week of next year's diary: Gina on the 2nd, supervision with Beth on the 5th. He knew how much he needed the latter, and how much he was dreading it.

With just one supervisee, an old stalwart, due at two o'clock, Patrick still had two hours to fill. He locked up and headed off to a local pub, stopping at a newsagent's on the way. The pub served a good steak sandwich and he enjoyed a relaxed and extended lunch, a rare treat, even if he ate alone with only the newspaper for company. He concentrated on the sports pages: a good result for the Owls, they were climbing the table and things were looking up. By the time he parked in his usual spot back at the Mill, he felt better than in a long time and told himself he should get out and do this more often.

Chapter Thirty-Three

BEFORE SETTING OFF FOR work, Patrick sent Mitchell an email cancelling the following Thursday's appointment, stating he had decided not to proceed with therapy at the current time. As he pressed 'SEND' he reflected on having chickened out, not so much of therapy, but of informing Mitchell why he was giving up on him. An explanation would at least have provided Mitchell with something challenging to take to supervision.

In aborting therapy at such an early stage, Patrick felt not only relief, but sadness, for what he had tried to explain to Mitchell in that second session was something, so far-reaching in its implications, he had never dared voice it before. 'Burnout,' Mitchell had chosen to call it, quite missing the point. 'Burnout,' rather like shell-shock, at least carries some semblance of honour by pointing to the hell you've been through. Patrick had no desire to hide behind false notions of burnout. What he felt himself to be suffering from, and from which he saw no possible escape route, was something far more insidious: the creeping realisation that his considerable training in seeing both sides of situations, and all his years of listening in, had effectively conditioned him out of the capacity for spontaneous, impassioned engagement with his fellow human beings. Patrick thought at first he might have found, in Mitchell, a man who, even if he did not share the condition, could at least imagine and explore what it might be like. 'Clients give you more than one chance,' Patrick was fond of telling student counsellors and supervisees, 'if you don't hear what they say the first time, they'll say it again, perhaps even a third time before giving up on you.' Patrick realised he'd given Mitchell only one chance, but his wound was gaping and Patrick couldn't face the prospect of revealing it so soon again. Therefore, he'd abandoned his place on Mitchell's sofa and deleted client-Patrick. He imagined Mitchell sitting at his basement desk, writing him off, *Case closed – by client.*

But as the morning progressed, with Patrick attending to various admin chores, he found that Mitchell wasn't to be so easily extinguished from his thoughts. It seemed there was more at work here than Mitchell's defences. Reluctantly, Patrick began to listen in to his own. A father's voice, that's what he realised he'd gone looking for, and what he'd always lacked. A father's voice at the end of a phone line, 'Dad, thinking of applying for a mortgage, what do you think?' 'Dad, we're decorating, any ideas on removing woodchip?'' 'Dad, I've been picked for the First Team, come and see me play?' And he realised this last request was the one carrying the most weight. Financial advice you can get on the high street. DIY tips you can get from a book. But it needs a real live father to come and watch you play. And Patrick thought of the empty space in his wedding photo, the empty space beside his mother. On the day that he stood up so publicly, trying to be a man. And how he had never been able to raise a glass with his own father and drink to them both being dads. And how he could not phone his father up now, and say, 'Dad, Maggie's left me…' It wasn't just that his dad was dead; he was never there when he was alive.

And he remembered Mitchell's voice that first evening, a voice rich as velvet; the kind of voice a son could climb into the lap of, breathe in the strong whiff of tobacco, and wrap himself up in its hearty maleness. Mitchell had been there for him that first night; more truly present than any man before, and he'd given Patrick an hour of damn good fathering, the kind of fathering that allows a boy to be tender without being pulverised. And Patrick heaved a sigh of regret at having sent the email. He glanced at the BACP Directory up on the shelf; there must be other experienced therapists, as good, if not better, than Mitchell. Or maybe he should bite the bullet, tell Mitchell he'd changed his mind again and ask to be restored? He tapped his fingers on the jotter, removed Mitchell's card from his wallet, and rang the number. It was engaged. He waited a minute before trying again. Still engaged. He waited a few more seconds, dialled directory enquiries and requested the number of the Sheffield Wednesday ticket office.

243

At a table by the window overlooking the Tyne, sat two women a generation apart, hunched over *lattes*, oblivious to the other customers. The younger one's chin rested between the heels of her hands, her palms cradling her cheeks as she stared intently into the other's features. The older one avoided eye contact, her face and hands making constant adjustments, as if endeavouring to squeeze from the recesses of heart and mind some explanation that might satisfy, not only herself, but also her young and reluctant companion. Suddenly the younger woman let out an exclamation that could have been shock, but was quickly followed by anger, and the two young men at the nearby table ceased their conversation and were now looking across as the older woman's hand reach out to calm her agitated companion.

"Don't shush me!" the younger woman hissed, and one of the men resumed his own story in a vain attempt to drag his friend's attention back where it belonged. Moments later, a chair leg scraped the floor and the younger woman ran for the exit. Her companion rummaged in her handbag, slapped a five-pound note on the table and headed off in hot pursuit.

The man's story was now fully on hold.

"A lover's tiff?" he suggested, to the one who had been more engrossed in the goings-on at the adjacent table.

"No. Mother and daughter," said his friend, assuredly. "The mother's tasty. Probably envy," he suggested, with a practised nonchalance.

"Whose?"

"The daughter's, of course, can't be easy having such an attractive woman for a mother."

"Could be the other way round, daughter's got youth and a firm body on her side."

"Huh! You clearly didn't clock the mother, anyway, the trouble with you is you only hear what your cock tells you!"

"And you're so very different?

"No, it's just that mine's more discerning."

A black VW pulled off the A1 into a service station, and parked over to one side, away from the amenities. The woman driver made a call on her mobile; she was crying. Just when she expected to be diverted to voice-mail, the other person answered.

"Hello?" he clearly hadn't checked to see who was calling.

"Gavin, it's me."

There was a brief pause.

"Hi, um, can I call you back?"

"Yes, no, I'm on the motorway, I'm upset. I need to talk."

"Look I really can't talk now, I'm at Vicky's."

Maggie's mouth froze, and her reply came from her thumb, which instantly aborted the call. She quickly tried Pat at his office but got only the answer machine; she hesitated, but left no message.

Chapter Thirty-Four

THE SEASON TICKET DROPPED onto the mat first thing Wednesday morning and Patrick found it on his return from work. He browsed the accompanying fixture list; if he did make the flight to Ireland he wouldn't miss any home games as the Owls were playing away over the Christmas period. He flitted through the booklet of numbered tickets that provided a new structure to his existence beyond that of his work diary, and he wondered how many he would ever use.

He stared out of the window into the cul-de-sac where every house but his stood festooned in festive lights of some description: a giant illuminated Santa clambered over one roof; lines of simple white bulbs draped through tree branches; neon-blue icicles clung to the fascia board of the large property in the far corner, and Patrick felt a small shard of defiance at his being the only house devoid of any testimony to the season. The Christmas cards still lay in a pile on the breakfast bar; he thought of standing them up on the mantle-piece but made no move to do so. He located the single response received to Maggie's carefully crafted note; a card bearing a line from a couple they had met on holiday in Greece a few years back, *Our thoughts are with you both this Christmas.* He wondered if they'd sent an identical one to Maggie. He realised most people would have already posted their cards by the time his and Maggie's were dispatched, but nevertheless, he could not avoid feeling a touch forsaken. 'People just don't know what to say,' he thought, trying, as usual, to see the other's point of view. "But they should bloody well try!" he snapped, a conviction at once tempered by the realisation that for many years he had pointedly failed to nurture any friendships himself.

He poured himself a small glass of Paddy, selected a Dylan CD and settled down in the front room. For once, Dylan's lyrics failed to claim him, and the thought occurred that he hadn't heard from Nuala or Maggie all week, and gave them both a call. Nuala sounded well enough but was on her way out to a party, but informed him that she and Jack would be heading off to spend Christmas with his parents up at Hexham, tomorrow or the day after, depending on the state of their hangovers.

"Oh, your parcel arrived, thanks, Dad; I haven't opened it."

"I should hope not."

"I'll take it with me to open on Christmas morning. I've posted yours and Mum's off yesterday, I'm sorry I left it so late. I'll phone you Christmas Day, promise."

Although he had already given his blessing to the arrangement, he winced at the thought of not seeing his daughter on Christmas morning. He offered to phone her instead, but she explained that her mother had given her plenty of money so her phone was well stocked with credit.

"Try me on my mobile," he told her, "there's a chance I might be in Donegal with your Auntie Rose."

"Oh cool! Give her my love. And remember, Dad, her name's Roisin!"

"Yes, I know. I'll try."

Patrick hung up reluctantly, knowing full well that she was only doing what sooner or later every child must do; he just wished she'd done it later. He couldn't blame her for opting to spend Christmas with her boyfriend's family, the alternative being a self-conscious Christmas dinner *a deux* with her newly separated father. Jack's parents' farm represented the obvious solution. The possibility never occurred to Patrick that their daughter might have seriously considered spending Christmas at her mother's.

After several rings Maggie answered.

"Oh, it's you. What time is it?" she sounded drowsy.

"Eight-thirty, or so, no, nearly nine," he replied.

"I must have fallen asleep."

"How are you?"

"Been better, and you?"

"Okay. I've just spoken to Nuala."

"Ah-huh, what did she have to say?"

247

"Not a lot, she said you gave her some dosh and she was heading off to a party with Jack. How was she when you saw her on Monday?"

"Feisty. I tried talking to her about our relationship, such as it is."

"Ours?"

"No, hers and mine."

"And?"

"Oh, Pat, I don't know," she said wearily, "I don't know what goes wrong between her and me, it's like me and my mother but in reverse. I tried explaining some things to her but we just ended up having a spat in a coffee house; she ran off, I ran after her, chasing her down the walkway beside the river. It was a right scene; my heel broke, I fell over, tore my tights and grazed my hands and knee, I was in a right mess. She came back to help me and we ended up in tears together on a bench in the rain. She took me back to her room, got me cleaned up and we had a good talk, the best one in years. She then walked me into town to buy tights and shoes. When we said goodbye we had a hug, a real hug, before she dashed off to meet Jack and I drove home."

"Feeling all kinds of things I'd imagine."

"Pat, I just couldn't stop crying. I pulled in at a services and phoned you but all I got was your bloody machine. I couldn't face leaving a message."

"Ah right, I had a silent call."

"I learned something, though," she added.

"What was that?"

"It wasn't Sam's."

Silence.

"The pregnancy. It wasn't Sam's. It was Wor Jackie's."

"What? I don't understand, she told me how it happened, her last night out with her mates before she left home for Uni. She and Sam got drunk and it was an accident."

"Well, 'drunk' and 'accident' are probably true enough, but it wasn't her last night at home, and it wasn't Sam. It was virtually her first night up at university. She lied, I think, because she felt so ashamed. It was her first night out with Jack, easier to present it as an accident back in her old life rather than admit to messing up the start of her new one. Making believe it happened back here with Sam, who she's known for years, somehow helped her feel less shame, at least in your eyes. She finds it bad enough having me for a mother, she can't bear the thought of you turning against her."

"I'm stunned," said Patrick, "what made her tell you?"

"I asked. I had my suspicions after the phone call when she first told me, then when I saw them both together the other weekend, I just knew. Didn't you ever suspect her story?"

"No."

"You know Patrick, for one so wise, you can be surprisingly gullible, and I don't mean that as cruel as it sounds. I quite like your innocence, it's less scary than your insight."

Patrick said nothing. He was still reeling from the revelation.

Maggie then filled another gap in her estranged husband's knowledge.

"And it wasn't her girlfriend who collected her from the clinic, it was Jack … Jackie, got it? He borrowed his Mum's car; he'd told his parents about the pregnancy from the outset."

Patrick clung to the phone, suddenly devoid of the power of speech.

"Pat, you still there?"

"Yes."

"Well, seeing as how it's the time for honesty," Maggie went on, "it wasn't you I telephoned first from the services, it was Gavin. He couldn't talk, he was back with Vicky, his wife."

Silence.

"Pat?"

"Hmm?"

"I thought you'd gone."

"Not yet."

"What do you mean?"

"I'm thinking of going to Ireland for Christmas; Roisin has invited me to stay with her in Donegal, that is if I can pick up a flight this late in the day."

"Oh, I see. Well, um … I don't suppose I'll see you then?"

"Guess not."

More silence.

"What did you want?" she said, at last, fighting back the tears.

"What?"

"You phoned me. What did you want?"

"Um, I don't know, nothing in particular, just thought I'd ring."

"Oh, okay." And Maggie wondered if her disappointment was as apparent to him as it was to herself.

"Pat …" she had no idea how to end the sentence, until the words slipped from her lips, "you take care."

"I will, you too."

And after another awkward silence, it was Patrick who hung up first.

He could recall no other telephone conversation with so vast a gap between how little he'd said and how much he'd felt.

Chapter Thirty-Five

NEIL WAS LATE, A quarter past nine and no word received. Patrick tidied his desk, gave its surface a wipe and noticed a grey smear of dust across his palm. He promised to give the office a really good spring clean before starting back in the New Year. When Nuala was at home he used to pay her to polish, vacuum and give the windows and small kitchen area a thorough clean. Now it didn't get done so regularly and he wouldn't trust anyone else not to nose around.

Patrick was agitated. He'd begun to bank on being able to book a flight and get away from all things familiar over Christmas, but as yet, he'd done nothing about it. He knew there were bridges to build with Roisin and felt ready to try, but what if the flights were full? He had no plan B.

Nine-thirty. Neil wasn't coming. Patrick scrawled *DNA* in the case-notes and placed the file back in the drawer, half-expecting Neil to waltz through the door in that very moment and announce, 'Bet you thought you'd got rid of me, eh?'

He didn't.

Ten-thirty. The door half-opened and Grace's face appeared.

"May I come in?" she asked.

"Yes, do! I'm sorry," he said, "I never seem to hear your knock. You should try giving it a real thump next time."

"And *you* should buy a doorbell," she replied.

"Touché!" he smiled.

"Here's a parcel for you, the postman must have left it at the door."

Patrick took it from her and put it down on the sofa next to his coat.

"David not with you?"

"No," she sighed, "David won't be coming here again."

Just for a moment they caught each other's gaze, but Patrick said nothing.

He led the way through to the therapy room. Grace removed her topcoat, tossed it onto the far chair and sat head in hands, massaging her cheeks, before giving a huge sigh and flopping back in the seat.

"Welcome back, Grace," said Patrick.

Grace closed her eyes and sat still for some moments, allowing Patrick took the opportunity to observe her: more casual than usual, well-fitting blue jeans, white tee, short suede jacket, long scarf tied loosely about her neck, Grace still managed to evoke an appreciation of style, but her demeanour spoke louder than the clothes.

"You look shattered, Grace."

"My plane was delayed, I didn't get back until eleven o'clock last night and walked into an almighty row that woke up the younger kids, who began crying and the older one came down and started yelling at David, it was awful. David had already packed my things in bags and had them lined up in the hall and took great pleasure in informing me he'd instigated divorce proceedings. He also told me he wasn't wasting any more money coming to see you as he's had a bellyful of being taken for a ride."

"Taken for a ride?"

"Oh, by me, but by you too. He was furious over the letter and he's threatening to lodge an official complaint and have you struck off."

Despite his regard for professional ethics and the seriousness of any prospect of an official complaint, Patrick felt surprisingly unperturbed by this news. He waited until it was clear Grace showed no sign of continuing before taking up the reins.

"It was a difficult decision, Grace. Your letter commenced, 'Dear David,' but you addressed the envelope to me. You asked me to read it aloud to David, but made no mention of me giving it to him. You see, it contained references that could have been put to other uses, for example, should the situation between you and David end up in court."

Grace looked perplexed.

"The letter contained several references to your mental

252

state, 'going off the rails', being 'like a mad woman', and having a 'nervous breakdown', things that could be used to make a case against you having access to the children.

"Oh God, I never thought. I just poured it all out; I may be an evil bitch but it seems I'm still too honest for my own good, or perhaps I should say, too naive?"

"The letter is yours, Grace. I'll fetch it from my desk now if you wish?"

Grace shook her head.

Ordinarily, Patrick might have gone on to ask about Grace's perception of herself as naive, its origins and function in terms of her own self-concept, and within the relationship dynamics between her and David. But these were no ordinary times, for Patrick Chime, therapist and separated husband, had missed his client this past fortnight and was jealous of the time Simon had enjoyed with her, wandering freely through a foreign land, sharing rough footpaths, plates of *tapas,* and a soft warm bed. And so instead he asked how the time in Spain had gone and what thoughts and feelings she'd brought back before being hit with the news of the impending divorce.

Grace explained that it had been the most wickedly selfish act of her entire life, and, despite the consequences, she had no regrets. She'd enjoyed the first evening with Simon at the hotel in Leon, but by the time they set off walking the following morning she sensed his unease at her presence.

"When you walk with a partner," she explained, "it is to them that you address the little asides, those casual remarks about the beautiful countryside, the precise length of the chain tethering the angry farm dog, or the disgusting diesel fumes belched out by lorries thundering along the road bordering the footpath. When you travel alone, your thoughts are your companions and you're freer to engage with the locals you encounter along the way. Simon is a travel writer, well used to journeying alone, he was also ten days into his walk, and I think he found it difficult to adjust to me being there. He said near the end that it was like the two of us were locked inside a bubble, and he found it claustrophobic. Oh yes, I even walk too slowly for him!"

"So much for Simon's feelings, what about yours?"

"When I boarded the plane it was like being a young girl again, full of hope and excitement, but scared it would all go wrong, and of course it did, because on the flight home I remember thinking I had travelled all that way to meet a man I thought was someone else."

"Happens all the time," said Patrick.

"Do you think so? When I was a little girl, I used to believe there was just one special person on earth for each of us, the one-and-only made just for me and nobody else, and I used to get scared, what if I couldn't find him? How awful it would be because I'd have to make do with being alone, or else marry the wrong person, and for the rest of my life my special person would be out there looking for me. We might even pass by along a crowded street, close enough to touch, and neither of us would have realised."

"Sounds like a rather grim fairy-tale," he suggested.

"Nightmare, more like," she replied.

"Well, as scripts go, it's more tragedy than comedy. But that was when you were a little girl, Grace, what about now that you're a woman, what does your script say now?"

"I don't feel very grown-up. More like a teenager who has gone off the rails. I keep expecting to hear my name announced over the tannoy and have them come to cart me away."

Patrick gave a hint of a smile.

"What's so funny?" she asked.

"It's the little girl talking, Grace, the one who believes in fairy-tales, in magical acts of rescue, and dire punishments. On the one hand you're saying, 'If only I could be rescued by my one-and-only, that special person who is out there somewhere,' and on the other hand, you're saying, 'I've been a bad girl, I've gone astray, and deserve to be dashed on the rocks.'

"Crazy woman, eh?"

Again Patrick's face revealed the trace of a smile.

"You're doing it again!" she accused, almost laughing.

"I know," said Patrick, still smiling, "I'm sorry, I guess it's just my way of saying that, despite what you think, it's not the end of the world, and you're not beyond the pale."

"Try telling that to David, and I'm not sure my children would agree with you, or my neighbours and friends. I can just imagine my girlfriends' husbands telling them, 'You keep away from her, she's bad news that Grace Reynolds!!'"

"Darling."

Grace froze. She was as taken aback on hearing the word, as was Patrick flustered by his use of it.

"I'm sorry, Grace … that was so silly, I suddenly thought you'd made a mistake. Do you remember that first time you came here and were about to introduce yourself as Grace Darling? Well, just now, I'd momentarily forgotten that your name is Reynolds."

"I wish it wasn't," she replied, without any trace of humour.

"I'm sorry, Grace, that was really remiss of me, I don't know what made me forget your name just then."

Patrick knew he was apologising too much, but feared that his Freudian slip had given him away, and feeling his face flush, strove hard to get back on track.

"As for your friends' husbands," he said, picking up the earlier thread in an effort to shift the focus, "people get scared when they see their friends' marriages start falling apart, it shakes their own foundations."

"I suppose you're right," and now Grace was the one to offer a glimmer of a smile.

Silence.

He swallowed hard and tried to breathe more slowly, still unsettled by his earlier *faux-pas*.

"What are you going to do, Grace?" he said at last, once his heart had slowed to a reasonable level.

"I don't know. What I'd more or less decided as I trailed along behind Simon, was to come back and tell David that I'd look for a house to rent, hopefully within walking distance of home, so that the children can come and visit under their own steam, after school and so forth."

"So David stole your thunder?"

"Yes, but it didn't feel like that at the time."

"How do you mean?"

"I was trying to sort things out calmly, to minimize the hurt, whereas he just seems motivated by vitriol. As I'm the one who wants out of the marriage, David doesn't see why he should be the one to leave. So, I'll just have to be the baddie, and bite the bullet. I just wish it didn't have to be so hateful. Why can't couples part on better terms, why do they have to fight and lay out snares and traps that only inflict more wounds on themselves and the children?"

"Even when a break-up isn't acrimonious, it still hurts, there are still wounds."

She looked into his eyes and saw he was no longer smiling.

"What about the children?" she asked.

"What are you asking me, Grace?"

"If they'll get over it? Do you think they'll be all right?"

"Tough one," he replied. "I don't know your children, but if you want me to answer in generalities then there are statistics that point to the negative consequences of parental break-up on children's school performance and other forms of measurable behaviour. But the flaw in that argument is that your children aren't percentages or generalities, they are small persons and real individuals, and the fact remains that not all individuals experience things in the same way."

He paused, and saw she was hanging on his every word.

"Look, Grace, there are plenty of people out there who'll line up to tell you that most people who divorce later say they regret it. But does that mean they actively wish they'd not pulled the plug on their marriage, or does it mean they still feel some sadness about what happened? Anyway, how do you figure out whether you'll be one of the majority or the minority? You can't. And it's the same with children; I've known people who have grown and matured through the painful experience of their parents' divorce, and I've met others who've suffered long-term damage as a result. A lot depends on what's gone before and on how the adults handle the separation. Too many people rush quickly into new relationships and expect the kids to seamlessly adjust to having a new step-parent. I suppose the main difference between kids' and adults' positions is that the kids don't have much choice, whereas ..."

"I do," Grace interrupted, "that's what you're saying isn't it? I've decided I want out of my marriage and my husband and the children just have to put up with it. The fact that David's now the one instigating divorce doesn't change the fact it was me who brought it about."

"No, it doesn't," he replied firmly, "and it doesn't change the fact that this marriage was made by the pair of you, and trying to unravel exactly what belongs with whom is frankly nigh-on impossible, and if the reason for doing so is simply to apportion innocence or blame, then it won't help your relationship one jot, nor will it help your children who will only find it all the harder to cope with their own ambivalent feelings. Whether it's a marriage, or a life, that has come to an end, the healthiest and most appropriate thing to feel is sadness, not blame!"

Grace looked stunned, taken aback by the passion and authority of his words.

"Quite a speech," she said at last.

"I'm sorry, I have a tendency to do that sometimes, you see, therapists don't always just sit here going 'ah-hah' and giving the occasional nod."

"I wasn't complaining. It's good to have the chance to talk like this, and to hear your views. Most of the time all this stuff just goes round and round inside my head. I tried talking to a girlfriend but she just told me I should go for it; easy for her to say when it's not her children who'll be affected. Besides, she's the one who would soon find her way into David's bed once I was off the scene."

"Hmm. Well, if you and David do split up, it is inevitably going to disrupt the children's lives and it will take time for new patterns and structures to be established, and for everyone to get used to them."

"But do you think they will?" she asked, plaintively.

"There's more chance of that if their parents keep making it clear that they're divorcing each other and not their children, if the parent who moves out continues to live close by, and if each partner shows patience and tolerance and resists the temptation to use the kids as pawns in their own personal battle."

"But it's one hell of a step to take, isn't it?"

"Yes, it is. And I can't tell you whether or not you should take it. You have choices, Grace. You can try and cram yourself back into a marriage that no longer fits, and which you long to leave; or you can take your own life, which I guess was what you hinted at in your letter when you spoke of being close to the edge, and just think what a legacy that would leave for your children. Or, you can leave David and attempt to put in place some new structures that will enable your kids to eventually see that although their mum and dad no longer live together, they are all still family. But whichever choice you make, you can't get away from the fact that your actions offer your kids a model of how to be in life, whether it's how to knuckle down and make the best of an unrewarding situation for the general good; how to turn your back on life because it's all too unbearable; or how to strike out for what you want and face the consequences, despite others not liking it."

Grace looked hard at Patrick, her face calmer than before.

"I married the wrong person, that's the plain truth of it," she said. "You know I think I realised that a very long time ago, but by then I was pregnant with our first child. I hoped that by being loving and caring, I could turn David into the kind of man I wanted him to be, but of course it didn't work."

"Why should it?" Patrick asked. "Don't we all yearn to be loved for who we really are, rather than what we might be manipulated into becoming?"

"Hmm," she paused, "love as manipulation? I'll have to think about that one. Anyway, I tried knuckling down, as you put it, for many years, I suffered in silence, wore a smile for the kids and a mask for David, avoiding, or pretending, in bed, until eventually it all wore too thin, and that's when Simon popped up."

"Good timing, eh?"

"Yes, but the wrong person."

"You're not alone, Grace. There are lots of men and women in your position, and they all handle it in their own way. Some hang in by clinging to a secret get-out clause that once the kids have left home, that's when they'll make their escape."

"I've tried clinging to that thought, but I really don't think I could survive till then."

"Well, it's your call Grace, or David's. Sometimes, making that decision feels like just too much responsibility and many unhappy spouses long for their partner to make it for them, even goading them into being the one to pull the plug."

She eyed him suspiciously.

"You think that's what I've been doing?"

"Not consciously, Grace, but isn't that what's happened, if you look at the bare facts?"

Grace sighed.

"I used to lie in bed at night after David had sex with me, I put it like that because that's what it was, something he did *to* me rather than *with* me, and that was my fault as much as his, because I never really gave him much encouragement. Anyway, I used to lie there afterwards, listening to him snore, and I'd imagine that one day, he'd be on top of me, the weight of him thrusting away, getting no response as usual, and suddenly he'd stop, roll off onto his back and say, 'Look, Grace, we both know this isn't working, it's time we faced up to that and split up, I think it's for the best, don't you?' I so longed to hear him say that, but, as time went by, I realised it was never going to happen. I tried imagining David meeting someone, like that girlfriend of mine that lusts after him. I almost wish she'd make a play for him instead of just repeatedly telling me what a gorgeous hunk of a husband I've got. I used to fantasize about David saying, 'Grace, there's something I've got to tell you, I've fallen in love with one of your friends and I want a divorce.'

"And then you'd have your freedom but without the responsibility of having laid claim to it."

Grace stared hard at him.

"In a way, I suppose you're right, that's what's happened, I've provoked David to the point where he's had enough."

"Yes, but rather than owning his share of responsibility for the breakdown of your marriage, it sounds like he's laying all the blame at your door," Patrick stated, not entirely innocently.

"Isn't that where it belongs?"

"Look Grace, if you want to be condemned," and his voice sounded impatient with her now, "there are plenty of moralising know-alls out there only too ready to point the finger at you. If you want forgiveness, go see a priest, or better still, look for it over time in your own heart. It's not my place to dish out blame or forgiveness, or approval for that matter.

I'm here to listen and to try and help you understand what's going on inside you."

"I'm sorry, I shouldn't have asked."

"You asked because the emotions you're grappling with feel too big to contain, so you look outside yourself for condemnation or approval. We do it all the time; most of the world religions thrive on it. What you've shown me over the few times we've met is that what is happening to you involves far more than just a long and unhappy marriage; I think you're engaged in a struggle you've endured throughout your entire life, a constant wrestling match between duty on the one hand, and pleasure on the other."

"How do you mean?" she asked.

"Well, we've barely any time left today, but I could sum it up like this: your conscience is telling you to knuckle down and adhere to the role of dutiful wife and mother, whereas your heart implores you to leave David and start a new life. It's a struggle between 'ought' on the one hand and 'desire' on the other; all of us struggle with that to a degree, it's part of being human, but for some of us it's a struggle that plagues us every day of our lives. I imagine it's a struggle you've had since being a little girl. Only now it has come to a head and you're compelled at last to address it. And you need to address it, Grace, otherwise, regardless of whether or not you leave David, you will carry that conflict with you wherever you go, and whoever you live with, and unless you resolve it you'll find that it's a recipe for perpetual unhappiness."

"Perpetual unhappiness? That sounds like a death sentence," she said.

He glanced at the clock, but knew he had to finish what he'd started. "The recipe reads like this, Grace, if I do what my conscience dictates, then each day I die a little more of unhappiness – but if I follow my heart's desire, then guilt eats away at me and destroys any happiness I might find."

She looked ashen.

"It sounds dreadful, like there's no way out."

"Which is what made you feel so close to the edge and even consider ending your life. But there is a way out Grace, and I don't just mean divorce; whether or not you leave David isn't the point. You need to examine how, and why, obligation and desire have become such dreadful enemies, and find some way of reconciling them; for until you do, I doubt you'll find much peace within yourself, let alone the happiness you yearn for."

Grace didn't fully comprehend all his words, but sensed that there was something here worth pursuing, and at this moment in time it seemed the one thing worth clinging onto.

"Can you help me find peace, Patrick?" and whether the look in her eyes was need alone, or of need laced with desire, Patrick was unsure, but it was a look that pierced his heart and he knew that more than anything, he wanted to say 'yes'.

"I'll try," he replied, "we can try together, Grace." He could have sworn he felt himself blush.

Grace's vulnerable smile made him wonder again if he'd given himself away, and he was relieved when at last she spoke.

"I don't know what the future holds," she went on. "Can I still come here? I need someone, I mean somewhere," she hurriedly corrected herself, "somewhere to talk about what's going on, and try and make sense of it all?"

"Count on it," he said firmly, and stole a glance at the clock. "Look, we've run over time and we must stop for now. Grace, I'm going to be away over Christmas …"

"Christmas," she said, wearily, "we've all got that to get through next."

"Well, it would help if you and David could get your parental act together over the holiday period for the sake of your children. I realise it won't be easy for either of you."

"No, but we should try."

"Look, Grace, I'll be back here for you on Thursday the 3rd of January, at the same time." He wrote it on an appointment card and handed it across.

"Thank you," she said, and began writing out a cheque, "sixty pounds?"

"Forty-five, you're no longer with David, remember? But I'm afraid my fees increase to fifty pounds from January."

"It's worth it," she said, handing over the cheque.

"What will you be doing over Christmas, Patrick?" she asked, as he walked her slowly to the door.

"Me? Trying to get my act together, I expect, across the Irish Sea," and he was instantly aware of having said far more than was necessary, or justifiable.

"Strange, I've occasionally wondered if you might be Irish?" she replied.

And for once, being thought of as Irish did not offend Patrick in the least, in fact he was glad of it, although gladder still at the evidence that Grace sometimes thinks of him in his absence. That discovery thrilled Patrick, and made him look into her eyes, a look she returned, a look lasting no more than a few seconds, but which cut so deep he had to break the moment by forcing a thin smile and looking away before touching her lightly on the arm. It was either that, or kiss her.

"Take care, Grace, I'll see you in the New Year."

"New Year? Yes," she said, exhaling deeply, "New Year, new life."

And as Grace Reynolds, née Darling, turned and headed off along the landing towards her new life, Patrick stood alone in his doorway, watching every step that she took.

"Grace!" he called out, far louder than was necessary. "Your letter?"

"Oh! Um, would you take care of it for me, please Patrick?" she asked, before disappearing down the stairwell.

"Take care, Grace," Patrick whispered, before closing the door, going directly to his desk and feeding Grace's letter into the shredder.

Patrick finished his notes and was about to put away Grace's folder when he recalled a vision of David, outside the office door, demanding to be given Grace's letter, and his parting shot as he stormed off empty-handed, 'Damn the pair of you!'

'The pair of you ...' Patrick mulled over the phrase several times. 'This was not just about my refusing to hand over the letter; if that was the case, he'd have simply said, "Damn you!" Maybe at some level he sensed the strong bond between Grace and me, or was it just a blast of hot air in response to the powerlessness he felt as a cuckolded husband?'

Patrick briefly reconsidered whether David might have had a genuine right to the letter?

'Well, it's academic now, of course. Of course, I could have written to David, acknowledging the conflict over the letter and our difficult parting, and ascertained whether Grace's reporting was correct, that he would not be returning for any further appointments? Perhaps I should have written, it might have lessened the likelihood of a letter arriving on the desk of the B.A.C.P.'s complaints department. Then again, things could get a whole lot worse,' he told himself, as he closed Grace's file and put away his pen; 'Never mind keeping a letter, I could end up being accused of stealing a client's wife.'

Patrick sighed, and straightened the jotter. Another year completed; a mixed year all in all; work with his supervisees had gone well, apart from the one who'd fled to Mitchell. A varied clutch of clients: the abrupt and frustrating ending with Margaret, in contrast to the long, painful, and much more satisfying one with Sarah. And Beth's words came back to him, 'You've never done better work,' and Sarah's own message in her Christmas card, *Thank you for restoring me to Life.* 'Yes, not a bad year,' he thought, all things considered, at least until the last two months. And of course, the work goes on, with Grace, Neil, Gina and the rest. 'After all, what else am I good for?'

He collected up the few Christmas cards from the windowsill and apart from the one from Sarah, which he filed away amongst her notes, threw the rest into the bin; New Year, new start. He went to gather up his coat and noticed the parcel left earlier by Grace. It was the size of a breadboard and as heavy and hard. He sat down on the sofa, and stripped away the brown paper; whatever was inside was covered in cheap Christmas wrap but accompanied by no card or message. He wondered if the gift was actually from Grace, and although he'd have expected classier wrapping, he still half hoped it might prove to be from her. As he tore apart the final sheet he revealed the book's title, *DEGAS The Man and his Work,* and he knew at once who had sent it. The book was not new; the top and bottom of the glossy dust jacket curled up like a stale sandwich and bore a small tear along the bottom edge. He examined the inside cover for some message, but there was none. Idly he thumbed the pages. There were many full-page colour and monochrome plates, as well as sketches down the sides of the dense text. It seemed a hefty tome in more ways than one. One section was given over to Degas' studies of nudes. As he flicked the pages, Patrick's took in the numerous sweeping curves, of arms, backs or shoulders, as the women stretched and yawned, bent double to dry between their toes, or twisted awkwardly to scratch some itch in the small of the back. These were not your idealised classical forms, nor your modern-day waxed and airbrushed young things; these were real women, rotund, middle-aged housewives and whores, engaged in the physical everyday reality of their bodily existence. Patrick was aware of a contradiction here, the paintings and drawings seemed deeply voyeuristic, and yet the models showed no evidence of exhibitionism, as if these women, oblivious of being observed, were freed from artifice, and revealed as they truly were, in the act of pulling on a stocking, fastening a corset, brushing their hair, trying on a hat, climbing into, or out of, the tub. And as his hand turned the leaves, Patrick dipped in and out of the text, gathering lines as he browsed: *Who was he? Degas never wanted us to know ... Works of art must be left with some mystery about them ... Boundaries were no longer so clear as before ... Degas would easily have known what the interior of a brothel was like ... Parisian art world gossip held that Degas was an inadequate lover ... It is as if the scenes are being witnessed by an outsider paying acute and avid attention, but quite unrelated to that subject ... Degas' life lacked any consistent fulfilling romantic or physical attachment to a woman ... he frequented brothels as a convenient outlet for a fragile sexuality ...* He read on until he turned another leaf and his eyes fell upon a half-page monochrome print that seemed strangely familiar, although Patrick couldn't say from where. The scene depicted was of a dimly lit bedroom. A woman dressed in a petticoat kneels in front of the fireplace, her back to the man who, it seems, has just entered the room and who now leans back against the door as if to survey his share of the prize they have waited so long to claim. Patrick scanned the footnote, *Interior, oil, c.1868.* He gleaned from the text that the painting is Degas' interpretation of a scene from the Zola novel, *Thérèse Raquin*. Apparently, Thérèse had embarked upon a lustful affair with her husband's best friend. The pair then murdered her feeble husband and laid low for a year in longing and anticipation until they were able to wed. The author argues that the painting depicts *not a scene of domestic violence, or rape, as some critics suggest, but the moment in which the prize, the lovers have waited for so long, eludes them. For the woman cringes on her knees in shame, and the man stands paralysed by the door, illustrating how often in life that which has thrived on lust, flounders and dies through guilt and shame.* And there in the centre of the painting, upon a round occasional table, lies an attaché case, its lid left open, which, under the pallid glow of the ceiling light, made it appear to Patrick almost exactly like a lap-top computer.

Patrick snapped the book shut, took a deep breath, quickly gathered up coat and book and made for the door. Just as he grasped the handle, it moved. Patrick gave a pull and felt a momentary resistance from the other side before it gave way and the door swung open revealing a be-suited man in his late thirties brandishing a warrant card.

"Mr Patrick Chime?"

Patrick assented.

"Detective Sergeant Campbell, sorry to disturb you sir, I wonder if might have a word."

"Come in," said Patrick, opening the door wide.

They two men sat opposite each other on the two sofas in the reception area. Patrick was too intrigued to think of offering any refreshment.

"I'm investigating the sudden death of a Mr Neil Higgins, we found this card in his pocket and wondered if you might be able to shed any light on what might have happened?" Patrick stared at the business card, proffered by the police officer, but made no move to take it from him.

"This *is* one of your cards, sir?"

"What happened?" asked Patrick.

"Well, that's what we're trying to ascertain. He fell from a bridge in the path of a Metro train, killed him instantly; didn't do a lot for the train driver's Christmas either. Looks like suicide although the driver didn't actually see him jump."

Patrick's thoughts were spinning.

"Patient of yours was he, Mr Higgins?"

"The people I see here are not patients, and I'm afraid I can't confirm the identity of any of my clients without their permission."

"He can hardly give that now though, can he, sir?"

"That's not the point."

"He did have your card in his pocket."

"So you said."

"Look, sir, I appreciate your work here is of a confidential nature; I'm not asking to examine your case records at this time, it's just that we're dealing here with a sudden, violent and unexplained death and we just wondered whether you might have been able to shed any light on Mr Higgins's state of mind. That's all."

"No. I'm sorry, officer, I can't help you."

"Very well, sir, sorry to have bothered you," replied DS Campbell, politely enough but with an underlying note of frustration. "I'll take my leave then. For now," he added ominously, and made his way to the door while Patrick sat motionless on the sofa.

"Detective-Sergeant," Patrick called out as the officer opened the door, "… thank you for informing me."

The policeman, looked back over his shoulder, and for a brief moment the two men stared into each other's features.

"Merry Christmas, sir," replied the officer, wearily, and closed the door behind him.

Patrick went directly to his desk; his immediate inclination was to phone Beth but he broke off mid-dial. He unlocked the drawer, removed Neil's file and felt impelled to pore over it from cover to cover, to find some indication, some important clue he'd overlooked, but halfway down the first page he stopped, took a deep breath and knew he must get out into the open air. He locked the office and strode off around the lane that encircled the mill. He failed to notice the brown mongrel dog that crossed his path, or the kids on the bit of adjacent wasteland whose football bounced just behind him. By the second circuit, he had begun assembling his thoughts into some kind of agenda. One: phone Beth and if she can't speak now, arrange a telephone consultation at the earliest opportunity. Two: take Neil's file home so it is to hand when speaking with Beth. Three ... Patrick realised with surprise that not only had he come to the end of his list, but that his feet had come to a standstill. He imagined there would have been so many more things to do, but of course, those are for others to attend to: DS Campbell; the pathologist; the train driver's workmates, GP and family; Neil's mother and her partner, Graham; Neil's employers; the registrar of deaths; the vicar; funeral directors; gravediggers; and of course, the Coroner. The only thing for Neil's therapist to do was to think, to feel, and to know, but not to say a word.

Patrick knew that a client committing suicide is probably the worst fear of any counsellor or therapist, and one that his supervisees bring to their sessions with him fairly regularly. As Patrick wandered back upstairs to his office, he remembered what he tells the least experienced amongst them: 'Most suicides take place in prison cells and psychiatric hospitals where there's round-the-clock care and surveillance, what makes you flatter yourself that a weekly hour of conversation with you will prevent someone bent on killing themselves from doing the deed? Don't afford your role a grandiosity it doesn't deserve; sometimes a counsellor or therapist's place is simply to be left feeling shitty.'

Feeling decidedly shitty, Patrick hauled himself back upstairs, made a coffee, rang Beth and listened to her husband's recorded message, 'We shall not be available on this number until the 2nd of January. Thank you.' It bore all the succinct smugness of a man glad for once to have his wife to himself. Patrick replaced the receiver and as he bent to close the drawer of the filing cabinet noticed the red light on his answer-machine flashing, indicating two messages. The first was silent and lasted just a few seconds. The second contained a female voice that sounded middle-aged, with a slight Yorkshire accent.

"Hello, We need to speak. Please ring me on the following number, as soon as you get this message ..."

The caller left no name, but the code indicated the Barnsley area. He played it again, and then a third time, during which he changed his mind more than once about whether to comply with her request. Patrick saw no reason to obey the demands of an anonymous caller, but then it occurred to him that the caller could well be Neil's mother and he shivered at the prospect. He played it through once more before picking up the phone and dialling. A woman's voice answered, simply reciting the number.

"I don't know who to ask for," said Patrick, "someone at this number left a message on my answer machine, saying we ought to talk, was it you?"

"Patrick Chime?" the woman asked.

"Yes, I'm Patrick Chime, who is this?" asked Patrick, annoyed at being toyed with.

"My name is Connie."

"Connie who?"

"Just Connie."

"Do I know you?"

"No, although I thought you might have heard of me by now, I've certainly heard of you, he spoke of you all the time."

As Patrick's lips parted to say, 'Who are you?' he realised he already knew the answer.

"You're …"

"Yes, and like I said, we need to talk."

Silence. Patrick flitted through the memory bank of the hundreds of cases he'd worked with down the years, but could find no precedent for this. He recalled his first Relate trainer's old adage, 'When in doubt, say nowt.'

"Look, Connie, I realise who you are, but I'm afraid I'm not at liberty to speak with you."

"Listen," she said, "don't think I don't know about discretion, because I do. I cared about Neil, probably more than you realise, and there are things that need to be said, and things that need to be heard, he's due that much. And don't kid yourself that some vicar he never met, or his few paltry relatives will be saying those things at his funeral, because they won't; it's only you and I that really knew him, and we need to talk."

"I'm sorry, I can't talk to you. I'm hanging up."

"Wait!" she shouted. "He said you were like this, elusive, hard to get through to. He's dead, will you get that through your head, Neil's dead! And there are things I need to say and things you need to hear."

Patrick was trembling. There was something in this woman's voice, something so urgent and familiar, that he could not turn away from. It was that same passion that had made him spout off at Grace, and, having recognised it for what it was, he knew he would agree to her demand. He asked whether she would come to his office, but she explained that her car was off the road being serviced. He took down her address and said he would be there well within the hour.

On the short journey Patrick's heart raced but his foot kept easing off the throttle, as if trying to warn him that this adventure was a perilous idea. He realised only too well that such an intrusion into a client's life, albeit a dead one, was ethically out of order, besides which, his guilt and embarrassment over his earlier foray into Neil's cyber world made it even harder to justify any further incursion into the world of flesh and bone. However, there was something in this woman's voice and words that compelled him to overlook his usual ethical constraints. It wasn't just her passion, he realised, as he took the rural underpass beneath the M1 motorway, Patrick was no mere slave to passion, it was the authority in her voice, '... only you and I really knew him ... there are things that need to be said, and things that need to be heard... he's due that much.'

As he drove through the outskirts of town, Patrick contemplated the Neil he had known, the tortured soul, torn by the fissure between overarching ambition and grandiose desire on the one hand, and pathetically low self-esteem on the other. 'For one who trusted so little, Neil expected such a damn lot,' Patrick repeated the phrase several times, it was like an escape valve on a pressure cooker, enabling him to complain about the task in hand, but continue on with it. Patrick thought about the yearning for wholeness, the alpha and omega of his philosophy, the healing of the splits that abound in the outside world and which echo the more substantial splits within the inner world of the psyche: the struggles between order and chaos, between love and hate, pride and shame, power and helplessness, trust and suspicion, or desire and obligation; he knew that it is the healing of these inner schisms that our unconscious mind yearns for above all else, and that we will defend against so vehemently. Patrick recalled Neil's struggle to reconcile his longing and his disgust, borne so poignantly in his purloining of the character, Degas, and the artist's final failure to deliver, resulting in his cyber-execution at the stab of a finger. He recalled Neil's struggle to reveal his relationship with Connie, an expression, it now seemed, of a deep longing for reconciliation. 'He's due that much.' It was to these words of Connie's that Patrick kept returning, reciting them over and over as he drove onwards towards this clandestine assignation between representatives of what he increasingly realised were not altogether dissimilar trades.

As he approached the town centre, Patrick's heart slowed to an acceptable pace and his foot settled more steadily on the accelerator, for he now knew why he was making this audacious journey: Neil would have wanted it. Neil would have wanted these two independent observers of the shadowy corners of his existence to bear witness to a life that failed to live up to its owner's aspirations. It was one last thing that Patrick could do for him and there was no way Patrick could have instigated such a meeting; it had to be at Connie's suggestion or not at all. Patrick had made his decision and, whatever the B.A.C.P. Ethical Framework might suggest to the contrary, Patrick convinced himself that Neil Higgins was indeed due that much.

Chapter Thirty-Six

THE VICTORIAN TERRACE MIGHT once have been quite attractive but now bore a somewhat seedy appearance; a lone tree bisected a pair of lampposts, only one of whose lights were aglow. On the opposite side of the road, a bare pavement, with ribbons of rubbish nestling against the railings protecting the railway track below. In the gathering gloom Patrick scanned the house fronts. Only three displayed a Christmas tree in their front window. It was well past four o'clock, as he sat at the wheel perusing the location. There was no one about, and several empty parking spaces on the lamppost side of the road, made him conclude that parking alone over here by the embankment was too conspicuous. His liaison was at number fourteen; a house with just a small silver artificial tree in the net-curtained window lit by white lights, and the first available parking space was several doors along. He manoeuvred the car, took a deep breath, stepped out into the biting cold and glanced in both directions before approaching the door. The paint was flaking but he was reassured by the glow emanating from the bell push and gave a grin at the elaborate series of chimes that sounded from within. The door opened until grabbed by a security chain.

"It's Patrick Chime," he proffered, and heard the chain being slid back and as the door swung open he was confronted by a woman of similar age to himself, round-faced, beneath a mop of chestnut hair, probably dyed, not much over five feet tall, dressed in voluminous, crushed-velvet purple trousers and a loose-fitting cream silk shirt, giving little clue to the shape of the body underneath. He hadn't known what to expect, but it wasn't this.

"The back room," she indicated along the hallway with a nod of the head, "we'll go in there."

She led the way along the narrow hall, opened the door and

271

bade him enter while she hovered in the doorway.

"Tea? Or coffee, if you'd prefer?"

"Tea would be fine, thank you. No milk or sugar."

"Earl Grey?"

"Lovely!" he said, raising his eyebrows.

"You needn't sound so surprised," she replied pointedly, before disappearing down the hall.

Patrick took a deep breath. 'One-nil to you,' he thought, and looked around the small sitting room, taking in the open fire with its elegant Victorian tiled surround, and recesses either side of the chimney breast, one of which embraced a table bearing a small combination television and DVD player, the other bore shelves of books from floor to ceiling. In the centre of the room, two small sofas at right angles bordering a rather attractive Moroccan-style rug, which appeared quite new. An old fashioned standard lamp illuminated the bookshelves and Patrick edged closer to appraise the stock: paperbacks mostly, their spines well worn. Arranged in alphabetic order by author, many of which he didn't recognise, holiday reading from the look of it, but others he did: Dickens, Zola, and several Bernice Reubens. He stepped back. On the wall behind the television, a small brass light illuminated a framed print, which caught Patrick's eye and he drew closer to inspect. The frame was attractive, plain wood housing a cream mount, at whose centre sat a moustachioed, bespectacled, elderly-looking man in a tweed jacket, cardigan, shirt and tie. The subject seemed familiar, the style and composition suggestive of a doctor or scientist of the early- to mid-twentieth century. Patrick peered at the title in a small cut-out window at the bottom of the mount, *James Joyce, by Jacques Emile Blanche.* He was still regarding it when the door swished open behind him.

"It's nothing to do with Joyce," she said, "I tried reading Ulysses when I was young, it was the thing to do but I got nowhere with it. I bought the print because I liked the image. It reminded me of someone I once knew."

Although aware of a pang of interest, Patrick knew it was not his place to ask.

Connie placed the tray down on one of the sofas, pulled up a small occasional table, set the tray upon it, assumed a seat and began to pour. She clearly saw no need to issue any invitation to sit down, so he helped himself to a seat on the adjacent sofa.

She handed him his cup and poured herself one too.

"No lemon, I'm afraid."

"I don't take it," Patrick proffered a smile.

"Well," she said, sitting back and crossing her legs, the cup nestling neatly in her lap, "we meet at last."

Patrick felt ill at ease. Unsure how to behave; his intention was to err on the side of caution.

"At last?" he queried.

"I've known about you since Neil first went to see you, that must be, what, four months ago? I know he only recently told you about me, just the other week, wasn't it."

'Two-nil,' thought Patrick. He noticed her hands as she took frequent sips from her cup; small, they sported several rings, mostly silver, one with a large black stone, possibly jet, and a number of metal bangles adorned one wrist. On her feet, a rather exotic pair of black slipper-shoes with pointy toes, tiny kitten heels and an appliqué design. He looked into her face and neck and realised she was older than he'd first thought, certainly into her early fifties. A pair of long thin silver earrings framed her face and swung with each tilt of her head; her face was interesting, bearing the look of a woman of substance.

"How did you hear ..." he paused, aware how hesitant his voice sounded.

"Of Neil's death?" she queried, bluntly.

'Three-nil, this is embarrassing,' thought Patrick.

"Yes," he replied.

"It was on the Look North news on Tuesday: 'Local man in death plunge from railway-bridge, hit by passing train, police appeal for witnesses.' I thought you might have seen it. He was named in yesterday's Yorkshire Post."

"I've not switched the TV on in days, or seen the papers."

"You clearly believe in keeping in touch with the world."

Patrick took her jibe on the chin, and merely pulled a face.

"But you already knew what had happened when we spoke on the phone?" Connie pointed out.

"Yes. A policeman came to my office not long before you must have left your message, he was looking for background information, apparently they'd found one of my cards in Neil's pocket."

She gave a wry smile, the first glimmer of warmth.

"I've never bothered with cards, no telling who'll get hold of them."

"So err, how do you ..."

"Find my clients?"

He stared hard, and said nothing, but she recognised his interest and began to fill some of the gaps.

"Look, I'm a widow. I have a small income from my husband's pension and the life insurance money, so this is not a full-time occupation, thank goodness, just a sideline that has served me well for the past nine years and I'll have you know I pay tax on every penny I earn."

Patrick's eyes narrowed, giving him away.

"As an astrological consultant," she explained, at which Patrick allowed himself a half smile. 'Three-one.'

"After my husband died," Connie went on, warming to the rare opportunity to speak openly of her trade, "his boss, Larry, called round to see me on several occasions. We became good friends, and in time, well, much more. Larry was a good man; he helped me out in all sorts of ways. Of course, he was married, and there was never any question of that not being the case. And so, each time he paid a visit, he would do some repair job around the house or perhaps bring a small gift of some sort, until there were no longer any jobs that needed doing and one day he simply wrote me a cheque. Well, before long, that became the norm. Three years later, after three weeks not hearing from Larry, his best friend turned up at the door and informed me that Larry had had a heart attack and the funeral had been the week before. So that was the end of it, not even the chance to say goodbye, that's what hurt the most. Larry's friend had known about our relationship for some time and he continued calling by every now and then, and before long the pattern became established much as before, but this time without the original pretence. He's since introduced me to two other gentlemen and I see them each two or three times a month. It's all very discreet."

"And is that how you met Neil?" asked Patrick.

"God no. I was in a small café bar in town. I go there most Fridays for lunch, and sometimes call in just for a coffee and to get out of the house. One morning I noticed this young man sitting alone with a book, he kept glancing across at me. Not ominously, I didn't feel intimidated or anything like that. I smiled back, and we fell to talking, you know about books and Barnsley being the back of beyond. He was nervous to begin with and I could tell he was, well, interested in me, you know, in that way. Now, I'd no illusions about competing with anyone of his own age on equal terms, but you know, most men need mothering in one form or another, even if it comes in a form they don't immediately recognise. I enjoyed chatting with him and I liked the attention, then, just as I got up to leave, he upped and asked me out. I refused, of course, but told him I sometimes go there for lunch on a Friday and he was free to say hello if he was ever in the vicinity. He said he worked shifts but said he'd see what he could do. Well, next week, there he was, clutching a bunch of freesias, no less! I knew right then that I was going to have to tell him, there was no way I could cope with him other than on a business footing, I've lived an independent life too long and could tell he would want too much, and I wasn't about to jeopardize the life I'd carved out for the fancy of a rather sweet, but very intense, young man. We finished lunch and he insisted on paying the bill then said we must do this again, and that's when I said there was something I had to tell him. We walked to the park and sat on a bench where I told him emphatically that, although I liked his company, I was simply not in the market for a relationship. He said it was because of the age gap, and I said it wasn't that at all, I just couldn't cope with an exclusive relationship with anyone at this time in my life. He was distraught and said he really wanted to see me again. I told him that he might not if he knew more about me, but he wouldn't let it rest and kept insisting that he found me very attractive, until in the end I just told him the truth: that at home I entertain a small number of regular gentlemen visitors for services of a sexual nature in return for financial remuneration. His mouth fell open. Well, I said the word before he got the chance. It's not a word I use very often, too many connotations of pimps and young girls on the streets hooked on drugs. I expected him to run a mile but he took it in his stride, even seemed quite excited by the prospect and asked if he could visit me in that way. I told him I'd think about it and agreed to meet him at the café the following week. I half expected him not to show up but there he was waiting, no flowers this time, mind you. Well, we drank our coffees and I brought him back here; I suppose I was taking a bit of a risk, really, but I think I'm a good judge of character. There was something more about him than his neediness. I can't explain it; I just knew he wouldn't turn nasty. Well, he's been seeing me on and off ever since, usually once a week, sometimes twice; then one day, he'd simply not turn up and I'd hear nothing for several weeks. I used to find it infuriating, the way he blew hot and cold, but after a while I got used to it, that's the way he is, or was. I suppose I could have charged him something when he made an appointment and didn't show up but I could never bring myself to do it; it would have felt like punishing him and, well, despite what you might think, that's not something I'm into. Eventually he'd ring up and apologise, and next time would bring flowers or chocolates as well as my fee. Touching really. I'm gabbling, aren't I?"

"It doesn't matter, go on," Patrick could see she needed to talk, just as he needed to listen.

"You see, I've not been able to talk to anybody about him. I've been so worried over the last few weeks; the last time he was here he was so agitated with himself, about various things, you in particular. I've never seen him in such a state. I wondered if he'd taken any drugs, but he said not and was angry that I'd asked. Apparently he'd just got the sack at work, did you know that?"

Patrick shook his head. 'Four-one.'

Connie sighed.

"I was really concerned about him and told him I thought he should ring you. You see I had this awful feeling something was going to happen. I even looked up your number after he left here last Sunday, I was on the verge of phoning you myself, but realised you wouldn't be at your office late on a Sunday evening. Monday came, and I didn't feel quite so worried as the night before, well, things always seem different in the morning, don't they, and so I pushed it aside. Now I'll never know if it would have done any good."

"I doubt I'd have engaged with you even if you had rung," Patrick tried to reassure her. "At most, I would have informed Neil that you'd contacted me, but I couldn't even have done that because I never saw him again. Now I know why."

"Did he ring you?" she asked, beseechingly.

"He just didn't show up for an appointment, it was the first time that had happened. I didn't receive any word from him, but I did have a couple of silent messages left on my machine, maybe that was him," said Patrick, exhaling deeply.

"You know, he talked about you a lot," she went on, "you meant a lot to him; he really admired you, Patrick. But you also infuriated him because he couldn't get away from the thought that you were just playing with him; he couldn't believe that you really cared!"

Her words cut deep, and her use of his first name and the intimation of her rising anger brought him up short, but Connie wasn't yet done.

"He said every time he asked anything of you, you turned it back to him. What if he'd rung you, and told you how close to the edge he was? What would you have told him – 'Well, it's your life Neil, it's down to you!' – is that all you'd have said?"

Patrick stood her gaze, but offered up no reply. Connie's lips tensed, parted, closed, and then parted again as she leaned forward, searching for words on behalf of a young life wasted.

"He just wanted to know that you cared!" she screeched with a passion that bounced off the walls and made Patrick shudder. Her hands clenched in fists, she was trembling, her face right up into his, she stared into his features and put to him the question he'd been summoned from the close confines of his therapist's chair to hear, and it was issued with the clean edge of a cut-throat razor.

"Did you, Patrick? Did you *really* care?" and she thumped the base of her fists down hard, first onto her own thighs, and then hard onto the arm of his sofa, and tried to utter the question once more, "Did you …" but the words would not come out and the words dissolved into sobs.

Patrick fought back the impulse to flee. He felt like he was back in Infant School, the day the exasperated student teacher caught him flicking powder paint and made him stand up before her at the class front and say why he thought it clever to act so stupid. He had hung his head in silence, but the teacher would not relent, staring into his face, repeating her question, over and over, 'Why? Why? Why? Why?' until at last something gave in his chest and tears of shame began to trickle down his cheeks, only then did she allow him to slink back into anonymity at the back of the class. But now he was no seven-year-old boy; he was a grown man being called to account under the penetrating, accusatory stare of a prostitute. He should never have come here today, but there was no going back; he had come because he owed it to Neil, and he had come because of Connie's words: 'There are things that need to be said, and things that need to be heard, he's owed that much.' And Patrick knew he must stand his ground and try to answer the question, still posed so accusingly by the eyes of the woman who sat before him.

"Connie, you're asking me the very question Neil posed time and again in therapy, and which he was so tormented by, and I cannot convince you of the answer any more than it was my place to convince him. But what I'll say is this, if I didn't care about Neil, I wouldn't be here now, just as I imagine that if you didn't care about him, you wouldn't have rung and asked to meet me."

It was the right answer. It was the only answer. And no sooner had he voiced it, he became aware of having taken hold of her arms, and squeezing them, gently, but firmly. He let go at once, embarrassed at the gesture. And yet Connie seemed to have visibly softened. Her rage spent, her sobs subsided, she looked soft and vulnerable.

"I'm not so sure any more," she whispered. "I scream at you for not doing more for him, but I'm angry at myself for not making that phone call last Sunday."

"I imagine you did rather a lot for him," Patrick responded, relieved that he was no longer the object of her scorn.

She shot a piercing look that startled him, until he realised what he had said.

"Connie, I *wasn't* being salacious! Really," he insisted. "What I meant was that it sounds like whatever else Neil received here, he could talk to you, perhaps in some ways more freely than he could with me."

"That's the thing," she said, clearly reassured, "we *did* talk, and it wasn't all sex you know, far from it. He was always talking and asking me things, about all sorts; I never knew what was coming next. He was strange, you know, he asked if he could just sit and watch me ... dressing, undressing, brushing my hair, putting on my make-up, even ironing, would you believe?' She smiled and shook her head. Imagine a young man paying good money to watch a middle-aged housewife wearing stockings and a slip as she does the ironing! Neil was in his element just being allowed to sit and watch and chat away. Then he started on about wanting to photograph me: in the bath, towelling myself dry, applying make-up, getting dressed, that sort of thing, but I always refused. He said he'd bought a digital camera and promised no one would ever see the pictures but him, but I still said no. Anyway, he wouldn't let it rest and we fell out over it, big time. He accused me of not trusting him, and he was right. He offered to pay me extra but I still refused. There was no telling where those pictures would end up."

'I can well imagine,' thought Patrick, now sitting more relaxed in the sofa.

"Connie, does the name Degas mean anything to you?"

"Yes. Neil talked of him a lot. I'd heard of him before. He was one of the impressionist painters, wasn't he? That's all I really knew about him until I met Neil. Neil loved his paintings. He brought along a huge book full of Degas' prints and we looked at it in bed one afternoon. There were ballet and horse-racing scenes but the ones Neil was most taken with were the paintings of women, many of them were nudes but not like pin-ups, these were women in their bath, getting dressed, combing their hair, trying on a hat, even doing the ironing! He said that Degas didn't paint outdoors like the other impressionists, but locked away in his studio. Neil said that he was like Degas, a sort of edge person, who didn't get on easily with others. According to Neil, Degas never had a proper relationship with a woman and became a blind and lonely old man whose talent wasn't appreciated until after his death. Neil said Degas painted women as they really are, rather than posed by the artist, or camera lens. The prints he showed me were different from any other paintings of women I'd ever seen, women dressing and bathing, brushing their hair in dark, rich interiors, quite mesmerising, even beautiful, in a dark sort of way. That afternoon was one of the nicest times I ever had with Neil, or with any man for that matter. As I got dressed he said that was how he wanted to photograph me, as I really am, not putting on an act. I softened a bit then and agreed to think about it before next time.

Well, for days I was in a real quandary over what to do. I wanted to trust him but couldn't be sure no one else would ever see the photos. In the end, I said 'no'. He was crestfallen, and I didn't see or hear from him for three weeks. But the real truth of the matter is that I've always hated having my picture taken; I was embarrassed, can you believe that, given what I do? I think Neil would like to have been an artist, but he said he had no talent. I suppose wanting to photograph me was the closest he came."

Connie talked on at length, sharing other memories of Neil, and all the while Patrick's head was spinning. He felt like he was with a client, listening to her story, teasing out the little nooks and crannies where joys and sorrows hid, but he was not ensconced in the secure, containing arms of his therapist's chair, he was sitting in a prostitute's parlour in the very house where his client had spent so much time, money and emotion. And the realisation that Neil had processed his therapy sessions with Patrick here with this middle-aged prostitute filled Patrick with envy and resentment at being kept outside in the dark. Of course, unbeknown to Connie, Patrick had discussed Neil with another older woman, behind both their backs, but he could justify that on clinical grounds and by the fact that he did not conceal from Neil the existence of his supervision conversations with Beth, only their content. But what really got under Patrick's skin was the creeping suspicion that Neil might have found as much, if not more, therapeutic benefit here under Connie's roof, as he did in Patrick's therapy room.

Patrick swallowed hard and his chest gave a stutter that he knew to be the forerunner of tears, a reaction that Connie failed to notice for she was too tuned in to her own grief.

"Neil was such a troubled soul," she said, pulling a tissue from her sleeve and carefully dabbing at her eyes. "Everyday life seemed so hard for him, he was always wanting more from it and always being disappointed. He never liked to talk about his family but I could tell there was little love lost there."

Patrick made no response; he was too full of his own feelings: sorrow over a life cut short because its owner deemed it unworthy; his own shortcomings as a therapist; and more disturbingly, his growing recognition that in his own way, he was as handicapped as Neil in his inability to relate outside the small, insulated therapeutic world he'd created for himself and his clients. Neil had accused Patrick of being a charlatan. He realised now that Neil had been mistaken only in so far as his geography; Patrick was genuine enough in his therapy room and role; it was outside in the real world that he found it so hard to be authentic.

Aware that Connie had ceased talking, Patrick looked up to see her staring hard at him. She recognised the vulnerability in his eyes and instinctively offered up a diversion.

"Do you see many people, Patrick?"

"Hmm. Between six and eight clients, who mostly come once a week for an hour," he replied, regaining his composure, "and a dozen or more supervisees."

"What are they?"

"Other counsellors and therapists who come to me to discuss their work. I usually see them monthly for an hour and half. They work in GP surgeries, universities, psychology departments; several are in private practice like myself."

"They're lucky, there's no one I can talk to about what I do."

"It must be lonely," observed Patrick.

For a moment Connie looked wistful but took a deep breath and sidestepped the question.

"I suppose you must hear all sorts, Patrick."

"You too, I imagine."

"Yes, but most of it's just white lies and games with me, pretending to be aroused when mostly it's little more than an act, saying the things the gentlemen long to hear. Deep down they must realise it too, it's a game isn't it; let's dress up and pretend we're not who we are, where we are, doing this thing for money. That's what I liked about Neil, for him there wasn't so much pretence; he never asked me to play act, or mouth sweet lies, he was just happy being here in my presence, savouring the moment, whether we were talking, or making love. You might think it odd for a prostitute to use that phrase when she charges for sex, but with Neil, that's what it was like, more often that not. I just happened to be paid for it. You know, I was really touched when he compared me to those women in the paintings; it felt like the greatest compliment anyone had ever paid me. Maybe I should have trusted him more, but I could never quite bring myself to say 'yes'. And now it's too late. I'd put a whole damn album of photographs in his coffin now, if only I could."

Patrick said nothing to all this, for he knew that in time he would have to submit his own pocket of regret in front of Beth. Besides, Connie was not yet finished.

"It was only afterwards, you know, after sex, that sometimes Neil got depressed and was full of contempt, when he saw himself purchasing moments of happiness in dark corners for the rest of his life. You see, Patrick, I think you were his way out; I was just the mother-wife substitute who was there for him to keep running home to, and to provide a little light relief.

"It's a beguiling notion Connie, but I doubt it was that straightforward. It sounds to me that Neil received a large measure of acceptance and value from you. Maybe he did turn to me for rescue, but he couldn't stop seeing me as way above him, and looking down with contempt."

She returned his searching stare, but made no attempt to contradict his estimation of his role in Neil's psyche.

"Connie, like you, I have clients, and like you, I charge them by the hour. Like you, I get paid to provide a secret, personal, and highly intimate service for people I might not be at all inclined to spend time with were it not on a business footing. In fact, we each sell the kind of intimate personal attention that most people out there would expect to find in a close personal relationship for free, whether that is in the form of physical comfort and sexual favours, or rapt attention and understanding. And, I imagine, we each hold back aspects of who we really are? You say your job is based upon pretence? I've been increasingly pondering the extent to which mine is too: a pretence maintained and concealed by boundaries and rules, of where and when we meet, and what I will do, and won't do, for my clients. Don't prostitutes also rely on boundaries, of time and place, and no real names, or no kissing on the lips?"

Connie gave a small nod but said nothing; she didn't need to, she was eager to hear more.

"Isn't our willingness, Connie, to get intimate with our clients dependent upon those very boundaries? Take those away, and our care and desire evaporates. My work is easiest when clients respect those boundaries; it becomes difficult when they challenge them or start enquiring too closely what lies on the other side of the fence. Those boundaries enable them to suspend disbelief, and value what they receive from us. But that's what Neil wasn't prepared to do, he repeatedly challenged the boundaries by questioning the illusions, but he also refused to let them go."

"The illusions?" asked Connie.

"Yes the illusions. When you dispense sexual favours in return for cash, don't you sometimes have to work hard to create the impression you're enjoying it, when, if you were not being paid, or if you'd met the person outside in the real world, you wouldn't want to be doing it with them at all? And isn't that the reality that most of your clients choose to forget in order to reap their rewards from the exchange?

"Years ago," she said, "when Larry used to visit me, after we'd had sex, he'd sit with me in the kitchen drinking tea, it was lovely; the best part of all, if truth be told, and I always felt sad when he left. But you see Larry didn't start out as a client, not like the others; I gave myself to Larry for free. He *chose* to give me gifts, at first in kind, and later in money; and I was glad of it. I did feel uncomfortable, the very first time he left me cash, but then it just became our regular practice, and we both got used to it; he'd place the money on the mantelpiece when he arrived, and I'd remove it after he left. Nothing more needed to be said. Well, of course, now it's all turned into a proper business, negotiated upfront in advance. But since Larry, none of my clients ever came into this room, they only ever see the front room downstairs and the back bedroom and bathroom upstairs ... until Neil that is; I made an exception for him. There's a utility room beyond the kitchen where the ironing board sits; Neil would sit in the kitchen with the door open, drinking tea or a bottle of lager and he'd watch me, and we'd talk," Connie welled up and fought to contain the tears, "It's funny how you'll bend the rules for a special one. Would you like to see?" she looked at him beseechingly.

Patrick smiled knowingly,

"No, Connie, it's yours, and his."

Connie looked sad, and took a deep breath before returning to Patrick's treatise on the similarities between their respective professions.

"Well, I'll grant that you and I each fulfil a need, but unlike you I don't have any certificates, or a nameplate on the door."

"No, not even a red light?" and the warmth in his eyes won her smile.

"I had a client once," he said, feeling a sudden impulse to share more of his work with her. "She'd been coming to see me for a very long time and one day she told me that she couldn't imagine a time when she wouldn't be able to see me, because it was what was making it possible for her to go on living. I told her I understood how she felt, but for me the very opposite held true, the only thing that made it possible for me to go on seeing her, was that, right from the outset, I knew it would end. I wonder if the real difference between our professions, Connie, is that yours has an investment in your clients continuing to use your service, whereas my job is to make myself redundant."

"I hate endings," Connie said. "I'm no good at them. I never leave; people leave me. I think that's why I'm better at relationships in this business than living life for real. Most of the people I've ever really cared about seem to die. Perhaps it's me."

"You should see someone about that, Connie."

"I couldn't afford your fees," she replied.

"You might be surprised!" he said, and gave a wry smile. "Anyway, I'm not so different. At any given moment in my work there are clients I'm just starting out with, others are in the throes of ending, and several in between. And I never get to hear the end of their stories. People get on and people get off, but the roundabout of therapy keeps spinning round and around. The trouble is, I've been on it so long I've become part of the roundabout, and I'm not sure any more where it ends and I begin. When you're on it, it feels like you're moving, but it's just an illusion, you have to get off the roundabout in order to go somewhere, and I've been going nowhere too long."

Connie stared into his face, transfixed.

"When I was a little girl," she said, "I loved the slide and the swings but was always scared to go on the roundabout, all that whizzing round and when I tried to get off I felt so dizzy I couldn't find my feet."

"Connie," he said, biting his lip, "I think you understand me more than you know. You see, dizzy is exactly how I feel much of the time these days, and it's as much as I can do to stay on my feet."

"Perhaps *you* should see someone about that, Patrick!"

"You're not the first person to tell me that Connie, and I have tried. I thought the problem was finding the right therapist, now I'm wondering whether the someone I need to see isn't a therapist at all."

Connie gave a hesitant smile.

"More tea, Patrick, or something stronger?"

"Thanks, Connie, I'm tempted. But you've given me more than enough. I must go."

"Christmas calls, eh?"

"After a fashion," he sighed, "it's going to be an odd one this year."

"It's always an odd time for me," she leapt in, "my gentlemen friends all have their wives and families; I'm like a tree with no lights or baubles, wearing only my thoughts and my solitude, it's eerie. I'm not the suicidal type, Patrick; I've always known there are people a lot worse off than me, but if I was going to end it all, then Christmas is the time I'd do it. But last year was different, last year I saw Neil on Christmas Eve, and again on Boxing Day, but not this year."

"No, not this year, Connie," said Patrick, "maybe that's something else our jobs have in common, the more we grow into the role the harder it is to live without it."

She stared hard at him, wanting to know what made him say that, but he was no longer looking at her, he was getting to his feet.

"Connie, did Neil ever mention the possibility of taking his own life?" and he was suddenly aware that this was the question he had driven here to ask.

"That's what I've been racking my brain trying to remember," she replied, "but I'm almost sure he didn't, certainly not directly," she replied. "Did he say anything to you?"

Patrick paused before replying.

"I think I missed it."

For some seconds, they stood in frozen silence. Connie looking hard into eyes that steadfastly avoided her gaze.

"I must go," he said at last.

Connie rose to walk him to the front door. They never reached it.

It was a strange coupling, neither a business transaction, nor enflamed by lashings of lust. More a ritual act, as if in the fusion of their two parts, there was the possibility that Neil could be conceived anew. Of course, it didn't work, but it fulfilled some need in them both. It was unclear which of the two initiated the kiss at the foot of the stairs, but the kiss was joined, and it enabled Connie to take him by the hand, lead him upstairs, and give without being asked; the part of a woman that opens, enfolds, and allows a man to roar and plunge until he is spent, and becomes, once more, a puny, helpless baby in her arms. But Patrick did not roar as he came, he whimpered, and cried. And afterwards, much to Connie's deep satisfaction, he laid still and soft inside her until sleep all but claimed them both.

It was the creak of the mattress that roused Connie. She saw that Patrick was sitting on the edge of the bed, putting on his socks.

"You can take a shower, you know. You don't have to rush off," she said, knowing full well that she would not shower until morning. Tonight, she would sleep with the smell of him upon her.

"Thanks Connie, but I've got to go. I've got to pack a bag. First thing tomorrow I've a plane to catch."

She wrapped a long silk robe about herself, and accompanied him downstairs.

"I'm sure the neighbours have their suspicions," she joked, as she slowly led the way along the hallway, "but I keep myself to myself, so rest assured, Patrick, I shan't tell anyone you've been here."

"Me neither," he whispered, and immediately wondered whether it was Connie, or Beth, that he would end up betraying.

She reached for the front door knob, and heard him draw a deep breath, as if bracing himself for the outside world.

"You're not at home for Christmas, then, Patrick?" she asked, holding the door only slightly ajar.

"Home? I'm not sure where that is any more, Connie. I'll be trying to pull myself together somewhere, Ireland I hope."

"Well, if you're ever in the vicinity, and at a loose end? I wouldn't charge you, you know," and she was as embarrassed at having made the offer, as was Patrick moved by receiving it.

"Thank you, Connie, thank you," he said warmly.

And with that, the therapist touched the prostitute gently on the arm, descended the four stone steps and strode off along the pavement as the front door closed silently behind him.

Patrick stood by the car rummaging for his keys and imagined Neil doing the same thing on this very spot so many times, feeling flushed, spent, or full of self-loathing. He searched each pocket once, then a second time. Satisfied they were nowhere about his person he took a deep breath and sought to clear his thoughts. Did he place them on the arm of Connie's sofa? They could have slipped down the side of the seat. Or had he put them down on her bedside table? He was about to turn back up the pavement when he noticed the bunch of keys protruding from the steering column. He grabbed the door handle, climbed inside and tried the ignition. It wouldn't start. 'Shit!' He gripped the steering wheel and gave an almighty sigh. He turned the key again but heard only the starter motor clearing its throat. He tried a third time and at last the engine caught and fired. His foot coaxed the throttle and the old Saab edged away from the kerb, its driver completely unaware of the tears trickling down Connie's face as she leaned back against her front door; or the glass tumbler being pressed hard against the adjoining wall by her elderly neighbour, whose wizened wife's acid gaze peered out from behind their net curtains. He was conscious only of the need to get home, try and book a flight for Derry in the morning, and then lose himself in sleep.

Chapter Thirty-Seven

PATRICK LIFTED HIS GAZE to meet the stare of the executioner, whose eyes glistened on a surge of new-found power, whose instrument was aimed directly at Patrick's heart. It was Neil who filled the gap in their conversation.

"I think about you a lot, Patrick. You know, something's been bugging me ever since I first started coming here. I've been trying to figure out what it is, and you know what, I think I've finally worked it out … you're not what you seem! I've suspected it for some time; I just hadn't been able to figure out who you really are. Then, as I was driving away from here the last time, the thought occurred to me that maybe *you* don't even know who you are! That's quite a trick, when I think of what you do for a living. Oh, don't get me wrong, you're good, Patrick, you're very good; you turn tricks like a real pro. I bet you're sitting there right now thinking all this is a heap of projections streaming out of an untrained mind, but you're wrong; it's not me, Patrick, it's you that's not for real. It dawned on me late last night as I sat staring at your business card; I didn't see it at first, I couldn't get past the front that you present to the world. It's like when I come here each time, I climb the stairs and approach your door and always have to look at that brass plate, so fine and formal, with its row of letters of qualifications and membership of this and that association. And you know what, I hate it. In the early days I actually thought about breaking in one night and unscrewing it. I really did long to do that. I imagined what it would be like to turn up for my next session and find just four holes in the wall, and I wondered what you'd say. Then I realised you wouldn't say anything; you'd have just had it replaced; perhaps something a little more modern and stylish, a little less solicitor-like. Then last night, I had this brainwave. You tried talking to me once about my 'inner child'. And how I need to

289

get to know him and care for him. Well, last night, I set about trying to imagine yours. I pictured you as a little boy out in the playground before the school bell goes, standing on the sidelines, looking on enviously as the other kids rough and tumble and chase each other about. You're standing on the sidelines like a sad little kid who doesn't know how to play. You've got your school blazer on, your school cap perched tight on your head and a leather satchel strapped across your chest; the label through the little plastic window reads *Pat Chime*. And that was when I saw it. It came to me in a flash, why didn't I see it before? Pat Chime, you're an anagram! Let's play a little game, eh Pat, why don't you re-arrange the letters and let's see what you come up with?"

Patrick's eyes remained fixed upon Neil's finger, all the while caressing the trigger of the gun that was still pointing at his heart. And no smart riposte could Patrick conjure up to meet Neil's challenge, no empathic response, no systemic re-framing, no behavioural confrontation or psychodynamic interpretation to assuage Neil's taunts, and neither could he solve the anagram. When it came, Patrick's response emanated not from his lips, but his hands. The wooden, sweat-soaked arms of Patrick's chair began to creak under his vice-like grip; they strained and winced, gave and groaned until, unable to withstand the pressure, the wooden arms snapped like two cream crackers, sending showers of splinter darts flying across the room. Neil raised his hands to protect his face, and as the whole room began to shake and shudder the gun slipped from his grasp and fell to the floor. Neil drew up his legs and cowered in the seat like a dog on bonfire night, and as the earth tremor increased in intensity, the two framed Degas prints of intimacy and isolation, *At the Café,* and *L'Absinthe* slid from the walls and the glass frames smashed upon the floor. The booming sound wave shattered the windowpane littering the carpet with glass shards and daggers, and the whole room shuddered as if the very bowels of the earth were laying claim to it. Clinging to the severed arms of his chair as if they were crutches, Patrick's body was now forced back into the seat under incredible G-forces, and he saw to his horror that he was starting to melt, shoes, socks, trousers, flesh and bone, all charring, disintegrating and turning to oil before his eyes; oil that oozed and soaked into the carpet and chair cushion. And as he watched his body melting from the feet up, Patrick sank lower and lower in the therapist's chair until, at last, only his head remained upon the seat, every muscle and tendon in his neck and face straining to avoid being sucked out of existence. With his mouth gaping like an old carp's, he sucked one last lungful of life, before Patrick Chime, *M.A., M.B.A.C.P. Senior Accredited Therapist,* stepped for ever out of his own frame of reference and disappeared into the upholstery.

When he awoke he was lying on his back, white-knuckled hands gripping the duvet, and each foot feeling desperately for the other. He sighed with relief, for although awash with sweat, his body had not melted and bore no bullet hole. He glanced across at the radio alarm, it showed 05:47; he'd set it for six. A plane, that's right, he had to get to the airport to obtain a standby seat on a flight to Derry. He knew he should get up but his heart was still pounding and the image of the gun came back to him. Something about it didn't feel right. If Neil had really wanted to attack him, surely he'd have come armed with a knife, to rip him open and see what's inside. 'But of course,' thought Patrick, 'the gun, like the rest of the dream, wasn't Neil's invention, it was mine, and the theme was guilt; the guilt of a therapist who misjudged the depth of his client's despair, and the guilt of a man who has hidden away too long behind his therapist's mask. There was a score to settle, that's what the dream said. Summoned by guilt, the hit-man cometh, gun in hand.'

Patrick pushed aside the gun-toting Neil of the nightmare, and tried imagining the real-life Neil, climbing up on to the parapet, before launching himself into the path of a hurtling train, and the vision of the driver's face a split second before impact; the driver's horror-mask an indictment of Patrick's own failure. 'Did you jump intentionally, Neil? Was this your final judgement on real life, and therapy? Or were you simply high on a tide of drink and drugs, devil-may-caring your way along the precipice just for the sheer hell of it, when startled by the train whistle, you lost your balance; an edge person to the bitter end?'

Patrick switched off the alarm, stretched out an arm and snatched at the curtain. The stillness of the cul-de-sac surprised him, so accustomed had he become to the recent gales and the antics of fairy-lights in the neighbouring trees, left on through the night; now just the yellow glow of a solitary street lamp and the beaming face of a single illuminated Santa penetrated the gloom.

Patrick sank back onto the pillow reflecting on the course his life had taken these past two months: a private earthquake had pulled the ground from under him and he hadn't seen it coming; he'd been caught unawares and now here it was happening again as a strange new sound claimed his attention. He closed his eyes and listened out, imagining it might be the central heating pipes creaking, mice up in the loft, or the streetlamp outside the bedroom window gently humming, until it dawned on Patrick that what he was hearing was nothing more than the echo of his own silence. He threw back the covers, sat up sharp on the edge of the bed.

"Listening … it's what I do," he said aloud, and he shook his head, "but if I'm not a therapist, what else am I?"

He didn't wait for an answer but took a huge gulp of air, hauled his tired body upright and wandered through to the bathroom to take a pee.

His gaze followed the eager stream as it jiggled and frothed the surface of the water, and he thought of a fortnight free from listening in; the blessed freedom to close his eyes and ears anytime he wished, the freedom to leave process and understanding to its own devices, and the freedom to be himself. Hurrying the last stubborn drips into the bowl he stepped into the shower where the cold, sharp jets chased the remaining beads of sweat from his body. He stood motionless, allowing the rivulets to slide down his skin, and thought of the forty-five pounds an hour people pay him to hear their stories, and the thought occurred that, rather like the Wedding Guest held in thrall by The Ancient Mariner, Patrick's curse was the compulsion to lend an ear to endless tales of woe. He turned off the shower and watched the stream gush and thin, and as the last dregs swirled and gurgled, he wondered if it was not only his marriage, but also his career that was fast disappearing down the plughole. Then he remembered his forthcoming fee increase to fifty pounds an hour, and he shivered, not at the cold, nor in shame, but at the true cost of a life spent listening in.

Wrapping the towel around his waist, Patrick perched on the side of the bath. He imagined Christmas morning: Nuala, happily ensconced with Jackie's family up on the farm in Hexham; Maggie, alone in her new apartment, awaiting the call from the lover who cannot be there, or the one from the husband who could, but will not. And he thought of his clients: Sarah, now living rather than merely surviving; Margaret, the tumour in her breast now having spread to her marriage; Jake, at last facing up to the cost of being true to himself; Gina, ever-determined to give men the one thing she believes they will value; and Neil, free at last from the vain struggle to be someone he isn't.

And finally, Patrick pictured Grace, focus of a forbidden love that had yet to speak its name. 'Is it really love,' he wondered, 'mere desire, or just plain devilment, that makes me want to fuck my way through the boundary that has always kept me in my place?' He noticed Maggie's razor left on the edge of the bath and dismissed the impulse before it even had chance to become thought. Sitting on the side of the bath, for once stripped of his therapist's mantle and his clients' projections, Patrick thought back to the nightmare; it had truly terrified him at the time, and again when he first awoke, but now it felt like a gift, for he realised that the dream's message lay, not just in its content, but in the fact that he had woken up in the nick of time. He stood up to finish drying, and as he twisted around to reach the small of his back, he caught a glimpse of his reflection in the bathroom mirror, like a strange echo of one of Degas' scenes from the *salle de bain*. Patrick stood up, let go the towel and stared at his reflection. Naked but intact, he breathed a sigh of relief. 'It's time I bought some new clothes,' he thought, 'I've not only got a plane to catch, but a life to live.'

Acknowledgements

My eternal gratitude to the wisest, sharpest, and most child-like woman I've ever met: Dr Kathleen Smith, who, more than anyone else, made a marital counsellor out of me. The character of Beth, was loosely based upon Kathleen. Sadly she passed away shortly before this novel was published.

I must put on record my appreciation: of my 'real-life' supervisor, Anthea Green, Fellow of the BACP and all round good egg, whose continued support for my writing endeavours and our many conversations about the issues raised within this novel have been invaluable to me; and of my friend and colleague, Ruth Whittaker, who held my hand as I took those first faltering steps into the world of writing, and who always wielded her red pen with love and honesty.

Heartfelt thanks to Hazel Cushion, MD of Accent Press, for showing sufficient passion for my novel to convince me that hers was the publishing house to go with. And, to her husband Bob, for so succinctly identifying the specific aspects of my manuscript that needed further work. I hope I have done them both justice.

I feel compelled to acknowledge the part played by countless clients of mine, in various settings spanning almost thirty years, those I listened to well and long, and those I misheard all too often; all of whom have helped educate me in the shadowy heartland of sexual, marital and personal relationships.

But most of all, I must thank my wife, Kim, who for some reason, goes on loving me, and who endured the months of neglect when I shut myself away in my study writing the first draft of this novel, and who voiced not a single word of complaint (until it was finished!) At the time it felt like being slapped with a wet fish, but, looking back, darling, I guess I had it coming.

For more information about our books please visit
www.accentpress.co.uk